O AMERICA

ALSO BY WILLIAM LEAST HEAT-MOON

Blue Highways: A Journey into America

PrairyErth (a deep map)

River-Horse: A Voyage Across America

Columbus in the Americas

Roads to Quoz: An American Mosey

An Osage Journey to Europe, 1827–1830

Here, There, Elsewhere: Stories from the Road

Writing Blue Highways

Celestial Mechanics: a tale for a mid-winter night

O AMERICA

DISCOVERY IN A NEW LAND

WILLIAM LEAST HEAT-MOON

UNIVERSITY OF MISSOURI PRESS
Columbia

Library of Congress Cataloging-in-Publication Data

Names: Heat Moon, William Least, author.
Title: O America : Discovery in a New Land / William Least
    Heat-Moon.
Description: Columbia : University of Missouri Press, [2020]
Identifiers: LCCN 2019034840 (print) | LCCN 2019034841 (ebook) | ISBN
    9780826222046 (hardcover) | ISBN 9780826274427 (ebook)
Subjects: LCSH: Physicians--Fiction. | Slaves--United States--Fiction. |
    English--United States--Fiction | United States--History--19th
    century--Fiction. | United States--Social conditions--19th
    century--Fiction. | GSAFD: Historical fiction.
Classification: LCC PS3608.E276 O24 2020 (print) | LCC PS3608.E276
    (ebook) | DDC 813/.6--dc23
LC record available at https://lccn.loc.gov/2019034840
LC ebook record available at https://lccn.loc.gov/2019034841

NATHANIEL TRENNANT,

KING'S COLLEGE, CAMBRIDGE UNIVERSITY

CLASS OF 1836

MY AMERICAN EXCURSION
to
THE BUFFALO PRAIRIES

THE LOGBOOKS OF A PHYSICIAN

Nathaniel Trennant, M.D.

April, 1848

⁎

Aboard the Packet Ship *Narwhale*

I HAD RECKONED to begin this log of my voyage to America with a unicorn rampant. Instead, the Atlantic Ocean commandeers my words. This morning I heard from a witness: During a downpour last evening, a young Polish father (who spoke no English other than *tonk you*) came from steerage to set out a pail to catch rain. When the storm abated, he went below to bring up his daughter of ten weeks to wash her in water free of salt. Sprinkling her from the bucket, he held her to the bulwark, still wet from the storm, as was the deck, both infant and his hands slick with soap. As he was wiping her, the ship got thumped by a rogue wave reportedly occasioned by an ungodly large pod of breaching whales, and he lost his footing, sending him hard against the rail and knocking the child from his grasp. Overboard she went, the bucket following to bob like a tiny boat.

Though shaken by his fall, he nevertheless instantly bounded up and looked whither she had disappeared, and despite not seeing her in the water twenty feet below, he pivoted over the rail into the ocean, to rise gasping to the surface, his head turning madly to spot her. The cold water at once clamped closed his airways, rendering him utterly unable to draw a breath, all the while the ship sailing onward. Eight hundred tons under full canvas in a ten-knot wind cannot halt in less than a mile to allow the lowering of the ship's cockboat. Struggling, he managed to grasp the bucket. His daughter was not in it. Said a passenger, "He snagged the bucket but not the baby."

I learned the helmsman had earlier shouted to the father to beware the slick deck and stay back from the bulwark, but the man, understanding no English, seemed to take the words as encouragement for paternal love and care.

As ship's doctor, it was given to me to inform the mother when she was brought to the captain's cabin along with an English-speaking Polish woman. I had little idea how to express the monstrous events, and I fumbled in trying, news the mother mitigated by believing what she heard had to be nothing more than incompetent translation; she stood rigid until the truth penetrated, then sank insensate to the deck. Events were not to end there.

About midnight the helmsman noticed a shadowy figure leaning over the port bulwark near the location of the incident. It is not unusual for somebody, especially one from steerage, to go to the rail for fresh air or to lean over to disgorge a fouled cup of water or a putrid potato or simply to answer to *mal de mer*. When the helmsman looked again, the shadowy figure was gone, and he assumed the person had returned to quarters.

At dawn I heard cries rising from below, and soon there came a rap at my door. Captain Finn asked me to come forth and help calm a clamor threatening the quarterdeck. A dozen Polish men were loudly demanding he take action to find one of their women missing from her sleep platform. Difficult it is to hide on this ship, the only place being the hold, but since it was secured as best could be, the search was brief. We had no conclusion other than in the cover of night the young mother had thrown herself overboard. And so it was.

The little family's voyage of great promise had come down to an accident, a reflex, and a decision, leading to three beginnings towards a new life terminated even before we had crossed the tenth meridian. Captain Finn gave, as his shipboard duty, an approximation of a service for the lost ones, translated into Polish by the afore-mentioned young interpreter. Remembrance was the best that could be done.

A matron quartered across the passageway, one who affects a certain gentrification, said to me in a surety able to relieve the disquiet death brings on, "Once the child fell, God in his wisdom saw to the taking of the others." I could only respond, "Some wisdom calamity is." Answered she, "Yes, the ways of Providence are marvelous to behold." I turned to the silent horizon and did not speak what I was thinking: at sea, how swift the change from deadly boredom to deathly ceremony.

Following the loss of the little family, at last I have opportunity to open my journal as planned before fell happenstance intervened and forced me to address such a dark beginning to my entry into the grand American experiment. I can now launch this log as my notes of the last few days intended.

Had it not been for the horn of an Abyssinian unicorn, I would not now be bound for America. Under me is a Yankee packet ship, 120 feet of oaken hull, creaking planks, and groaning ribs, all of it ready to sail although for now moving only by rolling port to starboard, a ship progressing nowhere, holding in place as if sunk into the cobbled bottom of Plymouth Harbor. We (I in my cabin) are awaiting an inspiration of wind to fill sails and push us on to the Channel and send us off towards the dark-forested coast of the New World.

The enemy of an ocean crossing, more often than the sea itself, is tedium, and to answer that I have before me a journal—quarter-leather, parchment sheets with gilt edging—a fine thing to serve as log of my journey howsoever distant it may run. The book has almost the height of my boot. On the first page I have, somewhat grandiloquently, inscribed a hopeful title (more to break in a new quill than to identify).

For a voyage, nothing so occupies one's mind, dispels ennui, and compresses time as does a pen scribbling to record events of passage. Sea or shore, the most express means of getting through hours is to put words on paper, even if all that occurs in a day is the recording of it. Is not the *punishment* inherent in a prison sentence the infliction of inescapable monotony? A human dreads boredom only a bit less than death.

It is but happenstance—in truth, a long procession of them—that I am here afloat. Plan and plot, calculate and contemplate, reason and reckon as we may, is not the doing of our days often little more than following random events? Circumstances arise and accumulate, change and vanish as we drone along, imagining ourselves masters of our minutes, directors of our destiny. If America is my destination, then it is that alleged horn of a unicorn which—I am tempted to say—*pointed* me westward. Saying it requires me to explain it.

In this, the twelfth year of the reign of Victoria, the London College of Medicine asked me, a physician and would-be adept in natural philosophy, to deliver a lecture in defense of rational thinking. The assigned title was "A Fantastical Bestiary." The topics were sphinxes, gryphons, minotaurs, hippogriffs, basilisks, wyverns, and a dozen others, each illustrated with a hand-painted lantern slide. In attendance, on liberty from his ship, was one Captain Eben Finn, an American of about six and forty years, more burly than stout, a man fitted to commanding the likes of boatswains, coxswains, gunners, powder monkeys, fearless younkers, or even a gang of able-bodied seamen bent on mayhem destructive to the operation of a ship of the line. His authority is superintended by a gaze of latent threat like that of a puma fixing its prey.

He is, nevertheless, not without humor, often expressed with bluntness typical of a New Englander. Although his education was self-achieved, his mind is nimble and eager for enlightened conversation, especially on long voyages with men not inclined to the spoken arts. As admiralties the world over have long noted, *slowness* of intellect makes for good sailors. In that calling, intelligence is a distraction: amongst the rigging, nothing more than the mother wit of a house spider is necessary. And a good grip.

At sea, says Finn, no deprivation—not even want of connubial comfort—requires more endurance than a lack of lettered interlocution. On some crossings he must depend entirely on two shelves of books in his quarters; still, there always comes a time when even ably written words fail to match well-spoken words. A book can speak to you, but only the mad speak to a book.

His belief, so I presume, led the captain to examine a pavement placard depicting a rearing unicorn advertising my lecture for that very evening a fortnight ago. When in port, as often as the demands of captaincy allow, Finn leaves his ship for holiday in London where he takes frequent constitutionals to sustain strength in his legs, those ambulations with a staff in hand, not to fend off a bounder but to aid his stride, the stick serving to regulate him as a pendulum does a clock.

The unicorn rampant drew him into the Garden Lyceum and to a seat front-row center and directly before the podium. During the performance, he held upright his staff. When the audience applauded politely, he stood and thumped the shaft on the floor, alarming the gentlemen beside him. As the company departed, he approached me to say, "If I might, sir, you deny the existence of unicorns, but what do you make of this stave given me by a hunter named Nunavik on the island of Greenland? Is it not the horn of a unicorn?"

He passed me his staff to examine: five feet long, of apparent ivory, its entire tapering length lined with spiraling flutes, the upper end finished with the carved head of a sea animal and the tip capped with a brass ferrule. "Most certainly an exquisite piece," I agreed, the captain responding, "Yes, but from what creature?"

"On the evidence of its length," I answered, "and its fluting, and the carving of a flat-faced mammal, and its ivory composition, *and*, most significant, that you came upon it in Arctic waters, I have to conclude it is the tusk of a narwhale, called by some the unicorn whale."

"You deny, Doctor," said he, "'tis an Abyssinian unicorn?"

"At the risk of offending your opinion," I replied, "in three centuries of explorations, many a traveler has returned with an unverified *tale* of unicorns, but never so much as a vertebral *tail*. Evidence of unicorns, Captain, remains even less than for those famous minikin angels able to dance on a pinhead. Less than nothing is negligible evidence indeed."

"You, sir, are a man of science?"

"I attempt to be."

His coloring rose, not from anger but from laughter. He took my hand and shook it vigorously and said, "My dry-docked packet flying the house flag of the Blue Anchor Line, she's the *Narwhale*. Christened by this man before you. The placard outside the theater, the rampant unicorn, led me in to test your knowledge. A slow-witted, gullible fellow is a man to be left ashore. But one with observant eyes and a well-stocked mind, an inquisitor of some capacity, now *there's* a rover to invite aboard."

Again he shook my hand, saying, "After requisite repairs, the *Narwhale* sails for New York in a fortnight. If ever you've longed to go to sea, then I can offer a cabin. Without cost to you. Next to mine. A man informed in physic and natural philosophy would be welcome. You need bring only your seabag, medical kit, *and* conversation. Let me inquire, sir, in your speech, do I hear an isle of the Caribbees?"

"Saint Kitts born, Cambridge educated," said I.

Thus, this happenstance of a placard displaying a mythical beast rampant has brought me to a becalmed ship—its sails furled— and into my cabin, and now before me a journal, pen, and inkhorn. I understand *where* I am bound, and I have a slender notion *why* I am outward bound, but I am quite lacking awareness of *what* I am bound for. That alone is reason to go forth, to take the exterior measure, and to look into the interior contours to learn what lies beating at the heart of an exploration. Perhaps this endeavor is beyond my capacities, as medicine sometimes does my capabilities.

I must admit I wavered on making the Atlantic crossing to America until I recalled the words of founding father John Adams: "Democracy never lasts long. It soon wastes, exhausts, and murders itself." His assertion—and a mythical animal—have brought me here this evening.

And now, as I write, I remember my mother saying just before she died, "Go forth laddie! Find the North Pole and carve your name on it! If you don't, you'll discover only the Land of Lost Opportunity. It's but ten paces down the Road Not Taken."

(I append the company emblem from a sheet of ship's stationery.)

PACKET SHIP NARWHALE

BLUE ANCHOR LINE

NEW YORK – PLYMOUTH

On our second morning at anchorage near the mouth of the River Plym, vagrant breezes gathered to fill our sails and move the *Narwhale* to a wharf proximate to the location the Separatists of 1620 embarked for a place they would also name Plymouth, in Massachusetts. Whilst docked, we took on some hundred steerage passengers, and the ship's boy retrieved Captain Finn from his coffee in the Cod and Cockle before we cast off our lines to await the seaward tide. When the wind shifted towards open water, the first mate signaled the boatswain to send younkers into the high rigging of the mainmast, and those fearless lads, showing human evidence of our possible arboreal ancestry, scurried upward and unfurled enough sail to take slack out of the anchor cable. Seamen leaned into the capstan bars, the chain rising clankingly as the flukes rose into the sunlight, and the anchor was made fast against the ship. More canvas dropped, and the *Narwhale*, assisted by the tide, came around, and we put out for the English Channel where gusts freed from the constraints of land sent her tonnage westward.

The spires of Plymouth fell away, and our bowsprit, as if the horn of a monstrous narwhale (or an Abyssinian unicorn), pointed towards the Atlantic. The boys scrambled about the rigging, fore and aft, and soon the ship was abloom with canvas, her sheets luminous with sunlight and straining full under the wind. To America!

Against the blue of sky and sea, the sailors exuberant to be moving, their chanteys descended on us from the lofty webbing of cordage, all hands vibrant with the promise of destinations beyond—except for one Irish lad not yet out of his nonage, a boy new to the ship, who appeared paralyzed in the rigging about halfway up to the topgallant. His terror-struck eyes were fixed to what was beneath him—not the deck but the white caps of the Channel below, exposed by the roll of the ship.

A pair of fellow younkers scrambled to talk him down, or, I should say, *mock him down*. Upon realizing all standing between him and a calamitous consequence of gravity were only his feet and ten sweaty digits grasping oily and swaying shrouds, he clamped himself in place like a barnacle.

An old tar silenced the mockery, and climbed up to the boy to accompany him to the deck. Once seated, the lad continued to tremble, his red-eyed shame buried in his forearms, his mind filled with the dread of knowing he would still have to undertake the ascent nearly every day of our crossing. I leaned over him, careful not to make any gentle motion others could later taunt him with, instead letting my bodily motions suggest I was lecturing him. What I said, *sotto voce*, was on the order of *his* first clamber took him higher than had *my* first climb some years ago. Never having served at sea, I spoke a fiction. Pretending to scold him further, I said, again softly, "Courage, my young hearty!"

Our second mate, assuming I had given a good dressing down, pulled the boy up and marched him to the forecastle, and there put him against the surety of the starboard bulwark and set before him a pail of oak pieces to whittle into belaying pins. He said, "Next time aloft, boy, remember, *one hand for yourself, one for the ship*." The lad, his eyes yet red with humiliation, looked up at me, and I gave him a secret wink-and-nod.

The wind blowing fair, we slipped down the Cornish coast; where purchase was possible for webbed feet, cormorants and shags festooned rocky ledges. On the cliffs and in the water, birds nudged and bumped and crowded one another in pursuit of the sea bounty. My pocket spyglass revealed cormorants holding sodden wings aloft to dry in the sun whilst others paddled and dived, some hauling up an eel the length of my forearm to be deftly tossed up to turn the spiky fins back so the fish might slide down the long throat, gullet to gizzard. It was as if the neck of the cormorant was designed to accommodate the shape of an eel, fish fins notwithstanding.

The northern shore was an interchange of open reaches of sheep pasture, some few above tin mines with stone engine houses like castle watchtowers. From those shafts have come men to cut and lay American rock into piers and foundations and canal chambers, all sturdy underpinnings to Yankee industry, each an economic sill to support a democracy.

The sun was not yet at meridian when we passed beyond Lizard Point and Land's End and on into the Atlantic. Abruptly, all England was behind, and within an hour it had vanished and before us lay an invisible New World.

———

Affluent passengers come out to the fresh air but soon find it more than bracing, and retreat to the grand saloon—also called the *salon*—their places along the rail of the main deck taken by immigrants from steerage, almost entirely Germans and Poles desperate for a few drafts of clean air—cold or otherwise—and the chance to clear their lungs of the close quarters below. Refreshed, they too leave the wind-blown topside to go again into the dim 'tween decks and air thick enough to insult the nose. Seeing passengers disappear like moles descending into their tunnels, I feel the privilege of a private cabin as if it were iniquity.

Alone at the rail today, I looked upward towards the invisible ecliptics the sun, moon, and planets follow in their own apparent glide towards the New World. The name Land's End surely brings to mind among each of us how our embarkation must inevitably lead to aspects of lives forever finished: homes, farmsteads, family and friends all now beyond reach. Every immigrant carries a little bundle of clothing wrapped in a sheet or blanket. They also carry a bigger—if unperceivable—bundle of hopes wrapped in a dream to be fulfilled in a constitutional democracy present on Earth not yet three-quarters of a century. Only in the past year has it assembled itself—from the Atlantic to the Pacific, from the Rio Grande to the Canadian forests—into a contiguous three million square miles now bestriding a continent. A collection completed through conquest and purchase, sabers and dollars.

Was ever a country so blessed in its geography? Within sight of both its eastern and western coasts rise mountains like ramparts against foreign intrusion. Centered among those ranges lie vast lands capable of feeding their own people and some share of the world. From terrestrial and oceanic advantages given by nature itself, a potential global power has come forth to change all nations. But will America prove to be a mushroom popping up overnight or an oak growing slowly to dominate its forest?

And what of its *human* nature? Predicated on the single concept of liberty, a nation born out of blood, bullets, and bayonets created a loose and fractious confederation able to defeat the world's mightiest sea power. The important word in that sentence is *fractious*. Now, one might ask, can this noble experiment which is America survive the bumptious nature and ignorance of its own citizenry?

I think answers may be found in the lives of those who have gone to America to take up the experiment. I plan to go where previous foreign visitors have not so I may consider what they have ignored: the plain facts of daily life as exposed in places others have deemed dull, backward, unpromising, or too remote to reveal who Americans are and what their country is. A plan to *disclose*, perhaps even *expose*, what is at the heart of this fortunate land so able to absorb cultures and assimilate peoples and turn itself into a nation of *fortunes*: a quest to discover antecedents of what is to come.

Thus this question: Is America alert to the inescapable threats to its continued existence as a body politic? Threats not from without but from within? A mansion may fall not from storm or fire but from the insidious jaws of unseen termites and wood beetles gnawing from the interior outwards until foundational timbers collapse, to leave residents and their beds and pots and kettles buried in dust. The second President has written: "There never was a democracy yet that did not commit suicide."

In an assay like this, where do *I* belong? For me many things are at end—some I hope to see vanish. Yet in other ways I want to learn what the great experiment might work on me. Is my journey an expedition or a personal experiment? But is not discovery the purpose of both?

Expedition: from the Latin *expedire*, "to extricate." And *experiment*: from *experiri*, "to try." Each term expresses my reasons for boarding the *Narwhale*. An expedition to try to extricate myself somehow, somewhere in the new land. But from *what* am I seeking to extricate myself? From more than the ghostly appearances?

Another Latin word is also fitting: *expiate*: from *expiare*, "to atone." Will I become an expatriate who gives his time to wandering through a journal, pen in hand, merely expatiating, leaving his life unlived? But *expatiating* once meant "to wander freely." Is to figure the way to find the way? Let the travel direct the traveler? So, Doctor Nathaniel Trennant, at age thirty-four, what is it to be?

About the *Narwhale* herself, I have said nothing, a conspicuous omission given I will be resident here for the next thirty or forty days. Everyone aboard—from shipmaster to the youngest in steerage—hopes it is no longer than an extended month before the American coast appears on the horizon and we can disembark into the New World for new lives. The ship is a typical packet, a square rigger of three masts—fore, main, mizzen—each carrying as much sail as possible since rapidity of crossing is the purpose of a packet. Painted on the foretop sail is the house emblem, a blue anchor on a field of green, an impressive image when the wind blows it into full expansion. Good it is to be driven by fair winds rather than smoky coal.

The *Narwhale* is American owned and American built of live oak, cedar, and locust, her masts of Maine white pine, and her hull sheathed in copper to fend off teredos, those mollusks capable of devouring timbers from the inside to leave planks so eaten into hollowness even a casual wave can knock the hardest oak into powder. She is somewhat tubby—I mean to say, *blunt of bow*—constructed to transport on eastward return trips all the cargo her below-decks can hold, the result being her prow butts waves so that we continually hear the voice of the sea and feel the whack and thump of water resisting our presence, and at times retarding progress. Because packets carry no armament, she has false gun-ports painted above the waterline. I cannot imagine the fakery deceiving a pirate.

Of her several decks, highest is the forecastle forward; all the way abaft is the poop deck, or quarterdeck, surmounted by the ship's wheel, the binnacle standing in front of the helmsman. Immediately below is the captain's cabin with the only enclosed, stern view opening to the leagues we have put behind. Forward from the poop—both starboard and port—are four dozen passenger cabins, double berths each but for mine. On the same deck is the dining saloon, with a skylight valued by us all for illumination and ventilation. Also forward but separate is the deckhouse, with galley and crew dining table. Nearby are two frightfully cramped pens: one for poultry, another holding a few sheep and pigs, all to be slaughtered, roasted, and served up by our steward. At times we can smell the beasts and fowls yet to suffer the knife as we partake of a meal made from one of them, an experience conducive to checking some appetites.

Beneath the main deck and running almost the length of the ship is the massive hold carrying English cargo of woolen textiles and roofing tiles. Above is a partial deck, only thirty feet wide, to house steerage passengers on claustrophobic sleep platforms—four or five bodies per berth—each stacked so closely as to allow one to lie down but never sit up. On the return trip eastward, the steerage deck will carry not humanity but more cargo—baled cotton, Yankee cheeses, tobacco. Between the rows of bunks are two long tables with benches for meals or cards or backgammon or checkers.

Forward of steerage, in the forecastle, are quarters with berths for seamen, mostly New Englanders, a space only slightly better than steerage, its betterment due to fewer bodies pressed into proximity. Were it otherwise possible to give an accurate picture of passage, I would leave unspoken how we in cabins have pitchers and washbowls and chamber pots. Those in steerage have a pair of iron basins and eight pails to haul down seawater; as for that most personal of necessities, several slops buckets behind a curtain serve the purpose. Only the poverty steerage folk come from makes these woeful contrivances bearable, a tolerance assisted by their dreams of a golden future now but weeks ahead. There is no justification for these crudities other than the demands of corporate ownership to extract maximum financial profit from a voyage, the poor a helpless target for ignored regulations intended to reduce costs and enrich a company.

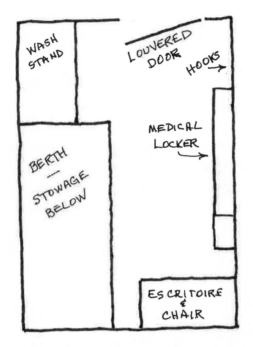

The physician's cabin—sketched here—is less spacious than the captain's quarters, but sufficient for a crossing. The louvered door admits air as well as noise—which just now is a clamor on the main deck. I leave my pages to look into it. (It was here the little family perished, and of that I will say no more.)

5 April

Last evening the captain invited me to dine with him in his comparatively spacious quarters. The meal was roast fowl along with English strawberries still fresh enough to enjoy. We sat to eat immediately, Finn hurrying through the supper before leaning back until I cleared my plate. He captains a conversation as he does a ship, expertly and in full command of the direction. Talking acutely, he listens only to come up with a question opening to his desired topic. This is not to say his talk is unworthy.

He poured brandies and passed a box of long and slender Dominican cigars, adding, "Brandy and a good cigar promote the human brain into meditation or discourse, and the finest discourse is meditative. Yes, Doctor?"

"I'm not a smoker, but tonight I'll engage with you," I answered. Immediately he was off onto a subject he had, I believe, foreordained for supper. "I'm a Yankee of the seas," said he, "though I do have a home, a place I'm rarely able to visit. My first billet was as an apprentice navigator on a whaler—the *Flying Gallinipper*, she was. I made but a single voyage with her, twenty-six months, New Bedford to the North Pacific and again home. To see grand beasts of the deeps cut and boiled down to oil was not to my liking. I returned to the house to find my bride gone off to parts no one could say, and in her stead was my sister, a woman good and true, but with an inherited torso too much like mine—which is to say, she's a spinster. The house is now hers to use as a schoolroom to teach ten young scholars and—where she allows it—I keep books there. Those not here on board."

He motioned towards two facing bookshelves mounted to the bulkheads.

"You notice above, what I'm reading on this sailing. Opposite is a shelf of fifty volumes I term Finn's Fifty. The two score and ten most significant books for me."

He stood to take down *The Consolation of Philosophy*. Inscribed on the endpaper in the careful script of a navigator was a question:

—Humanity is rational?

"It's my persuasion," said he, "an educated reader should maintain two bookshelves: one of current readings, the other of works of enduring personal worth. As one grows, the second shelf will evolve. What's important at age twenty may prove to be piffle and bunkum at forty. Such a book then goes into the general collection, replaced by a recent discovery. Changes become less frequent as I age, so now the Finn Fifty serves as a virtual spiritual *autobiography*—written by sundry hands—reminding me who I am. Who I've been."

I started to inquire about human rationality, but he continued before I could get my words out.

"At times, I'll take down one of the Fifty to reread in its entirety, but more often just to think about certain passages. Fluent expression of acute perceptions we rarely come upon from pens today. Do you find readers are now accustomed to thin gruel?"

As I nodded, he already was off into another topic, this one a recommendation, since I'm a physician, of Robert Burton's *Anatomy of Melancholy*. Then he veritably leapt towards Finn's Fifty to pull forth Thomas Browne's *Religio Medici*, turning pages to read aloud a marked sentence:

> Great account and much profit is made of unicorne horne, wherein notwithstanding, many I perceive suspect an imposture, and some conceive there is no such animal extant.

I smiled in recognition, and he asked, "Tell me, is there a living writer who could compose a like sentence?"

"No one wanting to reach the common reader." Having the floor briefly, I seized the opportunity to say Dr. Browne was the source of my challenge to the captain's narwhale hiking staff that had introduced us and led to his offering me voyage to America. A new topic not immediately coming to his mind, the captain said, "Well then, how about another brandy?"

6 *April*

Awakened at two a.m. by an agitating dream, I went topside to the transom to watch the following sea, our progress easy but not swift, the foam of our wake reflecting from a gibbous moon and leaving a long silvery trail whence we have been, a path disappearing even as it bubbles up. Over our leagues of sailing we have left no lasting mark, and to look eastward where lay England, it seemed I had only imagined those miles.

I stood near the capstan to observe the black ocean ahead not yet inscribed by the ship running towards *terra incognita* lying onward, although we now foresee not every one of us will arrive on the American shore. I stayed so long I could discern the Great Bear having ranged across the sky as if it too were in quest of new territory. Then I returned to my cabin to set down these night thoughts, musings in the dark.

Is the miracle of language how it allows us to retrieve time? I remember the weather of yesterday, but of Tuesday last, scarce recall remains save what I have written here; yet, when I peep deeper into the written repository where memories reside, words permit me to relive that Tuesday. It is as close to life immortal as we can assuredly know.

In the material realm, what we term *the present* doesn't exist unless we arrest it from its infinitely rapid passage: the moment a *now* arrives is the same moment it vanishes, too brief to apprehend, attend, comprehend, or transcend what just happened. To halt its progress in order to *realize* it, our noblest tool is a pen, say, this one a primary feather pulled from a mute swan's left wing (its angle fitting my right hand), dipped in lamp black from my inkhorn to record a present event for recollection and examination. So here sits the scrivener holding an insubstantial quill once borne among clouds and now descended to put into flight words ascending in a human brain to forfend against the inevitable erasure of what we have earned with our days. If we cannot truly grasp the present except through memory, and we cannot see the future except through imagination, then the present does not belong to us, lying as it does beyond our capacities, coming and going faster than even our ceaseless planetary and solar motions.

When the *Narwhale* arrives on the western shore, we will have gained seventy degrees of longitude, ten degrees of latitude, and covered almost four thousand miles. So I ask: What will remain of those degrees and leagues the day after, or in the years following, or at the moment my eyes close forever? If this journal can capture pieces of our passage across the sea, then one day it might provide answer to a question from a descendant: *How got ye into this territory?* If we give credence to the Magi, so fine it would be to read an account from Balthazar telling of their travails towards the splendent, westerly bound star.

8 April

It has been two days—can it be three?—since I last opened this journal, a rough sea and a round of nausea numbing my urge to dip my pen. I think I am now gaining my sea legs.

Memorandum: The death of the family a few days ago brought into my sleep a return of the keening specter, the Woman in White, facing away from me, hiding her expression, arms seeming to cradle something, her form growing larger until she woke me. I had hoped the Atlantic, the pitch and plunge and roll of the *Narwhale*, would wash her into the deep, silence her, and allow me to escape what has become an obliquity of the night.

To clear my mind, I passed part of the morning on deck to toss quoits with the men. (We use rings of hemp rather than iron to prevent injury to the planks, and the stake is a broken chair leg.) Others stayed in the dining saloon to play chess, checkers, backgammon, dominoes, whist. To the approbation of all, the ship moved along under a full press of sail, so much so I went to the binnacle twice to check our course with my dear pocket compass, noting with satisfaction we had knocked off several degrees of westing. I stood above the transom to watch our following sea and consider how each league we leave behind is one more we will not have to cover again. Onward our destiny! Because of hindrance from prevailing winds and currents, sailing the North Atlantic westward usually requires sixteen more days than the eastward run, and for that reason seamen term our route *sailing uphill.*

This afternoon, a fellow from Coventry, an amiable man who plans to buy an apothecary shop in Philadelphia, asked a lad—by chance the very ship's boy who had frozen aloft on our departure—to take an empty gin bottle and hang it from a line attached to a yardarm. I watched him ascend the rigging, cautiously but without stopping, to tie off the bottle; again on deck, he smiled, and I slipped him a half crown. The man of Coventry opened a leather case, and put forward a brace of well-fashioned Italian pistols and a contest to see who could hit the bottle first, the winner gaining a jug of West Indies rum. A coin flip gave me the initial shot.

I missed, but in self-defense I note the heave of the ship and the sway of the bottle made marksmanship more luck than skill. After each of us had a dozen failed tries, I nicked the bottle enough to knock its bottom off and leave the remainder swinging to and fro from its neck like a hanged man. At supper, I uncorked the rum at our table to share the cheer.

A woman in a group known surreptitiously among the crew as "the Gilded Ones of Kent," about whom I will say more anon, asked, "Does our good doctor intend to turn our dining saloon into a common American saloon?" I called upon her to observe that the portions were of a size not to inebriate but merely to jollify. "Let it be just so then," said she. I note here that this Mrs. Bentley—in the company of Mr. Bentley, a maker of textiles who intends to open a manufactory near Boston—commonly refers to those in steerage as *our inescapable dregs,* and complains of the odor rising from below on warm evenings. She is a handsome matron of later years, but taking to her requires one to view poverty as an unavoidable economic annoyance; further, one must acquiesce to her belief that all other minds should carry only her certainties. She would empty a room of all opinions but hers. Mr. Bentley, lacking physical stature, seeks to overcome, may I say, *shortcomings* through expansive self-regard, and in that endeavor, he succeeds.

11 April

Our ninth full day at sea: this morning Captain Finn summoned me to attend a German woman with an infected forearm who lay ill in steerage, which I had not yet visited although I circulate among the immigrants topside. Our exchanges are limited to smiles and nods but for those few possessing touches of English; I asked our young interpreter how to say, "Forgive me, but I don't speak German (or Polish)," an apology always warmly accepted and often followed by a handshake. As for the two nationalities, segregated by language, they are tentatively beginning to mix as if making themselves ready for the *American melting pot*, a phrase they all carried in mind even before embarking.

Taking my medical kit, I went below to the woman; she lay forlorn on a wooden platform sleeping three others, one an unrelated male. In the dimness and confusions, the press of humanity makes it difficult for anybody to get more distant from each other than an arm length, requiring everyone into continual dodging and turning sideways so others may bend or pass. Over her was a damp and sour blanket. The interpreter, a Prussian named Zofia, assisted me in accented but precise English. The German patient, Irena, was apprehensive, and I spoke to calm her, saying she would be dancing by tomorrow night; she smiled, knowing there was scarcely space to stand let alone dance.

Her forearm, wrapped in a soiled cloth, had sustained a three-inch laceration from a fall into a cargo box. The flesh was morbid with suppuration but not gangrened. Twice I had to request a glomeration of the curious to give her air, stale as it was. Upon seeing her injury, the more squeamish gasped, considerably alarming the patient. Zofia, young as she is, forcefully ordered them back. I explained the wound must be cleaned before bandaging it, but once done, she would feel less discomfort. Irena bore up well, and when I finished wrapping her arm, I said she would live to reach her new country, and in words I believe were English, she answered, "I am living tomorrow to see America!" She put two fingers to her lips and raised her hand towards me and said, "I zink God now to bliss you."

12 April

This morning I returned to find Irena sitting up, and under the dim glow of the hanging oil lamps I replaced the bandage. Only then did I have opportunity to take in the steerage deck and request Zofia to accompany me and translate where necessary. Of exquisite proportion, a diamond of the first water, she is three and twenty, and fair enough that in the dimness of steerage she appears illumined from within, a glowing in the gloom, a face to absorb light to release in darkness. When she speaks, her words come forth like fireflies, glimmering with help and hope.

Even though the *Narwhale* is one of the newer Yankee packets sailing the North Atlantic route, the conditions in this *'tween decks*, as the sailors term it, its low overhead requiring tall men to duck, are only marginally better than in a pen for shipping cattle. Sitting just above the waterline, the area is subject to a near constant crash of the sea against the hull, noise blending with voices suspiring a range of human conditions: crying infants; grandmothers praying in Polish, German, or impaired English; men calling out to scold obstreperous children.

A continual scurry of rats scavenges in clefts and corners where debris accumulates—rags, bones, rancid biscuit putrefying with maggots—filth from previous voyages. The air is rank with poorly washed bodies, slops buckets overturned by rough seas, the deck permeated with regurgitations of bad food or from seasickness. More worrisome are incidents of a looseness of the bowels, which

I trust is not early indication of dysentery or worse, cholera. The unpleasant irony in this instance is that cabin passengers tend towards the costive, a consequence of an unwise diet of meats and cheeses with few vegetables other than potatoes. Below, the problem reverses to *different* inadequate fare—too much biscuit (the unleavened flatbread New Englanders call *crackers*) and stale cheese washed down with water only days from putrescence and now beyond the tempering of vinegar. Tainted or otherwise, precious little meat is available in steerage.

In fine weather, the people go up to the main deck, but space allows no more than three dozen at a time. (The raised poop deck is restricted, and a steerage person stepping under the rope is soundly shouted off.) Cabin passengers have a continual worry about contracting illness from steerage—a not unwarranted concern—and I think none has gone below, and few will engage in any way with those whose journey to America can require half a year's wages.

Is the lure of the Golden Land so great, or is it the motherland was so miserable? Captain Finn says some of our steerage folk, within weeks of alighting in America, will deeply long for the old country, and will approach him in New York to hire them to earn their passage back home. A destitute woman may resort to prostitution to buy her family a return ticket. These are émigrés never spoken of in the emigration guidebooks, those pushed towards a new world by insolvency and misery, fugitives from poverty, war, repression, political impotence. And some are indeed actual fugitives fleeing justice, ones who present considerable risk not only to other émigrés but also to cabin passengers; one rogue male attempted an assault on a teenage girl in steerage and was severely beaten by his neighbors. So I heard.

Captain Finn terms an immigrant seeking return a "retrogressor," and will not take him aboard for fear his tainted experience could lead to trouble.

As ship's doctor, I encourage those below, especially children, to escape the squalor and malodorous air and come up into the sunlight, but as I have said, space on deck is at a premium in all but foul weather. (Captain Finn will not allow children on the main deck unless under watch by an adult.) At the least, exposure to fresh sea breezes airs clothing and pulls away noisome dampness from it. I write *clothing*, but the truth is many of the garments are little more than tatters and shreds; women, their dresses frayed thin, wrap themselves in shawls unable to block wind hardly better than were they of cheesecloth.

And, to be sure, simply *seeing* sunshine further freshens spirits, yearnings, the humors, and reminds people of the reasons they are undergoing the ordeal of steerage. In good weather, no one departs an open sky without feeling the spell of sea and sun refortifying resolve and endurance, reawakening dreams of America, revivifying aspirations to hold misery in abeyance. Those unable to reach the main deck must abide in the wretched dimness below, assisted only by prayer, friendship, and belief in the ancient nostrum "This too shall pass." Among the company of Germans is a rabbi, and alongside Jews coming to him is now a contingent of Christians who, having no priest or parson aboard, wish to celebrate similarities rather than argue differences, perhaps recognizing before a creator, a kneel might serve as well as a *daven*.

The voyage continuing, minor illnesses increase, making Captain Finn cautious about asking me to go into steerage, his fear being I will contract a malady to preclude my being of use to anybody, especially the cabineers. As fearless a mariner as he is, bearing fatigue better than any man I have known, ready to face the Atlantic or an angry sailor flashing a marlin spike, he *does* lean towards accommodating cabin class beyond a true democratic impulse. Still, he recognizes the threat in steerage of an outbreak of smallpox or cholera or typhus. He knows, other than fire, nothing else so imperils an immigrant ship.

In the lower hold are twin freshwater storage tanks of iron imparting a strong ferric taste inhibiting the beneficial practice of regular hydration. I have posted notices above and below urging all to drink water even if they vitiate the iron flavor with vinegar or cinnamon or a bud of clove, but such ameliorations are scarce in steerage. For everyone, the fresh water is, if I need say it, only for drinking. Cold seawater is for bathing. Even the air in the dining saloon, when the overhead hatch is closed because of weather, has turned somewhat more humanly odoriferous. During the rainstorm of yesterday, a few males from below decks and four of us from above went out with bars of soap, and tried to wash body *and* the clothes we were wearing. Several, encouraged by the ship's physician, stripped to their nether garments. The rain was nippingly chill, and uttered among us were jests about, what I will term, *shrinkages*.

14 April

With each day, the fresh water tastes evermore of iron, and that encourages steerage folk who have *some* specie to buy beer or rum from the cook or certain seamen who packed their seabags with spirits; happily, exploitive prices make drunkenness uncommon, and it will become even less so as the voyage proceeds and the supply dwindles. Among both men in steerage and ordinary seamen, liquor has been used to gain the attention of a few women who find it necessary (so I prefer to think) to exchange favors of the flesh for intoxicants they then trade for foodstuffs to feed a child. Two of them are with husbands who must endure this shame.

Yesternight at supper in the saloon, whilst Captain Finn was engaged elsewhere, I brought up conditions in steerage, only to be interrupted by a husband in the Gilded Coterie who said my topic was unseemly in the company of ladies. A woman not with the Kentish folk said sharply, "Let our physician speak!" As I resumed, the table emptied of all except six of us. How deplorable those who could ameliorate life in steerage choose to remain ignorant of conditions only inches of oak planking beneath them. Upper-deck passengers smell those below, but few will engage them. If I put my stethoscope to the thorax of a member of the cabinocracy, I would hear naught but the feeblest *pitapat* of a wizened heart.

Too slow have I been to realize among immigrants to America there also will forever be those lacking any democratic impulse, *their* American dream having no place for egalitarianism. And so, I fear, the seeds of oligarchy *and* plutocracy are surely aboard this ship, even among those in steerage. My foreboding is part of the great question about the survival of the American experiment.

I see now one of the reasons I am here: my journal, which I packed along to help occupy time by reconnoitering the experiment whilst reckoning my own past, need be more than a mere record of days and miles traveled. I must turn it to purposes beyond self and make it akin to the afghan being knitted by the lady across the passageway who sits quietly crocheting to create out of her arrested hours and the imprisonment of a sea voyage something useful. I resolve to direct my sea-necessitated physical immobility into a mobility of mind, to do what the dumb animal cannot— reckon circumstances, turn inevasible limitations towards service, and view this ship as an expression of the great experiment itself.

My purpose may rise from the scratchings of a pen. Out of an inkpot, meaning rises. And so, a single life recently thought lost might be regained to offer something *of some use* to somebody.

16 April

I have become aware no one in steerage is suffering more from the restricted space than three dozen children. Those not unwell or listless from confinement struggle to stifle the unbounded energy and impetuosity of hale youth. Cramped as they are into a hell of boredom and unrelieved idleness, the children's initial excitement about a sea voyage has worn down into fragile tolerance, their enthusiasm eradicated, the realities of ocean travel making them either restive or phlegmatic of spirit.

I traded the purser seven half crowns for a fistful of shining sixpence. Captain Finn allowed the children onto the poop deck where I seated them and gave each a sixpence, a sum most had never before held. Using a half crown they could see more readily, I held it up, let them study it, touch it, then *abracadabra*, made it vanish. In their various languages, they cried to see the conjuring again. Over the next hour coins disappeared only to reappear; I pulled them from the scarves of girls, found them under the caps of boys, and one in the shoe of a passing boatswain, all in a demonstration of my meager sleight of hand. "Come tomorrow," Zofia translated, "and our magus will teach *you* the magic," and they went below, grasping tightly their shiny coins and, I trust, looking forward to a morrow.

Having descended twice into steerage, I could no longer walk the main deck or lie in my berth without awareness of what existed beneath, a human misery to be atoned for only if those immigrant souls succeed in finding a truly new world they now so unshakenly trust in even though their evidence is nothing more than words; to a certainty, stories spoken or written constitute much of the basis for belief in the American experiment. And so, a grand question: Are those attestations substantial enough to hold against the destructive tyranny of self-interest?

17 April

With the approach of the first storm of note, a crewman taught me to anticipate foul weather by its telltale signs: low-lying clouds, a ring around the moon, a school of dolphins moving swiftly downwind, distinctive swells in the sea. Indeed, distant lightning flashed, the air grew heavy and sailors hurried aloft to furl the sails. As the wind began to blow from thirty-one points of the compass (it missed west-by-northwest), three men fought to master the tiller to maintain control of the giant rudder. With all hatches battened down, steerage and even topside cabins became stifling, the oppression eased only slightly by North Atlantic air gaining access through the most narrow of chinks. Below, impossible it was to undertake any activity other than retaining oneself within a berth; those folk lay on their crowded platforms, rolling into each other time and again with the regularity of the waves. Once the sea calmed, seasickness further befouled the air.

The constraints of having to stay inside leave the children predictably unsettled. Aboard is an old salt, a Nantucketer and friend of the captain's, one Caleb Button, who knows tales and tells them dramatically, some of them possessing an element or two of truth; his grizzled beard and wrinkled visage lend him a seaborne authority respected even by the hardened jack-tars. Several children have learnt my quartet of sleight of hand and are teaching others, so a different strategy was in order. I assembled them near the quarterdeck, Zofia present to translate, first in Polish, then in German. Old Button launched himself into yarns: a whale hunt, a mutiny on a privateer where only his swordsmanship saved him, a large seabird carrying off a wicked girl. Within the hour, as if planned, a corroborative occurrence lent itself to his fable.

A fulmar, exhausted from the storm, flapped in to perch on one of the yards above the helmsman, but soon dropped to the binnacle, where the children could almost touch the bird. It had no urge to return to the air and sat composed as the old salt modified his recountal to say the creature might eat a child unless fed scraps, a detail sending six moppets to the cook to beg him for tidbits from the garbage bucket. The fulmar, spotting the offerings of offal, rose from its crouch and made a gruff chuckling until Caleb pitched it a piece of pork fat.

A German man, angered by seeing the creature given humanly edible food, pushed forward with a belaying pin in hand to club the spent thing, his motivation not pointless brutality but rather securing provender to, if I may, *flesh out* the sorry rations of his mates below. The children—inadequately fed as they were—protested, valuing the entertainment of a *marblehead* (in sailor's lingo) over its potential nutriment. The German nevertheless came on, club raised, the bird still unwilling to fly. A Polish girl, by no means the tallest, ran forth to grab at the pin, and even this uproar did not disturb the fulmar, although sufficient to make the man stand down. I warned that the behavior of the critter might indicate disease and it should not be consumed; after we dispersed at sundown the bird vanished. Later I learned the poor fowl was taken below to be butchered and eaten.

I was not surprised: for the last week, any steerage rat caught below has found the same fate, including one girl's pet she discovered under her bunk; having paralysis in its hind legs, it could only drag itself. She nurtured it with what she scrounged. Once fattened, unbeknownst to her, it disappeared, only to be cooked, and on the sly fed to her. Zofia said, "Her papa thought it more important to keep his daughter alive than amused."

A related event: a German boy, skilled with a slingshot, twice managed to kill a rat then sent to the cook—with a few pence in bribe—for roasting. With a little salt—*and* an appetite—rodent flesh is sweetly esculent. So says Zofia.

18 April

This morn I was awakened by gunfire. Of three porpoises swimming alongside the ship as they are wont to do, one had been wounded so it could not dive, and two seamen got boat hooks into it and were pulling it on board, a heavy and bloody task eliciting a heated discussion about to whom its parts should go. Captain Finn intervened, silenced the argument, and assigned three dozen cuts to cabin passengers, the rest to steerage. Our meat-heavy menu makes it easy for three of us to decline our portion, thereby pleasing the Gilded, not one of whom needed more meat.

The remaining mammal going below was the first fresh animal protein provided, other than rodents and one fulmar, since leaving Plymouth. For the children, the porpoise head, intact though emptied of brains, became a fabulous exhibit. By this afternoon, Caleb had ready a tale about a sea beast swallowing a disorderly boy.

The young are picking up bits of English in a vocabulary heavily nautical and touched up with marine life: *mast, yardarm, binnacle, pirate, jellyfish, octopus, walrus*. Also phrasings: *chock-a-block, bilge pump, sheet the sails, trice up the jib*. And, inescapably, several *sailor's blessings* (never corrected by the parents, who understand scarcely a word of profanity). In concern for his health, aged Caleb is not allowed in steerage, so Zofia helps the children retell the tales, however ineptly, to their sickly mates confined below.

19 April

Our days have fallen into repetitions, events I have already reported on, although yesterday Mrs. Bentley of the Gilded Coterie of Kent, as wearied as the rest of us, at supper let loose an expulsion of complaints, soon checked by one of the twin sisters, Celia and Cecily, traveling to join family in Michigan. Celia said, "Please, Missus Bentley, remember you are on a wooden ship at sea. We all are aware of tribulations and insufficiencies. We recognize our lives are on short measure here and will be for a time undetermined. It behooves us not to continually fuss about inescapable inadequacies. The comforts of your fireside simply aren't available now. Think of those below!" Though scowling, Mrs. B drew herself into a haughty silence for which we all were grateful.

Cecily came up to me after the meal to say, "Were Celia and I to offer money to the ship's cook, would he make a little extra food for the immigrants below? A nourishing soup could be made from the marrow bones and meat trimmings he throws overboard."

Recently I learned the ship's larder was full of bags of dried lentils the crew refuses. I found the cook, a Jamaican with a perpetual tobacco pipe, along the rail where I broached the twins' proposal. He was amenable to the bribe in exchange for a daily kettle of lentil soup to be quietly sent to steerage. Should others in the cabinocracy hear of it, their frugality of empathy might create trouble.

Grumbling about a headache and feeling logy and gassy, Mrs. Bentley recently came to my cabin. Judging from the ship's menu of excessive carnivorous fare, especially salt pork, and from her breath and cadaverous pallor, I concluded the problem was likely obstipation of the bowels. I compounded a cathartic of Culver's root, the whole time thinking what she truly needed was not a purgative of the intestines but a lavage of the soul.

She will remain in her quarters, her husband looking after her. We are grateful for reprieve from a person so able to gasify a conversation (or a closed room). In her absence, Mrs. Bentley's oligarchic mouthings are now taken up by her friend, Lucretia Hardwig, who complains about Caleb's yarns of sea monsters and a sailor gone mad who tore off his tunic and ran about frenzied— and *quite naked*. Averred she: "Never a Bible story! Never mention of anything Divine!"

In response the next day, the old salt told a graphic version of Jonah and the leviathan, describing the monstrous size of its pizzle and how, once thoroughly dried and trimmed, a whale's penile bone makes a good walking stick. To prove up his anecdotes, he showed one he bought in Madagascar. Adults studied it amused—or aghast. It furnished distraction, something valued almost as much as a porpoise filet. (Zoological note: prepared phallus of porpoise sailors consider a delicacy of the deep.)

Caleb's tales—and *details*—are in demand, with the young now imploring for the capture of a whale. In their growing English vocabulary, a new word of a genital nature has replaced the popularity of *walrus* and *matey*—even girls have been overheard whispering it. Given the importance of any reprieve from ennui, I am glad for a touch of cetacean reproductive physiology.

The 20th inst.

Mrs. Bentley, recovered from her previous distress and favorably inclined towards my herbals, has come again to complain, this time of insomnia. The ship's medical cabinet, as is standard, contains a store of laudanum. I prepared a tonic from a few grains of it added to a jigger of rum. Having Mrs. Bentley catch up on her sleep can only be a boon to us all; I had to rely on the pledge in the Hippocratic Oath in order to dispel my notion of making it longer lasting than her restlessness required. To alleviate the discomfort of *one* can be to ease it for many.

Now, if only her second-in-command, Miss Hardwig, would ask for a soporific agent of my own devising. She has taken up the testiness of her friend, and her voice has become ever more harping and shrill. A wasp sting in the ear would be preferable. She recently groused to Captain Finn about the singing of sea chanteys, in her words, "bawdy songs of rowdy sailors."

On a long voyage, any music should be welcome. Yesterday she demanded the captain confiscate all liquor and pour it overboard. Wanting to avoid complaints to the company on our arrival, Cap'n nodded agreement and later ordered the ship's sergeant to collect every empty bottle he could find and fill each with bilge water. Calling the matron forth this afternoon to witness the dumping, he made certain she could hear a smirking Irish sailor say, "Mates, tonight there'll be a school of tunny half-seas over stumblin blind through Davy Jones' locker," to which she answered, "Better drunken sea creatures than seamen."

This evening the ship's carpenter, an Italian fiddler, took up his instrument and from atop the forecastle cut loose with a tarantella, pleasing those from steerage gathered on deck for air. They listened and clapped, then sang, and men began pulling onto wives, sailors offering hands to any female near, or, failing that, grabbing one another. Such a confusion and snarl of contrary motions I have never seen: a jig entangled with a schottische, a mazurka fouled with a rigadoon, a confoundment of footwork heretofore unknown to have come from human legs. I looked across the tossing bodies, and on the forecastle ladder *she* was standing, her radiance turned towards me, and I went to Zofia, and we joined the crush, laughing at our clumsy cadence, our discordant steps expressing not our heads but our hearts, and the fiddler played madly into the pandemonium.

For those from steerage, it was the first time since boarding that joy overwhelmed weariness and apprehension, smiles overcame scowls, and laughter overmastered despondence. Captain Finn reminded cabinocracy it was not drink lifting hoi polloi spirits but music. Not till then had the expectations and dreams in steerage risen higher, nor had their confidence in emigrating been stronger. As for the Gilded Coterie of Kent, I can only hope the ship's supply of laudanum and rum will hold out.

22 April (I think)

Everybody, from cabinocracy to steerage, is keen to leave the sea and set our feet on American *terra firma* to begin pursuing the lives we have imagined, no one more eager than I for change and the challenge of making my way into the American experiment. O to get free of these hampered days! (I happily note winds have begun favoring us.)

Rumor—the lifeblood of shipboard scuttlebutt—is circulating about the freshwater tanks dropping low. *Fresh* is a relative term here. From a Devonshire river, the water came aboard only a degree or two better than out of a ditch. Further, some table fare in steerage is going rancid or rotting: turnips and parsnips withering, potatoes wrinkling. In the dining saloon it is also evident our food is declining, as biscuit and oatmeal occupy a growing portion on our plates.

I had noticed Zofia starting to look peaked, but she assured me she was well enough. Her brother, Henryk, awakened me at midnight. (I was relieved to discover it was not the Woman in White tapping at the door.) We went below where I found on a crowded sleeping platform Zofia, feverish and mumbling out of her head. Her temperature: 102 degrees. Henryk and I carried her to my cabin to place her in my bunk, and immediately I made two febrifuges, one of willow bark, the other a Labrador tea. I laid out a pallet for myself on the deck nearby whence I could monitor her breathing, but my exhaustion put me to sleep till sunrise.

Though her lips were parched, she lay peacefully, and when I whispered her name she opened her eyes slowly and in Polish asked for water. It is useful the Blue Anchor Line permits the ship's physician to keep a full cask of fresh water for medical treatment. As stale as it is, she drank six ounces whilst I prepared another round of teas. Her temperature: 100.

She murmured something I couldn't make out, and I told her she must continue resting. I sent word for her friend Irena to bathe Zofia and wash her garments. I was relieved inspection turned up no lice. Throughout the day, I applied to the back of her neck compresses chilled with seawater, and by evening she was able to sit up, her temperature down another degree. She at last spoke, asking had I bathed her? No, I replied, it was her dedicated Irena. She smiled, an expression of modest relief. Her night was without incident.

23 April

We are in our third week, everyone hoping cautiously it marks our voyage beyond halfway. The morning began with three noisy children chastened for attempting to cadge coins from the cabinocracy, money they hoped to use to bribe the steward for a few uneaten morsels from our overloaded plates—biscuit, a bit of meat, a withered beetroot. I wish that was the only untoward event, but I have not said all.

Zofia, fully recovered, found me on deck and led me to a woman who gave birth three days ago to a son weighing but four pounds. The pitiful fare in steerage impeded sufficient lactation, and when I arrived, the infant was dead at his mother's dry breast. I asked to take the child to my quarters for preparation. She refused. Only after forceful persuasion by Zofia did the woman release the little corpse, already stiff with rigor mortis.

For the mother I prepared a lenitive Zofia took to her as I washed the child and wrapped it in a clean remnant of sailcloth. Captain Finn came to the rail to officiate, and the diminutive bundle was lowered into the Atlantic along the fortieth meridian, a detail I noted on the death attestation. The shrouded body, so tiny on the sea swell, looked like a bubble as it bobbed briefly before the sodden sailcloth pulled it down. Watching, I wondered what potential legislator, inventor, scientist had just been sent to the sea bottom and forever lost to America.

I think the burial was the cause of the reoccurrence of my nocturnal haunting about the Woman in White carrying her small fardel, but this time she turned towards me to hold up what she cradled, and I violently awoke, perspiring and shaken. I did not return to sleep, unable to shut down remembrance of the death that launched me on this voyage. I am a Jonah who cannot escape a decision to flee, but no leviathan exists to save me from what continues in pursuit. Now, as I record these events, I recall the timeworn adage in medicine: "Physicians get to bury their mistakes." But even at that, this *Herr Doktor* is inept, because his mistake lives on to walk the night and render retribution.

24 April

In the morning, with no requests for the ship's physician, I wandered into the dining saloon to sit listening, abstractedly I admit, to the day's *debate*, a thrice-weekly quodlibet concocted to pass time when chess or whist or checkers wears thin for those of the cabinocracy who term themselves not *emigrants* but *colonists*. Deliberation topics change but never move far from plutocratic interests. The issue today was betwixt Madison's position at the Constitutional Convention and what here was considered a Jeffersonian vision of American democracy. Mr. Bentley took the Madisonian argument, expressed in Madison's own words: "A decent society must protect the minority of the opulent against the majority." The opposition (if it may be so termed) was vaguely Jeffersonian: "While democracy is to be desired, it must recognize certain social and economic limitations necessary to sustain it." Once again it was clear, if the cabinocracy view those in steerage as essential to a free economy, there remains this question: What degree of remuneration should their *economic necessity* entitle them? Whilst often reminding us all of their belief that *inequity is inherent in reality*, the cabineers implicitly embrace privilege.

It seems a more genuine debate might be had between, say, Sir Walter Raleigh and a person arrived on a slave ship, or even an indentured servant. Somewhere within such a conversation lies a more practical and just and more *enduring* definition of American democracy. As the men (only two women were in attendance) spoke their sentiments, I had to assume I was watching seeds from an old world being carried into the new realm, seeds that would sprout as does flax or hemp—the one used to clothe, the other to bind.

I left the group to its dialectic and glasses of sherry, happy to escape, ever more so when I saw Zofia speaking to a German child sitting by the mainmast, the girl holding something in her cupped fingers. When I looked closely, she explained what I heard as "*Ist cahfer.*" In her palm was a large black beetle. Zofia said the lass wanted me to stroke her bug, so I placed my hand next to hers to allow the critter to crawl over to me. Believing the most imaginative and inventive children survive best, I encouraged her with two of the few German words I know, *sehr schön*—which unleashed an outpouring from her. Zofia said, "She's telling how she found it in her bedding, and now she carries it in a sock." The child displayed a sock riddled with lice, keeping the beetle in better fettle than the humanity in steerage. I went to my cabin for a vial to give the girl to house her bug, and traded her one of my kerchiefs for the sock I carried to Captain Finn for his examination.

In vexation, he said, "What's it now?" Then seeing the lice, "Get the blasted things out of here! Deep six them!" My remonstration, as calm as I could make it, was this: If there be one louse, then there be a hundred, and if a hundred there be a thousand. The rank bedding and unwashed clothing in steerage are crawling with insectivorous vermin. We must begin airing and sunning bedding and washing clothes. He reminded me of the limited open-deck space, to which I said we can set up shifts of a dozen people at a time to haul up their blankets for ninety minutes of sunlight. He argued the wind would carry it all into the sea; my answer was we could use an extra spar to weight it all down.

Responding in words I will not forget, he said, "Doctor, the body louse was created for some purpose, so it is our duty to bear with them." Surprised by such a rejoinder from an intelligent man, I argued his thesis would apply also to bedbugs, fleas, ticks, and a world of mites; according to him, humanity was destined to go about chewed on by parasites bringing us illness and death. He smiled condescendingly, forcing me to say I was unable to imagine he would allow the *Narwhale* to arrive in New York as a ship to be quarantined because of an epidemic of typhus fever.

He said, "Doctor, those immigrants have my full commiseration."

In annoyance I answered: "Commiseration may ease a conscience, but it salves no wounds. *Remedy* they require, not *ruth*."

Finn rose to pace the cabin, staring for some time at the wind-blown Atlantic, his worriment being Germans arguing with Poles could lead to conflict. The threat of quarantine at last overrode his reluctance, and he said, "Very well, my good physician, it is then your charge to oversee the process of airing. You may call upon the sergeant at arms if necessary." I found Zofia, who led me to the de facto superiors of the German and Polish contingents, and together they drew up ten groups of about ten passengers each, every group having ninety minutes to air bedding twice a week, weather allowing, until arrival in New York.

The proposal assigned the groups—organized by nationality—the responsibility of drawing up seawater for the washing of clothing in several tubs. Bathing below with lye-water soap provided by the ship would be superintended by proctors male or female. A refusal to bathe would mean forcible washing by German or Polish marshals of appropriate sex. Further, a changing detail would four times daily empty the slops buckets and every morning swab down the steerage deck.

In setting forth these plans, I wonder how it would have gone without Zofia's translating and urging cooperation most effectively because of the respect she commands, estimation greater than that accorded her brother. Speaking of him, I asked did his dream of America include pestiferous infestation? She said, "Henryk's dream begins with a *d* and ends with an *r*." I considered, then said, "*Doctor?*" She smiled, "If only so! But no. I mean *dollar*. He says he will never labor in field or factory."

26 April

After only two days of airing bedding, the cabinocracy has begun complaining about the chance of lice blowing or crawling into their quarters (neither has happened), and Captain Finn appears to be weakening his stance, compelling me to write a message I copy here:

Good Captain Finn,

I must raise my voice against any change in the plan we agreed to. Current personal hygiene in steerage is not only deplorable, it is dangerous to our salubrious arrival in New York. The threat of an epidemic from the preventable miseries now plaguing steerage can only create doubt and despair in those afflicted and poison their American dream. When a dream withers, it becomes highly combustible, and the spark to ignite it is misery.

As steerage falls into ever more ill health, it will turn angry and dangerous to all of us, including those passengers who have your ear. But we possess means to prevent a contagion of panic and dubiety and broken resolve. If in even moderate health, those below can travel on, carried forward by the continuance of their largely blind faith in what America may offer them. When they disembark, they will look up to the quarterdeck to bless their captain for bringing them safely and in fine fettle to the promise of those fertile lands they imagine.

I subscribe myself, Nathaniel Trennant, Ship's Physician.

The captain continues to allow the airing, even permitting washtubs topside for easier access to seawater. Whilst each group comes up to spread their fouled and fetid bedding and wash their shreds of clothing rank with vermin, I explain to them the nature of body-lice infestation and its common concomitant of typhus, describing the disease in the most graphic terms I can summon— Zofia translating accurately, so I judge from the repugnance and fear on the freshly washed faces—fever, violent headaches, rash, and above all a threat of deadly epidemic.

As I finish this account of the delousing, I ask myself: For those aboard who survive, will their posterity comprehend the ordeals their forebears underwent to gain the American shore? How long before the anguish and tribulations of immigration will be lost from memory?

The tidy logic of sentences fails to convey the oppressive afflictions these people suffer. Will their children, their grandchildren—safe from the perils of a sea crossing and sitting at kitchen tables laden with food—be able or even willing to imagine the tribulations and distress, the raw wretchedness endured by ancestors to get them— *the descendants*—to the privileged comfort of hearths and beds in the New Land?

28 April

No sooner had I opened my journal (which has lain untouched these two days) than a great huzzah rose from the main deck, where the starboard bulwark was crowded with passengers who in their excitement trampled over spread-out bedding to look at a flat-topped iceberg drifting off the coast of Newfoundland. Even though the floe lay a mile distant, the sun illuminated the deep blue in the frozen clefts, a sight granted to few humans, including those who often cross the North Atlantic, and the beauty hushed the throng for some minutes until the realization: *That coast is North America! We have crossed the Atlantic!* Men raised their ragged caps in salutation, women lifted infants to see their new continent, and joy was pervasive. The voyage, at last, was nearing end. Those who go down to the sea in ships are a species differing from most of us terrestrial beings: they are to us as the terrapin to the tortoise, a duck to a dove.

The ship reduced sail and came to a halt in calm water. Six seamen lowered the jolly boat and rowed it to the berg, where three hands clambered onto a low shelf and with hatchets began chopping at the ice, passing full buckets to the boat, dropping it so near the gunnels I thought it would founder. As the sailors returned, all of us at the rail sent up a cheer, and by the time we were moving again, the ice had been chipped and put into casks. Rationing will continue, but our disquiet over running short of drinking water before reaching New York is now allayed.

I have failed to mention the captain permitted two former Prussian fishermen to cast improvised lines from the rail, although the distance to the water made control of them difficult. A greater problem was lures: it was virtually impossible to obtain anything that might draw in a fish; after all, we are eating all potential bait. One Prussian did manage to sneak a slice of salt pork onto his hand-fashioned hook, but word of the snitched meat immediately escaped and the poor fellow was loudly abused, and events turned even uglier when he brought up his hook empty of fish *and* bait. The boatswain broke up the fracas by shouting that the man was only trying to provide fresh food for those below decks.

30 April

Hope rose this morning we will see the Narrows of Lower New York Bay on the morrow, but an approaching packet of the Gold Diamond Line changed things almost beyond forbearance. We hoisted our signal flags to indicate the *Narwhale* wanted to deliver post directed towards Europe and receive tidings about conditions in often crowded New York Harbor. The *Rappahannock* out of Philadelphia shortened sails to pause for the jolly boat to bring over Captain Finn with our letters. The missives were entirely from the cabinocracy. Those in steerage, having few pens, little paper, and no postage, and many being illiterate, are thereby unable to send news homeward. Within an hour the captain was back. The report is not propitious.

Excessive traffic has congested the New York immigration station, backing up the harbor and filling the piers with arriving ships, and diverting sea traffic to Philadelphia and Baltimore. Our voyage will be lengthened by three days, winds determining. Were it possible, some in steerage would sign on as bilge cleaners in order to return east on the *Rappahannock*. As she glided away, saddened eyes followed her until she was but a white spot on the horizon. For a few, their westward dream has reversed to turn eastward; still, most are more resigned than plaintive.

Even our fare in the saloon shows age: meat desiccated, cheese rodent-chewed, potatoes turned leathery, sugar bowls empty. Mrs. Bentley, of course, is not about to accept the decline in comestibles and the altered destination without grousing, to the point that the woman who addressed her several days ago again stood to say sternly, "Please, Missus Bentley! Silence yourself so I may call upon our good steward to pour us each a glass of claret we may lift to expedient arrival! *Somewhere!*" And so we toasted.

Captain Finn has not been able to invite me to join him at supper of late, the demands of his duties requiring him elsewhere. It may be just as well. He is a man given to lecturing rather than equitable listening; still, it is disappointing to miss out on his knowledge so different from mine.

An hour later, Mrs. Bentley came to me for a soporific. Considering the relief it would give us all, from the medical locker and my kit I mixed a lenitive, thereby further reducing the ship's and my own supply of laudanum. If there be another delay, the only remedy to keep her somnolent may be regular administration of a shillelagh to the cranium. Mr. Bentley, I add here, is retaining his sanity through, let me term it, *inspiriting*; it would not be accurate to describe him as *drunk*; rather he is merely inert—a man dormant, a mammal ready for hibernation.

The many books discussing immigration to North America—which I now say with assurance are disingenuously rosy—do not mention those travelers who do what they can to sleep their way into the American dream.

May, 1848

---

2 May

THE FRESHWATER TANKS now ring hollow when a fist is played against them, a not unwelcome sound since the liquid within—I cannot term it water—is so far gone off even vinegar or cloves fail to make it palatable; worse, this putrescence is one of the causes of the increasing incidence of dysentery. Dispensing water from the several wooden casks of melted ice floe is under continual watch by a seaman, a baton at his side. I have to wonder, were we to continue indefinitely under present conditions, how long before all aboard—from captain to steerage—would lie dead, the *Narwhale* floating on, a ghost ship with tattered sails, broken spars, her timbers slowly admitting the ocean, until she finally slides down to a salty berth beyond the Sea of Nowhere.

Yesterday my gloom led me out to the forecastle and the rail just behind the bowsprit to catch full-face the Atlantic wind. It soon revived me, and when I turned aft, I noticed Zofia whom I had not seen but at a distance in two days. I invited her to my quarters for a cup of tea made from the fresh and clear iceberg water drawn from the cask allotted to the ship's physician. Her fever had not returned, and other than being thin, she looked well, spoke coherently, and had regained her *joie de vivre*. As I brewed us a pot of souchong steeped in precipitation that fell when the Vikings roamed these waters, we listened to the melting ice pop, an effervescence of thousand-year-old air filling our cups.

From the forecastle we could hear a Polish girl singing a folk tune the Italian fiddler knew, and when he ran shy of notes he improvised, and when she ran short of words, she followed whatever emotion she drew from his music and turned it into song. Zofia said the girl was telling a story about leaving her farmstead near Rumia; we could only guess what the Italian was imagining; when the girl finished her lyrical tale, a boy stepped forward to sing of his Bavarian home, and so it went whilst we talked.

Now, a day later, I struggle to recollect all Zofia said, often distracted as I was by watching her radiance, her elegance even in torn clothing. Her father, a printer, died young in one of the perpetual clashes between Poles and Germans, conflicts drawing in Austrians and Russians, as is common in the history of West Prussia, a province at times in the German Empire. Her mother, a seamstress, now lives with a sister, both of whom Zofia hopes one day to bring to America. I had not known her Polish surname: Lewandowska, although in times past, when necessary, she used her father's German name, Schnarre. National hostilities make variation useful.

Speaking Teutonic and Slavic tongues, she formerly had temporary employ with the family of an American ambassador. Resident in his house, she taught the three children German. It was through them she improved her English: she would read— aloud and in English—a nursery rhyme and then translate it to German before explaining it in English.

Over the past year, the children introduced her to the poems of Edgar Allan Poe, *Peter Parley's Tales about America*, and Irving's *Sketch Book*. In her emigrant's bundle of possessions she carries a pamphlet containing the Declaration of Independence. With some pride, from memory she quoted in her sweet accent, "We hold these truths to be self-evident, that all men are created equal, that they are endowed by their Creator with certain unalienable rights." I applauded, so she added, "We mutually pledge to each other our lives, our fortunes, and our sacred honor." Until she recited the sentence, I had never really heard the beauty and power in those plain words. She said, "The ideas are so noble. They made me want to go to a land where that is the way people live."

On occasion as she talks, she will pause to hunt for the proper English word, raising a hand to indicate I should not divulge it before she can recall it, most of the time correctly, although *apprehension* continually eludes her. At times I lose her meaning, not because of language but because of her—how shall I term it? Dare I say, *bewitchery?* Of my response I doubt she is aware.

The American family, of Prussian extraction, recently returned to Buffalo, New York and asked her to join them to continue the language lessons. When she thought she had spoken enough, she asked about my boyhood on Saint Kitts. She had to repeat her question to break her spell on me and make me aware it was my turn to respond. I poured more tea, as she surely was remembering better days in Danzig. To remind me of her request, she said, "Saint Kitts, you will tell me now?"

I said it was not much of a story and told of how I was shipped to England as a teen after my father, a medic on the sugar plantation where I grew up, was shot down by an unknown slayer for supporting emancipation, his argument being freedom and a fair wage will endure longer than forced labor comprising the total economy of the island. He often pointed out that whites are less than a minority—they are a fraction of a five-digit number, chips of white ice that, sooner or later, are certain to melt in the heat of the West Indies. The forced labor, entirely from Africa mixed with a thin strain of the native Caribs, would arise and take all from the masters, who will be driven out or butchered to feed the hogs. My mother claimed it was such opinions which cost him his life. "So you see," I said to Zofia, "on Saint Kitts and Nevis, generations have been enslaved because England developed a tooth for sweets."

As I spoke, she lowered her head and did not raise it until I stopped. She said, "And your mother?"

I explained Father was born in Pensacola, but Mother was native to Saint Kitts. I told how she did not live long after his murder, the reason I was sent to England to reside with my grandparents.

The bell for supper rang, and I deeply regretted Zofia would not be allowed to join us in the saloon. I offered to challenge the rule. She recoiled from the suggestion. All I could think to do was give her a box of ginger biscuits, the only food I had in my cabin. (I must begin thinking—*and spelling*—in American!) They are ginger *cookies*—quite possibly made with sugar harvested from a Saint Kitts cane field. She accepted the food so readily I knew she would distribute it.

But *what* for her? Something of no use to anyone else in steerage. In front of me was my small bookshelf. I took down a leather-bound pocket edition of Shakespeare's sonnets, and on a slip of paper used as a bookmark, I wrote, "Number 116." She ran her fingers over the smooth ox-hide cover, opened it to the title page, asked what a sonnet was. In the doorway as she was leaving she said, "Before, I never had a real book for my own."

Given the way destiny works these things, Mrs. Bentley, emerging from her cabin, saw Zofia. The Gilded One's lips uttered no words, but her eyes spoke paragraphs, and I turned towards Zofia. She had vanished as if I had dreamt her presence. To confirm what had just taken place, my disbelief getting the better of my reason, I looked at my bookshelf. Where the sonnets had been was a space. Never was a man so relieved to see an emptiness.

The 3rd inst.

This morning the rising sun overlay the vast American coastline, spread across the Virginia shore—here the Accomack Peninsula— an aureate gleaming as if truly a golden land. From both steerage and cabins of the self-styled *colonists—émigrés all*—passengers came to press against the starboard rail, shoulder to shoulder on the poop deck, the main deck, the forecastle, as we sailed south. The *Narwhale* canted so far to starboard, Finn ordered everybody ten paces back from the rail.

Some from below dropped to their knees, many crossed themselves, one Polish elder with cheeks wet with emotion raised his arms in thanks for a prospect reanimated, and the German rabbi spoke something in Hebrew for all to hear, then a cheer went up. If ahead lie two hundred miles of Chesapeake Bay, it matters not. A few more leagues will be as nothing when we can see the new land to port *and* starboard, and smell the waft from its forests. The wind blows out of the south, the weather promises fair.

4 May

By noon we passed into Chesapeake Bay via the entrance between Cape Charles on the north and Cape Henry on the south, a separation of twelve miles of open water, although both capes are in Virginia. Having to sail two hundred *more* miles northward, entirely within American shores, requires mental adjustment in a European mind: that distance would take a traveler from London to Paris. Yet, beyond the ingress to the bay, there is no town of size on the banks of this great estuary other than Baltimore, and its harbor is a dozen miles from the open bay. The cause of this urban barren is the Chesapeake shore being ragged not only with large and navigable rivers, but also with arms and inlets and embayments, especially so on the west; the eastward shoreline is rifled with what Americans call *creeks* (in England they would be termed *rivers*). Everywhere, islands are not infrequent.

The low terrain of the Chesapeake, whilst lending itself to multitudes of fish and wildfowl, will scarcely support foundations. To build a city here would be to see it sink, an American Atlantis, into the squelchy bottom so rich with mollusks and crustaceans. Supper tonight, freshly purchased from a waterman, will be a platter of oysters on the half shell attended by steamed blue crabs. In two hours, an oysterman and hunter could fill the ship's pantry to feed all of steerage for a couple of days—such is the munificence of these singular waters. My thoughts should be reaching higher than my appetite, but days of biscuit and salt pork will do that to a voyager. We were welcomed into the bay by a red-tail hawk accompanying us for a half a league.

The forests are broken by farmsteads, some with substantial houses and cultivated fields. For those in steerage—at least those able to come up on deck—to witness our passage into this plentitude must seem like the beginning of their long dream at last opening before them, a theater of the potential and possible, a land awaiting anyone willing to strive and labor, the very inclinations drawing them here. And what about those in the staterooms? I cannot escape the notion that if a family in steerage looks onto these forests and farms and fields and sees a cabin and a cabbage plot, the Gilded see cash from a land with a growing populace ripe for exploitation. As to me, what is it I foresee? A man tramping alone through a fogged forest, a dreamer shadowed by a nightmare?

5 May

On deck I listened to Zofia conducting a final English lesson: the children reciting names of the states, their pronunciations of *Massachusetts* and *Connecticut* and *Pennsylvania* coming forth in a variety of versions, a few even understandable. When Zofia dismissed them, she told me of consternation below decks over how the indigent would pay for travel to the New York pier where they had arranged weeks ago for links to get them to their destinations. I tapped on Captain Finn's cabin door, he greeting me unusually warmly, but before I could raise the issue of indigent transport, he pulled me inside to give me a slip of paper. To my surprise, it was a draft on a New York bank to reimburse me for service as ship's physician. I had thought my passage was my recompense, to which he said, "Doctor Trennant, when the *Narwhale* reaches quarantine at Baltimore, she arrives free of typhus, smallpox, and cholera. For that, I thank you."

Nodding, I said, "Nothing but dyspepsia, some lower-tract disturbance, and a few coughs. For the coughing, I've made up several doses of a demulcent to reduce the hacking whilst going through immigration routines. Have the elders encourage all coughers to use it in advance."

He placed his hand on my shoulder. "Nathaniel, in ten days will you join us as ship's medic on our eastern return?"

I required a moment to decide not an answer but a way to phrase it. Our voyage, I answered, has been enlightening, but my journey is not to the Atlantic—it is into America, into her heart, and on to the upper Missouri River country. I want to encounter the great prairies and plains and bison and the Indians who hunt them.

He then listened to the problem of disembarking indigents ninety miles from New York City. He agreed to my request for a meeting with an elder from both the Polish and German contingents and our interpreter to discuss assisting the insolvent to travel on north. We met an hour later. I proposed setting up a fund to assist their transport and laid upon the table my honorarium and specified it was to go first to mothers with children under ten years, then to the infirm, the remainder going to men with dependents. I have been assured single men can readily find temporary work on the Baltimore wharves.

The elders sat silent, leaving me to wonder whether my subvention had been received amiss. Then the German elder, Gerhard Schiller, an American citizen sent overseas to lead emigrating Mennonites, announced that his people were headed for southeastern Pennsylvania, only sixty miles distant from Baltimore. Changing into textbook English (Zofia translating into Polish), he continued: "My brethren are willing to invite any passenger to join us under our auspices. We ask only they respect our practices. If they consider our ways amenable, we can offer them settlement in Berks County."

I turned to Captain Finn to propose my argument: The Blue Anchor Line, having contracted to transport all of us to New York City, should contribute to the fund. Because a portion of any contribution would come out of his own percentage, he hesitated, and I said it was only *just*. (Zofia whispered to me the trade of two women had been on the streets of Berlin; now, with a bath and laundered garments, they would soon be well funded along the docks of Baltimore.) I brought up to him that some of our complement might have to prostitute themselves to gain fare to New York. Speaking for ownership, the captain agreed, *contingent* upon steerage passengers giving a scrub-down to the lower deck and its bulkheads. That was the best I could extract from the company.

Arrangements were made for a Mennonite council to administer the money, and I delivered the cough demulcent to Herr Schiller, explaining to retain it for use only when passing through quarantine. As we dispersed, Zofia (I almost wrote *my* Zofia), who had interpreted so winningly, came up to me to quote, "We mutually pledge to each other our lives, our fortunes, and our sacred honor," and she took my hand and said, "In America, now I am Sophie," then quickly went below to finish preparations for landing.

For the duration of the day, those in steerage worked in shifts organized by the Mennonites to haul buckets of fresh water to wash babies and adult bodies, launder clothing, and begin scrubbing the decking. And so goes our passage up the great bay until we will arrive at the immigration station.

7 May

The continuing shoreline of forest and farms and clearings fresh from the axe was cause for celebrations of impending freedom from want. As bedraggled and weary as so many were, now they sang snippets of folk songs and where there had been frictions amongst them was cheerful cooperation.

The Chesapeake, beset by watery intrusions the locals term *guts*, allowed our eight hundred tons of goods and humanity gentle travel all the way to the much angled Patapsco River, its wooded banks cleaved by tributaries, and there we began tacking a crooked course towards Baltimore, the most western port on the northeast American coast. As the river narrowed, the city rose steadily beyond Fort McHenry and Mary Pickersgill's immense garrison banner celebrated in national song; it was of such size I could not imagine its construction. Earlier, Captain Finn mentioned that a seamstress for Mrs. Pickersgill had sewn the *Narwhale* ensign. Because today observes some event, the giant flag was at full staff, but despite the breezy morn, the wind was not enough to lift the heavy bunting from the pole.

The inner basin of Baltimore is well enclosed, thereby forcing clippers and packets into a proximity to make the harbor from a distance look like a forest of masts and yardarms and spars, a woodland not of limbs and leaves but of shrouds and sails. Behind, at town center, are steeples and shot-towers and several limestone monuments of considerable height, the tallest surmounted by a marble statue of General Washington.

(I note here: Our stop at immigration was brief. All passengers, even those from steerage, passed through apace, thanks to the relative health of all. Captain Finn mightily relieved.)

The *Narwhale* made berth at a long pier, and when her last line was warped to a bollard, the seamen cheered our *official* arrival, an exultation echoed by everybody on deck. I searched for Sophie but nowhere could I spot her. My thoughts: a second woman lost, this one without even a farewell. My joy at arriving lay flattened.

Standing next to me on the quarterdeck were the Bentleys, who watched the waiting steerage folk with their pitiful bundles of ragged garments. Mr. Bentley said, "Prepare for the onslaught of the unwashed and unlettered."

I was surprised not by his words but mine: "Time to pull up the drawbridge and bolt the gate, eh Bentley?" They turned to depart, Mrs. B ignoring my adieu. To acknowledge receiving help is beneath her.

Once the staterooms emptied, steerage was allowed onto the gangway, and as quickly as could be accomplished, the bedraggled traveled the final hundred feet to American soil. There they clustered into groups, to stare and take measure of the country. Released from the mephitic air of the 'tween decks, they prepared to puzzle their way onward, registering more uncertainty and confusion than relief or joy. In their out-at-the-elbows clothing they were gritty Robinson Crusoes stumbling ashore of an unknown land: dazed, overwhelmed, unsure. *And* willing to begin.

I was distressed not to catch sight of Sophie anywhere amongst the throng. From somewhere, an insistent whistle seemed aimed at me although I could not see its source. Then, from the mizzenmast high above, I spotted our Irish ship's boy perched precariously in the rigging, and waving excitedly to announce his overcoming the peril of greasy ropes. I saluted him as I followed my equipage onto the pier. Looking at the homely ship that had brought us safely to harbor, I wanted a small physical token of her—a decking nail, a sliver of mast, a shred of canvas—but I found nothing. Out of necessity, as I was a tramper parsimonious of luggage and with miles beyond knowing yet ahead, it is just as well. After all, what is my journal but a memento able to speak somewhat better than a deck nail?

It was then I saw a woman, her face obscured by a large bonnet, walking briskly towards me, the low sun in my eyes making it seem she was emerging from the sun itself. She drew back the bonnet and spoke, "I was nearly swept away! The confusion!"

I embraced Sophie and she me, and I stood wordless until my composure returned. I pulled out my pocket memorandum and asked how to reach her in Buffalo. As she wrote in the address, she said, "Sonnet one-sixteen," and whispered:

> *Let me not to the marriage of true minds*
> *Admit impediments. Love is not love*
> *Which alters when it alteration finds.*

My joy deprived me of speech.

She was about to say something else when her brother barged forward, seized her arm, and tugged at her. She resisted long enough to say, "What is *impediments?*"

Watching her disappearing into the throng, I shouted, "Miles!" I don't believe she heard me add, "Let us not admit *miles!*" And she was gone.

With passengers cleared from the pier to begin finding their way into America, the Yankee sailors—shaved close, mustaches waxed, bodies scrubbed clean like a ship's deck—disembarked to initiate three days' liberty in the ancient quest of men come ashore fresh from the sea, eager to purge mischief resident in the loins. Ready for them along the wharves was a spectacularly rouged and powdered *posse comitatus* skilled in the emollients necessary to restore in deprived men something approaching reason.

I took up the central city, my legs still carrying in them the sway the sea infuses and makes pavement bricks seem as if in flux, unstable clots of mud. The first order of business was lodging. On recommendation of Captain Finn, I found the Indian Queen Hotel, a hostelry of considerable celebrity; it was booked to capacity. On I walked to the Fountain Inn not far distant: it too chock-full. Then to the Globe—nothing. Forward to the Eutaw House to fare no better. I asked a wearied clerk was the city always so abundant with transients, and he, astonished at my ignorance, said, "Why, sir! This is a week of big auctions."

"Ah-ha!" said I. "Livestock? Horses? Cattle?"

"Livestock? No sir, not at all. Auction of Negroes headed for New Orleans!"

I know not how to describe my surprise. I left to continue my search, failing twice again and beginning to mumble though appreciating the proximity of the inns. In one I do not recall the name of, I prevailed upon the clerk to tell me where I might have some luck. He assessed my appearance and said, "Missus Tolley's Rooming House is a stone's heave to the east. She keeps a good place, but it ain't fancy enough for a gentleman as is yourself." Foot-weary, grumbling, wondering whatever had possessed me to leave England, off I went.

Mrs. Tolley, a jolly exuberance of flesh, has a talent of dispensing disheartening words in such a way a listener feels uplifted for undertaking a fruitless pilgrimage. The hour getting on, I said, jestingly I hoped, I would settle for a manger in a stable, and she, "Oh, young sir! Even my stalls is full!"

And I: "With travelers?"

"Mercy no! Gentlemen's horses, sir!" That was the first time I envied those born quadrupeds.

Reading my expression, and sympathizing, she added, "I *do* have a storage room on the alleyway. With a bed. Mister Tolley is required to use it of a night when he comes home three sheets to the wind. In his cups he snores like a hog. It's clean and quiet, the chamber is. And the alleyway—it's used only in season to move livestock."

For a price matching its spareness, the isolated, ground-floor room is twice the measure of my shipboard quarters and the bed has a horsehair mattress; also a tall chiffonier, wash stand with pitcher and basin, and a table and chair convenient for making journal entries. Faucet and sink are down a hall, the bathhouse farther along. At the foot of the bed, a service door opens into the alley, but being warped, it cannot be bolted.

I found my way to the bath and, as if a Japanese, rinsed head to toe before climbing into a tub of *warm, fresh* water, an undertaking I never before thought a sybaritic luxury. Shaved, combed, outfitted in duds I had held for arrival, I gave my other clothing to Mrs. Tolley's laundress. Polished like a new penny, off I wandered down Pratt Street.

8 May

Last evening when I returned to the taproom of the Indian Queen for a pint of lager, the preferred beverage in this heavily Teutonic city, lying about were several copies of a local gazette called *The Weekly Trader*. Its format was more flamboyant than typical in England, but that is not what drew my attention. No, it was a full page of notices, all similar in tone and approach, five of which I clipped out to insert in my journal:

Ranaway, my black boy Harper—30 years old—both ears notched—two upper fore-teeth out—has been shot in the buttocks—much scarred on the back with the whip.

Ranaway, my negress Martha—age twenty—has lost right eye—two toes chopped off—escaped with iron band about her neck—may go by name of Jenny.

One hundred dollars reward for my black man Abraham— 40—looks older—branded on the right jaw—had iron collar with one prong turned down.

Absconded, my negro man Top—his heels have been frosted—has an awkward gait occasioned by being shot in the right thigh—left arm scarred by the bites of a dog.

Ranaway, a negro man and his wife, Nat and Priscilla. He has a jagged scar across his left cheek, two stiff fingers on his right hand with running sores on them; his wife has a scar on her left arm, and one upper tooth is out.

Before I could read further, a man, elegantly attired, fingers adorned with rings falling just shy of ostentation, sat down at the next table. Observing my cutting out the notices, he asked were I in Baltimore to sell or buy. Hoping he might mean livestock, I said I was neither dealer nor drover. He introduced himself as Henri Ducharme of New Orleans, and said, "I observe your interest in the absconders. If you're looking to buy a recovered runaway, I may be of service. I'm preparing a gang to leave Friday for Louisiana and Mississippi. I have blacks for field or house. Men, women. Children. All the highest quality." It was as if he were selling not Negroes but mangoes.

Stunned to find my curiosity in such a fell undertaking draw me into human trafficking, I said I thought the United States had abolished the slave trade four decades ago. I give here a digest of what followed.

"Indeed so with *African* importation," said he. "By your speech you're not an American and are unaware of our *internal* trade—which was not outlawed, thereby creating a vigorous commerce within the nation for slaves already here. And their offspring. What's more, in places, the *smuggling* of foreign slaves continues. In states below or near the Mason-Dixon Line, our trade thrives, perhaps nowhere more profitably than in Baltimore. Its location is convenient between North and South, along with the advantage of a variety of water transport. A ship is the only secure method to move a pack of slaves."

Pausing to evaluate my attention, he continued.

"You should realize, sir, when Mister Whitney invented the cotton gin he created a single instrument able to reshape our southern economy on historic foundations consistent with the ways of our people. A cotton field is not like an apple orchard, where the fruit of itself falls to the ground for gathering. A cotton field must be *picked*. Human hands are necessary to feed those gins. Picking is a backbreaking task. To admit the facts, no sound mind will pick cotton willingly except at a wage too extravagant to underwrite the profit. Regrettably, we are left with the necessity of compulsion. So you see, were freedom granted, a sane soul would seek any opportunity to leave. Hence, before you, notices of absconders are there to alert hunters who, for sizable rewards, will return illegals to service under their rightful owners."

He offered me a beverage of choice. Whilst wanting a whiskey to steady myself at what I was hearing so logically, dispassionately presented, I declined. I asked were he a plantation owner.

"I'm a purveyor providing labor currently unneeded in the North to an area where people may find work and provender and shelter elsewhere."

I could keep silent no longer. I brought up the notices describing notched ears, amputated toes, broken-out front teeth, brands burnt onto faces, backs rippled with scars from the lash.

"If a man owns cattle he must mark his property. If he owns a horse, he must break it to serve him, and for both animals he must provide secure pasture and shelter."

"Mister Ducharme," I said, "we're speaking of men and women and children. Not dumb animals. Not property."

"There, sir, I'll correct you. Defined by law, Negroes in service in certain states are *indeed* property. As with real estate or material chattel, slaves may be owned, bequeathed, traded, sold, or given away. In this instance, ownership is *ten* tenths of the law."

"You're not a slave owner?"

"I enable transactions among sellers and buyers. Other than my house staff, I own no slaves except during the few days from purchase to sale. Slavery is as old as humanity, and at this time it is an economic necessity that arose with the nation. If it's an error, then it's a foundational error. You may misperceive me: I am not a racialist. I don't see black skin, I see golden opportunity to make possible for thousands nourishment and shelter *which*—please note sir—stand between sustenance and starvation for blacks and some whites alike. If you remain in our territory, and take the time to examine what you see, you will adjust privileged notions and perhaps discover your thinking to be, let me say, *broadened*."

"For me, Mister Ducharme, permit *me* to say, the term is not *broadened*. It is *corrupted*. But I *will* continue in the territories, and I *will* examine. I grew up on a Caribbean sugar plantation. I've seen forced labor, and I must say what I've encountered here is of considerably greater severity."

9 May

Mrs. Tolley's supper was spitchcocked eels with greens and sweet potatoes, all quite good. One of the diners spoke of his purchase of two exceptionally fine Negroes, men of solidity he would transport to Kentucky in the morning; for tonight, they were being kept in one of the many slave pens in the area. Mr. Tolley, whose corpulence was only a stone or two from being unmatched, explained to me that jails hold blacks both before and after auction until they can be securely removed for transport. The confinements also were useful in retaining slaves whilst their masters undertook other business or *certain* indulgences.

In the parlor I recorded these events, before going into the evening to cool my brain, heated as it was by what I had seen and heard, arguments uttered calmly with chilling reasoning, positions America, sooner or later, will have to come to terms with, for everywhere within that dialectic lie toxins of disunion. Remarkable it is such a system has obtained for so long. Even now, at this late date, I have read about Abolitionists, even in the North, being threatened and thrashed, their pamphlets burnt, their printing presses broken.

Without plan I wandered along Pratt Street near the inner basin and its rocking ships and halyards slapping against spars and yards. Lacking awareness of the hour, I eventually realized I had no idea where I was until a carter aimed me back towards the waterfront. Almost immediately the pleasant sounds of the harbor were overwhelmed by tramping feet approaching. Trudging towards me was a cordon of twenty shoeless men, each roped at the neck one to the other, hands bound before them, their black faces—except for the whites of their eyes—invisible in the darkness.

I stopped a passer-by to ask where so many convicts were going, and his answer: "Not convicts, sir. Them sorry devils is from the slave pens on way to the auction. Some certain slavers doesn't like to parade them to public view more than needs be. So they moves them under witching time. You seen one you want to bid on?"

Another man, overhearing my query, said, "They's another gang coming. Some prime flesh in there. You signal me the one you want, and I'll get your bid in for him. Or, would it be a *her* you lookin for? I got some cream of the crop flesh."

To anybody around, my presence indicated I could have only a single interest—buying ownership of a human being. When I returned to Mrs. Tolley's, I went to the washroom and scrubbed away as if to cleanse myself of what I had seen. To encounter slavery face to face can leave one feeling guilt for being free. Cleansing did not work, and on my first night ashore in America I lay in fitful sleep. A question would not let go: Is human enslavement inhuman or all too human?

10 May

The night long, my half-sleep carried with it an unending shuffle of roped slaves towards oblivion, on and on soundlessly but for their sighs, their empty eye sockets turned to me, and in each a blind imploring. I would half-wake, only to fall again into a nether realm neither here nor there, an atmosphere opaque with misery. When others march to a dark destiny, a coward lies abed.

At dawn I rose, bathed to wake myself, and found Mrs. Tolley's breakfast table set with meats, cheeses, cornbread, and baked apples, but my appetite was that of an ill man, and I took only a glass of buttermilk until an idea roused me to eat: I would pose as a buyer and visit the slave pens to verify what I had heard about them. If I had been ignorant of the events along Pratt Street, then people elsewhere probably also know nothing of its details. Should the devil truly *be* in the details—and in *these* he surely must be—then such facts have significant import.

I had not far to walk to find a slaver's jail. Outside it, a Negro was distributing leaflets, a portion of one I attach:

CASH FOR NEGROES.

Persons having similar property to dispose of would do well to see me before selling. I am always ready to purchase:
** Sturdy men, aged 13 to 23: $500 to $650.
** Women of same age and quality: $300 to $500.
** The best field hands, same age: $300 to $400.
Sold separately or in lots.

I was refused entry inside the brick lockup, but admitted with the owner into an adjoining, walled courtyard about forty by seventy feet. It contained not a branch of shade from the hot sun, but there were two hydrants, three washtubs, and a clothesline; milling about were twenty-six men, twenty-nine women, five holding infants, and three boys. Half the men were shackled in pairs at the ankles. This group was runaways brought in by slave catchers, a lucrative occupation, said the seller. In the building, he explained, is a large cell for confinement after sundown. The purpose of this incarceration, beyond storage, is to inflict a sense of having no control over one's life, to weaken thoughts of escape.

The eyes of inmates bold enough to examine me revealed subsumed loathing but, possibly, two or three men tried to determine whether I might prove a kindly master. I lack capacity to convey the shame the hopeful expressions gave me. How I wanted to announce the truth of my visit! At one point, a boy of about four years, a bonny little fellow, pressed against the barred gate to gaze at me with the innocence of a caged puppy looking to see whether this white man would be the one to get him out from behind bars. For the first time, I truly *felt* slavery. By asking his name, I worsened things. The eyes of the mother were wide with fear I was about to buy her son and carry him off for who knows what purposes. By turning away, I intended to show I had no interest in bidding on him.

The entire time I was there, the owner rattled on about the care his *charges* receive—their feeding and clothing. It is true the people were not emaciated, although, despite their youth, none appeared to be robust. Their apparel was acceptably clean. These accommodations, of course, are to make them as salable as possible when they stand at auction. It was there I went next.

One at a time, except for a mother with babe in arms, each was forced onto a raised block for evaluation, and then the bidding began. Males came forth stripped to the waist for the purpose of exposing musculature, and also their backs for evidence of the lash; some flesh was horribly disfigured, the number of scars considered a tabulation of indolence, insolence, insubordination, or, most serious, attempts at escape.

Buyers studied the faces for amenability, *and*, so I believe, some slaves similarly searched the attitudes of buyers and turned a smile on any thought to be *just possibly* a gentler master than another. Customers toting a coiled whip received deliberate scowls promising a troublesome nature. Twice, a potential buyer demanded to see the procreative organs of a male in order to calculate generative capacity; thin, small-breasted women, if they carried no infant, sold for a price lower than those with greater mammary development and its supposed nursing capability.

When a family was separated, the lamentations were loud and continued until the distressed were ushered away to begin their trip downriver. Once the most vendible slaves had been sold, others were brought forward: a living gallery of backs horribly mutilated by knotted whips, ears notched or lopped off, toes dismembered, necks and wrists and ankles deeply scarred by iron rings and hobbles. This group was for purchasers who hired out slaves. Last came the elderly and infirm, only one of whom was bought (she for only two dollars); those unsold will be turned out to the freedom of the streets, to the slavery of poverty to beg their way. Few, I heard, survive the first winter.

I have learnt northern opposition to abolition and hostility towards Abolitionists survive on ignorance of facts I was witnessing. No sane person could watch such barbarism and cruelty and remain impassive. The logical deduction from this premise: whites embracing or tolerating slavery for whatever reason are not simply morally debased, they are mentally disordered. But then, perhaps the explanation lies within humanity, its very nature being inclined towards masters and slaves.

Black helots, disbound and given whips, could they as readily as whites physically compel obedience, extract labor, and inflict pain to make a life nothing more than a function in an iniquitous economy? I had just witnessed a Negro overseer wield a lash with grievous effect on another black. Beholding these actions leaves me feeling useless and helpless before this social and economic juggernaut. Once again I had a not entirely fatuous wish I had been born a horse.

At Mrs. Tolley's supper table—her old sheepdog snoring beneath—I listened to a pair of drovers talk about their livestock. A partial relief it was to consider the herding of animals rather than humanity. Because my purpose in coming to the States is to evaluate through actual experiences the American experiment, I am relying on that necessity to keep me from running madly down Pratt Street.

Earlier in the day I had seen a young black woman pulled from the cold water of the inner basin after trying to commit suicide before she could be shipped south. Saved so she can live a slave, this time with chains added. As she was hauled onto the wharf, I overheard a man say, "No slave has the right to kill herself!" Then, winking, "Unless she first pays recompense to her master." Said I, "A slave does then have the right to purchase her death?" He nodded, deaf to my sarcasm.

The table talk shifted to a report of an escape by a half dozen roped blacks on the way to the auction block. Within an hour, four had been captured—near our lodgings—and returned for the addition of neck irons, insidious contrivances of a ring with three or four iron prongs turned outwards to prevent the slave from sleeping in a preferred position.

On a table in the Tolley parlor, was an Alabama newspaper, the *Southern Slave Trader.* I clipped two notices:

** Found on the rail-road yesterday, a negro's head which the owner can have by calling at this office and paying for the advertisement.

** Taken in this city and committed to jail, a negro girl named Nancy. She is about 30 years of age, and is a LUNATIC. The owner is requested to come forward, prove property, pay charges, and remove her, or she will be sold to pay her jail fees. —F. P. Hume, Jailor.

11 May

I wanted to go out for a tramp yesternight, but my poor recent sleep and the disturbing events of the day sent me to my quarters. On entering I noticed the warped door to the alley had apparently blown open a few inches. I pushed the chiffonier over to obstruct it, and fell exhaustedly into bed in hopes I might dream not of events of the day but of bison and Indians roaming freely across the American plains.

It was not to be. No dreams were there of any sort till one with labored breathing from, so I perceived, a cordon of slaves, their chains rattling, plodding towards market, each looking at me from uneyed sockets. I awoke, the images evaporated.

Drawing a deep breath, I dozed off again just before dawn only to be awakened by a snore, the kind Mrs. Tolley's sheepdog makes under the dining table. Or perhaps it was Mr. Tolley come home in his cups to the room he is required to use until sober. I rose, stumbled to the oil lamp on the wash stand, put a light to it, and held it aloft. No Tolley, no dog, only the sparse furniture. But the snoring had stopped.

I lay down, and before I could fall asleep, the sound started again. It was coming from under the bed. *That damned dog*, I thought, and shouted for it to get out. When nothing came forth, I leaned over the edge to look beneath, and there, inches from my face, was another face, a dark visage, looking back.

My start was so violent I pitched onto the floor, scrambled to my feet, relit the lamp and carried it to the bed and knelt to shine light beneath. I had not been dreaming: there indeed, lying as far from me as he could go, his eyes wide with alarm, was a black man.

As discomposed as I was, I managed to ask what in blazes he was doing. Answer came there none. I said, "Sir, I insist you extricate yourself!" He made no move, and it was evident he was deeply apprehensive. I explained I was an overseas visitor quite outside the slave trade and from me he had nothing to fear. Having no alternative, he crawled forward slowly to draw himself upright, a dust ball stuck to the top of his head, making it appear he wore a tam-o'-shanter. He said, "Boss, I mightily need to piss."

Oil lamp in one hand, I pushed the chamber pot to him: it was a dewatering of considerable measure, and he thanked me. He was entirely well structured, meaning he would command a premium price, and would be hunted all the more intensely. Around his neck was a stout hempen cord, the kind slaves on the march to the auction block suffer under.

I walked to the other side of the chamber, turned, and asked was he one of the six who escaped that afternoon. He gave no answer. With one door visibly bolted and the chiffonier barricading the other, he had to be weighing possibilities of escape. I went to the hall door, unbolted it, and returned to the far side of the room. He watched closely.

Running his palms over his weary face, for the first time he took his eyes off me—if briefly—before saying, "Why did you unbar the door? Be you an Abolitionist? A do-gooder white trying to make himself proud by saving a poor darkey slave?"

"I'm a physician who happened to be born white. Who tries to fulfill the Hippocratic oath. Whatever else I am, I'm hardly a savior."

"Oath?"

"To heal whenever I can, to proffer a pisspot when I cannot. To realize sympathy may outweigh a surgeon's knife. And not to play God."

"I don't need sympathy. I need a knife."

I retrieved my medical bag from the chiffonier and took out my sturdiest scalpel and handed it to him. Gripping it in his fist as if to defend himself, he stepped back and began sawing clumsily at his noose till it fell to the floor. About then we heard voices and footsteps in the hall. He edged to the door to listen, holding the blade low, ready to thrust it.

When the hall went quiet, he put his ear to the door, then secured it. Uncertain what to do next, he kicked the noose across the room. "Why are you trying to save my neck?"

"I'm trying to keep it connected to what's below."

"You're breaking that oath."

"What are you saying?"

"Seems to me you're playing God." He stepped back. "But, what the hell, maybe *you* can do a better job of it than—."

He stopped, to assess further. "Your accent, you must be a foreigner. You don't know the penalties for helping a slave abscond. Fines. Imprisonment. You're breaking the law."

"That decision," I said, "is mine." He asked for water, then sat on the bed. "You have education," I said. "How is it you're in this dire situation?"

"A long story."

"Do you want assistance, or just an unbolted door?"

By then, dawn was edging down the alley, and yet he sat with no notion what to do.

"What else be in that medical bag?"

"Nothing of use, but in my head is something that could be of use."

I laid out an idea, at least as far as I had it developed. To initiate it, I would have to leave for an hour, and that meant he must get back under the bed *and* trust me. He said, "To escape being locked *up* by a white man I have to begin by being locked *in* by a white man?"

"This white man pledges not to betray you."

He stood, shook his head and murmured, "Either I be dreaming or I be gone crazy," and he pushed the bed into a corner and crawled under. I asked his name. From beneath I heard a whispered, "Cuff."

That being a not uncommon African name, I guessed this Cuff was lying, a defense a slave learns with his mother's milk.

12 May, morning

Before I left the sequestered man under the bed, I gave him a kerchief to stifle a sneeze or cough, and urged him to avoid sleep and the peril in a snore. I found Mrs. Tolley to pay for another night, being sure to give allusion to moving on tomorrow to business in *Delaware*. I asked about a sailmaker along the wharves, and there I went for ten yards of stout canvas and a couple of sturdy stitching needles and a spool of sennit. The cloth was an unwieldy and weighty package. I stopped at a butchery for a pound of hog entrails fresh from the knife, then to a sailor's exchange for a bleached nightshirt of heavy muslin and a large nightcap and trousers and a tunic befitting a merchant seaman. In the Bank of South Baltimore I used my letter of credit to top off my funds; while there I heard more talk of the slave escape, one Negro still at liberty.

A customer, a man of self-assurance beyond what is seemly, told me, "H. B. Ferrall and his mother-of-pearl pistol grips, he'll find the niggra. Nobody shakes that irascible man-hater. And he's going to be mad as hell for making him take an extra day to hunt the boy down. When *he* knocks on your door, it's with an axe. They say tain't without cause HB come to stand for *Hell Bent*."

Returning to my quarters via the alley, I was delighted to come upon a dead rat, a providential gift to my chicanery. Cuff lay somnolent under the bed, my kerchief bound over his mouth. I woke him, and he crawled out to wash whilst I emptied the chamber pot. He said, "No white man ever before emptied my slops."

I answered, "I think it's in the Hippocratic Oath: *I hereby pledge to carry my patient's slops hence*." Recalling that moment as I describe these events, nothing I had yet said or done gave greater evidence to Cuff for trusting me, a most beneficial response, considering what I was about to propose.

He watched as I wrote up—using my finest cursives and adding the unnecessary flourishes of a court scribe—a pair of documents. The first I titled PERMIT TO TRANSPORT and the second, WRIT OF MANUMISSION. I showed them to him, and he said, "Lordy, lordy, what be the doctor up to now?" From an old candle in the chiffonier, I melted a dollop of red wax to drop onto each sheet. With an alley pebble shaped like a signet I made an impression. The warrants looked authoritative. All was ready.

Here I digest the devisement I presented to Cuff: He was to put on the cap and nightshirt, whereupon I would wrap him in sailcloth sprinkled with droplets of pig blood from the entrails. Then I would sew up the bag, top and bottom. Inside with him the dead rat.

He recoiled. "No! No, no! No rat! No rat!" When I calmed him, he described bedding down on the floor of the plantation hut he lived in as a child, falling asleep to rodents gnawing in the dark. Being awakened by mice nipping at his face.

Reminding him of the slave catchers in search of him, I offered how a stinking rat could be salvation. A gift from Heaven.

"I prefer heavenly gifts," he said, "that don't bite when alive and don't stink when dead."

"Perhaps salvation lies in stinking to high heaven," I rejoined. He remained resistant, forcing me to remonstrate that his cover of darkness was past and we had not time to debate. "The mule cart I hired is due within the hour, so please lie down so I can sew you into the sailcloth!"

Hiding the rat in a scrap of material, I placed it between Cuff's feet, wrapped the canvas around him, and sewed him in, the stitches more those of a seaman than a surgeon. I had no more than finished when the mule clattered down the alley. From the bag I heard a muffled, "If this scheme fails, we both be dead men."

The drayman, a free Negro named Casper, helped me lift the bagged Cuff into the cart atop a bed of straw, and without delay the lop-eared mule hauled us to Pratt Street and on towards the old York road and the free state of Pennsylvania. At the limit of the city, as destiny seems to work its events, a pair of men on horseback overtook us, one grabbing the reins to bring us to a halt, whilst the other came up on his mount to look into the cart. From the mother-of-pearl-grip pistol at his side, I recognized him as H. B. Ferrall: an ill-born thing in befouled pantaloons, a bullet-head shaved to reveal scars, a visage lined by years of sun, a cheek distorted by a load of tobacco juice. Even more arresting were stained canine teeth, one broken and jagged, the other extended as if a fang. A visage to offend the darkest night. Casper kept his eyes lowered and hat brim pulled low.

Whacking his crop against our bag, Ferrall said, "What the hell we got here?" I explained I was a physician with the Delaware College of Mortuarial Medicine, where I did research on leprosy. Inside the wrapping was a seriously deformed and lethally contagious body of a leper. "Unwrap the bastard!" Ferrall ordered.

I answered that because of the risk of contagion, the county court would not allow it. Said I, "Any man coming near this diseased corpse, breathing in its exudations, is in immediate risk of contracting leprosy. The thing has a rotted nose. Which means next week you could see your nose swell with pustules and eruptions before it drops off into your hog stew. You could eat your own nose by mistake." I showed the document of the county Plenipotentiary of Leprotic Flesh, deliberately passing it upside down. He squinted at it, never turning it upright.

For once, I was grateful for illiteracy. Despite my warning, he dismounted to peer closely into the cart, and that's when he inhaled a waft of decaying rat. He recoiled and shouted, "You goddam quack! You and your nigga get your goddam load outta here before I shoot this poke of rot to kill the stink."

12 May (2 p.m.)

At the split-off from the Delaware road, we found a surface allowing us to proceed apace, pausing only at a creek for the mule to drink and for us to check our corpse, whispering to it to remain silent whilst I opened a seam enough to offer it water, reminding it to take only a sip, given the problem of a corpse sewed up in a canvas cocoon needing to relieve a full bladder. The corpse whispered, "My nose will never again be able to smell a fresh-baked buttermilk pie."

We crossed the Pennsylvania line, and just beyond stopped before a way-marker at an intersection. I set Cuff up to unwrap him, orienting him so the first thing he would see was the fortuitous village name on a sign with an arrow pointing ahead: **NEW FREEDOM.**

Staring in disbelief, he was quiet, tears on his cheeks, and then he exclaimed, "Glory, glory! Free at last!" Then, wiping his brow, he said, "Please tell me we be not in Delaware."

"We be not," I answered.

"You told me we were going to Delaware."

"I told everybody Delaware. Misdirecting slave hunters to allow us time to enter a free state."

I pulled out the merchant seaman's duds I bought on the Baltimore wharves, and Cuff changed into them as Casper and I buried the shroud of an ex-slave. Also an ex-rodent. Underway again, Casper said, "I gots to tell you, Doctor. You be not safe here in Pensvania needer. Man what stop us, ever colored know him."

"The slave catcher?"

"He no catcher—he *killer*. Come outta Hell. He born evil-headed like a cottonmouth. A man go make him mad an he hunt you down cause now he got poison for you. That trick you work, you shame him. Now he kill you. Mebbe Casper too."

I had not considered my plan putting the cartman in danger, and I began rethinking my scheme. At length I said we should continue on to York and mingle with the population. I explained to Casper that whites are often poor at distinguishing black faces, and also I doubted Ferrall paid any attention to him so probably wouldn't recognize him if he saw him again. HB would be hunting *me* and a mule cart hauling a long bundle. If the cartman trades his mule for a horse—my covering any difference in price—and tosses a crate of chickens in his cart, Ferrall will not likely detect him. I added, "You said it, Casper. Now he wants *me*, not you. He wants me even more than a bagged-up corpse he never laid eyes on."

"All well and good, but he still gone hunt you down an kill you like you a colored runaway. You done made the wrong man mad."

Evening of the 12th

On the east side of York, we halted at the Griffon Inn. Cuff, passing as my manservant, had to take a bed in the groomsmen quarters above the stable, and I realized being in a free state does not mean an *equal* state. On the dark side of twilight we met up in the paddock, where we stood far enough from the stalls to prevent being overheard.

He said, "Doctor, you might be crazy, but you be useful crazy. Otherwise I'd be chained in a slave pen, bleeding from fifty lashes and trying not to show the man he hurt me. And at daylight I'd be sold down south for bottom dollar because nobody will pay anything for a bloodied-up runaway. Once I got down there, I'd be whipped again just to stamp correction into my brain. Make sure I be broken. The rest of my life, those scars tell everybody I be trouble. Nobody trusts a slave whose history is carved into his back for all to read."

I reminded him we were now north of the Mason-Dixon Line, and he said, "When it comes to a runaway, the Line turns invisible. There be laws giving a slaver right to reclaim his property. And you, you can be liable too. You're a thief who stole a man's property. And you know what property means to whites. This is America."

That chilled our talk, and it was some time before he said, "It be not proper for me not to say the truth. My name be not Cuff. I be Nicodemus, but folks call me Deems. Mama, before she was sold off, she called me Nicodemus after my pet salamander. I be five or six. At night, I kept little Nico in a cow horn. Till a dog ate him."

"Your surname?"

"A plantation slave has no need of a last name."

I asked where these events happened. "In Virginia. Loudon County. About age seven or eight, the mistress of the plantation—a small one for raising feeder crops, corn mostly—she brought me into the big house. Mistress had special affection for me, especially when she began to teach me reading and saw how I picked up on it. She was a teacher at the Saint Benedict Latin School and Female Seminary. Every evening she sat me down for a Latin lesson. We also read Bible stories. A year or so later, we started reading from classics a boy might take to. The *Odyssey*. Or Caesar's *Commentaries* on his conquests. She had me memorize brief Latin phrases. 'Gaulia est omnis divisa in partes tres.' Or, 'Quis legem dat amantibus?'"

"The Caesar I recognize," I said, "but the second one?"

"Who can give a law to lovers?" He smiled. "She liked that one from Boethius. She went out of her way to be good to me, but then—."

In search of something, a man carrying a lantern entered the paddock, and as if a shadow, silent and swift, Nicodemus vanished, and I wondered would a day come when he will not have to live like that.

13 May

This morn I found Deems seated in the barn loft, legs crossed and before him a breakfast of beans and cornbread and a thick slice of bacon and a mug of coffee. That was the first time I saw him give forth an unrestrained, unconditional smile. He said he had been "the most part of hungry for three days."

Kneeling beside him, I laid out two possibilities: the first, since he was now a free man, whether he wanted to pursue his own independent course. The second, a proposal to join me in my reconnaissance of the American experiment, traveling at least as far as the country of the upper Missouri River to witness the great bison herds, meet Indians who follow the ancient ways, see the prairie sky turned white by stars. He asked, "I'd be your manservant?"

My answer, "Never. Ever."

He could become a retainer paid a weekly wage and fully possessed of the freedom to leave if a better opportunity opens. As long as he stays, I cover costs of the journey with the understanding my resources are sufficient but not unlimited. He to be responsible for his habiliments and personal pleasures. Deems could explain aspects of American life unknown to me.

"You want my answer now?"

"No need for that kind of expedience," I said, "but there is need for *expediently* putting miles behind us to reach the temporary haven I have in mind."

Making certain we were out of earshot, I set forth the plan: A German elder I had met on the Atlantic crossing, Gerhard Schiller, was a leader of a contingent of Mennonites headed for Berks County in southeastern Pennsylvania, some fifty miles distant. The sect, typically strict and fervent Abolitionists, would surely grant us sanctuary until the slave hunter abandoned his search. "A daily stage wagon departs here for Reading at ten this morning," I said. "Which road is it for Nicodemus?"

"I never found adventure in the life of a houseboy. Toting things here and there. Scouring pewter. Shelling snap beans. But you talk about meeting Indians. Herds of bison. My answer is, *I be ready for Reading!*"

To pass the time before departure, the day being warm, we moved a short distance beyond the stable to a pasture and sat to watch the horses graze. I invited Nicodemus to tell me about the Virginia plantation—*if* he was so inclined.

I have not yet noted that Deems is approximately of my stature, his coloration more inclined towards mahogany than ebony, his hair trimmed close. His eyes are large and widely set, and with his smile and articulateness, he presents himself well, even winningly when he wishes. As far as he can determine, he is just past his twenty-first year, but he has no record of his birth, and his parentage is uncertain. His mother was sold away, and he knew naught of his father other than he was a slave hired for a harvest.

The plantation owner, James Reilly, was generally a tolerant man, lacking the brutality in many of his white neighbors, and among Negroes in the county he was thought a good owner. The weekly provisions of corn and cuts of pork were not stinting, and his slaves were given seeds and allowed gardens and a few chickens. Each dwelling, more hut than hovel, had a hearth and *chimney* rather than just a roof-hole that not so much let out smoke as let in everything else. Trusted slaves were allotted planking to lay floors in their huts and to fashion into beds. Because the Reilly family was of a vigorous religious bent, there was no labor on Sunday except during planting and harvest seasons; instead, Sabbaths were devoted to long sermons and prayers led by the plantation mistress, Angeline Reilly, a tall blonde of grey eyes and pronounced cheekbones, an elegant woman of early middle years, who conducted herself as if aristocracy. The Sunday service was often about acquiescing to one's station, putting oneself in the hands of the Lord without grievance, and living peaceably to gain the *Life Hereafter*.

Nicodemus said, "Slaves learned dedication to duty and acceptance of destiny equal docility. At Christmas, there were small gifts—a comb, a lump of maple sugar, a length of satin ribbon, a nickel."

Reilly gave leave to fiddles and singing on Sunday—but no dancing—understanding as he did controlling slaves through enticement instead of the lash. Said Nicodemus: "One man can hold out an apple to get a horse to come to him, or he can hire four men with whips and ropes to move it his way."

The whipping post, although visibly placed, went unused. When the lash was required, a miscreant slave was taken out of sight: Reilly believed word about *who* and *why* would immediately spread, and within hours others saw a bloodied back developing into thick ridges of keloid to serve as a visible and permanent warning of what insubordination or impertinence could mean. Reilly never marked his slaves with amputation, branding, or knocked-out front teeth. When a slave did abscond, he—or she—was simply never heard from again, leaving the others to the darkest conclusions. One girl managed an escape but returned on her own the third day. She was not whipped but prayed over and chastised for ingratitude towards the Reilly family; she had seen a frightening world beyond the plantation, and how it left her hungry. She was encouraged to tell her tale to others. Deems said, "Reilly's smart, but being smart isn't being good." Once a female turned fourteen, if well favored, he might take her into the house, and the girl she replaced went to the auction block. "My half sister was one of those."

I said, "Missus Reilly didn't object?"

"What could she do? Things like these be invisible before courts, the church, the community. Acceptance has the force of law, and it doesn't require whips or jails."

The trumpet from the Reading stagecoach sounded at the Griffon, and we hurried to board and join four others. Deems— wanting a view of the new territory and, I think, not wishing to create an issue about his presence—climbed up to ride alongside the Negro coachman, and off we rolled, drawn by four fine steeds.

A drizzle yesterday left the fifty miles of road to Berks County filled with mud holes, what Americans call *loblollies*. Crossing a miry stretch, the driver would order us in the coach to keep the stage balanced to prevent over-tipping. He would command us to lean out the port window, or move to the opposite side, then back again, a continual shifting that knocked off hats, whacked skulls together, all of us finding the event more amusing than annoying. After a head knocking, a passenger might say, "And a good day to you, madam!" or "Ah, we meet again!"

And so we rode until the wheels found a trench that dropped us to the axles. The horses strained and plunged, the driver popped the whip, and all of us alighted into the quagmire to ease the load, and still the coach remained stuck. Nicodemus retreated to a farm and persuaded a boy to bring a team of oxen to assist our horses, and with much labor the four beasts hauled us out of the heavy slurp onto a solid stretch of road, and off we rattled, the young driver now more alert to "chugholes."

The exertion and shared adversity created a sense of camaraderie among us, and a jolly Philadelphian opened his portmanteau to produce a large flask of excellent brandy to pass around. By the time we reached Reading, 'twas said we were the muddiest and merriest coach to arrive in many a season.

14 May (very early)

The stage halt was at the Ewe's Tail Tavern, a commodious inn with rooms available and allowing Deems to stay in my quarters. I wrote to Sophie to give word we are headed to Schiller's Mennonite farm. After supper we took a constitutional into the town center.

Traveling *à deux* doubles the necessary challenges of going alone but affords chances to share and escape the desolation common on a solo journey. I requested Nicodemus to continue his story. Nobody ever before having asked about his life, he was surprised by my interest. I said, "If a man wants to get to know a fellow, go on a long tramp with him. Here we are, ready to begin a long tramp into America." I quote him now as I try to record his words with accuracy:

"Miss Angeline, she," he said, pausing. "Teaching me reading and some arithmetic, she didn't do that with other colored children, but she saw I had good capacity. She brought me into the mansion, made me a houseboy, even gave me a small cubicle called the cockloft on the attic floor near the kitchen girls. As with the others, I was washed and scrubbed and trimmed. Miss Angeline—this is odd—she insisted the boys born on the plantation be circumcised. Although a devout Christian, she told me her father was Jewish. She was mad for cleanliness. I guess that's the reason."

I said I had wondered about the practice for a slave.

"She was gentle with the house coloreds. To prevent the field hands from heckling us, she let us take extra food out to the huts. Chocolate cake, gooseberry pie, sugar cookies. The children out there had to treat us fair, without jealousy, or they got no sweets. Of an evening, mistress and I sat on the porch in summer or in front of the hearth in cold weather, and read to each other. Eventually, she stopped calling me 'boy.' Instead it was 'little darlin.' You see, she was childless. As I grew, it became 'my dear.' Life was good, I had a plum of a placement. Then one warm night it all changed."

Deems hesitated, finally saying, "Maybe I ought not go on." I answered, if he considered it significant, I hoped he would continue. After some minutes, he broke his silence.

"I was about seventeen," he said. "She tapped on my door. Nobody knocked for me. She apologized for missing my lesson. I was propped up in bed by an oil lamp. Reading *The Pickwick*

Papers. Mistress sat beside me and said to continue. I was nervous. We'd never been on a bed together. I started on a page. Stumbling more than usual. She told me to quit fidgeting. I read on, making mistakes, mispronouncing, saying, 'Mister Wickpick.' *Mister Winkle* came out as 'Mister Tinkle.' But I—. Then, then—.'

Nicodemus had become much discomposed, walking without speaking until he said, "Then, *then* I felt her hand slip under my nightshirt. I froze, and she told me to read on. So I did, but I had no idea what I was reading, then I began stuttering. Stammering. Stopping. She ordered me to control myself. 'Just read!' When her fingers could go no further, I dropped the book, and she raised my shirt all the way, and, and, and she, she blew out the lamp."

We went along, wordless, before Deems said, "Nobody else knows this. From then on when the master was in Washington on business, she would sneak up to the cockloft. I told her we ought not keep, keep doing this. She told me to behave and not be intransigent. 'Rigid, recalcitrant houseboys'—those were her exact words—'forfeit *privileges.*' She said, 'Do I have to report you've been obstinate?'"

Here another long silence before Deems resumed, slowly: "I flaunted kissing the kitchen girls so Miss Angeline would see me and maybe lose interest. All that happened was getting scolded for impropriety. Master Reilly, he thought she protected me because of the reading we did. Miss Angeline, she reckoned I'd learned my lesson. I don't mean a *reading* lesson. She figured now I would be more accepting of inescapable circumstances. More considerate of her wishes."

He made a cynical chortle and said, "By then, I was so worried about inescapable circumstances, I couldn't, I couldn't *perform* anymore. So she introduced other, other *things.* I was uneasy all the time. I couldn't even finish Mister Pickwick's adventures. I came to fear our reading. I tried once to avoid it, and she promised a whipping."

Deems observed my response to his story. I kept my eyes on my feet. He said, "You come out of England. You may not see the threat. See the danger. I was trapped between a master's lechery and his wife's lust. If I stopped the—what should I call it?—the *reading*, she'd likely turn on me. If I obeyed her, how long would it be before Master Reilly found out? When an owner wants to, he forces a slave into flight so he can be shot as a runaway. A runaway with a bullet in the back of his head—that be all the proof the law needs."

It was now past midnight, and neither of us was certain which direction our inn lay. We turned about nevertheless and Deems continued. His words were coming forth in an unburdening.

He said, "Eventually, I was shifted out to work in the stable. I figured I was safe there. But I was stupid. I didn't prepare for the inevitable even though I always believed the truth had to break loose. One evening, months later, I went out to bring up a horse. Master Reilly came roaring into the stable, screaming for me, 'Where the hell's Deems? Drag him out here!'"

Nicodemus paused to collect himself, then he said, "You never saw a slave disappear so fast. No time to say goodbye even to my people. By morning I was across the river and into Maryland, and the next day I was beyond Gaithersburg and making for the Pennsylvania line. All I had was the clothes on my back. Not a damn thing more. Flat out unprepared. I didn't have a map. Not even a hat. I moved only after sundown and got twisted around and ended up covering some of the same territory twice. No money for food. I stole from vegetable gardens, and that was when I got caught, hiding in the weeds and eating a carrot. I got chained up and sent to the pens in Baltimore."

The 14th inst.

With the morning coach, a traveler out of Baltimore, a drummer of notions, arrived and overheard Deems speaking to the clerk. As

I came up, the Baltimorean was accosting Nicodemus: "How is it, boy, you talk like a white man?" Having encountered this challenge before, Deems answered forthwith: "Laws, boss! Dey calls me Parrot Bird, cause I kin talk to any critter dere be in de woods. Or in de feel. De Lord, he done give me a gift, dey sez, and sometime what I heah jest come right outta me. Cain't help it." He followed with a turkey gobble, then the yip of a red fox.

Seeing me, he returned to words: "Mas'r heah, he doan lemme talk like a feel-hand no mo. He bring out de whip iffen I does. Now, boss, when we moves on to Delware, den he let me talk liken I wants. Yes suh, over dere in Delware where we goan. Ain't dat so, mas'r?"

Managing to restrain laughter, I floundered to say, "Now don't you go getting clever, Cuff. You go up and pack us for New Castle. The company is expecting me on the morrow." The drummer huffed away, unsure whether he had been mocked.

Before heading off to hire a horse cart, at the reception desk I glanced over a *Baltimore Sun* from a day earlier. Amongst news about the auctions, I found what I was hoping not to find: a notice naming a white physician as a stealer of slaves, and alongside, an accurate description of an escaped male possibly going by the name Cuff. The reward offered for his capture was eight hundred dollars, and for the arrest and conviction of the doctor, the reward added another four hundred dollars, both to be paid in cash by James Reilly of Loudon County, Virginia. The recompenses were atypically high, suggesting an impassioned owner seeking more reprisal and revenge than mere return. Deems and I met beyond the stable. The gist of the discussion:

Our pointed references to New Castle and Delaware should— we hope—continue to misdirect the hunt long enough to allow us to reach the Mennonite farms, now only eight miles distant, but escape necessitated departure the moment the horse cart arrived. To cover the true direction of our exit, I had the cartman take a circuitous route through the perfectly gridded streets of Reading before striking off northeastward towards Oley Forge and Gerhard Schiller's farmstead. Fortunately for two wayfarers keeping watch on the road behind, we rumbled along at a tolerable clip.

For the first miles, I cursed our flight's impairing my goal of traveling America in order to experience the nation plainly. Then it came to me: I am indeed experiencing America as she is rather than as presented in the immigrant guides and as I have often heard her touted by Americans touring Europe, visitors who commonly fail to mention Negro servitude or, worse, they present it with a kindly face.

Stopping three times for directions, we neared our destination, a scatter of Mennonite farmsteads among gentle hills, a grouping united by social ideas and practices, all somewhat more liberal than those of neighboring Amish. Among those beliefs, we trusted, was a strong abhorrence of slavery and a willingness to assist a man into freedom.

It was noon when we caught sight of Schiller's community barn and two-storey house, everything neatly tended—as is common among German settlers here—and, I must note, tidier than many farms we have seen among citizens Mennonites refer to as "the English." A boy rang a large clapper-bell to announce our arrival, and without delay Herr Schiller came forth to greet me and express thanks for my medical help on the *Narwhale*.

He is a tall man of wide-set shoulders, long-bearded in the traditional way—top lip and upper cheeks clean shaven; hair of length but precisely trimmed; black jacket over a blue shirt; trousers sustained by braces; his head under a wide-brimmed black hat. In accordance with the belief of the plain people that the Devil seeks places to express temptations of vanity, nowhere on Gerhard or any other Mennonite—man or woman—was even a single button. Instead, he was fully behooked.

I inquired about two of his émigré contingent I had treated on the *Narwhale*; a broad smile attended his assurance they prospered. After introducing Nicodemus, I explained the imminent menace we both face and the apparent vehement resolve of a slave owner and his slave hunter. We requested temporary sanctuary, saying we would contribute labor as recompense during our sojourn. Herr Schilling escorted us to what was effectively a frame bunkhouse for unmarried men, currently occupied by only one. Before Gerhard promptly departed—Mennonites rarely show celerity in anything other than returning to work—he asked me to examine a man who had fallen onto a hay rake and suffered several punctures. Using his parlor, and assisted by Deems, I examined the injury, dressed one wound the size of an American dime before cleaning and wrapping three less serious others. The patient was embarrassed at having no English to express thanks, letting his countenance carry gratitude.

Interested in my treatment, especially the palliation of the largest puncture, Nicodemus queried me on the procedures and the prognosis. His words put one more idea into my brain: What did he think of becoming not a retainer but a nurse apprentice? He answered he was without qualifications, and I said, "Deems, you have the qualifications of concern for others attached to a versatile mind."

At the supper table with an assemblage of the brethren, I presented my medical apprentice, who was applauded. Though Deems was much moved, his eyes remained dry, mine less so. Never before had he received an accolade, especially from white hands.

22 May

The day after I saw my first patients in Gerhard's parlor, word went around the Oley Forge Mennonites had a physician in temporary residence—a necessary announcement, but one opening us to discovery. Now, Mennonite men, women, and children could come to the Schiller house for treatment. In the subsequent consultations—for sprains, coughs, rashes, a case of pinkeye, a bee sting, a bean in a child's ear—Nicodemus observed with dedicated attention. It was the first time in his life of enforced service to others that his work was not toting things or polishing boots or setting rattraps.

And so, for a week now, our days have passed, some with Deems helping in the training of horses whilst I set type in the Mennonite print shop at a neighboring farm. I also have found opportunity to write to Sophie in Buffalo and to sketch Nicodemus. If a human face is a map of one's affections, then his quizzical smile runs northwest to southeast. From the evergreens of Oregon Territory to the everglades of Florida. (Both which I hope one day to see.)

As I drew, he said, "The plantation had a Welsh pony named Arthur. After King Arthur. That pony could run, but I wasn't permitted to ride him. My task was to bridle him up. I remember, when I put the bit in his mouth, the sweet smell of his breath after he'd been in the clover."

In speaking with Germans new to America, I am uncertain whether I accurately interpret what I see in the remaking of Europeans into American citizens, everything filtered through Mennonite credence and customs, especially through aspects more practical than religious. Out of respect, Deems and I attend their services where commonsense and general moderation dominate fervor; we find them sensibly tolerable.

Husbandry pervades all Mennonite life, from farming to their pervasive thriftiness and disdain of ostentation and their insistent tempering of material hankerings. I admire the ways they support one another and practice an orderly economy driven by principles beyond greed. Here the continuing question is not *How to gain more?* but *How to do with less?* Successful they have been in stemming the American compulsion towards materialism.

The outcome of their approach renders a calmness among them. The Gilded Coterie of Kent now seems so distant, and I wonder whether the Bentleys would be capable of discovering anything of benefit among these plain folk for whom trumpery is repugnant.

British and French travelers to the States have made much of the pervasive enthusiasm Americans hold for mercantilism, the evaluations often unflattering. More than a decade ago, on his peregrinations to this nation, Monsieur Alexis de Tocqueville wrote in his *Democracy in America*:

> Americans are consumed by a desire for riches, which carries in its train a host of disreputable passions: cupidity, fraud, bad faith. Their sovereign goal is to make money. On the other hand, no or little shame attaches to bankruptcy; it is common in all cities.

Although I take no substantial issue with Tocqueville's opinion— he being a balanced percipient of American democracy—I do note, as far as I remember, he never visited a Mennonite or Amish community in the States.

Did he disqualify those immigrants for their keeping themselves apart? To be sure, Mennonite belief in building a life not upon pursuit of wealth and a gathering of material goods is ignored by Americans beyond the farms of the plain people, who show no desire to evangelize for their ideals. It seems to me this New World experiment would proceed more justly and equitably, more democratically and less plutocratically, if all citizens were to value affluence of mind as much as affluence of pocket. It would serve the nation to consider alternatives to the rise of corporate oligarchy transforming itself into a school of hyenas ready to transform democracy into a jungleocracy: eat or be eaten. I note here publication of Thomas Hunt's recent *Book of Wealth, In Which It Is Proved from the Bible That It Is the Duty of Every Man to Become Rich.*

Whilst Nicodemus and I admire Mennonite insistence on honest governance and devotion to education of the young, we have met older members with no interest in learning English or new ways suitable to an unfamiliar continent, a different climate, a changed social order. These are immigrants who care not to become *German-Americans*, instead content to be merely Germans living in America. They are believers in Paul's epistle to the Corinthians: "Come out from among them, and be ye separate." Or, in their own words, "Be ye not conformed to the world."

But is separation not antithetical to the American project? I see evidence of this in the image of the severed serpent and the attached phrase in the famous cartoon appearing in Mr. Franklin's *Pennsylvania Gazette* a century ago: **Join, or die.** Questions logically follow that admonition: How can the poisonous *separation* of races continue in the experiment? Why do citizens so disregard the very name of their nation? Is it not the *United* States rather than the *Divided* States? Their national motto is *E pluribus unum*: From many, one.

24 May

On two occasions Deems and I attended a community *sing*, where his tonal richness was sufficient to cover his lack of the German tongue and make his a welcome voice. One evening we were asked to contribute thoughts to a weekly meeting, where I volunteered a few words—Gerhard interpreting—from an English perspective about American social advancements, although I reminded them, I was a colonial by birth, Saint Kitts born. My remarks were tempered by my affection for America, and the response was polite if modest, perhaps because Berks County Germans in the last century threw vigorous support not to King George but to the American cause.

Nicodemus was called upon to address his experience as a slave; he was circumspect but truthful. The applause for him, happily, was more resounding than for my musings, an indication these brethren are looking not back at a war but forward towards means to heal a racially divided society. One man, Wolfgang, stood to say passionately (translated by Gerhard): "A war may end with one battle, but ending racial division requires many." If Wolfgang is correct, the issue becomes: How many battles will occur before the American fabric is torn irreparably apart?

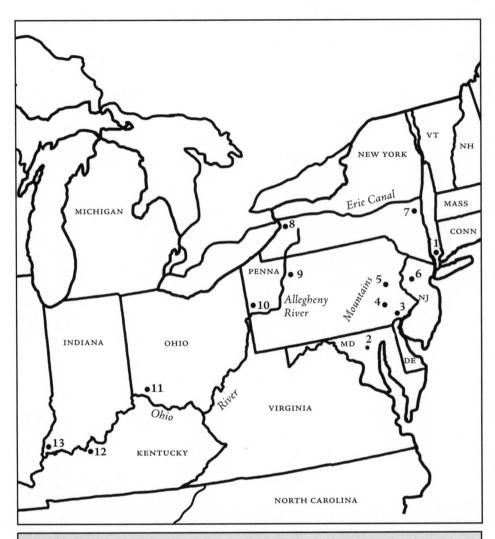

Key to Map

1. New York City, New York
2. Baltimore, Maryland
3. Philadelphia, Pennsylvania
4. Oley Forge, Pennsylvania
5. Pottstown, Pennsylvania
6. Hope, New Jersey
7. Albany, New York
8. Buffalo, New York
9. Warren Pennsylvania
10. Beavertown, Pennsylvania
11. Cincinnati, Ohio
12. Louisville, Kentucky
13. New Harmony, Indiana

June, 1848

---

3 June

NEAR THE END of our third week with the Mennonites, I received a reply to my letter sent from York to Sophie in Buffalo. I subjoin it here:

My dearest Doctor T,

We have arrived safely in Buffalo via an Erie Canal packet boat. Our voyage into America surpassed my expectations for introducing me to the country and reassured my decision to emigrate. I have given the children their first lessons here, and they, with much relish and some argumentation over personal style, have corrected these sentences.

I trust your travels proceed as you wished. You told me you would visit Elder Schilling, so I write in hopes this letter reaches you with its invitation to include Buffalo in your long itinerary (the children debated the meaning of that word). Their mother says it is the proper one and approves they discuss issues of language. As do I.

I am liking my life in Buffalo. There are enough Poles and Germans here to support a grocery of foods we knew in Europe. And the fresh fish from Lake Ontario and Lake Erie I prepare with recipes from the Old World. Did I ever thank you for the kind and effective way you helped me recover from my fever on the ship?

Your dedicated friend, Sophie.

Her missive was the promising news of the morn; the other news partook of a darker cast when promise deviated into menace. Through the Mennonite chain of orally transmitted information, word came in from Reading about a hostile man prowling the town in quest of a white doctor who stole a slave out of Baltimore. Because such hunters thrive along the Mason-Dixon Line, my innate optimism suggested the search could be for any number of white men or slaves. Sheltered within a community of ardent Abolitionist Mennonites as we are, slave-hunting here should prove difficult among people reticent to divulge information leading to Nicodemus's being returned to bondage. He, though, is considerably less sanguine, believing as he does our Delaware ploy may have played itself out. His words were: "If that pistoled demon is the hunter creeping around these parts, then coming this far shows we be on his *death* list." Thus, between the treat of Sophie's letter and the threat of Ferrall's list, I began a new month of my American quest.

For the lore Nicodemus offers, he has become quickly beloved by the Mennonite children who speak a mélange of German and English. Yesterday he described for them a variety of snares and gins for catching small game—possums to birds—all of which went onto the tables of slaves who tolerate any sort of meat.

He was asked to name all the creatures he has eaten: raccoons, bullfrogs, woodchucks, muskrats, bobcats, red fox, deer, even rats. And, ten kinds of birds, from larks to wild geese. There were grimaces at the mention of rats. Said he, "If it was flesh and could be caught, it got eaten." He explained how a diet from nature was encouraged by slave owners since it kept expenses down whilst providing their Negroes with meat to maintain their ability to work or improve their salability on an auction block. In graphic terms, Deems described a slave auction, the children listening wide-eyed.

Today he made for them a little gin of wire for snaring mice, and a larger snare of rope for a muskrat or a woodchuck or a wildcat. The biggest trap he ever built caught a young black bear that fed the plantation slaves for a week. His audience did not believe him. Challenged, he escorted them into the lofty community barn and seated them below a sturdy crossbeam holding a pulley used to hoist heavy loads into a wagon. He lifted a child so she could run a length of rope onto the sheave, and from there to be drawn forward by three sturdy boys standing twelve feet away; to the other end of the rope he tied a slip knot to make a loop two yards in diameter which he laid on the barn floor and covered with some of the straw thrown down to keep cattle manure off the planking.

Nicodemus whispered to the three boys before sending another—a strapping, cocky lad named Luke—to walk off a dozen paces then advance towards the loop. When Luke stepped within it, Deems signaled the trio to jerk the line taut, ensnaring Luke around the ankles and yanking him off his feet as they hoisted him upward towards the pulley to leave him hanging, his inverted head at eye level with the other children. Nicodemus wrapped the free end of the rope to a post, then gave Luke a spin, the boy's smirk now erased by wooziness, and there the upside-down youth hung like a steer ready for a butcher's knife. The children looked on in alarm, before laughing as the malapert begged to be lowered to the barn floor. Then they jumped and applauded, and, as if he knew the outcome all along, Luke attempted to regain his conceit by rising into a deep bow.

"And that, my young friends," Nicodemus said, "is the way you catch a bear hungry to eat your liver." All the striplings were now eager to be hoisted and swung by the heels, but Deems declined the entreaties, telling them first to practice making a gin to rid the barn of rodents.

4 June

Today I made time to sequester myself with my memorandum book and glean notes of the last several days and to write to Sophie, assuring her I planned to include Buffalo as Nicodemus and I travel on westward towards the Upper Missouri country. I was still writing when Frau Schilling, in some agitation, entered to pass on a report of a blemished and besmirched stranger roaming the valley and stopping at farmsteads to ask after two men—a white and a slave—the white wanted in Virginia for theft of *property*. That term should lead Mennonite householders, with their dedicated opposition to slavery, to remain close-lipped. Further, the hunter's flaunting "a gun of the hand" (as the people term pistols) makes him a dangerous pariah. If this hunter indeed be Ferrall, then Nicodemus and I will have to come up with something more effective and more lasting than a wrap of sailcloth and a dead rat. But what does one do against a man crazed by vengeance and driven by lust for our blood?

I have reached the point of no longer being willing to flee to escape a maniac trafficking in human lives. Before me is no wealthy patient who can be calmed by a snifter of laudanum-laced liquor. Whilst my medical bag does contain arsenic compounds for treating ulcerative abscesses and syphilis (as practiced by Hippocrates himself), to use poison to *treat* a bipedal abscess hell-bent on killing us, is out of the question. For now. There has to be means short of murder.

Setting type in the print shop this morning, I fell to thinking about the excitement the children evinced when Nicodemus demonstrated various gins and snares, and it was then I got the idea. Deems and I went to Gerhard to lay out a plan: if Ferrall indeed comes in search of us, one of the Mennonite boys will sound the bell. Till then, we can continue comfortably in the calm, sensible life of the plain people.

5 June

This afternoon, a Sunday, the rabid-brained Ferrall turned up, his foul temper and pearl-grip gun of the hand disquieting Sabbath activities. Deems, Gerhard, Luke, and I quickly assembled in the dim barn to rig the pulley block and lay out a loop of rope. We waited inside behind a wagon until Ferrall burst through the door. His eyes not yet adjusted to the low light, he paused, then began loudly cursing for Nicodemus and me to show ourselves. We remained silent. He came on, swearing, halting again, this time inches short of the loop hidden under the loose straw. From the shadows, I made a derisive catcall intended to outrage him further and draw him forward.

Spewing the most scurrilous language, he stepped smack within the loop, whereupon Deems and I yanked the rope tight around his ankles which threw him violently to the floor. In a flash, Gerhard and Luke also took hold to hoist him upside down, his knife falling from his belt as he drew his pistol to fire an errant shot at the pulley. Deems kicked the gun out of his grip whilst the three of us hefted and secured Ferrall so that his inverted head faced our knees and he swung back and forth, *tick-tock*. To further his disorientation, I gave him a twist to set him rotating, whilst he slavered and slobbered and spat vile invective such as I never before heard. The man apparently had been sleeping in the woods during his search, and he exuded a stench beyond what I thought a human could carry, which worsened when the spinning caused him to start choking up belly-soured beer and a half-digested squirrel.

Gerhard pinned his arms as Deems and Luke bound him head to toe, and with a strip of flour sack, I tightly blindfolded him and wrapped his mouth to shut him up, although he growled and gurgled till he began thrashing, twitching, and jerking like an angleworm on a hook. A young woman he earlier knocked to the ground entered the barn with four other sturdy women and walked up to punch him in the belly, causing him to retch into the gag the last of the beer. Gerhard reminded her to respect Mennonite passivity, but he was smiling when he said it.

We loaded Ferrall into Schiller's enclosed carriage of the design common among the people here, tied him down and out of sight, and four large farm boys hauled the flouncing madman to the jail in Reading. As we were packing him off, Gerhard listed some of the charges to be brought against him: trespass, assault on a female, discharging a gun of the hand inside a building, and six violations of the Sabbath. When Schiller boarded the carriage he said, "For many days, he will see the world through bars of iron." Let us hope so.

6 June

Later I told Nicodemus, even with the crazed hunter temporarily jailed, we still must put significant mileage between him and ourselves, and that will affect further our tour of inquiry which I prefer to conduct at a pace more conducive to survey of the territory. I have grown apprehensive about disruptions to our explorations. Without additional hindrance, I want to establish proper means to fulfill the reasons I have come to America. I cannot accomplish my purpose if pursued—or killed—by an armed man crazed by hatred of all he is not.

I took the opportunity to ask again whether Deems wished to continue with me or strike out on his own, and he answered, "That day will come, but until then I like this odyssey you're creating. If you be Odysseus, then I'm your crew of one."

Nicodemus relishes the freedom of the road and being able to travel far beyond the five hundred acres of a Virginia plantation. And, I add, his desire to encounter Indians of the great prairies and plains inspires him. Only a few weeks ago, he was resigned to be forever curtailed in his movements, never able to discover the nature of the world, forced to live only to serve the liberties of those who enslave him.

Tomorrow morning we will pay our respects to the Schilling family, buy two horses from a neighbor, and ride northward for Hamburg, on the Schuylkill River where it passes through a forested divide in Blue Mountain, a remoteness to help us shake a pursuer. Once again we will be on our way westward whither red men still live by the bison and bow.

7 June

Both our horses are spirited jennets good for the hills ahead. With our early departure, they made short work of the fifteen miles of handsomely cultivated country leading to the Schuylkill River and the bank-side village of Hamburg, founded only some sixty years ago by German immigrants and bearing their signature orderliness, evident in the precision of the street layout. Expecting nights in the open, we bought oilskins and two bedrolls and swapped out my clumsy English portmanteau for a duffel; also a pair of carpetbags of size and ingenious design allowing them to be used as sleeping pads. At a bakery next door we picked up two hefty loaves of rye bread and a wedge of Amish cheese.

Near the limit of the village a carnival was setting up a tent, and through the raised flaps we stopped to watch an acrobat rehearse his leaps onto a cantering pony, jumping down only to bound up and alight on its unsaddled back, then leap to the other side, and, in a single motion, once more onto the horse. Again and again the muscular man jumped, until he missed a mount, and went topside-totherway. He lay unmoving whilst the animal continued circling. The carny folk rushed forward and, for the first time in my medical career, I heard, "Is there a doctor in the house?"

When I reached him, somebody asked, "Is he dead? If he is, there goes our show." He who inquired was the proprietor of the carny, and what he saw was not a fallen man but fallen profits. As I checked the acrobat's vitals, he slowly opened his eyes. Seeing me, he said, "Who the hell are you?" and tried to sit up. Deems and I kept him pressed to the ground whilst explaining what had happened, and still he tried to rise as if to get atop his horse. Then he passed out again. We carried him to a bench to lay him down, and for a third time he came to and attempted to stand, saying he was all right, the owner happy that his acrobat could perform tonight. I recommended against it, warned of vertigo, but the dependence of the carny people on gate proceeds overruled me. The proprietor's gratitude was hearty, and he took me aside to hand me an envelope of dollars. Because I had done nothing, I refused it, but he pressed it on me, saying, "You saved the performance. It's yours!"

8 June

This morn, Nicodemus and I turned our horses towards a road that departed the cultivated fields for the bends of the Schuylkill River as it escapes Blue Mountain, a long and narrow and abrupt ridge of the heavily wooded Alleghenies which for a century and more have been a major barrier to the westward expansion of white civilization. Riding into the cloven rockiness, one wonders how so small a river could have ever made its way through stone and a thick wall of forest that resist human penetration. The track was as level as the river and only feet above it, but the road began making a twisting ascent of Blue Mountain, and dwellings became cruder in construction, and—of more note—fewer. At last we were alone.

We talked about the determined migration of Americans into tillable territory farther west, immigrants following paths of the indigenous ones who have passed and left so little behind we had a sense of entering a land primeval, abundant of leaf and twig and rank growth fresh from the creation. Our conversation caused us somewhere in the gloom of unbroken forest to miss a turn, but we did not realize it till sundown, and by then we were deep within the wilds. To one who grew up on a Caribbean Island and the domesticated lands of the English Midlands, this American wilderness is unnerving, made yet more jungled by the cry of alien bird voices. No, I am the alien. In the declining light, it was obvious we would find no inn, and the southern sky was assembling for rain. Yes, we had our new bedrolls and oilskins, but Blue Mountain was another country.

The ascent rose high enough that wherever a break opened in the trees, we could see hundreds of feet *down*. We were so perceptibly up, our jennets became aware of the climb. My inexperience had led me to assume along American roads we would come upon, as in England, lodging every so many miles. When reality ruptures innocence, the brain can be stunned by its naive blindness. On Blue Mountain we would pay the price for my failure. Nicodemus, accustomed to a dry bed in a plantation mansion, must now endure a mistake attributable to me.

From another rocky aperture to land below, the view seemed to mock us: a farmhouse identifiable by a window gleam, I recognized as having passed earlier. For the previous half hour in the dropping light, we had somehow been circling. When I turned to look forward at the narrow road, a more dismal and desolate forest I have never seen; to point up the inhospitality, wolves offered their native choir to the night.

There could be no descent of the mountain once the dark completed itself, and that meant no choice other than to continue into a wildness sparse of all but desolation. I questioned whether my ignorance would forever endanger those trusting me. Was that not the source of my nightmare about the Woman in White? My incubator of dread? I failed a loved one who put credence in a physician lacking not only raw knowledge but also foresight.

Without warning, something unexpected overwhelmed me: an exhilaration from challenge. A surge of confidence lacking any rational basis, a boldness I can ascribe only to a mind weakened by weariness, the most common travail of the traveler. But watching

Nicodemus beginning to slump in the saddle, my sense returned and elation evaporated.

Then, beyond a bend in the road appeared a misty light like the eyes of an animal reflecting a torch. I called out to Deems, who was almost asleep atop his mount. He stopped to let me catch up. I asked what he made of the glimmer. Said he, "I think it's salvation." Salvation, if such it proved to be, was a cabin of ill-cut logs and one small window whose glow was all but extinguished by dirt. The potential for salvation was this: in the American outback where inns are few or none, it is the custom of the country for a rambler to knock on the door of a dwelling and request to buy food or a night under a roof.

Our tired horses forced us to dismount and walk them, then abruptly they snorted, flared their big nostrils, Deems guessing they smelt a barn. In the dying light we entered the yard of the cabin, and there a man was splitting logs for his hearth just then leaking out a splendid spire of wood smoke. He was bearded, sag-eyed, begrimed, and so worn away that with any further diminishment, the frontier would have absorbed him as it does dreams. Our sudden manifestation out of the mist was as unexpected to him as his to us. Although he quit chopping, he kept the axe in hand.

I hailed him to introduce us and comment how we came to be there, and he said, "Did ye come to buy a jug?" Whatever a jug was, yes, I would buy one. Henry Foster suggested we step into the cabin, where he would join us directly, saying, "Missus Foster is inside, but she won't disturb you. She ain't much of a talker. She's a mite crippled up, so you and your man go ahead on in."

The single room, intolerably close and dark but for coals from a dying hearth fire, was furnished with naught but two chairs, a table, and a bed. A broken-out windowpane was patched with a weatherworn felt cap. I could just make out Mrs. Foster seated rather rigidly, discomfited perhaps by our unexpected entry or from one of us being Negro. I greeted her, apologized for our unexpected entrance, and we introduced ourselves, and I told how we had lost our way. She listened attentively, nodding, though that might have been only a flickering from the hearth reflected in her spectacles. We stood awkwardly, holding our hats, trying to retain smiles, until I commented on the dropping temperature and asked would she like me to add wood to the coals.

Henry came in, shucked off his worn jacket and shook it vigorously as if to dislodge the chill, then stirred the coals, tossed on a log, and said he guessed she had not introduced herself. "This here's my wife. Miss Dorsey. Her health has seen better days, but she's a durable woman. Comes from hardy stock. Welsh." As the fire rose, I saw she wore a neatly pressed gingham dress, her hands folded primly in her lap. The flames increased to reveal Deems staring rudely at her.

As the room brightened I noticed Mrs. Foster's face was the color of tanned leather, the tint of her nose not quite matching, her grey hair pulled into a bun, her eyes sunk into the sockets, her desiccated lips exposing her teeth to create more grimace than grin, more a scream than a smile. Dorsey Foster was mummified.

Henry lit a taper. "You recollect I mentioned she don't bother nobody, so if you want to put down on the floor in front of the hearthstone, she ain't agoin to keep you awake with idle chatter. Or there's the barn. Not so warm though."

He opened a floorboard and from the cavity withdrew an earthen jug and three grimy glasses to pour a transparent liquid known among Americans as "white lightning." The drink had the single virtue of burning warm our cold throats. Foster raised a glass, "To Miss Dorsey," and we answered with ours. That was the first time I ever toasted a mummy.

Here is Miss Dorsey's story as I collected it from Henry:

Ten years ago, whilst he was down in Hamburg for supplies, a winter storm rolled in unexpectedly early, which happens in the Alleghenies. He was prevented from returning to her for three days, but once home he saw snowdrifts up to the eaves of the barn, and the cabin door blocked by ice; it took an hour with a poleaxe to clear it, all the time calling out to his wife as he chopped. Inside he found the house empty of her but no indication of anything amiss other than her wire egg-basket most visibly not hanging on its peg. He went to the hen-yard attached to the barn, and came upon three frozen chickens half buried under a little avalanche off the roof.

He concluded she had taken her basket and gone into the woods to dig roots and fungi. For the next three days he searched all the locales where she hunted edibles. On the fourth day he rethought his conclusion: whilst gathering, she had disturbed a mother bear. He could not speak the conclusion. He spent several days looking farther afield in hope of finding a sign of her. Finally, he undertook the long trip into the village to post a notice requesting word of her whereabouts. He began to think: Maybe it had not been a mother bear. What if she ran off on her own accord? Was he not too old for her?

Winter was a long spell of loneliness and self-recrimination and confusion. In late April he awoke to ice sliding off the barn roof, and he went to the hen-yard to check on the chickens. Along a trailing edge of the heaped snow he glimpsed something out of place, a piece of blue gingham. Again with the poleaxe, he cautiously chopped away, and there underneath it all lay his wife, face down and frozen fast to the earth. In her left hand was the egg-basket and in it four eggs, frozen but unbroken. He went to the house and made himself an omelette.

He had to wait until the next afternoon for the spring sun to melt her free so he could lift her into his wagon and cover her with a blanket to take his beloved down the mountain. She had lost her ears and most of her nose, and she was still frozen through when he got her to the mortician. Henry's only relief was she had not run off with another man.

"Mortician done a good number on her," he said. "Even whittled her a nose. Out of maple to match her skin. Sort of. The hair, he combed it around her head to hide where her ears was. After he done her up, I brought her home. I told him to set her in a sittin position. You see, I had the rest of my days to recollect how her and me ever night sat by the fire. Talkin about the day. Sippin my spirit makins. She loved her hearth. The best part of our day. We never overdrunk ourselfs. We just sipped and talked. I talked more. She was a good listener, and that's what I missed that winter— her sittin and noddin and listenin. And that's what she does now. Except for the noddin."

He paused to clear his throat. As difficult as it was for him, Henry deeply needed to share this story. "Knowin she been froze in the hen-yard all winter, I sure didn't think she wanted to be put back in this cold, mountain ground. And that's why she's here in her chair with us, warm under her roof. The last ten year, she been right where she always perferred to be."

Raising a toast to Dorsey, he added, "To say the truth, cause I need company up here, I couldn't see wastin a good corpse. Nearest neighbor, five mile off, is ol Tom Tripp, but he's turned so crotchety, cain't nobody stand him. I know her sittin here ain't reglar, but if you boys ever lose your woman, then try what I done. What you see here. I don't say much to her except when I go to bed. She's there across the room, lookin over things, sendin me thoughts, and I listen and tell her what I been up to. She don't complain anymores about livin up here on this mountain, not now with me here for her. Bein a settler, it's hard on a woman. Ever spring I take her feather duster to her and then wipe her down real careful with turpentine. Gives her a nice glow. But she ain't so smooth as she used to be. Peelin here and there."

It was some time before he spoke again. He said, "Tell me this. Who can say for sure she ain't inside there right now, listenin, keepin watch. I don't believe in no Heaven or Hell, but a body gotta go *somewheres*. So for me, it come down to just one worry—where they gonna lay us up? I done writ out a note to a church-lady friend, sayin to prop me up in my chair next to her, shut the cabin and stick a torch to it. If it's a cold day, we'll go ahead on with warm feet."

9 June

Nicodemus and I last night chose the barn over the warmth of Henry's hearth and its unmoving human fixture. A corpse might be a clinical matter to a physician, but young Deems was considerably put off by the notion of lying next to withered feet ten years dead. Even in the barn he slept fitfully, and only at last did the calming sounds of Foster's pair of nags bring him repose. Spending a wakeful night together lost in the mountains, one comes to know a fellow traveler. For young Deems, he had opportunity to enlarge his conceptions of death and the human corpus—and love.

We rose at dawn, washed up in the cold water of the barn-lot trough—whether freshened for us or the horses, I could not say. Henry was at his woodpile, although he already had splits enough to carry him and Dorsey through whatever remaining winters lay ahead. But then, in this mountain isolation, an axe and a log provided something to do beyond looking into the unchanging regard of an eyeless wife.

Delighted to see us, he began talking, a steady outpour of verbiage I have no detailed memory of other than as an expression of the loneliness inherent in opening the remoteness of a new nation. Inside, Foster pulled the table to the hearth, slid forward his wife in her chair, gave me the other one, and set out a bench for Deems and himself. Unfortunately, the arrangement had the woman (is that the correct term?) directly facing Nicodemus, her inexorable gaze fastened on his every move. The flicker of firelight glinted in her spectacles in a way to make it appear she had not empty sockets but eyes—*animated* eyes. Henry served boiled oats drizzled with treacle, boiled eggs, a boiled rasher, and boiled coffee, not the worst ever put to my lips.

He said, "Some day this ol mountain will have people up here. Folks will wander into the territory and overflow the valley, and then they'll climb up the mountain like it was a island. Things won't be so lonely then. Missus would love that. Course, her and me will fall short of them times. And that's too bad cause loneliness rides hard on a woman. Sometimes I ask myself if she ain't better off like she is."

I paid for our food and lodging and the jug of gullet wash, and he said, "You fellas, you come again and visit us. This here door of ours ain't never locked. What's the need of a lock up here anyways? And you can bet she ain't gonna chide you for muddy boots," and gave out a jovial chortle.

We mounted up, and Henry directed us towards the eastward-bound Pine Creek Road down the mountain. It is clear, to travel athwart the numerous sheer ridges of eastern Pennsylvania is not the most expedient way west. Before the *Narwhale* shunted me away from New York City, my original plan had been to sail up the Hudson River to the Erie Canal and from there roll on west, but why struggle across the forbidding and parallel Allegheny steeps one after another when we can sit back and float our way into the heart of America?

"On the canal," said Deems, "I hope we'll not happen upon boiled porridge watched over by a cadaver."

Again on level ground, we conversed more readily, especially Nicodemus, in whose mind a mummy yet glowered. Three or four times he used the word *ghosts* in such a way to suggest belief in them. Had he, I asked, seen a ghost yesterday? No, but he had seen the start of one. If ghosts truly exist, I argued, would not some sort of emanation visibly hover near its source?

"I catch your drift," he said, "but in the dark, some science just doesn't hold up."

10 June

We struck out for Pottstown in eastern Pennsylvania. By comparison with our ascent of Blue Mountain, the two dozen largely level miles to the village we accomplished almost speedily. In areas recently opened for settlement, the American farms, while not as *in trim* as those of Mennonites, showed crops rising in ravaged plots of stumps with dead trees heaped for burning. Unlike so many European travelers, I see this destruction necessary to the initial stage of conquest of the forest.

Nevertheless, I sensed a paradise lost, and I could understand those who say Americans treat this plenteous land as just another commodity. Thus far, no matter how strenuously they exploit their natural resources, bountiful nature offers more. Always, over the next mountain lies unbroken land to be taken and turned to profit. No one yet seems to consider a day of reckoning, when extraction can no longer drive the economy. Then what happens to polity and governance? With Americans not threatened by any neighbor, and their country richly abundant, the people are generally politically quiescent. And why not, as long as there is so much ground ready for the taking? As we talked, Deems quoted Virgil: "Sunt lacrimae rerum." *Events have tears.*

Arriving in Pottstown, a village on the verge of becoming a manufactory of iron, we put up our horses with a hostler. A pair of slouching rapscallions tracked us into the stable, the whole time keeping close watch on Nicodemus before approaching him in a neighborly manner to ask where he hailed from, what his trade was, and his name. He answered he was James of Pittsburgh, here to sell a quarter-ton of pig iron. I stepped in to say he was my engineer and we had business to attend to, and off we went.

Beyond earshot, Nicodemus said the rascals had the look and approach of crimps, men who kidnap blacks—including freedmen—and smuggle them south for auction. Crimps are known to conglomerate along the Mason-Dixon Line, where exist easy pickings of fugitives trying to gain the Underground Railroad.

"They be not driven by contempt and hatred *that* make them stupid," he said. "They be driven by money—to kill me is to lose dollars, and that makes them tricky smart. They set traps, and I don't mean loops of rope. In me they see a black man made of gold. They feed themselves and buy their whiskey and whores with flesh the color of mine."

10 June, afternoon

Our time on the road has distracted me from mentioning the envelope given me by the carny proprietor: my surprise was not it contained money, but rather the *amount* of the money— twelve uncirculated, fifty-dollar banknotes. Because the recently organized United States Treasury has not yet begun turning out soft currency, regional banks answer the need for paper money by printing it, some with handsome bills; but it is local tender only as good as the bank itself.

The notes the carny man gave me were turned out in Philadelphia, making it prudent to have them proved up and cashed before leaving the state. Nicodemus wandered away to buy boots, and I went to a bank. A teller examined the currency, saying it was well printed, and began to exchange it for a letter of credit when he caught an irregularity. "On every bill," said he, "is a misspelling. *Pennsylvania* has only two *n*'s."

To verify his analysis, from under the counter he pulled out *Bicknell's Counterfeit Detector*, and, surely enough, the booklet depicted currency like that given me, the misspelling mentioned. He wanted to destroy the bogus notes, but I said they might prove useful down the road to light a campfire. Having done nothing medically to help the carny performer, I was amused, not dismayed.

Deems failed to meet me in the bank lobby. My continual concern that one of my plans might throw him into a slaver's hands flashed through me, and in considerable apprehension I hurried off to seek him on the street. He was nowhere to be seen. In full anxiety, I went to the stable. Preparing to mount up was the pair of crimps who had questioned him, and locked in a horse stall and bound at the wrists was Nicodemus, looking most anxious. I demanded of the miscreants the meaning of my engineer, a freedman, being so detained. The earlier casual manner of the reprobates had turned dour and of more significance, they were now wearing pistols. One blighter came close to my face, his eyes befitting some mongrel species, to say, "Ain't no way this here colored boy is a freedman. He's a damn fugitive. We know one when we see one, and this one's headed back down where he come from."

"And where would that be?"

"Delaware."

"You're quite mistaken. He hails from Pittsburgh and can prove it. He's in the employ of the Great Western Mining Company of Pittsburgh, Pennsylvania, a company producing iron for the United States military. Armaments. This man is widely respected in Pittsburgh. He's on the mayor's council. You steal him, and Great Western is going to send their private police to hunt you down. Those men have hard bark on them, and they return their quarry dead or alive. They prefer corpses that give no bother. Don't make a stupid mistake and end up in a pine box two days after you steal this engineer of theirs."

"Well then, jackass, looks like you got to be the one to buy him."

"How much?"

"This young stud, he's worth eight hundred. Maybe more."

I remembered what was in my pocket. Said I, "I have six hundred in Pennsylvania banknotes. You can take them now or we can go to Philadelphia. If we do, then I'll need to have the sale legally witnessed there by a federal official. Standard procedure. Or, instead, I can offer you this: if we conclude the transaction here, I'll toss in a jug of whiskey."

The rogues stepped away to reckon the proposition, arguing over the split, then pushed forward to say, "Show us the money." Seeing the hostler had come into the barn, I waved at him to use his presence to expose the transaction. I counted out the counterfeits slowly, crisp bill by crisp bill, letting the crimps' eyes widen at the sight, making certain the hostler could observe it all, a disquieted Deems vigilant in the horse stall.

One of the scalawags tried to snatch the notes. Pulling the money back, I said, "No sir! You bring out my engineer, his hands untied, seated on his horse. *Then* the money and whiskey are yours."

The chief rapscallion seized Deems, cut free his bound wrists, ordered him onto his horse, and grabbed the bills to stuff into his shirt. The crimps headed south towards Philadelphia as we mounted up and turned north. Nicodemus roused his steed into a pace a shade less than a gallop. Once again we covered over our true course with several opposite-direction turns in the streets of Pottstown. Before two hours were out, we had gained Allentown and, without stopping, we continued to Bethlehem to pass through quickly and, I hoped, invisibly.

By the third hour we were in Easton, then on across the Delaware River into New Jersey, and there we halted at the Mouth of Lehigh Tavern, a genteel roadhouse, and gave our mounts over to the stableman. In the quiet taproom we took a secluded table allowing us to keep an eye on the doorway. I ordered two generous measures of peach brandy, a specialty of the area (our host claimed), and we sat back in vigilant relief.

Said Nicodemus, "Doc, the carny man's money—I'll bet you never before were so sweetly swindled."

Lifting my glass, I said, "Can't swindle a doc who did nothing. But you *can* cozen a thief to help a friend stay alive."

"I have to admit, you're getting damn good at dodgery. And this time, you didn't use a putrid rodent."

11 June

Eager to add further mileage between us and any thugs on our trail, we rose with the dawn, pleased with weather conducive to dry roads and swift travel beyond the grasp of those who would put us in the grave. Nicodemus, a capable horseman, led the way on the faster of our mounts. He was still feeling the threat of the crimps, although for my part, I was *almost* confident they were in Philadelphia to squander—or *try* to squander—their counterfeit loot. As we rode along, I imagined their faces when the correct spelling of *Pennsylvania* was pointed out to them.

Twenty miles on, we came upon the pleasant village of Hope in New Jersey, a settlement founded by Moravians who built substantial houses and community buildings only to have the village laid low within a generation by smallpox, forcing them to leave behind a burial ground full of followers. Of their constructions in native blue limestone, one is the Jenny Jump Inn, Mrs. Lola Stewart, proprietor, an amiable lady with a body shape analogous to a fluffed pillow. She provided quarters large enough to contain a side chamber for Nicodemus, who will have a window opening to a roof, accommodating a rapid escape. It appears, at least for a while, his lot will be keeping continual watch over his shoulder, a burden a free man ought never have to bear.

After a lunch of Mrs. Stewart's savory beef and hominy soup, Deems and I went to the front porch and a wide view of anybody entering the Hope crossroads. I had suggested we and our horses take a day or two of rest from the flight forced upon us. With our mares at pasture, we will relax here in the quiet parlor where a rover can update his journal. Nicodemus, spotting on a bookshelf, a copy of Chapman's translation of the *Odyssey*, said he would be happy to sit back in an easy chair and read, play a man of leisure as he had witnessed it on the plantation but had never been granted freedom to pursue. Said he, "A slave is to be seen at work or not seen at all."

Once again, his words awakened me to aspects of myself I have never examined. Until traveling with Deems, I had not considered my existence favored, but now, even were he to strike out on his own tomorrow, I will be forever indebted for his revealing to me the narrowness of a life of privileges, most of them not earned by me but bequeathed by forebears. To presume such prerogatives as a birthright—the common rule in my world—is to live blindly. In my ignorance, too often have I so lived.

He sat with Homer in a corner chair near a window, and I opened my journal to expand notes from my pocket memorandum book. An hour later—to twist the phrase—it was Deems and not Homer who began to nod.

At three o'clock Mrs. Stewart, a Danish immigrant, brought us tea and a plate of aebleskivers, apple cakes free of anything apple but the shape. Nicodemus, long accustomed to carrying a tea tray rather than taking tea from one, looked at me from the luxury of his chair, and said, "So this is what it be like to be white," and returned to Homer's rosy-fingered dawns of the Mediterranean Sea of two millennia ago. As for me, had we not endured a wearying, knockabout time to get to the sedate parlor for tea and torte, I might be taken for a fop.

12 June

Mrs. Stewart, noticing me scratching away in my logbook after breakfast this morning, mentioned a former resident of the house many years ago, a young French-Canadian from Montreal who had taught pupils in this very room. Some years later, our host had found in the attic a journal kept by the teacher when she was sixteen. "Hers was a sad story," Mrs. Stewart said. "Full of promise, she died in childbirth at two and twenty."

"Childbirth!" I said—or more accurately, *exclaimed*. "Was a physician present?"

"Her husband."

I put down my pen, sundered from my writing, and found myself forced back to the memory I have tried to leave behind. I had no doubt the Woman in White would soon reappear. When Mrs. Stewart called us for lunch, I asked whether she would permit me to see the journal.

Afternoon, the 12th

The diary is a bound octavo, each entry introduced by a date. On the first page, in a schoolgirl's hand, this:

> ROSALEE RAYNAUD, HER BOOK.
> IF YOU ARE READING THIS,
> CONSIDER YOURSELF A BUSYBODY!
> (This means you, Charlotte!)

The girl's brief entries presented the ordinary and inconsequential events comprising so much of daily existence, her words being iotas of an America in the year before the Louisiana Purchase. As I read, I entered the life of a girl shaped by the animated mind of a sportive mother. It was as if, finally, I was able to glimpse a different woman and *her* newborn, who might have been but who lived not even long enough to be given a name. Seeing my interest in Rosalee's book, Mrs. Stewart gave it to me. I insert four pages from it:

> **WEDNESDAY, MARCH 3RD**
>
> I must write about a scramble last night. A rodent of considerable size has assumed winter residence in the house, and has shredded my frocks, and after dark has the audacity to stroll over my patchwork counterpane, and wiggle its snout at me. When I was ready to climb

into bed I saw said rat making a leisurely trek across my attic room as if it were his, pausing to look—a glare, really—toward this human intruder who dared to interrupt his repose. I slipped into the hallway, shut the door, and ran below to grab Caesar and bring him upstairs. He immediately spotted the rat, and I stood by for a classic combat between two archenemies, *felis vs. rattus*. But my *felis* would have none of *rattus*. Humping his back, vocalizing, and retreating slowly, *felis* stopped at my feet. Clearly his idea was to let me remove the opponent. Overhearing my encouragements to Caesar, Mother came in on us, and then went for Hector, returning with him and tossing him toward the rat. It was an accurate pitch. Hector landed atop the rodent and caused it to go into a fury that alarmed both cats into attempting (unsuccessfully) to gain refuge under the bed, the very territory the rat was determined to have as his own.

I yelled for Mother who returned this time with a poker and a broom. My assignment was to block the beast from getting under the bed. *Toutes les animaux* held their positions, the cats as far from the rodent as space allowed. Mother swung the poker, missed, swung again and nearly clobbered one of the cats, which then raced for higher ground—the windowsill—leaving me to face off, broom in hand, the infuriated beady-eyed *rattus*. While I held its attention, Mother came from behind and knocked it a good one with the poker. Stunned but not dead, it rose unsteadily, and gimped toward the underside of the bed—**my bed!** I let fly another blow from the broom and thereby dispatched it. I pitied the thing, which apparently had not been informed—this house does not sanction rodent residence. The felines had to be carried down to the relative safety of the kitchen, resisting and scratching, all the way dreading what they calculated would be round two below. But, finding the rodent absent of life, their mettle revivified, and they hesitated only to verify its passing before tearing *rattus* apart for a late Wednesday supper. And that's how one rainy spring night ended in our old place.

SUNDAY, AUGUST 27TH

Last evening, housekeeper Emily lying abed, heard a light fluttering, tapping, tapping on the headboard, only soon to feel the same against her cheek. Rolling fast out of bed and running for a candle lamp. In a panic, hands all a-shake, she managed to light it. Nothing in her chamber. But, knowing the cleverness of *les fantômes*, she raised the light. Then she felt cool, feathery fingers on the back of her neck, and whirled so fast the flame went out. Our terrified Emily pressed herself close to the wall. Again a fluttery tapping, tapping, these against her leg as the naughty ghostly fingers fumbled their way up her *chemise de nuit* toward her nethers. She whacked blindly at the trespassing digits, again and again until she felt an ooze in her palm. So trembling she could hardly relight the candle, she looked at her palm covered in a creamy goo, and below, at her feet, lay a twitching polyphemus moth the size of a hummingbird. May such an event be warning to human residents to prepare themselves for frightful molestation by creatures who come calling in the night.

MONDAY, JANUARY 12TH

Grandfather and I took a perambulation up through the north pasture to search for his missing cow, the beloved

Elenora, who's getting on in years—her milk production can no longer fill a sauce pan, but he loves her so. We found Elenora lying against the fence at the far corner she often retreats to for a little bovine privacy. Her eyes were terribly glassy, and she didn't make any response to grandfather's mooing call. *Quel dommage!* Then he noticed her great stomach move as if raised by a deep breath, and he knelt to put his ear to her flank, and almost immediately he jumped back. *Sacrebleu!* There was a long rip across her big belly and much stink. He whispered one word, **Panther!** He circled Elenora to listen, then came up to me to say, "There's something moving inside her." Out of her carcass crawled a possum, shiny with blood. It gave us a nonchalant look and waddled off, gleaming in the sun like the Queen of Sheba. Peculiar are the ways of Creation!

THURSDAY, SEPTEMBER 17TH

Finally! Excitement! During one of Parson Flynn's interminable sermons. I was admiring my new shoes, comparing them with Charlotte's (mine are prettier), when I felt the floor vibrating. Things on the altar rattling. A rumbling, all of it quite ignored by the parson who loves the sound of his intonations. The shaking became apparent even to him, and he paused when small fragments of plaster fell from the ceiling frescoes of certain selected saints. Because Saint Anselmo is (was) directly above our pew, he is my favorite. In the excitement, people began frantically making for the door, but Mother kept Charlotte and me in our seats until the jiggle-joggle stopped. (We found out later it was a minor *tremblement de terre*.) Parson Flynn resumed and built the interruption into his sermon—something about sinners and the bowels of Hell opening. When I looked again at my shoes, on the floor was Saint Anselmo's naughty eye staring straight up my pinafore. *Mon Dieu!* A fallen saint! How jolly! Best sermon ever! Tonight I'm praying for another earthquake next Sunday.

13 June

Our time in the parlor this morning was roused by two men in a discussion—polite if fervid—about recent conflicts between native-born American Protestants and immigrant Catholics resulting in a hundred injured and twenty dead in Philadelphia, *the City of Brotherly Love*. The nativist group, the American Republican Party, supports prohibiting Catholics from voting or holding office, and has proposed legislation aimed primarily at recent immigrants.

As a foreign traveler, I should think the founding documents of America—the Declaration of Independence and the Constitution—would have settled long ago issues capable of creating destructive contention. But difficult it is for humanity—anywhere, anytime—to live up to an instrument of high and noble purpose. What does that tell us about a creature presuming to term itself *Homo sapiens? Does sapience* truly describe us?

Furthering recent national discord, argument continues over the annexation of Texas, a debate largely addressing whether it should have entered the Union as a free or slave state. For a nation expressly founded on the principles of liberty and equality, I find it incongruent Americans so often dispute the meaning of those very words. When the two men left the parlor, still debating, Nicodemus whispered, "Don't call *me* a fool, said the farmer shoeing his geese."

With the parlor again quiet, Mrs. Stewart came in to ask whether we might consider riding up to Blairstown to visit her niece whom she worries about. Nicodemus was immediately on his feet and waiting for me to put down my pen and get to the stable and saddle up. The north road kept alongside a brook much of the way, through fields and rolling, wooded hills. The domestication of the American land here was pleasantly evident, suggesting a transition to husbandry *can* be executed without total destruction of the natural wilds.

After a few miles I remarked to Deems that, in speaking to a white man, his bearing becomes more erect and formal. Is it a conscious decision to act so? He said, "Not conscious. More likely just being a plantation houseboy taught that slumping indicates disrespect. Before a captain, the private stands straight."

Nicodemus turned the question. "When you talk to me, in your voice is a kindly note lacking when you talk to a white man. It makes me want to say, 'Please, Doctor, don't be kind to me in that tone.'"

Unaware of my manner, I began, "A subtle indication of class awareness—" only to stop and try again: "If I spoke with less civility to you, and you slouched before me, then we'd create equality? Wouldn't we both be forcing it?"

"Maybe certain things have to be forced until they become natural," he said. "Accustomed. Behavior less calculated."

"Slouching and rudeness? Then right you are, you scalawag! For my part, the hell you say!"

He smiled, slumped in his saddle, and on we merrily rode, but I could not cease thinking how unconscious training in each of us impairs our deep wishes for a natural sense of equality. For me, I must find ways to keep politeness from becoming patronizing.

We had not ridden far when Deems said, "My hope be not for assimilation. It be for inclusion as a free man, to contribute. I was reminded of it this morning by Homer. Odysseus would not have returned to Penelope without the help of others—including winds caught up in a leather bag."

An open road and a good horse underneath are concomitants to meditation, and mine was about my social bearing and how it operates not just in matters of race but also in other dealings: a taller man looking down on one shorter, a parson supercilious certain he knows the mind of God, a physician because he knows the location of the pancreas.

Such prideful distinctions, even if unrecognized, are anathema to democracy. Barriers to tolerance. Who wrote that everyone we meet in some way is our master, our teacher? Is there *anywhere*, *anybody* incapable of teaching me some special thing? Even a mute's inescapable silence should at least expand my level of empathy.

But then, empathy lends itself to gratitude for not being in an unfortunate's shoes. A half crown into a legless man's cup as thanks to Providence for the gift of legs. In democracy, what is the proper use of empathy? And simple caring—is there an implicit if unacknowledged placing oneself above those cared about? Before a patient, is that the reason physicians display an attitude of superior intellect?

The advantage of traveling *à deux* is the opportunity to escape the great enemy of solo travel—desolation—but another person doubles the chances of disaccord. Yet, true education lies in complexity. For the last few miles into Blairstown, I rode along aware that Nicodemus, in many ways, is indeed a master to me. The best fellow traveler, as Captain Finn observed, is one with an observant eye and well-stocked faculties. Which indeed Nicodemus possesses.

We found Mrs. Stewart's niece at home with her sister, Harriet, both in their early twenties, women with grace and education to match. Harriet introduced Clarice who automatically extended her hands to us. Deems and I introduced each other, and I gave a précis of our brief time in New Jersey, the women nodding, Harriet commenting in response before inviting us to sit for tea.

As we told our tales, Clarice seemed to listen intently, but spoke not, her silence becoming unusual. Deems asked her a question—I do not recall it—and Harriet explained the silence.

On a boating excursion a year ago, the two women and a friend, George, were overtaken by a squall preventing them from reaching shore. The sky turned greenish and poisonous-looking, with wicked forks of lightning and shattering thunder as they never before had heard. A flash struck the bow of the boat, knocking loose several strakes, and leaving the man unconscious and Clarice stunned. Harriet felt pain throughout her body as if hornets were stinging her from within. When she had managed the punt to dry land, she discovered George lying in the bottom of the sinking boat and her sister staring blankly, revealing no emotion whatsoever—no terror, no tears, no talk. Friends ashore helped the boaters into a buggy and on to town. The man died along the way.

During the telling of the story, Clarice remained silent, expressionless, a consequence, I assumed, of the nature of the details. Harriet touched her sister's knee to draw her attention, then said, "At a stroke, God's bolt from Heaven damaged Clarice's hearing and erased her power to speak, and left her with no remembrance of her life *before* the event. Over the next few days it became clear to us she had no memories anterior to the lightning strike. Worst of all, her capacity for emotional response was obliterated."

Clarice sat as if listening, alert and inestimably lovely, but her demeanor, other than an occasional muscular twitching of her right arm, was disturbingly frigid, her mien unable to register anything other than a mechanical smile performed with only the lips. It was then I understood why Mrs. Stewart had asked me to meet her.

Nicodemus, wanting to ease the strained conversation, began a lively tale about a racehorse, speaking loudly. Halfway into the story, he paused when Clarice motioned with her fingers for a tablet on which she scribed, *The breed of the horse?* and passed the pad to Deems.

Harriet said, "My sister doesn't remember she's always liked horses, but she hasn't forgotten what a horse is. Something even this small now seems a blessing. She lost spoken language but not its written form. Her vocabulary remains. She reads again, and among our family she's inventing a system of signs to express herself with her fingers."

Nicodemus talked about our present mounts, and as he did, Clarice would occasionally cup her hands to her ears, and he would raise his voice until he was almost shouting. When he slowed for a breath, she would write two or three questions, with space for his answers, and pass him the pad for a reply. Using the pencil, he described our hopes for the trip to the American prairies to see bison and meet red men of the bow.

Clarice made a little sound, looked at me, and wrote, *Your travels, what is the motive?* I scribbled, *To examine the experiment that is America.* She read and gave her limited smile, one I realized, although it appeared otherwise, came from her heart. She wondered whether we would be afraid getting near a buffalo? Did we know sign language to talk with Indians? Would they cut our throats?

Over the next hour, we scribbled away in admiration of such an energetic mind refusing to be undone by a stray blast from the heavens. We promised we would send her a letter about our travels, with special attention to miles covered on horseback. She seized the tablet, and in large letters wrote, *Oh, thank you! One day I will ride again too!*

I was fascinated to observe an injured brain still bright, though bereft of its yesterdays, expunged of earned wisdoms, yet nonetheless cogent and at times even coruscating in its penned expression. I asked whether she enjoyed writing. Her answer, *Oh, yes!*

Harriet interjected, "She loves stories!"

On the pad I jotted, *Maybe you have a natural ability to be a storyteller.* I mentioned my journal, concluding nobody else had *heard* a single sentence of it; perhaps someday that might change. After all, I wrote, writers proceed despite being unable to *hear* an immediate response to their words, although I cautioned to consider detractors who do not *want* to listen to a story. No tale finds a universal audience. More are those who have never read Shakespeare or heard his words performed than those who have.

I watched Clarice as she scanned the pad. I hoped to see from her even the smallest expression revealing what she thought of my comment. She wrote an answer, then handed me the tablet. On it was, *I have a story now. It's about two strangers who come to call. And their horses.* I looked up. Her eyes said what her lips could not.

Evening, the 13th

Nicodemus and I returned to the boarding house, each mulling over what we had witnessed. It was as if Clarice were a newly born, entering the world with an uncorrupted mind but with comprehension appropriate to a young woman. A devil's bargain: to earn it, she has had to be deprived of full engagement with the human community, although I have read about certain types of deafness having potential to self-heal. As for dumbness, fingers and pens can assist releasing her from a prison of silence.

That is insufficient to offer Mrs. Stewart. My medical failings exposed yet again. All I will be able to say correctly and honestly, is that while Clarice has seen vanish much of two decades of her life, she seems capable of building new memories to carry her forward. As the years pass, how much of our first twenty do any of us remember? Clarice has now a rare opportunity to make herself into a person free from errors created by youthful ignorance and selfishness and wasted time. A chance to become both the sculptor Pygmalion and the marble sculpture he carves so well he gives it voice—*and* the capacity to love.

14 June

Last night it turned unseasonably cold along the eastern front of the Kittatinny Mountains. One of the horses needing care, Deems took his bedroll to the stable to watch over the animal. His sleep, as it turned out, was enhanced by the horse. I will explain directly.

Before retiring, I added several lumps of anthracite—mined not too distant from where I was about to burn them—onto the grate of coals lit earlier by an attendant. As I wrote journal entries, my vision began to dim, and a cold-water ablution did nothing to rectify my sight, now accompanied by a headache of increasing discomfort. My temples throbbed, my breathing became difficult, and within moments I was on the verge of losing consciousness. As much as my disordered brain would allow, I evaluated my symptoms for cause of the sudden attack. I rose, off balance, to stir my circulation before deciding to alert Nicodemus to my condition should I fall unconscious.

By the time I reached the stable, my well-being steadied, and improved further with drafts of cool night air, and I was again myself. The alteration was as sudden as the onset: my vision cleared and the pounding in my brain slackened. Glad I was I had not disturbed others needlessly in a house where only the month before there had been discombobulations following a death from cholera.

I went back to my quarters and lay down, but the symptoms soon returned. Once more I took myself outside until I again steadied enough to go into the room, the stove now cold, and lie down. A broken sleep overcame me.

At a breakfast of spoon bread and gravy, I happened to mention my strange malady to the attendant who oversees matters of the hearth in the house. Asked he, "Did ye bank your fire and open the window a smitch before bedding down?" Yes to the banking, no to the smitch. "Ah," he said, "'tis the anthracite. Our lady guests prefer it to a wood fire because it don't give off smuts or black smoke to mark a bonnet or dress. Get it lighted and Allegheny coal throws off a red heat quite in stint to the draft. It wants air—just like a body. No sir, not good to sleep in a shut room with anthracite."

Thus I learned another piece of American ways. Noxious anthracite belongs in the boiler pan of a locomotive, not in a home stove. Henceforth, my heat will come from a hickory cut down last season instead of from a tree felled last month out of a three-hundred-million-year-old Pennsylvania petrified bog.

A maidservant brought Nicodemus and me our washed clothing, and I mentioned again the anthracite. He said, "The stable was sweet with horse dung, and old Nellie and I had the sleep of innocents."

14 June (later)

Now that we are beyond the hunting grounds of crimps, I feel able to pursue openly my questions about America and Americans, but first Deems suggested an additional protection for his freedom. Back in Blairstown today, we visited the local gazette and printery to have the Writ of Manumission set into type to lend the appearance of a faithworthy document capable of misdirecting a deputy from seizing Deems. My ethical basis for printing an extra-legal writ is that of an Abolitionist: The Constitution—the law of the land, as Americans often term it—lacking explicit sanction of slavery, ignores the abomination. Therefore, any so-called fugitive slave law may be presumed meaningless. If, in the view of certain powers, my action to assist Nicodemus to freedom is seen as criminal, then I will accept that eventuation.

Whilst my writ was being printed, I thought to restock my medical kit of herbals and tinctures exhausted from treating patients on the *Narwhale*. In a haberdashery, of all places, I found a chemist—in America they are known as "druggists" or "pharmacists"—whom I asked for medicaments I was short of. He looked blankly at me and hesitated before saying, "I got none of them, but I got Doctor Dawson's Sagratone, and I got Professor Long's Longevity Elixir." Between the two, according to the labels, the bottles held cures for general morbidities, debilities, and infirmities, as well as fevers, cramps, flux, varicose veins, lethargy, palsy, Cupid's itch, dyspepsia, rashes, scurvy, corns, canker sores, warts, wens, and *the heaves*. Neither bottle listed its ingredients.

The—dare I call him a chemist?—haberdasher poured a cuplet of Sagratone and offered it. The nostrum, so my tongue told me, was largely blackstrap molasses, thinned with a few ounces of distilled spirits, and possibly a dram of laudanum.

At the medical college at Cambridge I had heard about such medicine mongers—this one also a hatter—who flourish in America, particularly in the out-country, where a widely spread populace cannot support a licensed physician or even a chemist, the shortage giving rise to medical quackery and pharmaceutical flimflammery, the only available resorts for a cure. If a sovereign remedy succeeds in not killing the patient, it will sell.

Curious about the haberdasher-druggist's knowledge, I asked did he have anything to ease the discomfort of angina pectoris? No. Myocarditis? Said he, "My what?" Did he have the common ipecac or syrup of squill? "Nothing here made out of squirrels." He suggested another panacea, one promising treatment of lumbago, dropsy, catarrh, gallstones, lockjaw, goiter, charley horse, general cantankerousness, and a dozen other ailments. I said I needed something for a tender coccyx, and he recommended eating only pullets and young hens; if it had to be a cock, then boil it.

It is a temptation for a traveler in a foreign land to view some individual aspect as diagnostic of the entire country, rather than a local peculiarity. Such assumptions lead to falsifications. Still, in our early days on the road, I have seen numerous avowed chemists who were also greengrocers or harness makers or cobblers or wheelwrights. And many a barber advertised the extraction of teeth.

As I listened to the haberdasher, Deems noticed a particular blue corduroy hat—not a cap, but a broad-brimmed headpiece designed for a man of fashion. When he joined me outside, on his noodle was the hat and on his face an expression of perfect aplomb. As we walked to the hostler, two smoothly coiffed young Negro women came our way, each slyly eyeing Nicodemus, who tipped his hat, drawing from them approving nods. Beyond earshot I said, "Well executed!" He answered, "For the first time ever, I felt like a citizen." Then, a sardonic smile, "A gentleman should show a chapeau as a ship its colors."

15 June

From Blairstown we bent our course northeastward towards the great North River, also called Hudson's River, where we hoped to board a steamer for territory yet farther north. The fine weather put our horses into good fettle, and they were ready to canter, so we knocked out the nine miles to Fredon crossroads, a place *freed* of everything but a conglomeration of signboards, only one of them giving directions. The others were nailed to fence posts, each board advertising one or another miracle nostrum or proclaiming cures for intestinal maladies or the discomforts of menses. Also: magnetism for headache, mustard plasters for rheumatic joints. The words *wonder* and *miracle* predominated.

In beautiful natural landscapes, a commercial sign is as a pustulous carbuncle on a lovely face. Over the last many days, our time in Mennonite country excepted, we had seen enough of these signboards to give credence to a phrase I heard among the plain people: "The mercantile mind distinguishes the English." But perhaps I am adducing evidence from too brief an acquaintance.

Our route passed through a land of scrub pine amidst rocky soil, handsome in a rugged fashion all the way into Newton, a county seat gathered around a town square, where under construction was a courthouse of severe, somber Doric columns seeming to say, *Ye who enter here shall not go unjudged.* It was near Newton, we were told, that James Moody, a local farmer and leader of a Tory band during the Revolution, conducted several successful raids, failing however in a plan to rob the archives of the Congress, his fiasco still praised among citizens whose respect for that assembly today is less than for body lice.

I wanted to follow up on my pursuit of American medical practice, especially so when we happened upon a painted sign for a doctor *and* druggist. Expecting another mountebank mediciner, I instead met Paul Michaux, a Belgian immigrant and licensed physician, resident in the States for a decade. Never has a church dome been more perfectly shaped than his skull, a half ring of white curls running from temple to temple. His command of English was excellent, and he welcomed my questions, ushering me into his storeroom to show me a panacea he had recently analyzed: Dr. Farmer's Miracle Formula—its label promising *NO SORE IT WILL NOT HEAL, NO PAIN IT WILL NOT SUBDUE*. Inside a box were three packets of what proved to be an admixture of unidentified herbs, barks, leaves, and dried berries. The directions indicated the ingredients be poured into a quart jar filled with one's preferred distilled spirits and shaken well to allow the alcohol to be infused by the *alleged* salubrious properties. Said he, "A patient isn't likely to be improved medically, but the intoxicated will little care."

His locker was able to resupply my medicine bag, and when so accomplished, Dr. Michaux gave me a tract he had recently published. I attach here his preface:

> To date, every attempt at federal regulation of medical practice and the dispensation of alleged medicines has failed, and the reason is clear: profits. Unregulated products are an enormous source of income in a pharmaceutical business driven by avarice and sustained by a susceptible populace wanting a ready cure for an ailment. In rural areas—and even in our cities—Americans are unaccustomed to a proper medical examination, and so they resort to quackeries often based on alcohol and opiates that leave an addicted patient. Because there is more profit in a suffering patient than in a cured one, even an otherwise scrupulous physician may concoct a nostrum and sell it himself. Nowhere is there scrutiny, analysis, or enforcement.
>
> In America, one often encounters unwillingness to recognize utterly unfettered liberty as anarchy: anyone may attempt anything anytime against anybody. In Europe, the term for such a society is *ochlocracy*, and where it exists, so does exploitation. Today we see American medicine driven by pharmaceutical manipulation of uninformed patients and by dedication to obstructing change.

Michaux told me, "In the States all I need do to term myself a doctor is to pay an annual business fee. Cash equals credentials. Fakery results. I'm formally educated in medicinal science, but any who are not may also purchase the title and immediately begin practicing medicine. I emphasize the word *practicing*."

Perhaps more than any nation ever on Earth, America depends on a wise understanding of the common good underwritten by active support for education. Believers in democracy, no matter how fair-minded, must always recognize the perils in stupidity and avidity. Failure to educate is the Achilles heel of democracy.

Noting the curiosity Nicodemus manifested in the laboratory equipment and a human skeleton hanging from the ceiling in his apothecary, the doctor pulled from a shelf a small book, *Pocket Companion to Human Anatomy*, and gave it to Deems, telling him, "If you study this, you'll discover whether your interest in medicine is genuine." On our way towards the New York state line, I watched him trying to read from the saddle of a walking horse. Could he make out anything at all? Pointing to his elbow, he sang, "Olecranon connected to the humerus, humerus connected to the ulna." And so I witnessed what may be the first medical education begun on the back of a horse in dusty stride.

16 June

We arrived just before sundown in Newton, a village surrounded by stumps and rock-bound fields furnishing more products to architecture than to agriculture. The inn was draconian simple, and nowhere did I see a single item lacking necessity for the hosting of guests. The compact barroom was barren of all but chairs, tables, and fellowship directed by the landlord who served more as a gladsome counselor than a proprietor, recommending his own apple cider and a plate of hoecakes with sausage from his father's farm.

Conversation with Nicodemus consisted mostly of his grilling me on the human skeleton, the introductory topic of his *Pocket Companion*. Part Two was musculature, Part Three the organs. To memorize the assemblage of human bones, he continues to sing a diagram of a skeleton as if a sheet of music, proceeding from the metatarsals upward: tibia, fibula, patella, femur, ilium. In his voice, the recitation today was melodious enough I heard it in my head for hours. Sitting nearby was a girl, four or five years old, who picked up the rhythm if not the pronunciation of the bones to give

Deems a cappella accompaniment. Considering the longevity of certain childhood memories, I can imagine her teaching the words to her daughter a couple of decades hence.

Looking about in satisfaction, I said to Nicodemus, "So this is how it is in America." And he answered, "This is how it is for white folks in northern New Jersey." Our host, overhearing us, said, "Welcome, strangers."

In these villages I have found nothing like a menu because Americans eat what is coming out of the kitchen that hour or they do not eat, but I have yet to see anybody turn down a proffered plate, no matter the provender on it. Were it a serving of oats from the stable, I think an American would put it away with dispatch as is the practice in the States—conversation ceasing once knife and fork are in hand. Our evening meal was cabbage soup, a thick cut of Kittatinny Mountain venison, and applesauce cake with a second pint of Kittatinny cider. Not wanting to affront local custom, I put it away with Yankee dispatch.

17 June

This morn we accomplished the fourteen miles to the New York line and onward to the village of Warwick well before noon. The American penchant for appropriating names of British villages and towns can work a keen disenchantment on expectation. An English tourist who comes into, let us say, the Warwick in the Empire State, finds not a pair of medieval gates each with a chapel, and half-timbered houses, and a castle holding a Holbein portrait of Henry the Eighth. To expect such of a building nation is a foolishness ending in invidious comparison, a common reaction of European travelers who inanely grouse that the rocks being dug fresh from the quarry have not yet been shaped, chiseled, and laid up into a cathedral.

The *American* Warwick, sitting at a crossroads, is a village of a half dozen lanes leading to a stone tavern and a few frame dwellings straight from the sawmill—although the inclement, mountain winters have wrought on them a patina of premature aging. At this point in the development of the United States, if foreign visitors seek the monumental on this continent, it is to nature they should look: American storms, lightning, winds, clouds, sunsets, forests, even starlight are all of a colossal nature able to draw forth a human response between awe and terror.

In Monroe we quenched our thirst and shared a large wedge of Yankee cheese and peppered flatbread before moving on towards the Hudson, the great estuary of the North Atlantic. The road made a half orbit of Bear Mountain, a singular rise overlooking a portion of the river known as "the race" for the rapidity and turbulence forced into the descending current at this most narrow and treacherous portion of the Hudson south of the Mohawk.

As a traveler, I have long found it intriguing to consider a particular spot where I might find myself and imagine others who have set foot on that very place. To stand on Pevensey Beach along the English Channel and visualize, *right there*, William the Conqueror beginning a conquest which would remake not just the island under his boots, but the language its people one day would speak, as well as the language of those on the opposite side of the ocean. In America, to this particular stretch of narrowed river have come Henry Hudson struggling against contrary breezes to get his *Half Moon* another mile up the river that would one day bear his name. And through this narrows also would pass General Washington and a thousand-thousand tourists wanting nothing more than a change of scene, perhaps on the way to view the falls of the Niagara at the west end of the Erie Canal.

Southward and beyond the tumult of the Hudson's water, on our way to Peekskill, we came upon a horse ferry, a contraption of a flat-bottomed boat with twin hulls, and in the middle a paddlewheel powered by a pair of horses on a circular, horizontal treadmill. An example of often-remarked *Yankee ingenuity*.

By accepting a tender atrociously low, I was able to sell our now unnecessary mounts to the ferryman, a rough-edged character whom a pair of travelers might thank for not thrashing them on sight. But truth was something other, for the fellow, hearing my speech, was eager to kill time before his next crossing by explaining local details of their "War of Revolution." Even though the encounter he described ended in a British victory, he spoke politely yet with pride in the pluck of Continental soldiers. On the deck of his ferry lay a pair of iron ellipses, a former chain, each link weighing 140 pounds and (observed Deems) the length of a man's femur. The ferryman said, "Them there's hunks of history at your feet. I use that history for an anchor, but seventy years ago them couplers was made from iron dug out of these Ramapo Mountains. They was stretched across this river right the hell here to stop the damn Brits—excuse me, the British."

How many battles of significance throughout time have been waged between leaders with the same surname, I have no idea, but the struggle on this river to prevent foreign (as it had become) ingress into northeastern America pitted General George Clinton against Sir Henry Clinton. Early in the Revolution, the General oversaw the assembling of a chain athwart this narrows to block ascent to Lake Champlain on the northern border and prevent isolating a corner of the fledgling nation. The links were supported by platforms of felled trees and by two new ships, the *Constitution* and the *Montgomery*.

Only fifteen months after hearing about the Declaration of Independence, the British attacked the west-bank fort anchoring one end of the chain. The outnumbered Continentals, following a day of fierce fighting, were forced to abandon defending the obstruction; that night they set fire to their two new ships and disappeared into the forested mountains. British sailors and marines went to hacking at the chain in the glow from burning masts and spars until by morning the way was open for invasion into the north country.

Sir Henry got word another chain was already under construction only six miles upstream. The second version proved worthy enough to become an important relic of American independence. The ferryman said to me, "Up there at West Point, you can see a number of them couplers strung around a monument. Without them, I'd be talking your lingo."

At our departure he put the horses into motion, their heavy steps being translated to the big paddles, and the weather-beaten boat, grandiosely named *Chain of Liberty*, moved into the current and turned towards the east shore; assisted by the tidal flow, the ferry soon brought us to the foot of the uplands, once the center of a preponderance of Toryism.

A passing farmer and his wife saw Deems and me standing perplexed at the ferry landing, and called out an invitation to carry us up to the village—if we did not object to riding next to four crates of agitated chickens. Off we went.

Despite all the dark and bloody history surrounding Peekskill, its finest structure is a new Presbyterian church built entirely of wood along Greek Revival lines, a style much revered in the States, although to my eye the architecture is more appropriate to matters of governance than of God, but then the Yankee mind is given to a certain conflation of the two realms—regardless of the oft-repeated catchphrase *separation of church and state*. In America, the church in need of separation always happens to be that of neighbors living across town.

17 June, afternoon

Businessmen hereabouts are not reticent about reminding tourists they are in the land of honored writer Washington Irving, and a delight it was to Nicodemus (and his memory of reading about

Rip Van Winkle) to see us lodged in the Sleepy Hollow Inn, a modest structure lacking any charm of his imagined version. A sampler hanging above the registration desk:

Rip required a twenty-year sleep.
With us, a single night does it.

We wanted only eight hours' sleep before boarding one of the steamboats plying the river from various points south to a variety of places north. Our intended destination was the debouchment of the Mohawk River, which is to say, in the era of engineered land, the Erie Canal, some hundred miles distant.

We took comfortable chairs on a front porch common to American inns in this part of the country. A Negro waiter brought us a pitcher of brandy punch, and as he poured gave a close eye to the dapper chapeau atop Nicodemus. I thought the scrutiny more curious than critical, but (I learned later) the curiosity was about Deems sitting in a catbird seat, information germane to a bounty hunter. The waiter's interest could carry special risk were Deems to display an attitude of superiority. To discourage exposure, he makes a habit of generous gratuities to Negroes, whether or not the service deserves it. Whilst I recognize his reaction as strategic, to me it is extortion, one more aspect of segregated life never before entering my awareness. To live always having to watch one's step and buy privacy is to be distracted from the greater journey of one's existence.

I asked him: What if, as a requirement of American citizenship, a white and a black who share some interests must travel the country as we do now, the purpose not to gain *self*-knowledge but to earn *another's* knowledge? Would abolition then be possible? He said, "If, at the start, the hearts are open and true, then I think *yes*, it's possible. If not, then I say there could be a slit throat. But to answer accurately, you need tell me the percentage of true hearts to bad. Mama used to call a ramble a 'gitalong.' She'd say, 'You gots to git along with each other to git on along.' It had application beyond footwork."

In the cooling evening we have now sought the quiet parlor where hangs a large map of America—Florida, Texas, and California not yet added. I am struck by the proximity of the Atlantic—in its extension of Long Island Sound—to where we sit. Although I have no precise idea of the mileage I have covered since leaving the *Narwhale*, I can see I am now no more than thirty miles from the ocean I left weeks ago, with the far Missouri country still two thousand miles distant. My initial reaction was, *Ye gods! Progress into America is impossible.* Many thousand steps of man and horse have gained me less than one hundredth of the national breadth. Deems is reading a thick book from the parlor shelves. His concentration suggests to me the shallowness of my thinking.

A traveler can measure a journey in miles. Or, the measure can be done differently. Instead of an odometer gauging linear distance, what about an odograph that gives a reading not in mileage or even in footsteps, but in experiences? A calculation not of leagues or length, but of breadth and depth. What if travel—or a life—is assessed by a depthometer, where the determination is not linear but submersive? As walkers, we see the road ahead, yes, but we also may see the surround to the right and left, and we may remember what now lies behind, perhaps even imagining what lies beneath, and maybe even a halt to peer up at what spreads out on high. How often does a wayfarer consider entering a center-place, an ever-enlarging sphere, an orb of growing experiences spreading out 360 cubic degrees? O, to dream the land we roam and thereby discover it through the dimension called *sleep*!

Had the *Narwhale* landed me thirty miles east of where I now sit comfortably ensconced, my boots would not need resoling. Deep travel is to be gauged not by paces but by enlargement of the mind, progression of the heart. To survey how deep wanderers have traveled, look not to the testimony of their soles but to the affidavits of their soul.

Snug in this parlor, I know the names of where I have travailed, but the greater *wheres* are those without name lying in a surround of everywhere else. Aboard our planet, I ride across the black skies, unable to calculate mileage; instead, I reckon my outings—my days—by other means. Because peregrination of necessity comes one step after another in linear mileage, to know distance can hold little significance. But to reckon the depth of our movement through the grand celestial orb, *that* measure must be *felt*. I recall and evaluate my journeys not by distance or hours but by events.

Deems, reading in his chair, I shall never forget my times with him. His very presence brings to mind images of our excursion: a devil out to kill us, a mummy seated at a hearth, a woman struck insensible by lightning, Mennonite children learning to snare a rodent. Had I not met Nicodemus and encountered events his life has brought into mine, I would be less able to imagine this journey, to remember it. And without memory, what would be its worth?

The 17th inst.

Just before the supper bell rang, I finished a letter announcing to Sophie our progress, but mostly I wrote about my good fortune in meeting Nicodemus. As I penned along, he was dipping into Frances Trollope's widely read account of her experiences in this nation a few years ago. If her *Domestic Manners of the Americans* resounded in Britain, the response here is quite the reverse, and the reason is opinions like this one Deems quoted to catch my reaction:

> I very seldom during my whole stay in the country heard a
> sentence elegantly turned, and correctly pronounced from
> the lips of an American. There is always something either
> in the expression or the accent that jars the feelings and
> shocks the taste.

The British, I can report from my education there, commonly travel with an attitude of empire: *We have proven our global superiority—need we say more?* Too frequently they carry a mental valise fully packed with smug surety of rightness and a vigorous propensity to allow predilection to transmute into prejudice. I do not disagree over a frequent lack of elegance in American expression, but in citing pronunciation, Mrs. Trollope ignores the offense her ears must register attending the many dialects in her homeland. Does she avoid the fishmongers of east London or venture out with cotton lint in her ears? To go forth with one's nose in the air may provide a fine view of Heaven but leaves unseen the earth one treads.

In reading travel narratives I often see an unwillingness to report as a simple observer working to describe a topic accurately, leaving judgments to the honored lector. One can speak of Mrs. Trollope as a bold woman traveling with a trio of children whom she saw safely through the vicissitude of frontier America for more than three years as she attempted to build a Cincinnati emporium for imported goods from Europe. *Or,* one can speak of her as a frequently peevish fussbudget eager for hasty conclusions and ready to draw invidious comparisons with her native land having a millennium head start to develop cultural institutions and monuments. Poor is the rambler who returns home with more prejudice than perception, more insularity than insight.

Travelers, so I said later to Deems, should be alert to how much escapes their notice simply because they have not been on the lookout for it. Eyes see what the brain prepares them to see. The reverse is also a danger: being so heedful of one aspect, they are blind to other details. Perhaps more than anything else, Mrs. Trollope's success manifests how bias can make for popularity with a selected audience. Humanity is given to take pleasure in demeaning the ways of those who differ, resulting in a reader feeling a comforting superiority that corrupts tolerance. In a democracy, the biblical injunction "Judge not lest ye be judged" can be of use. In matters concerning a wayfarer, it may be better coined as, "Judge gently—lest ye be judged a cranky bigot."

Said Nicodemus, "I'd like to tell her, 'Madam Trollope, somewhere you sat on some bugs that crawled up your butt and can't get out except when you open your mouth.'"

18 June

On making our way towards the boat landing below the heights of Peekskill, we passed a stationer's shop where I bought six pocket memorandum books, half for Nicodemus who wants to keep notes for his medical study. He was delighted, and before noon he made three entries in a precise hand, an indication not of years of opportunity to write but of dedicated schoolmarm instruction. He asked rhetorically, "Who could imagine jotting down thoughts is a joy?" Then he wrote that sentence into his memorandum.

By nine in the morn the steamboat *Mohawk Princess* emerged from behind a broad river bend, the first notable obliquity in the remarkably straight descent of the Hudson through this irruption of the Highlands—one more example of fortuitous American geography created in places as if to facilitate movement of people and goods necessary to a vast democracy. In the assembly of this continent, it appears nature has engineered geology to assist the American experiment.

The monstrously tall twin stacks of the *Mohawk Princess* fumed upward thick columns of smoke as if escaping the Hadean forge of Vulcan himself. When the boat came into full view of the Peekskill landing, she whistled her approach silently but visibly, the steam soon followed by sound carried forward on a southerly breeze. At the sight of the giant vessel, Deems broke into a buck-and-wing so sweetly executed those waiting to board thought him ship's entertainment. They applauded and tossed coins he picked up and gave to a porter too stunned to say thanks; the passengers were baffled, then, realizing their error, they applauded again, and two women came forward to hand the porter more coins. It is safe to say the man will not have another boarding like that. This event was noted by a well-dressed octoroon about to make himself known.

Once the mooring lines were affixed to the pier, a throng of day-trippers and commercial travelers crowded to the gangway. With no need for a stateroom, Deems and I found on the second deck a coign of vantage to observe our departure. The *Mohawk Princess* is three hundred feet in length, her beam only a tenth of that to create a narrow measure permitting swift passage upstream even against the 150 miles of tidal ebb rolling down from Albany. The paired housings of the paddle wheels give breadth to her hull and stability to her lofty construction, seen so splendidly in the height of the grand saloon, with its Corinthian columns extending up to the second deck and a stained-glass skylight above. Such opulence is the result of not having to contend with oceanic winds and waves. The *Narwhale*, built to withstand the North Atlantic, is a poor cousin to this elegant riverboat making our ascent shamefully easy despite the thrash of the paddles and throb of the anthracite-powered boilers.

Few passengers showed curiosity for the Hudson shores, preferring instead to focus on card tables, book pages, or the interior side of their eyelids, giving us an unpopulated rail to take in fresh air and the riverscape of this critical American artery. On the east bank from far downriver and proceeding on northward, tracks are being laid for the Hudson River Railroad as it promises—or threatens—to assume for its own the deep opening the river has so patiently chipped, chiseled, and chopped from mountain rock to reach the sea. Soon it will be river versus rail, steam vessel against steam locomotive, the future challenging the past until one ends dominant. For a nation the size of America, questions of transport are crucial to the role reciprocal commerce will play in uniting the people and shaping the nature of their democracy.

The *Mohawk Princess* had just rounded a small peninsula below an eminence named West Point when the fashionably tailored man who had watched Nicodemus give coins to the porter sidled in next to Deems to begin speaking—with some eloquence—about the river, its economic importance, the value Americans place on money, their willingness to tolerate certain unfair conditions to underwrite an economy, and the consequences of their acceptance of injustice. I attended closely.

At length, the gentleman, Joseph, inquired whether Nicodemus knew of the American Colonization Society. Deems thought not, till he recognized it through Joseph's description of its purpose: the successful establishment of a colony of free blacks in West Africa, an area called Liberia and only recently acknowledged as an independent nation. The exchange (which I reconstruct with help from Deems) was this, Joseph saying: "From your attire and conversation, I see you are not a field hand. Allow me, are you in servitude?"

"I've had a few years in that function."

"Are you a freedman?"

"I have my manumission papers."

"The text you hold, you're a physician?"

"I have interest in medicine."

"In Liberia are more than three thousand American Negroes, some of mixed blood, as am I. What we need to prosper further are educated émigrés. Should I continue?"

"I'm listening," Deems said.

"I extend to you paid passage to Monrovia, our capital, named after the author of the American Constitution. Once arrived, you'll have considerable assistance—provided by church and state both here and in Liberia—to support setting up a medical practice to match your qualifications."

"Leave my homeland? I'm free *here*."

"Free, perhaps, but what is your *degree* of equality of opportunity? Can you travel everywhere in America with no fear of the hangman's tree? Can you enter a bank and secure a loan? Can you sit in church next to a white? Will your children attend school in the same building as a white child? Can you cast a ballot for a senator or a county sheriff? Can you walk down a street without having to step aside? Can you safely look a white man in the eye?"

Deems kept his view towards the river. From his vest Joseph pulled a steamer ticket and said, "This is my return to Liberia in a week. Meet me in New York, and you can have one like it to carry you to true liberty among people who find it natural to be black *and* equal in opportunity. In a state where *our* Constitution specifically guarantees your freedom." He asked for Deems's memorandum book and wrote something in it, saying, "On Monday I'll be in this hotel. Let Liberia welcome you."

As he turned to depart he said, "Slavery will split this Union, and when it does, consider where you want to be."

This evening Nicodemus and I shared an early—and overpriced—meal aboard the boat, both of us saying little as we mulled over Joseph's proposition. Disembarking on the Albany pier, we found accommodation in a nearby hotel of some size—the rooms less so. In the bar, once emptied of a fellow loudly extolling President Polk's Mexican War, we were able to address Joseph's proposal.

At Cambridge, my reading about the Colonization Society indicated many whites *and* blacks consider the real intent of Negro colonization is not liberty but the reduction of blacks in America, *especially* the draining off of free, educated Negroes who are highly prone to challenge slavery. In their absence, the institution of human bondage can be preserved, an argument numerous slave owners put forth in support of African expatriation. *To Africa.* They—and also others who have no stake whatsoever in slavery—believe a freed Negro can never be successfully integrated into white society. Whilst the powerful economic force that is cotton could be operated under other systems—perhaps free people working under communal principles—there is no likelihood, short of revolution, wealthy planters of cotton will give up their massive portion of its immense profit.

How long must the poor wait? Is it truly in the American grain to say, *We cannot live concordantly, so let us separate?* Such a belief does not comport with the widely espoused maxim "United we stand." The American experiment struggles to rise above an economic principle known hereabouts as "the horse and sparrow": oats passing undigested through the horse fall to the sparrow.

Nicodemus took his time, but at last said, "If I still was a houseboy on a plantation, I think I might ask for a ticket. But not right now. We have our travels calling us on to see what America is. I know the Constitution doesn't recognize me, but the soil a man is born on, it can be deep in him. That attachment needs no document. Joseph's offer I reckon like this—I want to keep roaming the territory to see bison and Indians. To find out whether there's a place for Deems on this side of the ocean. If there's nothing, then maybe he heads off to knock on the door of the Colonization Society and puts out his hand for a ticket to the jungle."

He considered what he was saying, then, "I can't see silencing my voice by exile. Not yet."

Tonight the captain of the *Mohawk Princess*, Charley Tupper, came into the bar. Having heard he was a man to unloose a tale, I invited him to join us for a double brandy, one he drained in a gargantuan swallow productive of a thirty-year-old story from a rundown wayside inn: The captain, then a young stage-driver, was roused from his bed by a raggedly dressed drunk who had forced open the door of Tupper's room to demand money. Pretending to reach for his wallet, instead Charley picked up a long, brass candlestick and leveled it as if a musketoon at the intruder who backed away. Tupper lunged forward to pin the rogue between the door and the jamb, trapping the inebriate's left foot before he wrenched it free.

In the morning Charley found the heel of a boot near the doorsill. By chance, that evening he saw a man limp into a bar, the gait a result of a missing bootheel. Tupper's first thought was to summon the sheriff; his second was to stand the pitiable sneak thief a whiskey, and so he did.

He told another spirituous tale: In his second term as captain of another boat, the *Queen of Night*, he was observed taking a plenteous pour at the ship's bar by the owner of Eames Steamer Line, Commodore S. T. Eames himself. Believing a bluff was his best cover, Captain Tupper began talking business with the bartender in a way easily overheard. Finishing his whiskey, he noisily plunked onto the bar a silver dollar. The admiral approached and said, "What's this? You're made to pay for your drinks on the good ship *Queen of Night?*"

Responded Tupper, "As a matter of course, I find it's an effective means of interposing restraint on natural tendencies." Eames, satisfied his captain practiced sobriety *and* pecuniary honesty in paying the inflated steamboat price of a whiskey, clapped him on the back, and left. With the room again safe, the bartender poured Charley a second round and restored the silver dollar to him, thereby retaining the captain's goodwill.

19 June

Our canal packet sports a compact foredeck for observation. She is the *Narcissa*, named for the line director's daughter—a theatrical, self-centered woman, it is said. Departure was set for nine a.m., enough time for Nicodemus and me to wander the heart of Albany and its several edifices of civic affairs, pre-eminent among them the state capitol and the city hall, buildings of considerable taste in complimentary Grecian style: ionic columns supporting unadorned pediments, both buildings domed, the capitol surmounted with a cupola. The pair confer a classical cast to this part of the city, and point up the longing Americans—especially New Yorkers—evince for classical touches in architecture and nomenclature to lend the dignity of history and civic gravitas to infant endeavors. In a single state are the towns of Rome, Troy, Ithaca, Corinth, Syracuse, Ilion, Attica, Athens. In a corollary way, villages choose names of legendary heroes, statesmen, writers: Seneca, Ulysses, Diana, Cato, Hannibal, Homer, Marcellus, Scipio, Tully. If the appellations claim more dignity than their actuality will support, the choices are superior to, say, Fishkill, just south of us.

To hear from afar celebrated names whilst holding in mind the original entities attached to them can lead a traveler to expect a nation not only striving for greatness, but one presuming to have already achieved an illustrious antiquity. Deems, though, believes the nomenclature is intended more to attract investors than to hornswoggle an outsider. He argues the founders are suggesting, *Look not at what is, but towards what will be.* As a native-born, he perceives a most American proclivity I misunderstood.

The *Narcissa* has the requisite narrow beam for movement on a canal where the breadth of navigable water is often no more than thirty feet and its depth as shallow as four. Her bulbous nose is similar to her stern, so to determine whether she's coming or going, one checks the direction of the mules.

The lucent morning sky encouraged us to take a bench atop the cabin a few feet aft the bow from where a long line ran to the towpath and three mules, two of them rigged to pull the boat, the third mounted by a rider—termed the hoggee—whose occupation is to keep them moving forward. Eight tourists sat behind us, two men in silk hats; five ladies in billowy skirts and large bonnets, the women sheltered from the sun by umbrellas; and, slumped from drink near the stern, a wayward fellow who awakened and stood only to tumble overboard. Once fetched from the cold water, the dunking and the captain's vexation over time lost fishing him out effectively sobered him.

The opened windows of what serves as a salon and dormitory below us permit a steady murmur of idle chatter and passengers reading aloud to drown out noises, and one voice from a girl scolding the hoggee for cracking his whip to spook the mules forward. The beasts exerted themselves mightily to set the boat in motion, but once moving, inertia did a noteworthy portion of the labor to overcome the imperceptible eastward current against us.

I found a little canal map in a company flier. From the Albany pier to conjunction with the Mohawk River, the distance is right at eight miles. Two miles farther is the juncture with the Erie—or, as they say hereabouts, the Western Canal, a peculiar name given its west can exist only if it has an east. The route embraces some eighty locks and eighteen aqueducts as it makes two major rises and two large descents to arrive at the Niagara River almost seven hundred feet higher and nearly three hundred miles west to achieve the shore of Lake Erie and the enormous gathering of fresh water known as the Great Lakes extending all the way into the heart of America.

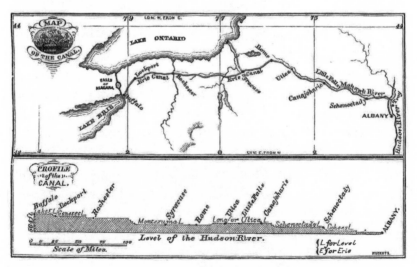

The seaward-bound current of the upper Hudson, about eight hundred feet wide here, is overcome by only a small margin through the labor of mules requiring more cajoling from whip-cracking than when on so-called flat water of the canal just yards west of the river. To enter this stretch of the Erie, a boat must ascend five closely spaced chambers, styled *flights*, a lovely word for the enclosures elevating a boat of several tons nearly two hundred feet. This eastern end is entirely excavated to gain passage around the wide and rocky, seventy-foot height of Cohoes Falls. Ingenious it is to use water descending to the sea to lift a boat towards the sky.

Surmounting fundamental laws of nature—in this case, gravity—is an integral aspect of the engineering of America. Pundits here and abroad posit that the nation, especially with its recent absorption of Florida and Texas on the south and California on the western ocean, has assumed more ground than it can hold both topographically and politically. These savants believe in physical limits to a nation, arguing that borders can be extended just so far before becoming stretched beyond sensible maintenance and defense. These naysayers fail to consider effects the inventions in transport machinery and communication will have on democracy itself.

Only months ago, Mr. Morse demonstrated his electric telegraph; it, along with increasing development of locomotive and steamboat power, will serve mightily to unify a far-ranging and sparsely settled nation. A tripper may now get from Portland in Maine to southern North Carolina in a couple of days. The ready transport of people and goods, and the transmission of ideas and news, will increase the structural stability of America with its far-flung corners and opposing opinions. Among the talents Americans have manifested in their initial three-quarters of a century—their national infancy—are ingenious enterprises to underpin the Union.

Again I hear an echo of Benjamin Franklin's alert to the colonies to *join, or die*—forever a requirement for American democracy. Undertakings such as the National Road, the railways, the telegraph, and certainly the Erie Canal, are commercial efforts to produce dollars *and* to develop and maintain unification.

Since 1795 the configuration of the American flag has been a symbol of diverse unity. Or unified diversity. What Americans call Old Glory soon to comprise thirty-nine separate components— stars, stripes, colors—functioning as a single symbol. The rest of the world flies flags almost always of only three or four distinct elements, yet the Stars and Stripes possesses a visual unity immediately recognizable even from a distance. Appropriately, of national insignias it is the most expressly manifold, and will be even more so as stars are added with further carving of states from the vast territory west of the Mississippi.

Americans will have to answer the question about territorial limits to a democracy: Can the Floridian share a bond with the Californian, or a slave state with a free state? Will their broad territory imbue them with so many differences as to prevent the equitable apportioning of an economy? Can distance between homesteads be overcome by proximity of purpose? If the country holds itself together, then perhaps the celestial pentagons now on the American flag should be replaced with earthly shovels and sledgehammers and survey transits.

19 June, evening

Seated next to me on the forward roof-deck this morning was a woman dressed not like others nearby, but in attire ready for hill and dale. Evelyn Lanier of Cobleskill, New York periodically raised a spyglass to observe soil exposed along banks of the canal before making notes and drawing maps in a ledger. Deems asked were she an artist or a cartographer, and she said, "Today, more the latter. I'm on the canal to search out sources of clay suitable for pottery.

What I'm using now comes from England and is too expensive for me to earn a living from ceramics."

Her fingers were powerful looking, able to tame a mule or a ball of mud. When she saw me watching her, she said, "Five thousand years ago the potter's craft was one of the earliest arts to appear in human history. Various forms of it beyond cook pots led to other arts. Sculpture and writing, the major ones. But in a new nation, conceptual arts are among the last developments."

I said numerous European travelers in America had derided the country for its scant achievement in the arts, commentators who ignore necessities such as first putting a roof over one's head and a supper on the table.

"In the instance of pottery," she said, "we have three million square miles in America to search out native sources of the best clays. That's what I'm doing—hunting exposures of potter's earth. Doing it the easy way, I admit. Sitting here, letting mules do the legwork."

Deems asked had she found any sources, and she showed a sketch map of a promising locale only six miles behind. "On my return," she said, "I'll get off the boat now and then and walk the towpath with a trowel in hand. Dig a few samples. Some of what I've identified might make good stoneware."

She watched me scribble.

"Our society," she said, "doesn't expect a woman to dig clay to throw on a wheel, but some eccentricity in my brain makes me prefer my potter's bench to a dinner table. At the wheel I'm in touch with Earth. Both meanings of *earth*. Both meanings of *touch*. *Also* with the ancients."

She finished her map, then said, "Egyptians believed their god Ptah created the world on a potter's wheel. And their god Num fashioned the first human on a wheel. The only tools necessary were fingers. I *suppose* those gods had fingers. Fingers are all I need to coax a glob of spinning mud to rise. As if it's alive. There's magic in beholding clay emerge from a formless lump into something. It's like a birth. Maybe that's why women take to a potter's wheel."

She stopped speaking and apologized for talking so much about her craft. Then, happily, she continued.

"When I'm at my bench, my hands covered in wet clay and looking like those of some strange earthen creature, my brain hypnotized by the spin of the wheel, I watch a wet clod transform and I wonder, *just who's the pot here and who's the potter*.

"I tell you, to observe something never before seen on Earth come into being—I don't have the words for the feeling. Of course, some of my creations are stillborn or fail to stand up properly. But once in a while misfits can be *reformed*. If only we could do that with humans. In Genesis, it says, 'God *formed* man of the dust of the ground.' If you think about it, a potter works to honor mud, one of the simplest products of the Earth. Fire it, glorify it. Keep it from returning to mud. At least for a while. Like us. We're wet dust only for a time."

On the high side of the Waterford Flight, our boat passed within hailing distance of the packet *Madcap Alice*, bound for the Battery in Manhattan. Standing on her cabin was a trio of young women who called and waved merrily to Nicodemus. He leapt upright to execute a stately sarabande, to which the women hooted and clapped, one of them artfully imitating his footwork. He said, "Why are my feet heading west when the ladies are dancing east?" That put me in mind to write Sophie to explain our necessarily deliberate progress towards her.

From atop the first chamber of the Waterford Flight, the canal will take us in upward steps four more times to enter a stretch of flat water before encountering additional locks leading to the village of Rome, where, by my calculation, the canal will have gained more than four hundred feet above the Hudson, only to make its initial westward descent, dropping a total of fifty feet to a sweetly recumbent landscape.

Once beyond Cohoes Falls, we joined or followed closely the Mohawk, in places twelve hundred feet wide and spreading into marshland. The river current here is insistent but composed as if it understands its run to the sea is nearly complete and it wants to conclude with quiet grace—the falls excepted. On the excavated ditches of the Erie, the Mohawk is but an arrow-flight distant; with the river flowing east and our mules pulling us west, the disparity in directions seemed to double our speed from three miles an hour to six, a welcome delusion for a dreamy man thinking about a woman waiting at the end of a canal. Deems kept an eye out for another approaching packet of dancing damsels but was rewarded with nothing more than clumsy bull boats carrying salt or rock.

I went below to get relief from the morning sun, and was immediately accosted by a Yorkshireman, one Thane Thorvald, an oddly visaged specimen of our species who inquired about my speech which to his ear, had not quite the ring of the mother country. When I explained my Caribbean background, he asked my evaluation of America. Human bondage and materialism aside, I said, I find its institutions generally worthy, its lands beautiful, and its citizenry welcoming *if* incurious about me, other than what I thought of their country. I agreed Americans were vain about the States and unreceptive of any view suggesting criticism, but then foreign tourists should consider the brief time—less than a century—the nation has had to aggregate itself into a functional democracy based on principles rarely practiced in human history. If their grand experiment is not without flaws in its attainable operation, it still holds promise—although not for *all* the world, as Americans so often imagine. Their version of democracy is unlikely to work everywhere. As I talked, his expression descended from bright expectation to dour disagreement. Nicodemus joined us, and Thorvald turned to him: "And you sir, how do you see America?"

Deems knew to avoid entrapment by a white: "The roads could be better."

"To be sure, but on abolition, how stand you?"

"I stand here a freedman."

"And those of your people who are not free?"

I interrupted to redirect us towards roads by adding that Britons ought to reckon the eight-hundred-year advance on their roadways given by Roman invaders, never mind the natives' soon managing to abandon paved pikes and let the entire system devolve into twisted lanes. Vexed by not hearing accord with his views, Thorvald said, "Well, sir, there's one thing you surely won't gainsay, and that is, nowhere in America does one find a satisfactory steak and kidney pie."

Agreeing, I said I preferred to abstain from rancorous comparisons that cannot possibly help mend frictions occasioned by two recent wars between the royal kingdom and the American state. "I decline," I added, "to provoke or further ill-will amid nations whose histories are so inextricably shared. For a visitor, generosity of opinion is a useful response."

In my mind were the many recent spiteful travel accounts from English pens about personal experiences in America since its independence. Some publishers have even dispatched reporters to these shores specifically to describe—with deliberate malice— American failings, an *approach* to fulfill a British desire for *reproach*. How deranged was it for a colony, so goes that thinking, by armed force to remove itself from an empire the envy of the civilized world? What arrogance, what blindness to offer hoi polloi democracy as a substitute for divinely ordained monarchy!

My jeremiad was sufficient to distract Thorvald from his pursuit of Nicodemus, although perhaps the Yorkshireman was yet fixed on steak and kidney pie. To nail the conversation shut, I said, "Do you disagree that, anywhere in the world, excessive national zeal is a perilous practice?"

20 June

Much similarity obtains among canal packet boats, the *Narcissa* distinguishing herself only in being but a year on the canal and still in Bristol trim. At seventy feet bow to stern and twelve in the beam, she is an arrow among cargo-carrying cannon balls. Her cabin roof, as is the style, is planked in pine to serve as a second deck high enough to allow survey of the land beyond the towpath. Topside are benches, a few chairs, and three travelers' trunks able to function as seating if one gains permission from the owner. At the *Narcissa's* bow and rising to the height of the cabin roof is a peculiar thing called the *knife*—a wickedly sharp scimitar to sever a tow line of any oncoming boat careless in pausing its mules to let its line go slack in the water so that we may glide over it. By law, packet boats receive preferential treatment at a lock or aqueduct in order to maintain their published schedules, a priority of right-of-way bringing on not occasional fisticuffs to decide precedence. Some packets hire a pugilist for the very purpose of establishing priority.

The cabin interior is a single saloon which in daylight becomes a drawing and dining room. In the evening it changes into a dormitory of shelves hinged to fold down from each bulkhead. They are more bunk than berth, more boards than bed, and on such narrowness heedless passengers turning in their sleep can meet up with the cold deck.

At mealtime, a long table is placed next to settees moved centerward from their day position. Sixteen ports, eight to a side, admit light; with nightfall four candle lanterns and a pair of hanging whale-oil lamps suffice. The American penchant for chewing tobacco necessitates five sandboxes for expectorate. Outside, at the stern and near the steersman and his long tiller, is a cubby with wash stand and a fat ewer of canal water, and a chamber pot more or less out of public view. Overboard the contents go.

Following our first dinner—served and eaten quickly and in silence, as is the American custom—Nicodemus and I took opportunity for a stroll between an unscheduled port of call and Vischer Ferry, a distance of about three miles. Although there was no time to loiter for observations, with brisk steps we walked the ten-foot-wide towpath, our boots guided around (in American lingo) road apples and ground sodden with equine urine. Whilst our nostrils rebelled, our legs rejoiced at the exercise; we considered the ramble another advantage over a claustrophobic coach even if the rate of our advance would be measured not by the hour but by a calendar. Still, like days of the week, progress is relentless.

Our finest packet enjoyment, however, is sitting topside in a quiet broken only occasionally by the steersman's trumpet to announce to a village *Narcissa*'s approach or departure. Free of swirling road dust, we move along, sliding through the territory, taking in America posteriorly: no rattle and rumble, no tossing cramped passengers to a coach floor, no thrust of skulls against skulls, no dozing excursionist leaning inescapably in to snore in one's face, no inevasible expounders on a topic without interest to anyone within earshot—which is everyone.

At what Americans term *sundown*, a curtain is drawn across the saloon to separate female sleepers from male, even those wedded to each other. The bunks, stacked three deep, drop down to leave us, once abed, laid out like so many parsnips and cabbages on a green-grocer's shelves, some parsnips clinging to the edge of the bed, some cabbages tumbling noisily to the deck, their *thumps* not waking others so much as does subsequent cursing.

In truth, though, a greater cause of wakefulness is not billingsgate but expostulations from human lungs, a response to having almost necessarily to lie on one's back. As the night proceeds, the cabin fills with an evening serenade which rises to a fully dissonant symphony of inhalations and exhalations, snores and gasps, snortles and snorks, sniffles and snuffles, puffs and huffs, wheezes and whiffles and whistles, aspirations beyond classification, and without fail, expulsions of flatulence, usually from the bloke above. Could a wind trumpet be attached to the various orifices, the walls of mighty Jericho would face a second challenge.

I add, with due respect, the volume from the distaff side of the curtain is only slightly less than from men, a lessening the result of fewer female passengers and the physiological diminution of lung and nasal capacity. After an hour of trial last night, I took a blanket to the cabin roof and lay down between the soft glowings of the bow and stern lanterns and not far from the drowsing tillerman, only to be roused by the captain himself and informed topside sleeping is not permitted. "The reason is this," explained he. "Should you awake and, forgetting where you are, sit up as we pass beneath a bridge, you'll leave your brains on a girder."

I found his argument persuasive and returned to the Nocturnal Symphony, and within minutes contributed my own trumpet flourish to the second movement.

Deems later claimed he had not slept, though on the two occasions I looked across the cabin at him, I saw a man in a slumber second only to those who repose in the eternal stillness of a marble crypt.

20 June, afternoon

We are in Schenectady to change mules and to discharge and take on passengers as well as a crate of hen's eggs, a tub of farmer's cheese, and three cans of milk for our provender, and for the mules a couple of bags of oats—the very fuel impelling our boat, a vegetable substance wonderfully better than the noxious anthracite driving an iron horse.

Schenectady, an old Dutch settlement, promises to become a city of some significance, with its industry of Durham boat construction and a college of science and the liberal arts. The town has progressed rapidly from its days as a producer of brooms and its ordinance requiring pigs to wear rings in their noses to prevent them from rooting up the streets. Under construction now is a factory to manufacture locomotives, a change promising to make the *Narcissa* an historic artifact.

A citizen of the city, watching us tie up, told me the dispossession of native tribes here years ago turned nasty when the Indians argued that the early purchase of the area by whites did not include sale of the soil but only the grass growing from it. The indigenous position, to no surprise, fizzled, a failure leading to a French and Indian force massacring what were then British settlers. In the words of one Christian of that time: "The cruelties committed no pen can write nor tongue express."

Hearing this, Nicodemus noted something in his pocket diary, a sentence I copied down: "Time can bury sufferings and leave us with ignorance equaling ingratitude!"

Between Schenectady and Amsterdam, the generally level land is given to agriculture or let remain in deciduous woods. Our leisurely progress is challenging passengers who boarded with us back in Albany. Their initial curiosity, no more than that of an egg yolk, already has been exhausted, so they stay below to gab or play cards or board games. Those who do come topside into the warm sun and gentle splash of water against the bow soon doze off, a forgivable response to having lain open-eyed through the concerti of the night. Despite my own effort for wakefulness, I joined them until Deems, as I had asked him to do, nudged me.

I may be casting a net too wide, but I perceive an inclination in American tourists to be content with simply being able to say "I've been there." A goal of little more than arrivals and departures. Depth of comprehension appears to be of slight importance, and so visitors leave Schenectady not with a sustainable memory of the college on the hill or the town center rising from the very edge of the canal, but merely of a place to be checked off a list of cities visited. To *know* where they have gone, to comprehend what they have encountered, to recollect what they have seen, for such they care not.

Nicodemus bumped me awake again, I thanked him, and he read me this quotation cited in a canal guide he had just bought:

> Unlike President Washington, who believed in the importance of canals and the necessity of water transport to the national economy, President Jefferson, considering the concept impractical and premature, refused to release funds to build the Erie Canal.

If only Jefferson could have foreseen what we are traveling is a watercourse effectively fertilizing its surround to bring forth not vegetative produce but bricks and stones growing into towns and villages that sprout up like so many potato and turnip patches and apple orchards, gardens of commerce and industry, their yields extending from the Mississippi to the Atlantic Ocean.

21 June

Because *Narcissa* has been detained at the east end of the great stone aqueduct over Schoharie Creek a few miles west of Amsterdam, the crew set up the gangway to gain access to shore. Snubbed in next to us lay a compact freighter transporting wheat, a canaler's boat fitted out at the stern with a flower box of geraniums and living quarters for a family of four, although how two adults and two young daughters could squeeze into that space was another waterway mystery. The kitchen held a small iron stove allowing them to carry their hearth east to west and back again and again: their bread kneaded on New York Bay and buttered on the shore of Lake Erie.

Nicodemus and I struck up a conversation with the captain and his wife, Fergus and Maureen Molloy, their girls peering guardedly through gaps in the stacked cargo barrels. Fergus had brought his bride from County Cork and found a job as a stoneworker repairing canal locks; but his ambition was larger. In his seacoast town he longed for a fishing boat of his own, though as the youngest of four sons, that seemed an impossibility. Hoping labor rather than primogeniture would provide him opportunity, he turned to America. Daily watching freighters pass by as he laid up stone, the young man *locked in a lock* longed to become master of his own boat to travel the country and meet people from ports near and far—his love at his side. He saved to buy a beat-up bucket he repaired to sell and earn a better boat he renamed the *Skibbereen* to honor their home village where the Irish Sea joins the Atlantic. Canal freighting is unending labor from early spring till late autumn, but when leaves drop, then Molloy can ease off and wait for a winter dry dock to perform annual maintenance.

As we talked, a four-year-old daughter, a pale blonde, came out, curious to get a close look at Nicodemus. With some pride the girl showed Deems her blackened thumbnail which had got pinched between cargo barrels. She did not mind the injury because she figured the changing color of the nail was indication she was turning dark like him, a welcome alteration to permit her greater freedom under an American summer sun. Nicodemus whispered slyly to her, "The doctor can fix your thumb, but he has no remedy for being white."

Deems lifted the child to her mother's lap and opened my medical bag. With a stylet drill I perforated the thin nail, the girl wincing only when the entrapped, dark blood oozed up. Mother was more relieved than daughter, and now, younger sister was envious she had no repaired thumb. Maureen insisted we take dinner with them, an estimable bowl of ox heart stew and soda bread and the richest butter I have yet come upon in the States.

With *Narcissa* again underway, I went to the roof-deck, where the warm afternoon soon put me into a doze until jolted awake by a sharp explosion. Who else but Thorvald? This time the

Yorkshireman was taking aim at any unsuspecting critter coming within range of the small-caliber, single-shot rifle built into his walking staff. A deadly if ingenious device.

He stood at the bow to bring down anything moving in the canal-side trees and marshy edges: squirrels, songbirds, sandpipers, a half-tamed duck. Behind us stretched a trail of bloody feathers and broken bodies, several twitching in their death throes. Gunning is his only pleasure in America, and the lone tolerability of this pointless carnage is it keeps his mouth shut. Travelers cannot go far without meeting somebody they wish belonged to a species lower in the mammalian order, one lacking speech. Say, a possum or a wombat.

Those believing in *natural justice*—retribution by nature—may see evidence in this: Concentrating on the next kill, aiming at a pileated woodpecker, Thorvald failed to heed the helmsman's alert for a low bridge. I, flattened on the deck, heard a gun discharge and a *thunk* of something against iron followed by a heavy *thud* as Thorvald fell near me. I confess to reluctance to embrace a Hippocratic oath requiring me to help any human organism. Nevertheless, I rolled him to a supine position to discover a lump the size of a grouse egg on his temple. I spoke his name, his eyes opening slowly to make sense of where he was, and he turned to me to ask, "Did I bring down the bastard?"

"No, sir," I answered. "A bridge girder did the only bringing down of bastards."

Afternoon of 21 June

East of Canajoharie we passed between the Adirondack Noses, spurs of impervious rock forming a gate-like exit from the grand Appalachian chain. On the north, Big Nose precipitously rises some seven hundred feet smack from the river edge, and on the opposite bank, Little Nose reaches up slightly higher but less steeply and impressively. Except for one of us, we on the roof-deck awakened to watch the *Narcissa* gradually enter changed topography; the exception was a forever torpid teenager who sleeps away his opportunities for experience.

The break the Mohawk opens into the mountains has been known to the native Algonquin and Iroquois for generations and used by them for purposes akin to those of the Yorkers—as Upstate folk term themselves—who have turned the great fracture to the service of the longest canal in the world. From near the Canadian border south into Georgia, there is no other commensurate water passage flowing eastward through the two-thousand-mile Appalachian barricade. Early in American history, the mountains were considered a potential natural barrier to the expansion of the nation into the fertile lands west where so much future wealth lies. Had the United States allowed itself to be thus circumscribed, its power and influence would be a shadow of what they have become.

Indigenous tribes have long passed back and forth in the Valley of the Mohawk River, but human travel today is much against the natural flowage, moving largely westward, the result of immigrants seeking homes and opportunity in the fertile land and growing cities to the west. Among the seekers aboard *Narcissa* are a number of New Englanders leaving thin soil they have exhausted for more tillable acreage in the Ohio and Mississippi valleys. There are also five families from Europe, each speaking a version of the English language often more charming than comprehensible.

The Mohawk remained comparatively narrow for a good distance, to Fort Plain, a village rising from a redoubt built during the "Revolutionary War," as Americans term it. When we slipped under yet another low bridge, a sphere of humanity dropped onto the roof-deck and rolled up to my feet; that ball was immediately followed by another, both orbs uncurling to stand and doff their caps to us. The youths, about twelve years old, bowed, pulled from their jackets a harmonica, and ripped into a sprightly melody from the hand of a young composer, Stephen Foster, they said. Deems knew the music to "Open Thy Lattice, Love," a title of indecorous suggestion all aboard winkingly comprehended. The boys segued into Foster's newest song, "Oh! Susanna," a capital piece of jollity.

The captain came forward to knock heads—I assumed—but no. He introduced the lads as his nephews who in season lurk under low bridges to drop like fallen angels to give impromptu performances in front of packeteers encouraged to reward the boys with coins. And so we all did, excluding the inflexible Thorvald, who found Foster's tunes "too damn jiggly." Said Deems, "That scarecrow's crabbed soul could use a little *jiggly-jiggly.*"

The rest of us took more entertainment from the songs than from the patchwork fields running all the way to Little Falls, a village with an exceptional prospect created by both its position above a major bend in the Mohawk and its setting within a craggy declivity. The houses mount a web of hilly and crooked streets of small, riverside industries, Yankee cheese–making chief among them. Little Falls almost lured me into departing the packet for a day to become again a landsman, a world where legs are of use, where bathtubs exist, where one may escape the Thorvalds among us, where the only concerto grosso for nose-trumpet is one's own. But thoughts of Sophie kept me aboard among the other bleary-eyed and poorly bathed packeteers.

Nearing its headwaters, the Mohawk narrows even further and wrenches itself into bends and bows, twists and turns, hooks and crooks to challenge efficient movement. Soon, though, the canal shifts to another engineered ditch, granting expedient progress quite lacking in scenery across its skewed miles of terrain with scarce topographical relief all the way to Utica, a sizable trade center. With the Mohawk highlands behind, now on the north horizon was the distinct assemblage of mountainous rock termed the Adirondacks, said to be more ancient than the Appalachian chain. This gap between geologies is yet one more indication of the good fortune nature has bestowed on North America, a view some citizens, perhaps in their avidity, propound as evidence creation itself does not want to see the nation constrained.

A freighter had made a maligned entry into a Utica lock to clog travel on the canal for two hours, a welcome delay Nicodemus and I turned into a foot tour of the town. The name Utica may sound indigenous, but it derives (so I'm informed) from an ancient city in northern Africa, and thereby belongs with those other names from classical history I mentioned previously. While *Utica* rolls off the tongue, it lacks a certain grace. But then, the town could have ended up with what the Oneida called the location: Yahnundasis. Or that of a Rhode Island village east of here, the one with arguably the worst toponym in the States: Usquepaug.

Nicodemus spotted a bookshop with a selection of journals almost matching mine of nearly filled pages. He also saw a human anatomy text—rather heavy for a traveler, but he was determined to have it now that he has twice read through the physician's pocket guide. His dedication leads me to believe his interest in medicine is sincere. Whenever I transfer observations from my memorandum, Deems uses that quiet to study, later asking me to expound on some particular medical topic. Relevant to his study was an incident of two days ago:

In the *Narcissa* cabin I overheard a white woman sitting next to me say to another, "Look at the colored man pretending to read a medical text." To her I suggested she ask him what a tibia is. Seeing the query as sport to expose his dissembling, she did so. Nicodemus stood, raised one leg of his trousers and touched his shin bone and said, "Tibia." Then raising his thumb to his thigh, he said, "Femur"; then he moved his hand to his right arm and said, "Humerus."

He perceived the bigotry behind her question, and he confessed he had wanted to point towards his coccyx and say, "Ass." In the South, such a response could bring on a lynching, and once again I noted his finely tuned awareness of what constitutes real danger—perhaps even in the North. I admire the insouciance Deems maintains among those who respect him not.

I suppose it is possible the woman intended not insult but only curiosity about a Negro reading a medical text she considered beyond common learning. If so, the incident reveals the parlous state between black and white communication, a condition either race may stumble into without malice aforethought. Both Deems and the woman had proceeded by that devil called *assumption*. Presuppositions and foregone conclusions are poisonous to equity, to democracy, to the acquisition of knowledge. If scientists do not presume they know an answer to an unresolved question, then should not ordinary citizens be wary of trusting their certainty about a human intention?

Throughout this cool day the sky has refused to yield its clouds as if a sleeper holding onto a quilt on a winter morning. Our silent, serene floating westerly lets me fancy we sit unmoving as the landscape itself slides by. Among us today, the liveliest are listless and the lethargic lifeless. I remained atop the cabin—now entirely alone—even Nicodemus staying below to read. The *Narcissa* passed close by a reach of dark woods broken only by a dismal square of ground choked with blackened stumps, and in the center of the lot an ineptly built cabin and a man repairing a *lean-to* with enough *lean* to collapse. A thin woman, sallow and morose, in torn garments watched us. I waved but she gave no acknowledgment. Passing her threshold day and night are manifestations of mobility and prosperity, central components of the American experiment, whilst she remains tethered to a clutch of dead stumps and a husband's dream of a new life.

How I would like to visit her lot in a decade! Ask whether the trial has worked out. Ask whether her days in this cut-open fastness have been worth the cost. Ask, does she still watch boats come and go and leave her bound to burnt stumps she first saw as living trees? Ask, does she ever imagine a gaily painted packet stopping to take her aboard and carry her elsewhere, to any *where* other than this Adirondack *where?*

22 June

West of Utica the hills resumed to encroach upon the Mohawk, before flattening again near Rome. A few miles shy of the city, at the juncture of the river and Oriskany Creek, one of our mules threw a shoe, fortunately convenient to a small mart with bold, block-letter words painted across the window panes: **GROCERIES & NOTIONS**. To blunt passenger complaints about lost time, our captain set us ashore at the shop whilst the mule was reshod. Slumped against an exterior wall, out of sight of the shopkeeper, sat an emaciated Indian woman—an Oneida, I was told. Her young son, a handsome lad but for his seriously misaligned teeth, was trying to rouse her from intoxication. She pushed him away, her chin dropping onto a necklace of blue beads in beautiful contrast to her bronze skin.

He slipped into the store to mix among the packeteers, and carried a loaf of soda bread to the counter, where the proprietor, knowing the boy was penniless, harshly ordered him out. Nicodemus picked up the bread and put a half dime on the counter. The man scowled at Deems but said nothing as he swept the coin into the till before turning to me and saying, "Yes sir?" I laid out a half dozen thick strips of jerky along with payment, which he accepted with a nod of thanks and a "Come again!"

In advance of an incident I will immediately report, I must describe here our fare aboard the packet. Yesterday we were served a choice of tea, coffee, bread and butter, shad, steak, ham, sausages, chops, potatoes, pickles, and black pudding. Some diners selected from the items, but others took a portion of everything to a degree their heaped plates resembled dumped garbage rather than anything culinary. This profligacy of the table is not unusual among Americans.

Outside the shop, we came upon the frail Oneida mother as her son tried to get her to stand. She was not yet thirty. I felt her pulse, but detected no abnormality for her condition. Attempting to wake her, I pinched her arms and called to her, all to naught. The son said what I think was, "She not safe here," and pointed to a ramshackle stable. "Safe there."

Deems and I carried the woman to a dry stall holding enough straw to afford her a pallet, and left the food with the boy and told him to bring her drinking water. The steersman was blowing his bugle to summon passengers for departure, forcing us to make a run for the boat. Thorvald had watched us move the mother to cover, and in a tone of triumph he had prepared for me, he said, "And now, sir, how do you find the experiment?"

I stopped and squared up with him to say, "Imperfect. As with every other endeavor created by imperfect mortals. Especially those who rebuke and scoff and do nothing about conditions they censure."

The 22nd inst.

At Rome, the Mohawk River turns sharply north towards its source. Our route was now via a completely engineered waterway of a dozen miles due west, to where it shies away from Oneida Lake to fetch up in Syracuse. We were losing daylight when the supper-bell rang, but I stayed seated topside in growing darkness relieved only by the glow of the forward and aft lamps. I could hear from the saloon the murmur of diners at work on a nine-course meal even though our boat-constrained inactivity left few of us with an appetite; but because food was served, bored humanity ate. The captain had told me the typical bodily gain for one traveling the length of the canal was ten pounds. The steady clink of cutlery from the cabin brought to mind the Oneida and her son.

They are my first encounter with that often deplored aspect of the American experiment—dispossession of native peoples.

Until meeting the Oneidas, my idea of the condition of Indians depended on a belief the dislodging and dispiriting and dishonoring of indigenous inhabitants was inevitable *anywhere* whenever a technologically advanced society meets up with a populace living at the edge of stone-age ways.

But what I witnessed at the canal store casts a different light on my inadvertently heartless misunderstanding of history and a concomitant and conveniently untroubled notion of inescapability. Whilst superior technology may indeed disrupt and displace, we can choose whether to eliminate or elevate; ineluctably, that decision lies entirely with the technocracy. Nowhere is it set down such supplanting must be executed with cruelty, greed, and dishonesty, yet those responses distinguish and disgrace the history of European entry into Africa and the Americas, North *and* South.

Hearing love of freedom loudly proclaimed in a tavern or reading about it coming out of the Congress, I question the integrity behind treaties between whites and natives, compacts clearly written with the aforethought of disavowing or disregarding them, particularly when dispossession is effectuated with arms. It is dispiriting to read of a President proposing removal of natives from their ancestral grounds for which the Congress appropriates a half million dollars to underwrite the expulsion. Nevertheless Andrew Jackson and his Congress have recently done just that.

And for what? To gain thousands of acres of half-peopled wilderness to be surveyed and parceled out and assigned *tribal* titles to its native possessors, disingenuous actions which will prove to be a preliminary step before extinguishing those titles altogether so the land may then be bought at a half cent on the dollar and resold at a hundredfold profit to *white male citizens*, a number of them scarcely better off than the natives. Colonizing is a brutal form of imperialism. Empires want territory, not its people.

A common practice here is to trade manufactured items to Indians for furs and skins at an exchange rate causing the tribes to become indebted and unable to escape the debt except by ceding lands. The honored William Clark of expedition fame helped dispossess the Osage of *fifty thousand square miles* which the government sold for pennies, often to speculators. Thus, the Congress appropriates Indian land and calls it "purchase." Clark, to his credit, later wrote that should he be damned in the hereafter, it would be for making that treaty.

Political hypocrisy and machinations, driven by greed, may not lie within the purview of *all* Americans, but they reside in enough of them to elect politicians who will enact legislation and draft covenants to dispossess Indians. When a founding document declares *certain truths to be self-evident,* and the first truth enumerated is *all men are created equal,* then one expects no distance between declarations and deeds. Although I regret to say it (given the respect I hold for many American institutions), such an egalitarian assertion is not the case today.

23 June

I know not whether I have adjusted to the racket of nose-trumpets or have been deafened by them, but last night I slept through all movements of the *Narcissa Nocturne.* When I was awakened by the steward preparing the grand saloon for breakfast, we were cruising quietly across farmed acres north of the aptly termed—if one looks at a map—Finger Lakes.

In the cool air of morning, the steersman was working his tobacco pipe so vigorously the fumes could mislead an approaching boat to take our packet for one of the steamers beginning to ply American waters. I found Nicodemus bent over his medical text. He had been reading about practices of Hippocrates and the oath still applicable more than two millennia later. Thinking of the Hippocratic phrase, *First do no harm,* Deems asked had I ever ministered to a patient I would have preferred to see depart this realm. I said there was one.

Said he: "Just one?"

"Perhaps it was two or three."

"But you treated them as you promised in the oath?"

"Yes."

"Did any live on, to your regret?"

"Within a year following one recovery," I said, "the patient assaulted and strangled a child, and was never apprehended."

"So you have no idea how many others died because you saved that one man?"

"What are you driving at?"

"Call it the Caligula question," Deems said. "Let me propose this: What if you had a little slate—a wondrous device like the master of electricity, Samuel Morse, might invent. On this slate you could write a name, then wipe the slate clean with the result that person vanishes into nonexistence. Into the Land of Never Was. An absence noted by no one. It's not murder, it's simple nullification. Total deletion. Under those terms, has there ever been a name you might mark in?"

"Other than my own?" He smiled. "Yes, I've treated a few patients—*only a few*—who could have qualified for erasure."

"So what should a physician do?"

"Keep in mind, whilst doctors may serve as the hands of whatever greater power they recognize, their actions and conscience belong solely to them."

The 23rd, evening

As if the current engineering of the canal were not remarkable enough, only some dozen years before work commenced, a plan was offered to use the water of Lake Erie by constructing a canal—an artificial river atop an engineered slope: a three-hundred-mile-long inclined plane requiring embankments the height of a fifteen-storey building. Americans, naturally attracted to grand designs, gave it consideration, but ultimately knew an improbability when they saw one, and decided instead to fashion locks and aqueducts and here and there dig through mire so oozy they could apply picks and shovels only in winter when the ground froze. Such a place the *Narcissa* is now making its way into—the big Montezuma Marsh.

The most dedicated and curious travelers understand that yielding to tedium is a failure, realizing as they do the need to resist the humdrum and look deeper. On a morning of slow miles, despite my efforts to stay alert to what might be hidden, remaining awake lay somewhere between difficult and impossible. Once again telling Deems to nudge me if he caught me dozing, this time without result because his head also fell into frequent noddins and bobbins. Twice I turned towards the stern to see how others were bearing up, and of the dozen human knowledge-boxes riding the cabin deck, the only one uplifted belonged to a child explaining to her dolly the trudge of the paired mules and the young hoggee astride one of the beasts; of the trio on the towpath, only the quadrupeds were awake.

And so it was *until* we approached the long, stone aqueduct curving sinuously into the heart of Rochester, a structure to awaken us all. A fellow who discharges continual complaints about delays near locks, for once expressed a wish for an impediment to give him a chance to walk the city. It was not to be. After a rapid change of mules, the *Narcissa* was again moving, this time into a cut permitting our vision to reach no farther than to the rock walls of the excavated channel. Traveling it became mobile incarceration, and I went below to transfer notes into my log. I looked at the bunks secured flat to the bulkheads, and thought I would pay a sawbuck if allowed to pull down a berth for an hour's stretch on it, this as we passed a sequence of villages calling themselves ports simply because citizens had built rickety wharves. As it was, without the continual rattle of dice in a backgammon game next to me, I would have been comatose again.

The helmsman's horn sounded to announce our arrival at the magnificently engineered Lockport Flight: five dual-chamber locks make it possible for boats, whether bound either east *or* west, to ascend or descend simultaneously almost 170 feet *from* or *to* the level of Lake Erie. Packeteers set aside dice cups and cards, or they awoke to come topside to watch us make our hydraulic journey upward. The durable and substantial natural stone ledge necessitating locks here is a continuation of the rocky shelf creating Niagara Falls twenty miles west; in a way it was as if we were ascending the massive cataract itself. Instead of the roar of falling water was the steady hiss of *rising* water raising thirty tons of *Narcissa* to a point more than four hundred feet higher than the place we departed the Hudson River. Once atop the Flight, we gloried in the aerial view eastward over the landscape engineers had mastered, not just at seeing long miles now behind us but at the aerial perspective itself. It was as close as a human—without a hot-air balloon—can get to lifting off heavenward.

Knowing our canal voyage was ending, we all remained alert as *Narcissa* made for Tonawanda and the Niagara River south of the falls. As the final miles slipped away easily—I want to say *swimmingly*—I knew in the leagues ahead would be many times I will long for effortless travel accomplished by the legs of mules. When we disembarked, Nicodemus went up to them, stroked their muscular necks, and with fare he had snatched from supper, gave each two carrots.

THE SECOND LOGBOOK

Nathaniel Trennant, M.D.

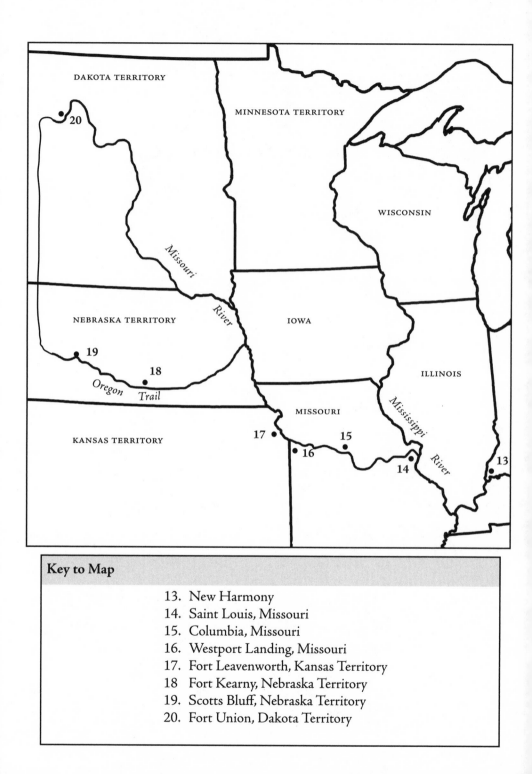

DAKOTA TERRITORY

MINNESOTA TERRITORY

WISCONSIN

Missouri

River

NEBRASKA TERRITORY

IOWA

• 20

• 19

• 18

Oregon *Trail*

ILLINOIS

KANSAS TERRITORY

MISSOURI

Mississippi

River

17 •

• 16

15 •

14 •

• 13

Key to Map

13. New Harmony
14. Saint Louis, Missouri
15. Columbia, Missouri
16. Westport Landing, Missouri
17. Fort Leavenworth, Kansas Territory
18 Fort Kearny, Nebraska Territory
19. Scotts Bluff, Nebraska Territory
20. Fort Union, Dakota Territory

24 June

THOUGHTS OF SEEING Sophie filled my mind. This morning I hired a chaise to take us the dozen miles into Buffalo and to the Hunt home of her employment to see her and meet the children she is teaching German. The Hunt family—and their lovely governess—would not return until evening. I left the house-maid a message inviting Sophie to a buffet at Hotel Cataract on the morrow. Deems and I took quarters near the city square (forgot the name) creating in Buffalo a pattern of streets radiating outwards, none of the central six running to a cardinal compass point, thereby forming an angled grid disorienting my usually reliable sense of direction. To enhance the challenge, a pair of crossing avenues dodge off at forty-five-degree angles from the others, as happens with L'Enfant's design for the national capital. To maintain my bearings, I tried to walk true compass headings, which forced us at each intersection into continual corrections; and so Nicodemus and I zigzagged a tour through the heart of the town by tacking as if sailing.

The unremittingly querulous Mrs. Trollope visited here a few years ago, and she describes Buffalo in her *Domestic Manners of the Americans* as "the queerest looking" of American cities. But it was not the street pattern troubling her eye; rather it was new buildings appearing to have been "run up in a hurry" despite what she saw as pretensions in wood: porticoes, columns, colonnades, domes. And the great lake lapping at the shore here was as nothing: she complained Erie was without beauty because it was neither a sea nor a river. (Is a horse, being neither cow nor pig, therefore without beauty?) To her, the lone interest of Lake Erie was her anticipation of its waters soon to flow through the crevasse below the ledge of Niagara Falls.

Failing to perceive the *reasons* for hurried construction blinded her to events in this young city expanding in all directions, even down to the Erie shore: new to Buffalo are a steam-engine manufactory, a medical college, an iron works to turn out plowshares, a steam-powered grain elevator, a brass-bell factory, and a maker of porcelain bathtubs. For Mrs. Trollope these developments were invisible to her whose attention fixed on young women wearing false hair and powdering themselves immoderately with pulverized starch; she glowered at "hollow-chested, slump shouldered American men" perpetually expectorating tobacco juice. A dedication to surfaces coupled with an unyielding bias weakens the authority of a witness.

Her incapacity—or unwillingness—to foresee what is happening in the States leads me to wonder what habits and changes in America I am blind to. To write as a traveler is at every moment in every location to expose one's ignorance and the difficulty of projecting a tomorrow from what one encounters today. Should I spend two seasons scrutinizing a square acre of New World forest, I still would fall short by half to grasp what was before me. In the instance at hand, however, this physician's prescription for Mrs. Trollope would be a daily physic of Epsom salts.

Several of her mope-eyed views allow me to come upon places she found wanting to discover something quite different, and in Buffalo those surprises lent the city a particular interest. But then, I was not there in January to undergo what residents term *lake effect*, described by our hotel clerk as, "Winter turned loose till Hell won't have it. Of course, that keeps Erie country from being overrun by milksops and mollycoddles."

25 June

This morn, Nicodemus accompanied me in a chaise to call on Sophie and, so I hoped, escort her to the buffet. I have not the words to describe my joy in seeing her again. I persuaded myself her smile revealed an equal sentiment. With the Hunt children observing, she modestly took my hand as I introduced Deems. Despite her scholars' clamoring to join us, Sophie was released for the afternoon. She passed me a letter from Gerhard Schilling, the Mennonite elder, and I slipped it into my jacket to read later.

The bounty of the buffet fulfilled the accolades paid it, and to judge by the two plates Nicodemus piled up—verging on the embarrassing—it was indeed a feast. He carried to the table thick-sliced corned beef, pickled oysters, New York cheddar, Munster cheese, celery and olives, melon wedges, preserved pear slices, and a cardamon custard, all accompanied by a pint of ginger beer. He concluded his meal with a slice of strudel and a *crème glacée* and Turkish coffee. Noticing our staring at his plates, he said, "Never like this down on the farm."

I confess to encouraging his appetite to keep him occupied long enough for conversation with Sophie. She spoke of her adjustment to American ways and of her progress instructing the children and their occasional corrections of her English, which have given greater naturalness to her expression. Although she was happy to be free from the conflicts common in Danzig and the consequent food shortages there, she felt momentary homesickness (*Heimweh*, she called it), partly eased by the sizable German and Polish settlements in Buffalo and the native-language community sings.

Of her stories, I was most interested in her description of teaching her pupils the Polish custom of telling fortunes by melting a candle and dropping the hot wax into cold water to create curious shapes the children read as if tea leaves. Candles are now scarce in the Hunt household.

Through one of my letters, Sophie knew a little about Nicodemus's tutelage in Latin language and literature by the mistress of the Reilly plantation, a parallel to her instruction of the Hunt children. Although she was not aware of the predatory situation bringing about his escape, as she inquired about his education the conversation seemed to be moving towards the behavior of the mistress. I grew uneasy about what could come to light. Deems deftly redirected the topic towards books and reading, citing a couple of relevant apothegms from Cato. The one I remember: "Rem tene, verba sequentur." *Grasp the subject, the words will follow.*

After an hour, Nicodemus excused himself for a walk to the new medical college and we went to the Hunts' veranda. I left my first journal with Sophie for safekeeping. At last she and I could converse intimately. Feeling she had spoken enough about herself, Sophie turned questions towards me with a Teutonic (or is it Slavic?) logic: my youth on Saint Kitts, my studies at Cambridge, my medical practice before leaving England. I foresaw where her curiosity was tending, and I considered trying to shift it before deciding that would be to hide myself. And then she asked the question.

"Have you ever been married?"

"Once."

"No longer?"

"No longer."

"With your permission, did she leave you, or did you leave her?"

"She left me."

Sophie dropped her head, and there was a moment of silence before saying, in the softest tone, "Why?"

I had to pause before I could answer, "She died."

Another silence, then Sophie looked up, her eyes keenly on me, and she said, "You would have told me soon?"

"Yes. But you should know, it's difficult for me to talk about. I, I—."

"You are still in love with her?"

"No. But I still love her."

"In English, there is difference?"

"I loved my mother, but I was not *in* love with her."

I shuffled about, not knowing how to explain the idiom or myself. "She's gone. I cherish her memory."

"What is *cherish?*"

"To keep fondly in mind. To be *in* love belongs to the living."

I needed to change the scene, and invited her for a perambulation around the square to take in the sunlight, and speak of other things. And so we did until it came time for her return; we strolled the short distance to the Hunt home, and what an excited welcome the children gave her. They had feared I was taking her away. Percipient as Sophie is, she sent them off to prepare a lesson, and I took her hands in mine to say, "I want to see you again."

She replied, "Tomorrow we depart for a fortnight in Boston."

"I'm thinking of time beyond tomorrow," I said. "Beyond my exploration of the American dream. To see you again—that means I don't know when. Or where. It means I'll find you wherever you are. Unless you say no."

She put her arms around me, pressed herself to my chest; then taking an audible breath, she said, "I want that too." She pulled from a pocket a small envelope, saying, "This is for later."

Without another word, without looking back, she hurried into the house. In the hotel, I opened the envelope. Inside was a daguerreotype. Her portrait.

26 June

My sleep went poorly until Deems gently wakened me from a midnight mumbling and tossing. He poured me a glass of water from our pitcher. Feeling I owed him a few words, I mentioned my recurring dream of the Woman in White; he listened intently but asked no questions, although I knew he needed to understand more. I said, "I believe the nightmare arose because of ambivalence I felt seeing Sophie again. She—*and you*—are the great gifts of this journey. But within me resides a voice saying I don't deserve such gifts. Not a man who has, who has *changed* another's life, who—."

He remained silent. I said, "Three in the morning isn't a fit time to discuss culpability."

Nicodemus yawned, extinguished the lamp, and lay back in his bed. In the darkness I sensed the apparition withdraw, and I said across the room, "Thank you for the water." He was already asleep.

In my wakefulness, I made the mistake of lighting a candle to read the letter from Gerhard Schilling. I should have waited till daylight.

> *Greetings to you, Herr Doktor Trennant,*
>
> *I trust you and Herr Nicodemus are well and your exploratory travels proceed apace. I send my apologies for the nature of this letter, but I must alert you to that scoundrel H. B. Ferrall who came uninvited and with malice into our community.*
>
> *After you left us, the circuit judge found him guilty of trespass, assault, and malicious mischief. Ferrall was sentenced to jail. While incarcerated, he talked of you and Herr Nicodemus, stating each day his determination to seek you out and bring you down. His hatred is strong. On several occasions he told the jailer he would be happy to hang for the murder of you both.*

Ferrall was visited in his cell by a man hired to pick up
your traces so the scoundrel can pursue you once he's released.
The talk of the reprobate disturbed the jailer. All of us here
are uneasy about your safety. He departed yesterday. Be on
the watch! He bears you the greatest ill will. I hope this news
reaches you soon. God be with you.

For your friends in Oley Forge, Penna., I remain,
G. Schiller.

Exhaustion finally allowed me to fall into a perturbed sleep.
In the morning Nicodemus read the letter. I tried to ease our
apprehension by counting how many miles *and days* we were
from Oley Forge, each mile, each day giving us an improved
chance to have covered our trail. My rationalization was only
modestly successful, especially after Deems pointed out that Herr
Schiller found us in Buffalo without ever leaving his farm, thereby
suggesting Ferrall may know where Sophie is.

From here forward, I will not sign hotel registers or buy coach
tickets in my name. For those purposes, I will become Jack Wilcox,
and Nicodemus will return to being Cuff.

I arrived in this country a free man. Now I am the object of
deadly pursuit, effectively a runaway enslaved by my beliefs. Were
it possible, the racial divide in America might be eased if whites
spent one day a month living under the conditions of simply being
born black.

27 June ??

Formulating a plan to head for the Ohio River and there to
steamboat our way towards the Mississippi, I presented the idea to
Deems over a simple breakfast in the hotel to give him opportunity
to pursue a route of his own design. His response: "As long as we're
getting on towards Indian country, I'm your fellow traveler. I be
Patroclus to Achilles."

"If that's the case," I said, "we must keep watch for a Hector."

"I think we already met a Hector. We didn't drag him by his heels around Troy, but we sure as hell hung him in a barn by his heels."

My intention is to make our way stage by stage via coach to the Ohio, the beginning leg to take us about forty miles from Buffalo to Gowanda. Departure was set for sunrise, and so it would have been but for the Lady and Major Botford, he of Her Majesty's Service. He was a mustachioed old campaigner and she of such volume as to prevent her from being able to raise a leg onto the first step of the coach. Deems and I reasoned a push upward from her stern would be unseemly. The Major, to be of use in elevating her, carried too many years, and their young niece carried too few. After managing her ladyship's right foot onto the step, Nicodemus and I climbed aboard so we each could seize one of the good woman's fully fleshed arms. Then we heaved. She rose all of six or seven inches. The Major helped replant her foot, and with increased effort we pulled heartily, and up she came, all of ten inches. And so it continued until we had her aboard and, like a sack of potatoes, deposited atop a seat. Who of the three of us was panting harder, I couldn't say.

The facing benches in the coach were designed for trios of adults abreast, or, one Lady Botford and a niece holding something in a hatbox. To join us, the Major assayed a hop upward, but it was as failed a hop as I have seen; on a second try he made the step and stumbled on into the coach, aided by nothing more than a groan, a curse, and an energetically induced expulsion of rearward wind. We three men sat opposite her ladyship and the niece.

Southward bound, our horses converted good road into expeditious passage. The girl, Annabel, fiddled with the hatbox, continually lifting the lid to whisper into it. The steady sway of the vehicle set us all but Annabel and me into nodding. To keep awake I asked what cargo she carried in the box. She opened it to show me twigs of oak leaves. Why was she carrying leaves? She said, "To give Copernicus cover." Who or what is Copernicus? She gave a gentle shake to the box and opened it again, looked in, and said loudly enough to wake the others, "He's gone!" The *he* in question proved to be a serpent, specifically, a copperhead she had secretly paid a nickel for.

"It's loose!" she shouted.

"What's loose?" the Major shouted.

"The copperhead!" Annabel shouted.

"Merciful heavens!" shouted Lady Botford before fainting dead away.

As if choreographed, in a single movement eight feet were in the air. The unconscious lady's legs were, fortunately, too short to rest on the coach floor now free of anything other than a small carpet bag, the same bag *almost* concealing the escaped snake eyeing us as it steadily worked itself into a coil. It was not a large copperhead, but when considering pit vipers, one withholds questions of mensuration, especially when they indicate a deteriorating temper. Folklore says a copperhead may become so agitated it can bite itself to death, and our reptile appeared as discomposed as we.

With a few moans, Lady Botford began to revive, eliciting from the Major orders to prevent her from falling off the bench, noting we would then be unable to raise her, and concluding with a hoarsely whispered, "And for god's sakes, don't rouse her!" Instead, she woke on her own, saw the riled coil, and forthwith returned to the safety of her faint. A problem in a full coach is having no place to climb save on another passenger.

Presented with a manifest enemy, the Major's military training had him prepared for the challenge, and he withdrew from his weskit a derringer, took aim, and fired at the snake, relieving it of its head and sending its dead eyes in an unblinking stare onto the lady's shoe whilst its torso writhed and twitched towards her. The pistol shot brought her to, and the serpentine gaze, now locked on her, sent her back under. Annabel, distressed and dismayed, sat in tearful silence as the coach rumbled to a halt. The driver opened a door to bellow at us, "What in tarnation is going on here? Who's firing a gun? Is that woman *dead?*"

The major, his reloaded derringer again pointed at the palpitating viper, needed not confess. It was then the coachman noticed the snake and a hole in the floorboards. In a volume greater than necessary he said, "You shot up my stage!"

"Had to," said the Major. "Copperhead!"

The driver bent close to examine the corpse, then said, "Goddamnit! This ain't no copperhead. It's a milk snake! You shot a hole in my stage for a goddamn milk snake!"

"Poor Copernicus," said Annabel.

Things proved worse than a misidentified reptile or holes in a floor. The Major had managed to separate not only a serpent cranium from its corpus but also a hub from a portion of an axle. We pushed milk snake remains out of the coach before rousing Lady Botford, who, on reviving, smelt gunpowder and said, "Is it Indians? Major, draw your weapon!" and gave unequivocal sign of a relapse.

After inspecting the hub and axle, the driver lashed pieces together with a length of chain so the wheel could now skid along if not roll. Disconsolate Annabel watched. Nicodemus said to her, "Let's find another snake," and off they went into the forest edge. I requested our baggage be transported to the next station once the vehicle was again running.

Annabel and Deems came from the woods, she smiling and opening the bent-up hatbox to reveal not a serpent but rather a most awesome insect: a stag beetle two inches long with curving and hooked mandibles almost the same length. It was a gleaming chestnut brown, spider-legged, and disconcertingly beautiful. At intervals it audibly snapped its pincers. Annabel loved its monstrousness and had already named it Nicodemus, Terror of the

Territory. He—the human Nicodemus—pestered it with a twig until the annoyed beetle clamped its mandibles onto the stick, and he said to Annabel, "That's an alert to mind your fingers." Adding as an afterthought for eager Annabel, "I wouldn't show it just yet to your auntie." As we struck off on foot for the Conewango Inn, I turned back to wave a farewell. Lady Botford lay prostrate in the grass.

Large patches of forest alternated with small fields set among wooded hillocks, giving the territory a lovely if lumpy look, and the damp morning air was rich with deciduous sweetness. We ambled along spiritedly, saying little other than to point out a yellow warbler warbling, a bright ruby of a scarlet tanager, and lazing at the margin of a vernal pond, a spotted salamander (surely a less threatening resident for Annabel's hatbox).

We slowed as the day warmed, finally stopping to wipe our brows. Seated against a massive oak, a man observed us, and when I called a salutation, he with effort pulled himself to his feet. His skeleton appeared more strung with rawhide than hung with flesh, long white locks straggled from under a broad-brimmed hat, and keeping him steady was a crooked staff made from a branch. He came forward, saying, "Hello, pilgrims! May I join you on your jaunt?" Without further words, he fell in with us, his step sprightly for a man four score if he was a day. But his balance wavered despite his stave, and he said, "Poor is the wobbling hiker who blames his staff."

What I report here are his words as Deems and I recall them. I inquired where he was bound. Said he, "Where else but elsewhere? I'd gladly tell you if I knew, and I should know by now, I've been asked so many times. If there's such a place named Onward, my answer is accurate, but then Onward's the destination for everybody every day. Whether or not we have it in mind. So my answer doesn't reveal anything other than a vague truth. I always hope *onward* also leads *outward*. Slipping inward impedes a good trek. And you gentlemen of the road, where are you bound? Notice I didn't ask your destination—that I infer because it's mine too. To be born obliges us all towards the same destination in the grand beyond."

Deems said, "The Conewango Inn."

"Capital objective! The hotelier there treats a vagabond kindly, and sometimes sets out a bowl of soup."

When asked his line of work, the fellow said he no longer followed anything one might call a *trade* or perhaps even *work*, and Deems asked, "You do nothing?"

"Ah, my young compatriot! One can't do nothing. An impossibility. To do nothing is to do *something*. Nothingness is, at the least, a concept, and a concept is indeed something."

"But nothing is something I can't see."

"Invisibility is no proof of nothingness. Can you see gravity?"

I mentioned Socrates and his famous utterance before drinking hemlock, "All I know is I know nothing."

Replied the old roamer: "But he knew that one significant *something*. If an untoward but seemingly unimportant idea disturbs us, we may say, 'Oh, it's nothing!' But, just to have thought it makes it *something*. We exist outwardly, but it is between our ears we truly live, which explains why—to the human mind—nothingness is a devilkin to chill the heart. It comes too close to *nonexistence*. Invisible as it is, a chilled heart is further evidence of a *something*. Once you feel the chill, you'll not forget its reality."

I nodded, and he said, "Each day I remind myself that I am only all that I am not."

"*What?*"

"We're made," he said, "from what we presently are not into what we will become. What we *are* is but an experiment in natural chemistry. Some human experiments are rank failures, others turn out rather better. A Caligula. Or a Galileo. Of course, many of us are not allowed a full chance to engage experiments. Many of us still await emancipation from one bondage or another. Subjugation works against experimentation, and that means it's unnatural. It goes against nature."

We introduced ourselves. He said, "I was named Peter, but the biblical weight of that cognomen was more than I wanted to bear, so I changed myself to Cedric. You've read *Ivanhoe?* I've found the burden of Mister Scott's imagination easier to carry about. It draws no expectations. To be a Cedric, as opposed to being a Peter, one also faces no jests of a bawdy, procreative nature."

Would he describe himself as a philosopher? He said, "Philosophy has many meanings. If your meaning is *inquiry into things*, then I admit to trying to engage in the endeavor."

As we walked, Deems asked what Cedric's line was before he became an inquirer.

"Oh, you're interested in *employment.* Let me see. Baker, drayman, cook, carpenter, mason, hod carrier, bank clerk, steeplejack, and once a pencilmaker. Now, if you mean true *occupations*, most often I've been *occupied* by the pursuit of *why's* and occasionally their consequent *how's*. But for some time I've been occupied as a simple rambler, a vagabond. A bindle stiff. A Bedouin who's lost his tent and camel. A mere trekker of byways and lanes and trails to inquire into the realms of nothingness each of which is *something.*"

"Why?" said Deems.

"A *why!* Cuff! You're catching on! 'Tis likely humans are the only critters able to ask a *why*. Is there a better metaphor of our passage into life than the journey? If we're alive and alert, then we may be said to *travel* through our days, each necessarily of a different cast—however slight—than the one preceding and the one succeeding. Every day a different village, another road, a different weather. I beg your pardon for reminding you of what you know."

"It takes money to travel," said Deems.

"I'm a fortunate grandson of a man of small fortune. One who devoted himself to wealth, a *potentially* honorable calling—depending on your definition of wealth. His definition was *pecuniary wealth*. Ah, *pecunia*! Of material goods, I want *of* nothing because I want nothing material. I have *nothing*, therefore I have *something*, and this particular *something* happens to be thoughts uncluttered by needless things. The result is clarity of purpose."

"And the purpose?" Deems asked.

"To become aware and behave charitably."

"But money—."

Cedric interrupted Nicodemus. "Money, like manure, is best expended and stinks less when spread about. A little here, a sprinkle there."

I asked had he once been a professor. "Did I fail to include a professorship?" he said. "It's just as well."

"What about family?" Nicodemus asked.

"Family? Family, one of the more perishable fruits of a life."

Deems asked whether he considered we were now walking through unrealities—this forest, the road, birdsong, our conversation. Cedric said, "Perhaps. Without our presence, *show* me those things. *Prove* their existence. But we *are* here, and you have named them from their potential unreality into temporary actuality."

Said Deems, "If that's the case then I'm going to name into actuality a beautiful woman serving up a cold cider and hot leg of, of *roast turkey!*"

"And so you have! I see her now, she of shapely form and a laden tray. You're a magician to call such fare spang out of nothingness and share it with me. But I don't eat flesh, so on my plate is something risen from roots."

"My magic still leaves me thirsty and hungry," Deems said.

"Of course," our vagabond answered. "Sooner or later, every philosophical proposition has a snag. For this snag, the solution could be at the Conewango Inn. Another mile ahead. Over the next hill we shall see it emerge from invisibility—some might carelessly describe as nonexistence—into a visible reality. There we can sup at the very verge—a divide—where all the waters in this territory change their flow from being North Atlantic bound to finding their way into the Gulf of Mexico."

?? June

Whilst we awaited the return of the morning stage bringing our equipage, the same one to carry us on to Jamestown, our host served up a Conewango Inn omelette of duck eggs and fried venison. He had watched us sharing a pint with Cedric yesternight and asked our views of him. "Perhaps peculiar by American standards," said I, "but less so by English measures. His brain does more than just keep him breathing and walking upright." Nicodemus added that Cedric had quizzed him at length on medical topics for reasons Deems did not yet grasp.

The eccentric vagabond had moved on at sunrise, whither nobody knew, leaving behind an envelope addressed to Nicodemus. Inside was a trio of hundred-dollar bills drawn on a Jamestown bank along with a note in a stately hand:

For your medical education. —Cedric of the Road.

Cuff of the Road was perplexed and rattled with excitement by such an unexpected sum. The innkeeper said, "Cedric has been stopping in here for years because I usually have something in the kitchen for him, but never has he offered a penny for it. He thinks me comfortably employed."

Deems said, "But three hundred dollars would buy his meals till he's toted to the grave!"

"His grandfather," replied the host, "owned a thousand and some acres hereabouts. When the railway moguls started procuring land for the line, they had to have—*absolutely had to have*—a long stretch of his acreage. The old man bargained hard and beat the tycoons. Cedric—his name's Peter—as the only heir, fell into the fortune. Up to then he'd lived on little or nothing all his life, and he saw no justification for change. So today he wanders this territory and passes out money where he believes it could do some good. Two men squandered their gift from him. Within weeks of losing their stash, they came to bad ends, one of them shot down in a gambling game. Now Cedric's doles are seen around here to carry bad luck. A widow, fearing for her children, refused his gift. Word of advice—don't let your unexpected fortune turn into misfortune."

Nicodemus was eager to get to Jamestown to prove the notes genuine, and as the stage bounced us southward, his mood shifted from anticipation to anxiety. He had hidden the money inside his stocking. I was watching him so closely I have no memory of the route; instead I was asking myself: Should I advise him on his financial windfall? To even broach the topic, would that be a white man's presumption a plantation slave has little concept of handling so much money?

Jamestown is a fine village at the outlet of Chautauqua Lake, another of the slender and beautiful bodies of water lying longitudinally across western New York. The citizens, many of them recent Nordic immigrants, are especially adept at wooden furniture, and the central street is as well ordered as a Swedish kitchen. Amongst the buildings we found the bank issuing Cedric's bills.

Waiting for a teller to examine their authenticity, Deems shifted from one foot to the other whilst looking about to evaluate the economic stability of the institution. The clerk pronounced the money genuine and accepted it for a deposit save for two small bills Deems later hid in his shoes, thereby hampering his gait, not from the notes but from his fear of rendering them unidentifiable. I suggested he try to walk naturally, otherwise somebody might suspect he had a shoe full of money. He said, "I can't because I feel like dancing."

The coach from Jamestown to Warren in Pennsylvania on the Allegheny River followed Conewango Creek into woods and fields and past small sawmills, eventually leaving us at a stage station, the Glade Run Tavern, where we found quarters and a simple but sufficient *table d'hôte*, afterwards repairing to the bar to toast generous Cedric. We talked about medical college tuition, calculating that the gift could carry Deems through his first year.

Our thoughts shifted to a darker but correspondent topic, one able to make his plans—and mine—moot: H. B. Ferrall. I reiterated my refusal to be driven from my goals by fear. "I'm roundly resolved to see America, and see the land I will. You wish to enter medicine, and enter you shall."

He answered, "And if we come upon Ferrall's mother-of-pearl pistol stuck down our throats? A revolver against a resolution?"

"Can you fight?" I said.

"Every slave boy learns to fight. In every way possible. Either he learns or he dies young. The question's not me—it's you."

"What! I'm trained in English fisticuffs. A contender in my weight class at Cambridge."

"*Fisticuffs?*"

"The fistic arts. Boxing with leather mittens and rules. No kicking, no eye gouging, no biting, no—."

"You think rules mean anything to Ferrall? Boxing mittens against bullets? I don't like the odds you keep putting forth."

"Nor do I, but I pledge to you, I refuse to flee."

Deems said, "If fleeing is out, then we have two choices."

"They are?"

"Hide or kill him."

Realizing the limited extent of frontier justice probably would be without effect, I said, "If the time comes to confront him, I will. I'm sorry I brought you into this."

"Had you not brought me *into this*, I'd be dead. A fugitive slave dumped into a Virginia hog pen. A colored boy sliced up for bait in a Chesapeake crab pot. A skeleton rotting in a Louisiana swamp. Doc, when you wrapped me and a dead rat inside sailcloth on a Maryland road, you protected my new freedom. Except for being taught to read, I've never had a greater gift. And now, because of me, your life is as endangered as mine. I do *not* intend to thank you by running away again."

"Then let's face—*as men*—what we must face. Not with fear but intelligence."

Smiling, Deems said, "Why not? All he has are a pistol and a knife."

"We have two functioning minds. And each other."

Later I thought about the deadly irony of two whites bringing gifts to Nicodemus, both of which have proved entailed: his plantation mistress teaching him to read and his friend the physician leading him to freedom. With whites' *help*, we have made him a hunted man.

28 June

At dawn we pumped bathwater directly from the river; instead of warmth there was volume, in place of relaxation, instantaneous morning vigor. The stage, only five of us aboard, headed south along the Allegheny, the route keeping close to the east bank of the river to use its ancient bearing through the undulating terrain to curve us around hills rather than up them; we negotiated areas where a careless driver could drop a wheel off the edge of the road and dump us butt over brains into the Allegheny.

Cabins were few, settlements fewer, and nowhere was anything that might be called a village. The territory still belonged to Terra, the forest heavy and wide without end. I cannot guess how long it will take to assume civilization onto such a wilderness and remove it from nature. Were it not for the ingress created by the

Allegheny River, I should think this dark fastness could remain under natural precepts for years, perhaps years beyond human measure. I admit to enjoying the unpeopled road and moving in a society of only five, one of us using the coach as a cramped dormitory. Our quietude was proper for an arboreal cathedral.

Then a hamlet at the junction of Tidioute Creek with the Allegheny. Being so surrounded by trees led Deems to ask, "Can Ferrall trace us across these lonely hills? This forest is one hell of an eradicator of tracks. When the dust from our coach settles, it's as if we were never here."

Near the juncture with Tionesta Creek, even its contribution of water leaving the Allegheny more rocky than deep, trees reached down to the sinuous if narrow flow. The breadth and straightness of a river stand inverse to its beauty, and as if aware of the principle, the Allegheny began twisting ever more and apparently losing interest in a direct southerly course, caring neither to search the hills for a way out, nor wanting to resist its master, gravity.

Franklin, yet another collection of disordered structures, sits where a creek joins the Allegheny. In the western part of America, one hears the term *creek* more often than *stream* or *brook*; in England, a creek is a small inlet or bay on a shoreline. Franklin has been an Indian camp, a French fort, an English fort, an American fort, and still it has remained sequestered in the forest of the Allegheny plateau that presses up against the Allegheny Mountains. I had not understood—or conceived—of America accurately before encountering this vast concatenation of woody hills, humps, heights, mounts, and steeps with their intervening valleys and hollows which finally dissolve at the western escarpment of the Appalachians, the only thing able to impede them short of cataclysm or doomsday.

Fully eager to dismount the coach to stretch legs and spine to resume a human profile, we were thirsty for a tilt of beverage in the

Venango Tavern. Considering the remoteness of our surround, the inn was remarkable: spacious without luxury, tidy without barrenness, and a taproom ready for fellowship with a barkeep whose pours were a liquid definition of generosity. Maybe what we felt was little more than the outcome of miles of bouncing through greenery wonderfully desolate of humanity. Whatever the source, our relief pulled from Nicodemus, *"Meum est propositum in taberna mori. Can't remember who said it."* Whoever it was, said it well enough for me also to resolve *on the spot* to die in a tavern.

The phrase almost came to have further meaning, an evil cast, when a ruffian entered, and both Deems and I briefly took him for Ferrall. He was not. In fact, he proved to be a boon companion for an hour. Deems offered later, "Our foreboding was anxiety speaking. Let's not forget Plato—'Nothing in human affairs deserves great anxiety.'" Reflecting, he added, "But then Mister Plato didn't have Hell Bent Ferrall in pursuit."

29 June

The coach departed so early we had time for only a hard-boiled egg and a chunk of buttered bread. Our stage companions were the Merciers of Pittsburgh on their way home. She was as lean and wan as he was round and rubicund, and in a second contrast, her words offered a question mark where his flashed dollar signs.

For all the warmth it held, the face of Asa Mercier seemed cast from pig iron. His brain, knowing more than it truly comprehends, let opinions stand in for wisdom, and within them mercantilistic ardor advocates for commodity over community. His heart, of beaten brass carrying the imprint of past poundings, was no longer malleable by anything short of a drop hammer.

Conversely, Mrs. Mercier possessed a lively curiosity and demonstrated an unusual trait in this country: interest reaching beyond merely where a stranger hails from. Whether Americans have not inquired about me out of simple incuriosity or whether they wish to avoid appearing to be pryingly inquisitive, I cannot determine, but rare it has been on these shores to be asked about *who* I am, *why* I'm on the road, *where* I'm headed, or even *which* state I find most worthy. To tag me as English—my Caribbean childhood rarely discovered—suffices for most to explain my entire life.

Loraine Mercier, however, filled the cabin with questions directed at both me and Nicodemus, some of them forcing us to obscure our identities and, twice, even to mislead her about the route of our travels and our destination. Fortunate it was that Mr. Mercier slept, because I have no doubt he would readily divulge anything he learned about us—provided money crossed his palms.

My questions to her brought answers right to the point but with little more until I asked for her thoughts on the future course of woman suffrage in America. She looked at me in surprise before responding.

"As you are undoubtedly aware, Mister Wilcox, recent discussions have raised to an unprecedented national level resistance to the practice of placing all power into the hands of only a certain classification of citizens. But today, the suffrage movement has become entangled and its progress retarded by the equally crucial issues of abolition and temperance. Nevertheless, I and so many other American women—including numerous men—will continue to insist our representative government must come to *represent*—rather than *restrain*—its electorate. Would you agree, Mister Cuff?"

With caution Deems answered, "I believe Plato argued in favor of a degree of equality for women."

"Perhaps so, Mister Cuff, yet, let us recognize you may gain access to the ballot box before I do."

30 June

We arrived so late last night at Beaver Town, Pennsylvania on the Ohio River, we had no choice of accommodations but a dormitory in a shabby hotel; the name of the place I either don't remember or deliberately forgot. Separately from Deems, I entered the building, signed the register under my *nom de guerre*, and was followed an hour later by Cuff. We went to opposite ends of the sleep chamber and did not acknowledge the other at breakfast this morning, and certainly not when buying tickets for separate cabins on the steam packet *Cahokia*. Deems had a Negro cabin-mate from Baton Rouge, Charles Rushton, who is in service to a gambler from New Orleans; even to Charles, Deems admitted no connection with me. Together, their pairing served our scheme by leading others to see them as companions. For me, when somebody asks, I say I hail from Norway and put a twist or two into my speech. I almost convince myself.

Beaver Town sits on a narrow flat at the base of a humpage of wooded hills where the Big Beaver River flows into the Ohio. For some reason, the *Cahokia* remained tied to the dock till ten a.m., an uncomfortable delay allowing a pursuer to close the gap. To avoid being seen from shore, I stayed along the port rail—the river side— out of sight of anybody on the wharf. Before getting underway, Nicodemus passed casually by to deftly transfer a note directing me to the second deck overlooking the dock, where, to buffer our conversation, he stood near an eastern European couple who spoke not a word of English. Just loud enough for me to hear, he said in a rapid, almost incomprehensible Negro vernacular, "Below, man in de red hat, pistol at he side. Be it ol HB?"

I stepped behind a brace for a covert look. The man was speaking animatedly to a dockhand in what seemed a dispute, an exchange keeping him occupied until our lines were cast off and the *Cahokia* moved into the downstream current. The last I saw was the pistoled man pass something to the other, money perhaps. I came back and told Deems I felt almost certain neither was our nemesis, and he said, "With our lives at stake, *almost certainty* is a penny candle in the sun."

Topside passengers being occupied by our departure allowed Nicodemus to follow me at a distance to my cabin, and there he said, "What if it *was* Hell Bent?"

"If so, he missed us, and the next steamer doesn't stop here till tomorrow afternoon. That gives us a fair lead."

"For me, three months and three hundred miles is a fair lead. Don't forget, the south side of the river is slave territory all the way to Saint Louis."

We set up a system to communicate: a note with an assigned time in Roman numerals—say, III.XV—to meet in my cabin. Every hour we will check our "postbox," nothing more than a crevice between a rail and stanchion. And so we begin our cruise down the wooded banks of *La Belle Rivière*.

The 30th (later)

Before noon a drizzle came on to obscure the shoreline and drive me into my cabin, not an unwelcome change. Deems and Charles played cards in the grand saloon—termed on this packet a social hall—heavy with the taint of cigars and expectorate boxes, both odors driving women to the smaller ladies hall. Whilst a sleeper snored away in the stateroom next to mine, I took up Monsieur Alexis de Tocqueville's recent *Democracy in America*. Before leaving England, to prepare myself for this journey, I read the first volume and packed the second into my trussery. On the Atlantic crossing, I made not even scant progress into a book become a prominent resource for European tourists to this vast, vital, voracious, and at times vagarious country. No other visitor has yet given a more masterful interpretation of the democratic aspects of the American experiment.

His judicious commentary and formidable erudition place his account above other interpretations of what is underway on this side of the Atlantic. Nevertheless, based upon his intellectual examinations here some fifteen years ago, his words are not those of a traveler. He came not so much to explore a country as to examine a concept: American democracy. But his sober-sided text smells of a scholar's lamp rather than people's lives. In his pages no women laugh or remonstrate for universal education, no expectorating men argue over horses. I never learn what Tocqueville ate for supper, whether his mattress had fleas, whether he noticed the distinctive scents of American forests. I hear him speak of capital punishment but I do not see a thief or a noose. I read of wealth but there is no clink of gold eagles. He writes of slavery but not of an enslaved woman floating face down in Baltimore harbor. His roads are without dust, his rivers without water, and his tavern floors have no spilled beer or cigar butts.

Perhaps this is as it should be for a work dedicatedly analytic, its expression decidedly abstruse. Young Tocqueville arrived here not to confirm but to educate himself, and in that way he stands distinct from visitors the likes of Mrs. Trollope or Captain Basil Hall, their jaundiced accounts expressions of travelers in quest of anything wanting in America when compared to the mother country. Further to his credit, Tocqueville resists preconceptions and prejudgments better than other observers of what this country is and may become. He did not arrive in search of an El Dorado or the picturesque or investment opportunities or to escape a despot or to spy on a nation deemed by some Europeans a threat to monarchical power. If the Frenchman is on occasion an aristocrat annoyed that his kid gloves lasted only one evening at a ball, he still inclines more towards a Lafayette than a George III. And never is he an indolent Charles Dickens.

As I write this in the relative safety of my cabin, I wonder how Tocqueville would have interpreted America were he dogged by a man determined to kill him. How he would consider the equalizing power of a pistol leveled at his head.

I put aside his disquisition for a constitutional around the *Cahokia* decks to study its construction, in part because the steamboat—that is, power from steam boilers—is looking ever more like a world-changing mechanical invention. Not long ago Robert Fulton's little steamer made its initial run up the Hudson, and the first steamboat on these waters was but four years later. Steam boilers turning paddle wheels is certain to remake the commerce of the Ohio and the bank-side towns and even, perhaps, change the river itself. What will be the results when steam is fully applied to rail locomotives to free them from geologically determined routes and allow passage through almost any terrain in any weather? I fear Americans are not contemplating the effects mechanical propulsion will have on their economy. On their democracy. On their lives.

The rapid increase in material prosperity steam engines have brought to this river valley and the resulting unmodulated growth in population are, to the residents, indisputable advances. Nobody questions whether American social institutions can stay abreast of such uncharted transformations and unforeseen destinations. Along the Ohio shores of forests unbroken only a half century ago, today are towns, settlements, and hundreds of burnt-over clearings. The constructs of human hands are not yet omnipresent, but where they appear, some of them are already wreckage. *Videlicet:* In our first hour on the Ohio, we passed three burnt-down cabins and two wrecked and abandoned steamboats.

Europeans have had generations to adjust from living in crude dwellings to life in timbered homes with chimneyed hearths and wooden floors and glassed windows. So: Is the American experiment proceeding more rapidly than its citizens can comprehend and control? How much of and how fast can the wilderness be safely turned over to humans? What is the cost per acre of the loss of woodlands? Costs reckoned not simply in monetary profit. Who is calculating the future? When I raise these issues with an American, I receive a look suggesting I must be simple to challenge headlong affluence. Perhaps so, but hasty and unreckoned change is not always a salutary companion to liberty.

The 30th inst.

This river of snags and sawyers and shoals makes the longevity of a boat that of a house mouse. The rather new *Cahokia* is a steam packet built for speed, her ratio of length to width four to one: 120 feet stem to stern, a beam of thirty feet, her draft only six feet. Forty staterooms of two berths each, and officer quarters on the texas deck.

Walking the decks earlier I met a carpenter, Andy Hulbert, who explained innovative features such as the twin water-tanks to fight fire, also wooden doors and hinged window-shutters, all of which can be quickly detached to buoy up a passenger if need to abandon ship arises. Ten years ago, near Cincinnati, Hulbert survived a steamboat explosion that marked his jaw with a cicatrix like a dueling scar. I report what I recall of his story:

"I was a deckhand, just a young dog on a Louisville packet. The *Hannibal*. Stokers in the engine room—the farmen—they sure as hell earned their name one night. Word come down, ahead of us was a rival, the *Bessie* out of Pittsburgh. Now, the boys had been into the whiskey barrel and was plumb drunk. They was feedin the boilers pine knots that burn fierce. What's more, they sprinkled them with rosin to raise steam fast to overtake the *Bessie*. Them flames busted loose into our fuel supply—sixty cords of wood.

"People was asleep in their cabins until they was woken by a loud commotion—panicked men tryin to lower the yawl before the lines caught far. The crew wasn't fast enough and most of them stokers went into the river and drownt in the churn from the paddles. Captain tried to steer us to shore, but the wheel-ropes to the rudder burnt through, and the *Hannibal* kept right on her merry way downriver. A course, the wheel ropes on this here *Cahokia* is metal chains. I live to tell you them chains—*and* them emergency water-tanks—they's the reasons I'm on board this steamer today.

"It musta been a sight on Earth, a boat on far stem to stern, flames seventy feet high. Decks full of folks screamin. Some of the people, their clothes was on far, and others, they was all but nekkid. I pulled a burnin nightie off one woman. The flesh on her back was meltin. She jumped into the river. If you never seen a lady on far, pray to your saver you never do. Them in the cold water, less they had a peg to hang onto, you seen the last of them. Some was lucky enough to grab a floatin somethin—a deck chair, a plank. Problem was, they was more people than planks and chairs. Folks fightin for a piece to grab.

"Then part of the cargo—whiskey barrels—took to explodin. For them boilers, that was all she wrote. They blowed up one after t'other. It rained down arms and legs. I got blowed sky west and crooked. But I landed in the water. My arm was broke. Figgered I was done for. Then the current shoved something into me. A flour barrel. I didn't have no time to start any prayin, so I can't say it was Heaven-sent. Luck, just pure luck. I got myself draped over it like a gun-shot hound until it jammed into a chunk of deck where they was a gal, and she tolt me to grab aholt, so I clumb on, and her and me floated downriver. A upstream packet comin on to rescue folks, its waves upset our float and thowed us off, but I got back on and managed to reach my good arm to her. She was about gone. I tried to steer with a hunk of drift, but my broke arm wasn't no use.

"We come to a person hangin to a footstool. She was all in. Gaspin. I snared the stool and got it over to our float. Stuck to it was a colored girl, daughter of a steward. She didn't have two ounces of fight left. Right about then I seen a man in a small skiff come rowin towards us. He was huntin floatin baggage and whatever else he could scavenge off the water. I called for him to take the women, and he said—*as God is my witness*—he said, 'How much you gimme for em?' Why, they wasn't a penny in my pockets. Nothin in them but river water. Then he rowed away and kept on scavengin.

"After a hour, we was washed up on a gravel bar. When mornin come on, a big steamer, the *Majesty*, she picked us up, and a doctor on board, he bandaged up the woman and girl, then he set my broke arm. The disaster killed ninety of us, but here's one upshot of it. The gal on the drift with me, she was right-down attractive. That winter, we was married. To top it off, the colored girl—one who lost her daddy in the explosion—we brung her in to work at our place. Dorothy. We found out she was pregnant. You see, they was *four* of us on that raft. That blow-up, it give me a family.

"It was three years before I could even think about ridin a steamboat again. I'll tell you this, times in church, sittin there lookin at my people brung to me out of calamity, I wonder if I oughta thank the Lord for them drunk stokers for explodin them boilers. But somehow that just don't seem rightful."

July, 1848

1 July

OUR CLANGING DEPARTURE from Ironton, Ohio woke me, and as I prepared to shave, a key rattled in the lock. Cheeks fully lathered, I opened the door, and there stood a sturdy, bare-chested Indian wearing leather leggings, in his hand a tomahawk, his face smudged with charcoal and russet. Whose visage gave the other the greater start, I have no idea. He was without expression unless war paint is an expression.

He pointed into the stateroom and said, "Bed mine," and to explain he held up his key stamped with "26." I grinned, the shaving cream, as it can do, surely making me look insane. I motioned for him to follow me across the passageway to cabin 26, and there I turned his key to match the numeral on the door so he could see the similarity between 26 and 29. His formerly immobile face flushed into laughter, and in he went.

A dance troupe of Shawnee men and women from Chillicothe, Ohio performed in town last night. At breakfast I saw the dancer again, and he smiled and said, "Nine is six stand on head." In England it is foolishly believed the rictus muscles of the American Indian are so inflexible, a person cannot facially express delight. It is also claimed native women prefer reticence when in the presence of whites; whether that observation is also inaccurate, I can say only I have not seen the Shawnee females engage with white men *or* women. Indeed, the entire troupe comports itself in a retiring fashion, perhaps because the barkeep denies them alcohol.

The Shawnee braves maintain *practiced*, stern visages and enjoy the role of fell savages hungry to slay an American. But with white children they show marked affection, smiling and lifting to their shoulders any child not intimidated; they even let the youngest hold a tomahawk. The whole time, braves are aware how whites perceive them—either as ferocious primitives or romantic, uncorrupted fugitives from an endangered race.

When I checked the covert postbox, Deems had left a slip with an **XI.XXX.** At eleven thirty I met him in my cabin. He told me his friend Charles said coming aboard this afternoon was a famous gambler who would draw special interest to the *Cahokia*. Among the throng might be he who is anathema. Deems recommends we watch all boarders from a covered vantage.

I went below to inquire of a crewmember about the gambler, whose name I heard as Lukee Luc Long, and I asked was he Chinese. Said the crewman, "What! He ain't no Chinaman! He's six-foot six of pure niggra as black as the ace of spades, but he's known as the King of Hearts. When he boards, he'll have a beautiful quadroon woman on each arm, and in their ears will be diamonds. It'll be a procession. Ain't a better gambler on the Ohio *or* Mississippi. In New Orleans, he's 'La Tontine': winner take all."

As I was to learn, Lucky Luke Longdon is a poker player welcome on any packet because of the well-heeled planters from the South and fat-walleted businessmen from the North he draws to tables in a social hall. Rare was it for any of those self-considered grandees to depart a boat with more in his pocket than he carried aboard. La Tontine's big season is after autumn harvest when cotton planters are flush with cash. To Lucky Luke, relieving them of some of the profit created by field slaves is not only lucrative but an act of due justice. It is said the King of Hearts is always amenable to a Negro needing—call it a *loan*.

About five o'clock Deems and I assumed a covert position above the gangway. Among those boarding we saw no one remotely resembling Ferrall. Last to enter was La Tontine himself and his brace of bronze beauties asparkle with gems, the group attended by a pair of bodyguards whose bull necks said all that was necessary. Trailing the entourage was a slight, weasel of a white man who, I learned, is known as the Fifth Ace.

The King nodded and smiled, shook a few hands, dared to tip his hat to white women, and spoke not a word. Deems had never seen such a procession of richly attired Negroes, and he followed as Longdon emplaced his court around a certain table the gambler preferred, a procedure requiring shunting to a corner four whites not at all receptive to being moved aside for a Negro, men apparently unaware of the role of money in American democracy.

A steward noted beverage orders—the King of Hearts taking only something clear and effervescent—and the demonstration began. The diversion, so said a man standing next to me, is called Ten Tontine and requires neither tactics nor skill unless nerve be a skill. Longdon invented the game and has become famous on the river for it. Its underlying purpose is to announce the arrival of the King and his specialty, high-stakes poker.

Theatrically, he opened a new pack of playing cards, removed the suit of hearts, and passed the remainder to an attendant. With flourish, his diamond-laden fingers fanned the thirteen hearts across the table before removing the face cards. Then he swept up the ten numerals and adroitly shuffled them before addressing the nine other gamblers, saying in a voice suggesting Moses announcing the arrival of the Ten Commandments, "If you're ready, gentlemen. Place your bets on the table." To match the King's wager, each contestant pushed forward ten gold eagles: a thousand dollars heaped up like so much gleaming gravel. A crowd pressed in to lay side bets yielding to La Tontine a percentage overseen by his bullnecks.

With a warning not to touch the cards until he spoke the word, Longdon dealt every player a single heart face down—deuce through ace. At his command, each man turned up a corner of a heart only enough to catch its value. Even he who had the low card might win a few dollars from off-table bets. The King said, "Deuce," and the no-longer-smiling chap cursed and turned over the two of hearts. Then "Trey," and the three exposed. The side bets were continually adjusted upward by those watching, and the groans from losing bettors matched those of eliminated participants.

At last only four cards remained unshown, one of them necessarily the ace of hearts. La Tontine said, "Eight," and turned over his own card. Then "Nine," and the game was down to a pair, one worth a thousand dollars in gold. In search of a reveal of misery or joy, the side-bettors studied the composure of the two gamblers and, interpreting what they saw, made their final wagers. With more dramatic pausing and resonant delivery, the King said, "Ten." A man stood, threw up his arms and hooted before showing the ace of hearts, and with minimal dignity and maximum avarice, swept the one grand of gold into his pockets, its heft nearly pulling his trousers to the floor.

I had lost track of Nicodemus. As deflated gamblers and a few losing spectators disappeared, Deems stepped up. Believing him a steward, players gave beverage orders he ignored to seat himself at the table, closely observed by La Tontine. Not an eye was on anything other than young Nicodemus, the men's faces indicating, *Who's this colored boy with the derring-do?* When bettors pushed their wagers of gold forward, I realized Deems had cashed in a portion of Cedric's gift on a game of pure chance, his odds of winning only one in ten. I tried to cover any indication I knew him, but the truth is I wanted to seize him and drag him outside. What the hell was he thinking? Gambling with his medical-college education!

The game began. La Tontine called: Deuce. Out. Trey. Out. Four, five, and six—all out. And Deems was yet alive. Seven. Out. Four cards still down. Then the eight went out. Nine. Out. Now a pair of cards left, one of them belonging to Deems. The other—*as fate would have it*—was the King's.

Side bettors were going silly: a young Negro against the black King of Hearts! With no more side bets, Longdon let tension build before saying resonantly, "Ten." Deems did not move. Waiting, waiting, La Tontine reached for his own card and turned it up: *ace of hearts.*

The uproar was loud. I joined a line of winning bettors who gave a condolent whack on the shoulder as they passed behind Deems, and when it came to me, I whacked him hard and said as if referring to his losing hand, "Ten to *one!*"

(After midnight)

I stood topside to view moon reflections off the dark waves and wonder what had just happened to our explorations, our lives. I reasoned, reconnoitered, calculated, and, yes, cursed before going down to my journal to write questions appropriate to an obituary.

What do I say to a man unpracticed with money? What could result from a former slave gambling for a thousand dollars in gold? How long before such an unwonted story makes its way up and down the river? How many slave hunters will get word of the game? Should I chastise Deems not for a foolhardy loss of a hundred dollars, but for endangering us and our plans, our dreams? What now of Sophie's future? Have I traveled six thousand miles only to see my journey, my days ended by the turn of a playing card? Has my friend remade three lives into a wager on a real-life game of Tontine, *winner take all*, with Ferrall doing the taking? Had I helped a man out of slavery only to watch him descend into, into *what?*

At one o'clock, Nicodemus tapped on the door and quickly slipped in. My face bespoke itself, and he said, "You're angry?"

"It would have been prudent to discuss it."

"I saw the game, saw a chance—."

"A ten-to-one chance of losing a hundred dollars and what we've been building. You signaled our whereabouts to every slave hunter between here and New Orleans. After all, it's a unique tale of two black men turning a card to win a thousand dollars in gold."

"I had to decide fast."

"*Fast?* Your decision means we have to leave this boat fast before word of your bet goes on downriver. *Fast* means a hunk of your windfall for medical college is gone in a flash."

"In a way yes. But in fact, no."

"What the devil are you saying?"

Nicodemus pulled from a pocket a trinity of hundred-dollar bills. I said, "Now what have you done?"

"Almost doubled my tuition fund. Cedric would approve."

"Oh yes. He'll bless you and lay a rose on your grave."

Deems said breathlessly, "The King, after the game, he had one of his ladies escort me to his stateroom. He likes *the spirit of bold enterprise in a young Negro.* His very words. He asked where I come from, and I said I'd been a plantation houseboy. From *Georgia.* He considered, then looked at one of his ladies, and she nodded. He said the tale of a former slave gambling against a rich black would have white planters ready to empty their wallets."

Stopping to see how I was taking the news, Deems waited for my response. I remained silent.

He continued. "Tontine said I'd turned his game into a way white gamblers will express their feelings about abolition. He thinks whites will want no slave getting ideas about running off to become a card shark, but others will want to bring down the rich Negro with the diamonds and beautiful women and kill off a game putting thoughts into the head of a field hand. *Or a house* servant. La Tontine said no white man along the river could resist the ploy, and we can practice it from Kentucky to Louisiana. David and Goliath. Slave versus king. Prince and the pauper. He said my pockets won't hold all the gold eagles heading my way."

"Did he say heading your way—*our* way—is more than gold eagles!"

"La Tontine, from his pocket, he gave me this three hundred. He said to remember four words: *Ploy. Predator. Prey. Plunder.*"

"And you decided to make us the prey and to hell with medical college just so you can become a famous Negro hustler. Our predator will need about two days to find his prey."

"I told Longdon I'd think about it."

"Think first about using Cedric's investment in your education to buy a bodyguard. Maybe the King will sell one of his."

"I'm still Nicodemus. Thighbone connected to the hipbone—I mean, femur bone connected to the pelvic bone."

In response, I sang, "Head bone disconnected from the neck bone, neck bone disconnected from the shoulder bones."

We sat in silence until I broke it. "Will you promise one thing?"

"What's the *one thing*?"

"The *one thing* is this: No slatterns, harridans, doxies, dolly-mops. No *filles de joie*, fizgigs. No fricatrices, no cockatrices. No trugs, trulls, or trollops."

"You're well versed in queens of the night."

"I'm well versed in treating syphilitics. The lesson here is this: Keep your damn pillicock in your pantaloons and your boodle in the bank."

2 July

The stone-paved levee at Cincinnati is long, broad, and sloped slightly up towards a veritable wall of brick buildings of repeated design punctuated by hundreds of windows opening to the Ohio River. Given the usual, minimal rise above high water here, the façades seem unchallenged by the tenure of the Ohio as possessor of the place. The city horizon is similarly long and low with but few spires and steeples breaking into the sky. The shoreline, to which steamboats tie up parallel to the river and in tandem as if canal mules, is impressive in its length although not distinguished by architecture. Perhaps the prospect of no other American city so adamantly announces, *Tradesmen!*

As Nicodemus and I waited to disembark, we watched the King of Hearts and his entourage exit with much the same ceremony as when boarding. Deems had learnt Longdon decided for his Tontine ploy any young Negro could play the role of ex-slave challenger, the less known all the better. Nicodemus was not disappointed, but relieved of the temptation.

Once in the city, we found a bank to deposit his cash. I said to him, "Like a mogul, you're on course to establish a string of bank accounts across America," and he answered, "Until only days ago, I never had more than a handful of pennies. I kept them buried in a fruit jar behind the plantation barns. When I ran away, I forgot it. If I leave it there, I'll never be penniless."

That gave me an idea: our boots need resoling, so why not each of us have a five-dollar gold piece bound within a heel? Companions to the bills sewn into my jacket lining.

We decided the delay in changing to another boat would impair the lead we surmised we had gained on Ferrall, so the boots could wait. Further, the attenuated memory Americans have for current news suggests the tale of the slave boy and the king might be evaporating already into obsolescent and implausible tittle-tattle. So we can hope.

A blow from the untuned steam-whistle called us, and the paddle wheels began a heavy and slow toiling to start us towards Louisville, 134 miles distant by water, ninety miles by wings of the crow. Away from the river valley, the country was generally rugged and forested above an assortment of bench lands and flats.

Our stopover in Louisville is extended because a barge broke loose to block the canal around the Falls of the Ohio, in low water an impassible rock ledge that until recently made the river, at least for boatmen, into two rivers, necessitating two boats, one on each side of the cascades. A woman aboard the *Cahokia* recommended entertainments along Market Street. "We're in an age of lectures," she said. The choice was "Phrenology: Doorway into the Mind" or "Adam and the Amendment." We chose Adam.

But for a few chairs at the front, the auditorium was filled—many folks curious about a female speaker. As we went forward, Nicodemus, the only Negro in the chamber, drew stares, but being in slave-state Kentucky, people took him for, to use local parlance, "my man." Americans are given to avoiding the word *servant*, preferring rather the term *help*, as in, *We have hired help*. It is part of the lexicon of their democracy, a toning down of class, even one embracing slavery. Deems, accustomed to such staring, was more at ease than I, even though he knew some in the audience wanted him in the balcony.

As the gas lights were dimmed, Mrs. Emma Ripley, a woman of stature modest enough to require an apple crate behind the lectern that she might be seen, began in an amiable manner, speaking with—for an American—untypically crisp enunciation and never in their hurried speech. Maintaining a temperate delivery, she discoursed with a passion arising not from anger but conviction.

Notepad on my knee, I realized keeping pace with her central arguments would be a challenge, so I nudged Deems to assist with his book. Her first words were, "Some of you present tonight may believe I am descended from Adam's rib. 'From man made God a woman,' says Genesis. Adam tells us he will call her *woman* because she was taken *out of man*. Ladies and gentlemen, I come before you to assure you I came from a *woman*. Out of Sarah Mae Dawson, wife of my father, Edgar Dawson. I ask now, any of you *not* taken out of a woman to please stand so we may learn the miracle of your birth."

At this, a clutch of tongue cluckers seated near went to work and thereafter clucked disapproval after every perceived impropriety or sacrilege.

"I am," Mrs. Ripley continued, "dedicated to be helpmate to my husband—as he to me. But I will not be defined by it. I reject biblical sanctioning of a myth that places women as descending from a male ribcage. I was born out of a pelvic region below a female's ribs. As were my brother and my son."

The cluckers could scarcely stay up with the proclamations. A further distraction was a dozing man, whose angle of repose became greater than gravity sanctions, slipping noisily to the floor. Mrs. Ripley waited for him to be set upright.

"We are engaged in three momentous battles," she said, "battles in which each contender will eventually earn victory. But not all at once. Our field is a Constitutional struggle to write amendments to form, in those immortal words—if grammatically negligent—*a more perfect union.* These amendments are the abolition of slavery, the prohibition of liquor, and the establishment of universal suffrage. Let me say them loudly and clearly: Abolition! Prohibition! Universal suffrage!"

With each term, applause rose, although that for the second was rather muted. She followed with, "These contestants, however, compete in the minds of our fellow citizens, and it's likely the writing of appropriate amendments will come independently. I put top priority on woman suffrage for this reason: Less than ten percent of us are enslaved, and even fewer imperil their lives with hard spirits, but more than half of us are female. Therefore, an amendment for universal suffrage should be the *first* order of business."

As she drew to her conclusions, she scanned listeners before asking, "Is it not ironic our national symbol is not *Gentleman*

Liberty, but *Lady* Liberty, yet we deny her the ballot box?" There was general if not universal applause.

Whilst the audience filed out, I read quotations Nicodemus had jotted down:

—Is our lot to darn and knit, never to hammer and chisel?
—In your handbag do you have money of your own, beyond a lucky purse-penny?
—Are we to be mothers of magistrates but never magistrates?
—Are we to be allowed a garden bench but not a seat on a judicial bench?

Having observed his note taking, a man said to Deems, "Missus Ripley's order of precedence is unlikely. Emancipation of Negroes must happen before enfranchisement of women. Resolution of the slavery question, because it's so patently economic, will be tumultuous and it will compel action. It will overwhelm all else. The irony is, were women's suffrage put first, it would lead naturally to abolition. A consequence of their voices."

Nicodemus dared to say, "I've met many a woman far from ready to unclamp the chains."

3 July

From Louisville downstream, the Ohio enters a run of thirty miles flowing every direction except due north in a succession of bights and obliquities appearing to be attempts to prove its dedication to the territory. In the leisurely evasions, the Ohio seems to lack destination, descent not its goal. But finally, to atone for deviousness, it abruptly reforms and cranks around to get the hell on with the business of rivers: flowing to the sea.

At the terminus of this straightness is a large oxbow and Evansville, Indiana; there we decided to depart the *Cahokia* to obscure our trail yet further. Deems arranged quarters in Mother Butler's Boarding House where we learned of a *camp meeting* across the river in Kentucky. Given the anarchy of creeds and the equality of dogmas and the engendering of self-appointed saints that American democracy produces, we prepared to observe the events.

A ferry left us on a bosky Kentucky shore with a trail towards a circular enclosure of about twelve acres cut into a woods. A perimeter of wagons, buggies, carriages, carts, gigs, and shays had formed, and within were dozens of tents. At the cardinal compass points stood a quartet of log altars six feet tall and topped with a bed of soil to furnish a hearth. The fire-stands were set as if a clock face: one at the noon position, another opposite, and one each at three and nine o'clock. Approximate to the altars rose head-high platforms intended as rostrums for sermonizers.

With sunset a trumpet sounded and four maidens dressed like vestal virgins put a torch to the wood atop the altars to efface the approach of night. Whether the blazes were reminders of the flames of Hell or the luminance of Heaven, I could not discern, although the smoke suggested more the hellish than the heavenly. The blazes, coruscating the dark, drew people from tents—moths to light—to pray or kneel or, in a few instances, to prostrate themselves on the humid earth. Several hundred souls sorted into groups at the foot of the platforms, and throughout milled spectators of whom Deems and I were two. I estimated three females to every male, a notable portion of them not far past their twentieth year.

Preachers ascended the platforms to begin declaiming, words eliciting loud affirmations of "Say on!" and "Amen!" and "Hallelujah!" In no time moanings welled up, followed by cries for salvation. To judge from the voices, we were in a Hades of iniquity and perdition and unabashed, unpardoned carnality.

A girl staggered out of a tent and towards the foot of a rostrum holding four clerical jawsmiths. One descended to lay hands on her convulsing body, and he cried out, "Sister! Young sister! Do you renounce your profligacy? Do you relinquish bad faith?" The weeping child chokingly obliged, and for her complaisance the man bent to kiss her forehead, her childish cheeks, her bared arms, stopping only at the verge of impropriety. Shouting "Hosannah!" he reascended the platform to spring into the air with impressive agility, pausing only momentarily to regain breath, calling out, "It ain't rainin tonight! Levitate for the Lord! Jump for Jesus!" Then he dropped to all fours and howled and yawped into the forest to such an extent that out of the darkness came answering yips and ululations from stray dogs. If ever I saw a skilled disciple from the ministry of self-aggrandizement, from the prelacy of self-sanctification, it was he.

Atop another rostrum a pair of fervid expounders, one bearded and dressed in white and brandishing the *saber of truth*, addressed a horned adversary dressed in black, face painted red, who wielded a pitchfork. A rousing clash began but ended unintentionally with the parson in white receiving a sharp tine to the gluteal area, which turned his posterior red, an outcome drawing more gasps than laughter, this verisimilitude attesting to the inevitability of Armageddon. Theirs was cracking good theater outperforming preachers offering nothing more than harangues and exhortations against trespasses without name and loud blandishments to all manner of penances. Believers responding with oblations of credulity.

As Deems and I roamed about, we jotted in our memoranda books, and we were twice rebuked for writing during *the Lord's hour*. A miscreant—whether his soul needed cleansing I cannot say, but clearly his earthly corpus did—accosted Nicodemus with an angry, "Why's a nigga-boy writin down what we're doin?" and grabbed at Deems. I pushed the rotter away, and he wheeled to swing wildly at me. I answered with a Cambridge right cross to drop him. Deems smiled and said, "The fistic arts?"

I acted because a Negro striking a Caucasian in a slave state could bring on a thrashing. Or, in a crowd of true believers able to fuse religion with racism, even a lynching. But, among so many souls throwing themselves down for spiritual uplift, nobody paid attention, the rank assailant nothing more than another decumbent body needing penitence. And a bar of strong lye soap.

We came upon a supplicant in a frenzy of sobbing before she fell to her knees and tore open her blouse and began crying out, "I back-slided! Oh, Lord, I back-slided!" Deems wondered how a young life—perhaps not without taint but hardly so bespotted as one day it will be—could become unremittingly fouled. She was quickly aided by a parson—ordained in the seminary of personal belief—who laid healing hands on her, his palms happening to land athwart her breasts, calling her to yield up her depravity, shouting, "Renounce sin!" while his hands kept right on healing until he apparently had massaged away her impurity, and she sat up to receive a blessing of kisses of salvation falling just short of where the massage had been applied. Pulled to her feet, she was relieved to have gained redemption through a simple "I believe!" brought forth by ministering fingers.

By this point Nicodemus and I were growing numb to men hoarse with imprecations. Encouraged by spectators, the goal among souls—more *earnest* than is commonly tolerable—was to outperform pulpiteers emoting nearby and prove your Gehenna greater than their Tophet.

Other items:

— A boy with a large black snake coiling around his arms and shoulders as the Devil does a soul.
— A woman sitting in a puddle and smearing herself with mire in admission of profligacy; to prove genuine her zealotry, tears streaked her muddied cheeks.

— A preacher speaking of sinners whose hearts were *darker than a closed Bible*, and suggesting sin is *excrement of the soul* more foul than any bodily expulsion.

— A man beating his back with a bloodied bag of horse chestnuts still in the pod, the spines lacerating his skin.

My thought: what need to deliberately foster misery, when the ordinary terms of the human condition ought to be sufficient to inculcate anguish in any sentient person?

The shrifts I heard sounded less about depravity and more like expressions of just being human—simple foibles inherent in our species. We observed no confessions of burglary, assault, rape, murder, treason. Exposed guilts were not criminal but mere lapses and slip-ups strong enough to support the brisk sale of Bibles, declamatory tracts, and admonitory plaques: REPENT. BELIEVE. SALVATION TODAY!

The best theatrics were from a sermonizer detailing his former days as a drunkard until being *washed in the blood of the Lord*. To illustrate his proposition, he picked up a whiskey bottle holding brown fluid, and took a long guzzle, then stared stonily at his audience to let anticipation build before, whilst standing, violently retching into a bucket at his feet. (My guess: his purgative was salt water colored by pork-fat gravy and laced with a woodlot emetic, perhaps bittersweet or boneset.) He ripped off his tunic to expose a tattooed cross extending from neck to navel, nipple to nipple. His face revealed his satisfaction with his righteousness among the tarnished and stained and sullied and defiled.

Nowhere did I hear reference to the immense cast of Christian saints, martyrs, apostles, disciples, prophets, church fathers, theologians. Not even biblical figures: no Moses, Noah, Ruth, Abraham, Esther, Esau. An entire pantheon had been reduced not to a trinity but to a single divinity. Unless we count Satan. And never did I hear the words *charity* or *benevolence*; never a call to repent for having set oneself above a neighbor or for keeping for oneself what might have been shared. The dominant sharing here was corrupted reason: disarranged minds too confined within their own perceived debilities to feel the needs of others.

Deems and I moved to a far corner where we could watch the sweep of a carnival of spirituosity. Lamentations rose loudly from reflections into rants, hallelujahs shifted into hallucinations, belief conflated with hope, everything sliding into graduated layers of communal hysteria requiring denial of common sense: preachments of faith dependent on innocence and ignorance led to self-inflicted wretchedness transforming into exhibitions of self-authored dramas of confected depravity intended to bring on a fervor considered necessary for redemption. Ardor more fanatic than ecstatic.

The goal was to wallow in admissions of imperfection before all who cared to gawk at a confession of wickedness shift from shame to sorrow to slobbering and on to presumed salvation. The result: a temporary repose of refortified belief scarcely distinguishable from delusion.

Eventually the altar fires collapsed into orange coals and darkness reclaimed the grounds as nature again assumed its ancient place, silence winning out as it must over the hullabaloo of humanity but failing before the rising voices of the night—crickets and whippoorwills and foxes—from which came no cries of perdition or fear of Hell or hope of Heaven. In a few hours on this boggy soil another day would begin.

4 July, U.S. Independence Day

Mother Butler's boarding-house manager, Hobart Earle, a bewhiskered, retired mathematician whose smooth pate has no need for brush or comb, was a member of Robert Owen's social experiment in New Harmony a few years ago. Serving breakfast on the porch, he sat to ask our views of the camp meeting. Deems said, "Watching those performances, I'm saved from salvation. But I see why folks come from miles around to witness such zealotry. It was a circus. I have a changed understanding of one biblical injunction: when sects forbid taking the Lord's name in vain, does *vain* refer to blasphemy or futility?"

Earle said, "The lure of observing humanity degrade itself runs deep in those wanting to rise above their own failures. One means is to reduce others. Mockery becomes servant to self-esteem."

I listened to them but added nothing, disturbed as I was by what we had witnessed: a forum of the mentally disordered where self-induced agitation evokes apprehension and disables minds. While recognizing my own reverses as a physician, I still believe less in attending to issues of the *soul*—however we define it—and more in curative remedies to counteract or at least palliate mental derangements. But the truth is, our pharmacology is yet too primitive; our *materia medica* has not progressed far from the nescience of centuries gone.

Last night people were crying out for help, for release from their debilities, but what I saw descending from those platforms differed hardly a whit from conjuration. Most of the moaning and suffering seemed about as genuine as the shams and dissemblances concocted by charlatans to benefit humbug and work their game on the poorly educated lacking capacity to consider things critically. To succeed, apocalyptic self-promotions depend on foisting off auto-deception. The practitioners establish a camp meeting to dispense hysteria, which converts not into cures but into manic exhibitions of psychotic behavior encouraged by perpetrators rather than true pastors. They know smearing the mud of guilt over a disturbed face is easier than assisting someone to think through confusion. Weeping is easier than reasoning. The result is a bamboozled aggregation swapping comprehension for confessions of deficiency. Say the preachers: *The fruit of sin is misery, and thou art a sinner. Ergo, thou art miserable.*

But what is the greater sin? Believers accepting hoodwinkery or pastors ignoring any call to charity? When a search for solace destroys rationality, the consequence can be termed madness. And the result is the freshly *saved* returning home to walk the lanes temporarily relieved of confusion but enjoying only the brief comfort of a validation failing rational analysis. That is a practicable definition of derangement.

Yet true it is, sin gives meaning and purpose: it makes a human count for something. No longer does one's life seem a cypher with the rim rubbed out. I cannot deny the efficacy of either reasoned or unreasoned faith—belief is captain of the human brain and renders possible much achievement, including the inculcation of an intellect at peace. But is achieving tranquility the noblest use of a human brain? Our goal ought to be to enter the boneyard with more than a serene mind. An intellect cocooned in silken quiescence is unlikely to fulfill its unique capabilities. A tranquil brain belongs only to a beast with a full belly. What a loss had Isaac Newton ignored falling apples to traipse about lacerating his back with horse chestnuts.

The Fourth inst.

Nicodemus took a stroll into the town center, keeping alert for our nemesis. I was only mildly uneasy about his exploration because Ferrall had never obtained a look at him. Whilst Deems was away, I continued on the porch and used the quiet to write to Sophie, alerting her to the dangerous and devious pursuer. Even more, I wanted to express my, my—what *is* the term? *Admiration? Adulation? Veneration?* But I mentioned only we are bound towards Saint Louis and I will inquire at the central post office there for any letters addressed to me care of general delivery.

Earle brought out a lunch alfresco, and joined me to inquire about my American travels. Partway through my précis—perhaps now more practiced than polished—he interrupted to ask whether I had interest in utopian experiments linked to the American democratic impulse. "Up the road only a few miles is New Harmony," he said. "American love of invention and our belief in the necessity of improvements—especially to the body politic—is at the heart of the successful framing of this nation. Across the country you can find our attempts to advance, not just with machines but also with the machinery of human society—Brook Farm, Economy, Amana, Oneida. The Shakers, the Icarians."

Soon after Earle went off to do his chores, Nicodemus came bounding onto the porch, breathless and impassioned over something he did not reveal until he calmed to say straightforwardly, "I think I know where my mother is. I was idling down Vine Street. I happened upon a black man holding the reins of a horse for a woman in a carriage. I nodded as I passed. Then I stopped dead in my tracks. Couldn't believe my eyes! I knew that man! It was Toby, from the Virginia plantation! Reilly's old groomsman. I turned to take a closer look. He wouldn't likely recognize me now. I said, 'Loudon County, Virginia! You taught me to ride! I'm Cuff! Patsey's boy!' He studied me, leaning forward, squinting. Then he said, 'You be Patsey's boy. Cuff.'"

Nicodemus had to slow himself down before he could continue. "Reilly planned to buy property adjoining the plantation. To raise money, he sold off six slaves. Mama and Toby were two of them. Sold downriver when I was about fifteen. Toby, he told me Mama got sent on to Saint Louis to a family named Heckendorf."

Never had I seen Deems so beside himself with excitement. He said, "I put my arms around Toby, and the white woman snapped at him, 'Tobias, leave the young man to his duties, and you do yours! Get us on home!' As Toby adjusted the reins he whispered to me, 'They say she be a good lady, *Missus Heckendorf. Missus Walter Heckendorf* of Saint Louis.' Toby wants me to remember the name."

Deems was ready then and there to run off for a long shot in Saint Louis and add another crinkle to our route. I suggested we could head there via New Harmony. The next coach north is tomorrow morning. We will be on it.

5 July

The twenty hard miles to New Harmony was rough road in an ill-assembled stagecoach rattling itself into its individual members; on the way a door fell off and two overhead ribs broke; the driver's attire was hung together no better, he losing on the way a sleeve and the thumb of a glove. Secured in my breast pocket was a letter of introduction from Professor Earle to our host at the Wabash Tavern, Bronson Wynch, a professor of moral philosophy, who came down the Ohio River and up the Wabash to New Harmony twenty-some years ago with the establishing group of men and women known as the "Boatload of Knowledge." That cargo of human brains included scientists, educators, artists, and reformers of several inclinations, each dedicated to answering the fundamental question of human existence: *What must we do?* Which is to ask, what course can lead to a more humane and creative human society? If not all aboard considered themselves utopians, each nevertheless wanted a scientific reconstruction of the body politic. The leader, Robert Owen, decided the place to put into practice a new order was the American West.

We descended the coach at the village tavern, a sizable two-storey brick building of elegance borne out of architectural restraint. All was in proportion, nothing extraneous or merely decorative. After reading the letter of introduction, Wynch proposed we begin with a walking tour of the village. Recognizing the import of New Harmony to the American experiment, I said, "Indeed!" Here I condense the story of the village as the professor gave it to us:

Thirty-four years ago German immigrants under founder George Rapp ascended the Wabash and began clearing the forest and draining lowlands and molding bricks of local clay to construct houses and public buildings where before there had been wilderness. Rapp, a dour man, drove the Teutonic folk with apostolic fervor and demanded unremitting labor, celibacy, and common ownership of property to fulfill *his* concept of a religious utopia. He permitted so little repose that within a decade his village of Harmonie was materially realized, its economy established, and its burgeoning success drawing envy from neighbors.

Having greater leisure from then on, so the history comes down, the German immigrants had more time to ruminate on other ways to live in a new country and commenced debating dogma and communal law. Within months of finishing construction, their discontent and resentment crept in like fog off the Wabash bottoms. In his attempts to maintain the accomplishments, Rapp resorted to a sham, possibly one he, under the strain of impending failure, brought *himself* to believe. He had carted from Saint Louis to Harmonie a large and peculiarly eroded stone slab and set it up in a conspicuous location in the village. Wynch pointed out the flat rock contained a pair of remarkable—perhaps *too* remarkable— footprints left by, so Rapp claimed, the angel Gabriel when he descended to manifest his blessing of the Harmonie undertaking. Rapp ignored that the original angelic landing spot was more than a hundred miles from the village.

A herald from on high and an earthbound autocrat proved inadequate to stem restlessness, and within a year of completing the village, residents were quarreling amongst themselves and with neighbors—their friction making mock of the name Harmonie. Rapp sold the entire village and its surround—door locks, farm stock, and gun barrels—to a Welsh industrialist, philanthropist, and critic of capitalism, Robert Owen. Thereupon a second social and economic experiment began exactly on the grounds and in the structures where the first had expired. Could an autocracy *confounding* the mind be successfully replaced by a democracy *unleashing* the mind to explore the chaotic corners of liberty? It is a question of surpassing relevance to America.

Owen rose from a childhood of poverty and malnutrition and eighteen-hour working days to amass a fortune giving him means to assemble ideas for an advanced industrial order based not on economic competition and exploitation but on cooperation and equipollence, ideals requiring not heavenly footprints but scientific learning applied to education and human rights and the belief in an ethic of *We, not I*. Owen's books, especially his *A New View of Society*, became templates to lay atop the topography of Harmonie and reinvent it as New Harmony, a village emancipated from poverty, malnutrition, racial discord, inequities of women's rights, and especially from the growing oligarchic power of the corporate few amassing wealth at the expense of the many.

Within two years, the tiny village had established national influence; distant from it a dozen other, related villages sprouted, and tiny New Harmony began making history exactly where the religiously autocratic Harmonie had collapsed. Despite differences in the two attempts, their fates were the same and the causes similar. Why do I say this? In both, self-interest struggled against a sense of otherness. Against avarice, intolerance, willful ignorance, and undisciplined individualism. A wish for utopia endeavors to stand against the culpabilities of humankind, and in that weakness may lie the seed to destroy American democracy. In New Harmony, profiteers skimmed the economic gains, workers gave no support to Owen's progressive ideals, and the experiment failed to resist manipulations by various enterprises widening the divide in material prosperity.

But it is significant, even cause for hope, that the science—in particular, geology—brought in by the Boatload of Knowledge, has survived here thus far. And socially, the exemplars of Negro emancipation and woman suffrage continue. I asked Professor Wynch whether Rapp's experiment had too little liberty and

Owen's too much. The ancient paradox of the kite: no restraint, no flight.

He said, "Perhaps true, but more to the issue, the failures arise within the constitution of humanity. Two sentences identify the *poisonweed* in the garden of democracy: *I want that. This is mine.* To care not what we may achieve together, therein resides the heart of human suffering and corruption, with the resulting desire for illusions and distractions from our self-created condition."

6 July

This morning Professor Wynch spoke of having difficulties with a resident who had recently suffered a concussion in a carriage accident that killed her husband. Forty years old, Eleanor Evans, an English émigré, was a teacher and the director of the annual Shakespeare performance. In fact, rehearsal had recently begun for *King Lear*, Bronson playing the role of Gloucester. Although imperious at times, she was respected by her thespians. The calamity left her in a coma for a week, and when she came to, she awoke as another woman, one who believes her husband, the King, is touring the crowned heads of Europe, and she, his wife, thus a queen, is to maintain the throne while he is in absentia. With partial memory loss, her magisterial manner advanced to render her intractably opposed to the guidance of attendants in the infirmary, staff she now considers courtiers or servants. She resists bathing—an unusual response from one formerly well groomed—and she has begun complaining of dyspepsia. Wynch thought I might help.

In a parlor of the women's dormitory Mrs. Evans kept herself apart from five others, she in a large wing chair, her gaze sideward as if to avoid them. From across the chamber we observed her for a spell, Bronson informing Deems and me of her behavior before and following the accident. What had been a vigorous and personable woman was now one increasingly discomposed, principally when staff insisted she cease her fantasy about being queen. Eating little, she scarcely moved, sitting morosely, speaking only to make a command, at times throwing out vile execrations uncommon from a cultured lady, and a few days ago blacking the eye of a young attendant who told her to awaken to the reality she "weren't no damn queen." Wynch whispered, "In the words of Gloucester, grief hath crazed her wits."

The professor led Deems and me towards her. When he called her by name, she snapped, "There are four vowels in *Eleanor*! Pronounce each one! Now, be gone, you jackanapes!" He waved us forward to introduce me as a physician from England here on a tour of America. She glared from under a crownlet she had artfully woven from strips of newsprint and tattered ribbons and withered flowers. As I stepped up, she sat ready to snarl. I bowed deeply and pulled off my hat to sweep it elaborately across my ankles, and said, "Great is the honor to come before the Queen."

Rising from my bow, I saw on her a slow change of expression and on Wynch astonishment. She said, "Approach, young man, that the Queen may see you!" And so I did. Studying me, at length she said, "What is your business with the throne?"

"Your friend in England, perhaps unbeknown to you, the Duchess of Trennant, sends you her warmest regards. Learning of your recent, shall I say, *your recent feeling not quite yourself*, she has dispatched me to offer my medical expertise in matters abdominal and cranial. My specialty, Your Grace, is dyspepsia."

"You presume to examine the Queen?"

"Only if Her Highness perceives the wisdom of it."

As she scanned the room to see what plot might be developing, I indicated to Deems to bring in my medical bag and a book, any book. She commanded, "Proceed, physician."

I asked for consent to take her pulse. No longer scowling, she turned her face aside and extended her wrist. Her theatrical training had prepared her for this role. To give Deems opportunity to find a book, I proceeded slowly, temporizing by speaking of cures for dyspepsia—a vegetable diet, warm baths, a forbearant attitude towards others. As I did so, I examined her eyes, her pallor, noting a sourness of breath. When Deems returned, I introduced Crown Prince Nicodemus of Upper Abyssinia, who brings greetings from his father, long an admirer of the Queen. I said the Prince was studying medicine under my tutelage. Deems executed a fine bow. She said, "The Crown Prince is a handsome princeling, and I shall inform his father he well represents Abyssinia. And now, Doctor, the Queen awaits. She has not all day."

"May I listen to the Queen's heart?" I queried, and she sat erect for the stethoscope; then Deems brought a book for me to open and show her, holding it as if on a salver. On the first page was a variety of fonts. Would the Queen read the title? She glanced down, then looked up at me querulously, and said, "I need no promptbook to read a title from Mister Owen's hand. I know it and I knew him. *An Explanation of the Cause of the Distress which Pervades the Civilized Parts of the World.* Do you wish to learn a title of an earlier opus? *A Plan for Gradually Ameliorating the Condition of Mankind.* There! Has the Queen passed your intelligence test? And you, physician, are you able to ameliorate the condition of sorry mankind? Or that of your Queen?"

I explained the book was not an intelligence test but one for eyesight. Would she read the small print at the bottom of the page? Fortunately, this amused her into a smile, shocking Professor Wynch. Squinting, she read rapidly, "The profits of this edition will be given to the association for the relief of the manufacturing and labouring poor. 1816."

"What else, wise physician? Do you wish to learn secrets of Mister Owen's life? He was one whose ideas people here were then unprepared to serve. They were—*like all humanity*—inadequately equipped in heart and mind for utopia. They thought only of themselves."

A convalescent limped by, carrying on a dialogue with a presence unseen by us, and the Queen said, "Ignore her, Doctor. She's quite the lunatic."

7 July

When next I saw Professor Wynch he questioned my encouragement of her disorientation: Wasn't such an approach only leading her more deeply into confusion? I set forth my thoughts for Eleanor's treatment. Her vital signs are within normal limits and give her a sound physiological base for recovery. She is able to perceive mental aberration in others. In her case, I want to try conciliation and cooperation with the world she has been traumatized into. Sympathy, not strife. Not contention, but comfort. Bless her, don't cross her. Continual correction and denial of her perceptions appear to work adversely. Note that her imagined magisterial realm functions with a certain internal logic: Things make sense within it. Cows don't sing arias, and kings don't grow mushrooms in their ears. By seizing on the part of her internal logic matching ours, we might be able to introduce more of ours back into hers. Attempting forcefully to disabuse her intensifies fractures in her reason. Remind her of what she once clearly knew. Speak to her of the noble attributes of a queen. Give her fantasies opportunity to heal her untethering from reality.

He said, "Eleanor does appear calmer. And this morning, without resistance or abusing others, she accepted bathing."

On my following visit to her, she was in her wing chair, but her crown of wrinkled paper and faded flowers was on her lap. I greeted her with appropriate royal formality. During my examination she said nothing, until I asked how she felt on this day of splendid sunshine. She said crossly, "I live." Then in resignation, "As must we all for our assigned duration."

I nodded and inquired whether Her Majesty thought a constitutional in the fresh air of early summer would serve her. To such a notion she looked surprised, turned towards a window to ascertain the weather, then said she would accept the counsel from her physician, provided he would accompany her. I went below to arrange for a carriage to Rapp's famous Harmonist labyrinth just south of the village.

Mrs. Evans, stepping from the building, blinked in the sunlight as if seeing a new world but then noticed the carriage and recoiled, complaining, "There's something about those vehicles—" and shrank back. I reminded I would be at her side for the short distance. She drew herself to her full height and glared at the chaise, then turned the dormitory porch into a stage. She intoned,

> Does any here know me? This is not Lear.
> Does Lear walk thus? Speak thus? Where are his eyes?
> Either his notion weakens, or his discernings
> are lethargied. Sleeping or waking?
> Sure 'tis not so!
> Who is it that can tell me who I am?

With ceremony, as I had requested, the coachman helped her in; to keep watch, I took the seat across from her and drew her attention to the calm air. When we reached the labyrinth and she had descended, she studied the circling greenery to comment that the beech hedge is taller and less well tended than in Harmonist days, the nave now evident only by the roof of a tiny *templum* of stone.

Would Her Majesty care to enter the circuities? Said she, "I remember the route, so I'll let you direct us. The amusement here lies in ignorance of the path. The hedges will test you and reveal to me whether your physic is to be trusted. Whether our court physician can perceive the way in. And, of more significance, can discover *the way out*. In all things, to enter is easier than to exit. One can stumble into a beginning, but it's more difficult to fumble out of a conclusion."

I append a diagram.

Leading her slowly, I noted the dead-end alleys were slightly less worn, enabling me to follow the correct path. She talked of the Harmonist concept behind the labyrinthine design: A pilgrim moves along never knowing in certainty the route to one's destination—to the heart's desire. The strong, never quitting the path, continue, enduring intimidations of blind alleys, willing to retreat from a dead end, always ready to wind back whither one just was, ignoring failure, picking up again the trace until at last the pilgrim achieves the center. Harmonists considered the journey as perhaps the greatest and most common of spiritual motifs, an emblem suggesting time and space, departure and arrival, beginning and ending. For them, the labyrinth was a figure of progress into enlightenment and internal harmony.

Eleanor said, "Hand in hand, the King and I have often walked these hedge lines. In sunshine and moonlight. Darkness adds intrigue. Not one of its blocked alleys we haven't stumbled into. He'd pull me down alleys to kiss me. Or he'd go in ahead and wait for me, refusing to answer when I called. I'd be glad to find him sitting in the *templum*. I needn't continue to the conclusion of those romantic strolls. The good doctor may discern it on his own. And stars! They make the path truly cosmic. To divagate! To get lost! To look upward to gain an intimation of where we stand within the Universe!"

Once inside the *templum*, she became meditative, eventually saying, "It all seems like yesterday. I so miss the King." She was quiet again before saying, "Let us remain here a bit longer," and she touched my hand. Then, without being aware of it, she called me by his name: "Oh, Johnny, how the days fly!" She rose unsteadily, set her feet, and recited Lear's plea:

> Let me be not mad, not mad, sweet heaven!
> Keep me in temper. I would not be mad!

At what I thought an appropriate moment, I said, somewhat theatrically myself, "Your Majesty shall *not* be mad! She shall recover to direct the play and lead her actors onto the stage where they will deliver Shakespeare's sublime sentences to lift an audience towards awareness."

Again in the carriage, she asked the coachman to drive slowly that she might take in the blossoming, golden raintrees throughout the village and bask in the glow they reflected into the afternoon.

Wynch was on the dormitory porch to meet us as we alighted, and when she acknowledged him, he said, "We rejoice at Her Majesty's safe return."

Playing Lear's words for her audience of two, Eleanor declaimed,

> Thou shalt find that I'll resume the shape
> which thou dost think I have cast off forever.

8 July

Nicodemus discovered me seated under a small arbor behind the inn, where I was putting into my journal the events following Mrs. Evans's carriage accident. I read him the entry so he could evaluate my report; he said he did not quite understand my approach in treating her. "You deplored the mania and hallucinations at the camp meeting, but you encourage the illusions of Her Majesty. Why shouldn't the staff press on her to set her straight?"

I said her disorientation is probably a temporary response of a rational mind protecting itself from the pain of realizing her husband is dead. Perhaps her wits can never be returned into reason, but if not, delusion may allow her to live in less sorrow. What happened to her is incontestably real. Unlike the camp meeting, her disability is not concocted hysteria arising from beliefs lacking the slightest evidential proof.

Thinking, Deems said, "The invention of oppressive guilt demanding repentance for something a newborn has no hand in? Original sin?"

"Among other evidence-free fabrications passed down for three thousand years by a host of desert tribes having only recently begun using sticks to scratch words and numerals into mud. Missus Evans is not at a campground in a dark forest of fragmented minds transformed by self-evoked mortification. Sorrow worked up into self-indulgent mania perpetrated by self-anointed charlatans. She's a victim of physical injury. The source of her incapacity is possibly a lesion in her brain. A reality deserving medical treatment. *And* sympathy and tolerance. If her disharmonious mind can never be reset to equilibrium, by our leaving her wits unchallenged for now, she can live without continual discord. *Pseudological phantastica* is preferable to torment. At the least, she won't offend her company with royal body odor."

Deems *may* have considered my reply for a moment before blurting out, "I'm in love!" I said only, *Again?*

"She's in the village choir, the New Harmonists, they're called. I listened to them practicing. She's a contralto. Oh, her voice!"

"Tell me more."

"Some years back, an Abolitionist helped her escape a Tennessee farm to cross the Ohio River. She made it to the Wabash when Owen was still here. He assigned the school to teach her to read. Words *and* music."

"Then she's older than you?"

"I don't care."

"And now you want to stay on?"

"The choir leaves tomorrow for a concert tour. The whole damn state. I'm thinking—."

"Of your mother in Saint Louis?"

His brow pinched, and he left the arbor, not returning for an hour, only then to slump into a chair. Did his contralto reciprocate his interest? She was *nice* to him. Civility and physical desire, I suggested, should be distinguished from love. They are as a comma to an exclamation point. He responded with a rasping sound of annoyance. Said I, "Deems, you're hardly the first male to fall for a female voice. But nobody is her—or his—voice. The rest of the person comes attached."

In vexation, he said, "Well, then, let's get the hell on to Saint Louis. Damn it all!"

9 July

Gloom hung over sunrise and above a glum Nicodemus, who was more sullen than sad, his youthful inexperience evident; he spent the initial miles in the stage in silent study of his medical text, finally speaking to talk about digestion. After some time plugging westward beyond the Wabash River, he said, "For me, seeing Mama is of the highest order. I'm her only surviving child. I'm the only thing in life she can lay claim to. Whoever fathered me, he disappeared twenty-one or twenty-two years ago. His name was never spoken. If we find her, maybe I'll find other things. Maybe who I am."

"You have a good idea who you are, Deems, even if some of your antecedents are a mystery. No one ever knows more than a fractionalized fraction about our deep ancestry. Nobody needs a genealogical chart to be of service. You can live up to being a distant descendant of legendary African king Cuff by contributing to the good of others. Perhaps atone for some of the rascals we all have in our pedigree."

The early start and good road carried us expediently through further miles of almost faultless levelness, tilled fields of corn and oats and lesser grains; at about fifteen-mile intervals were settlements, most lacking enough structures to be termed villages and certainly not towns, each entirely dedicated to serving the economy of the plowshare.

Even without the monotony of row after row of crops, the stage would still have become naught but a load of numbed humanity, although I may have been the only one who regretted slipping off. I am in America not to drowse but to observe. In a rocking coach, watchfulness is a most difficult phase of my undertaking.

A wobbling wheel forced a brief halt in Carmi—pronounced to rhyme with "on high," which it wasn't. When a blacksmith examined the wheel, I heard him tell James, our coachman, in an American phrasing able to leave an Englishman baffled: "Jimmy boy, she's jist plumb outta fix."

Across the road was the Ratcliff Inn, the landlord's surname not well considered for a lodge, one nevertheless offering a nice cup of tea in a parlor where I took to an unmoving table to set down ideas for my speech. On Wynch's commendation I have been invited to address the medical college in Saint Louis. I asked Nicodemus would he contribute a few words on the need for education for Negroes. "I've never done—, I can't see," he fumbled. "I can't—."

I interrupted: "Can you try?"

Ten minutes later I noticed him at another desk, scratching his head, then scribbling. To urge him on, I showed him notes for my lecture:

New Harmony may be the smallest American village to have influenced the conscience and practice of democracy in the new nation. What could be more experimental in this grand experiment than the various tries at utopian communities New Harmony inspired? Both utopias on the Wabash—one religious and autocratic, the other secular and democratic—were courageous in facing criticism and mockery of their challenges to an established social order. Yet, questionings are natural to a young democracy enamored of invention. Few are the adjectives an American has greater admiration for than *new*. Nevertheless, the dozen or more utopian attempts in America to improve the human lot have labored to survive beyond the lifespan of a dickey bird.

Two such endeavors on the lower Wabash River, in spite of broad differences, failed that longevity test. The first was a religious autocracy created and directed by an uneducated immigrant who constructed his idealist vision from trees and soil and clay and administered it through a heavy dosing of scripture. But the leader, otherwise shrewd, failed to address a *deeper* nature—the inclinations resident in people granted the liberties of democracy.

The second essay fully embraced democracy from its inception, but it too largely collapsed, this time by trying to improve humanity and its creative life through scientific reasoning, acknowledgment of complete equality, and progressive methods of education.

In the end, Harmonie and its sequitur, New Harmony, foundered despite contributions they—especially the latter— made across America, each of brief duration because of what appears to be the impossibility of humans reining in self-interest. Visionaries tend to see humanity as perfectible, despite abundant evidence we are flawed creatures possessed in near equal measure of caring and cruelty, generosity and greed, intelligence and ignorance. Our innate nature threatens every societal and political order we dream up. Freely and continually, we engage in behavior endangering not just our happiness but our very existence. Such comportment is another definition of madness.

Until we invent a mechanical man, perfection should not be the basis of a social experiment. Until we can take tin-snips to clip out a metal heart, until we can power a brain with Mr. Faraday's electricity, perfection is not in our future. In its place, though, is something simpler and immediately possible—at least in theory: dedication to tolerance of our necessary and biologically inescapable dissimilarities, variations built into our behaviors that have created civilization. Even if an ideal fulfilled is unlikely or impossible, it need not be without point. It can serve as a continual reminder of our nobler potential.

Because species by their very nature *require* diversity in intelligence—both in type and degree—a failure to master and practice tolerance is ruinous to well-being. That flaw in humans allows our intellect to go astray and behave ignorant of our highest interests. Yet one more expression of mental disorientation.

Is it not an achievable goal for the architect to respond as neighbor to the quarryman and steeplejack? For the physician to honor the plumber? The Calvinist the Catholic? The Hebrew the Hindu? The fundamentalist the freethinker? And yes, a white a black?

The lower our compass of tolerance, the lower our compass of democracy. Democracy should not be considered an absolute but rather something measured by its *degree* of humane liberty. I have foreboding the current degree of American democracy may not be sustainable. Indications I have seen on my travels are quite equivocal. Of even greater import: If the durability of this new nation is in doubt, then what does the American experiment portend for the rest of the world?

9 July, mid morn

With the coach wheel jury-rigged and remounted, the notes for my talk organized, and my beloved colleague agreeing to address a border-state audience about the need for equal medical education for Negroes, we pegged on across southern Illinois, past yet even more forest clearings of chopped stumps, fire-blackened stumps, stumps pulled and piled for burning, all among standing trees awaiting those fates. Miles of oaks and locusts and elms being swapped out for cornstalks.

Speaking from his plantation experience, Deems said, "Only the rich can afford trees. If a farmer cuts an oak, he can sell it once. But a field of corn produces year after year to feed a family and its animals, with maybe enough left over to barter for a skillet."

Nicodemus had recovered his emotional equilibrium and wanted to talk about the search for his mother. "All I know," he said, "is the surname of her employer in a city of—what? Thirty thousand souls?"

I replied that his hope must be that Heckendorf is not a common surname there. He considered, then answered, "Since the chance to find her has come up, I'm going to be mighty low if I fail."

Tourists who report nothing to see on any particular route of wayfaring need to get their brain rattled awake, and the stage rattled us awake every mile, but still my eyes struggled to observe differences in a place providing little relief in its topography. The *size* of America is remaking my ideas about it: abundance of land requires abundance of imagination.

The county seat of Mount Vernon, Illinois is notable for lying only seventy-some miles from Mount Vernon, Indiana. American settlers have taken up the territory, naming their villages and towns as if obeying a federal statute enforcing dearth of imagination and paucity of toponyms. Each state need have a Springfield. (Can any resident of any Springfield direct a visitor to the field where the eponymous spring rises?) How many Salems are there? How many Washingtons, Jeffersons, Madisons? Without the precedent Indians and their colorfully multifarious names on the land, the nomenclature of America would be thin indeed.

As if to make the point, the road took us into Mascoutah, an Indian word for *prairie*, I was told. To this traveler, its name was the best part of a sorry and inhospitable village where a constable gave Nicodemus the evil eye and kept close watch on us. When we reboarded the stage, his surveillance reflected a crudely lettered sign at the edge of the hamlet:

NIGGER DONT LET THE SUN SET ON YOU HERE

Some towns are agreeable enough once they lie behind. In the instance at hand, even if the next village down the rough road should be labeled Hell-on-Earth, we wanted out of Mascoutah.

The next name was, however, Illinoistown, and it sat on the east bank of the Mississippi River, across from Saint Louis. Our wait for a ferry afforded opportunity to try to comprehend the river width, a genuine task for anyone accustomed to what the English term a river. The Mississippi is to the Thames above London—beyond the estuarine portion—as a mammoth to a marmot, a hippo to a hedgehog, and not just in measure but in genus, because the difference lies not simply in breadth but also in muscle: contending currents, waves and whirls, swells and swirls, bubblings and boilings, the opaque water moving drift trees every direction a compass can indicate as well as what a compass cannot show—verticality. For a fellow who grew up drinking from the streamlets of a Caribbean isle, the Mississippi truly belongs to a continent.

The coming additions of California and the Oregon Territory will make the great river a discernible and comprehensible demarcation between the mountains on the east and those to the

west. Americans will be wise to prevent such a natural division—
as markers of partition can do—from becoming a social divide
discriminating not simply West from East but citizen from citizen.
Around the globe, any town limit, any county line, any border can
operate as a place of contention. If human reproduction succeeds
by blurring lines of separation with each conception, should not we
so-called Masters of the Earth hesitate to erect artificial barriers
among us? After all, the human brain and heart are results of some
thousands of years of crossed borders.

The finest prospect in Illinoistown is from its levee across
the river towards Saint Louis. In the words of Nicodemus, "The
best view here is the view out of here." The long midsummer
light allowed us to reach the Mississippi in time to make the last
crossing before dark.

A two-horse ferry transported stenciled crates and barrels of
merchandise from the East: dishes, salt, saltpeter, scythes, nails,
spikes, hammers, knives, rifles, pencils, books. On the crammed
boat, we sat atop the tools of empire whilst the river of empire
flowed beneath us. There were also ten hogs aboard—those beasts
of empire we did not sit atop.

10 July

Saint Louis, founded only eighty years ago, has a well-laid levee of
cobblestones rising gradually to the commercial edge of the city,
an easy walk, although our destination was the medical college, a
mile farther west. We hailed a cab to take us and our equipage to
the administration office of George Hancock, who had proffered
the invitation to speak to students and staff. He greeted us and
suggested supper at a near dining room. (Do not remember
the name.)

My lecture will be three days hence. I laid before him my
thoughts on American utopias and mental health, adding I trusted
he would invite my intern to conclude the talk with a call for the

medical education of Negroes. He said, "You may not be aware of issues concerning Negroes in this city. Because of our location at a nexus of slave and free states, we're a magnet for blacks suing for freedom. Plaintiffs argue their claims of maternal Indian ancestry, or being freed by an Abolitionist, or having an established residence in a free state. One slave, Dred Scott, filed suit a few years back, and it's still not settled. Powerful whites here and elsewhere underwrite challenges to the Scott petition, and thus far they've been successful in thwarting it. One of those wealthy men opposed to Scott sits on our board, and that makes Mister Nicodemus addressing us a thorny issue."

My response, evenly delivered to Hancock: "I appreciate the invitation and its generous honorarium to address your students. But I'm forced to say, should my intern not also be permitted to speak, I must decline."

Visibly disquieted, Hancock thought before answering. "If you'll allow me till tomorrow, say, noon, I'll have time to try to stitch together this rent." Then to Nicodemus, "I believe your words ought to be heard, but please consider the state of society here. Only a few years ago, a Negro—a muscular mulatto named Frank McIntosh. He was arrested for interfering with police discharging their duty in calming an altercation among black residents. On his way to jail McIntosh pulled a hidden knife and managed to stab one of the officers before cutting the throat of an assisting officer, who fell dead on the spot. Much spilled blood."

Again Hancock stopped to let us absorb the grisly murder. Then he said, "McIntosh escaped but was soon recaptured. Within an hour several hundred whites gathered at the gory scene and were driven into a frenzy by men shouting that hanging was too good for McIntosh. When the constable's wife and children arrived and saw his corpse in a pool of blood, they began screaming. Incensing the mob into demanding frontier justice. The crowd moved to the jail and broke in and hauled McIntosh out to chain him to a tree.

They piled brush around his ankles and ignited the tinder. His legs burned to the bone, and flames opened his body. His entrails were hanging out, yet he was still alive. For twenty minutes he burned and begged. It happened only two blocks from where we are."

Deems said, "I haven't cut any throats."

"Indeed, but a black man lecturing whites is offensive, and then to espouse Negro education can alarm the recidivists who see Negro education as leading to emancipation, and that's a threat— *the* threat—to the cotton economy. Among other economies."

Hancock calculated how to continue. "What you're advocating is a volatile issue. Only six years ago four Negro men were hanged, decapitated, and their heads displayed in the window of Corse's druggist shop. That location is across the street from where we sit."

Deems, shaking his head, asked, "How in God's name, did we ever get to this place?"

Hancock: "Who's 'we'? And what's 'this place'?"

"'We' is America, and 'this place' is now."

"I should not think," said George, "God has overmuch to do with it."

A strained silence until Hancock said to me, "If your decision is to press forward, I'll uphold your position."

Again on the street, Nicodemus answered Hancock, "If the medical college invites me to speak along with Doctor Trennant, I will. Briefly. Circumspectly."

11 July

Deems spent a restless night, hanging as he was between a speech on a dangerous topic and concern about finding his mother. At breakfast, as he added milk to his coffee, he said, "Oh no! Look at this!" The milk floating in his coffee formed a discernible death's head. "It's a sign about Mama," he whispered. "Or maybe the lecture. I'm being warned. Something bad's afoot."

I was slow to realize he was not jesting.

"Nicodemus, you're becoming a man of science. A man to hold the line against pernicious folklore. Unfog your mind! Start by drinking your coffee so your stomach can remedy your brain. Send your bugaboo into your bladder! Micturate your superstition!"

He took such a gulp he choked, then cleared his throat to down the remainder. "There!" he said. "It's done! I mean the skull. Bury me facing sunrise."

We left the hotel to find a city directory in the county offices. Standing side by side to read a long column of names, we noted six Heckendorfs. Many residences lie near the commercial area, allowing us to walk to three of the addresses. We discussed strategy. How to avoid arousing wariness? Should inquiry come from him or me? A Negro or a Caucasian? Our conclusion, less than foolproof, was the best we could think up: if a black answered, he would inquire; if a white, I would.

At the first Heckendorf, an attractive Negro girl, wearing a spotlessly white apron, answered. She seemed surprised by well-appointed Herr Nicodemus in his chapeau and gave him a coy curtsy. *Oh no*, I thought, *he's going to fall in love again.* She said the family had no other female *help.* As we stepped away, with a second curtsy she said to him, "Call tomorra night! *If* you wants to visit us."

The neighborhood rose in affluence the farther west we went, and at the second house, a Negro butler answered and barked at Deems and told him to move on before he—something or other. At the third residence, a white maid opened the door. I spoke what Deems and I had fabricated: "Madame, I'm with the medical college. I'm inquiring after a Negro woman who cared for me some years ago. My medical practice has provided me with circumstances allowing me to express a gift of gratitude to the goodly woman. Her name is Patsey."

The maid said I could pass the gift to her and she would see to it. I answered I couldn't do that, but I was prepared to leave a gratuity to whoever would lead me to Patsey. "How much?" she asked. I said I would need to ascertain I had found the *right* Patsey. She excused herself and closed the door.

In a few moments a lady appeared—Frau Heckendorf I presumed from her attire and German accent. She appraised me and Deems, then said, "Herr Doktor, vee *do* have a Patsey here. You are please to enter." She showed us into a parlor. Nicodemus fidgeted between anticipation and foreboding. There came a tap on the door and a Negro woman, quite aged, stepped in and at seeing us excused herself. Deems, disconsolately, said, "Not her. Not Mama." He was crestfallen. As we prepared to depart, a second knock, and Frau Heckendorf appeared, turned aside and said to someone, "You may enter."

Coming forward discreetly was a black woman in late middle years, who looked first at me, then to Deems, only to retreat as if alarmed. I introduced myself, but she did not take her eyes off Nicodemus, nor he his from her. She started to speak but stopped abruptly and covered her mouth. Slowly she said, "I know you. You be older now, but I *know* you."

He said, "It's me, Mama. Your boy."

"Land o' Goshen, chile! Deems! Oh, my chile!"

He went to her, put his arms around her, and she wept quietly, saying, "Lordy, Lordy! Praise the Lord! I'm reborn!"

I moved to leave, but he called me back and said, "Meet Mama." I bowed and reached to shake her hand, trembling as it was. Having no idea how to address her, I said, "Miss Patsey, a great pleasure." I offered my arm to Frau Heckendorf, and we left the room, and I made for the college to convene with George Hancock, whom I found in his office.

"Doctor," he began, "I've negotiated an accommodation—a strange one, to be sure, but it can allow your intern to speak for a few moments. The invitation is fortuitous *if* conditional. A quid pro quo from the resistant board member. Shall I continue?"

What Hancock proposed is this: Not far from the Mississippi shore of Illinoistown is a wooded island considered to be under no certain jurisdiction of either state. For that reason it is a dueling ground. A challenge has been accepted for this afternoon, and the duel needs a physician.

I waited for him to finish, but that was it. I said, "Are you suggesting I must witness the murder of a white man in order for a black man to be permitted to address a white audience? About education? At a medical college? This is madness!"

"You mistake me. One of the duelists is a man resisting your demand to have a young Negro tell us what we should do. *But*, he will give assent if you agree to serve as physician. Realize, the duel will be fought with or without you. A doctor present may save a life."

I walked to the window and stood there watching a bird. *How easy it must be to live as a pigeon.* A potential to save a life leading to a potential to open minds to universal education. I accepted— *provided* my intern would be allowed to assist me. Hancock said, "All is agreed then. A skiff will be at the levee at four o'clock to take you both to the appointment."

"What's the name of this odious place?"

"Bloody Island."

"The opponents?"

"Alderman Simon Stengel."

"And the other?"

"Ambrose Lort. Our board member."

The 11th inst.

On my return to our quarters, I found Nicodemus lying across a bed and reading a sheaf of papers. He said, "When you have the chance, you might be interested in these pages."

"From your mother?"

"She's not my mother. But then again, she is my mother. She said I was her *beloved boy*, but she isn't my mother."

"I'd like to comprehend perfectly what I don't understand at all."

"She's my mother's sister. Mama died three months after my birth. Patsey was childless. She'd been caring for my mother in her sickness, so Patsey made me her own and was allowed to keep me. When I was a boy there was talk about it, but I assumed people were trying to disparage me. I didn't believe them. Why should I? There could be no better mother than Patsey."

"How do you feel now?"

"She's the only mother I've known. There are more ways to motherhood than birthing." He rose, put an arm around me, and said, "Now I have a greater family than I had the night I ran away from the Reilly plantation. If Ferrall shoots me down tomorrow, I'll die happy I had freedom to learn a truth and find a friend."

I was reluctant to say it: "Speaking of shooting, I'm due in twenty minutes to attend a duel."

"Ye gods! What's happening here?"

"I need you to come with me."

"A day like this gets only *more* like this."

"You're right," I said. "One of the duelists is the racist board member." I explained the quid pro quo.

Walking to the levee, Deems told me the Heckendorfs treated Patsey fairly, even purchasing her a burial plot next to a friend in a colored cemetery. Viewing her resting place, she feels peace of mind, and seeing her boy again, she considers her life well lived. How fine to learn the child she had striven to raise properly—the one she had coaxed the plantation mistress to take into the house and clothe and educate to give him a chance beyond the poverty of slavery—wanted to become a doctor!

Although Patsey's vision no longer allows her to read, she wants him to send letters Frau Heckendorf will read to her. If she knows where her boy is traveling, Patsey will ask the mistress to write to him in return. I inquired about his father.

Deems said, "He was a field hand from a neighboring plantation. Got sold in Baltimore, and never seen again. All Mama knew was he had beautiful teeth and was too wise for his own good."

The 11th (continued)

Hancock, serving as Ambrose Lort's second, waited at the skiff to accompany us to Bloody Island. He carried a brace of dueling pistols purchased for this wretched occasion of settling a dispute over human bondage that degenerated into whether God countenances slavery. At that point, name calling began and two adjectives—*chuckleheaded* and *beef-brained*—triggered the challenge. Deems said, "A man is going to die over adjectives?"

"Don't forget God's outlook on abolition," I said.

When Hancock used the phrase *field of honor*, Deems said, "I'd term it a field of humiliation."

Hancock snapped, "Please! Within earshot of Ambrose Lort, watch your words!" As we crossed the Mississippi, George spoke about events in the history of Bloody Island: Most duels there end in a wounding rather than a death, especially those with an attending physician. Because the Code Duello requires seconds to try to mediate conflict, some duels conclude with a truce.

The most famous contest on the island involved Senator Thomas Hart Benton of Missouri, who only a few years ago fought two separate duels with the same opponent, killing him the second go-round. But the bloodiest was a duel involving a severely nearsighted man who, as the one challenged, had the right to choose weapons and distance: he called for pistols at five feet. The score settled by both men dying.

But the most peculiar duel, said Hancock, was a recent one in which the outcome was neither a wounding nor a death. A young Illinois lawyer and legislator, named Lincoln, had mocked and criticized in print a political opponent, James Shields, who responded with a challenge. The lawyer, a veteran of the Indian wars, chose cavalry sabers. At well over six feet, his height and reach gave him an advantage over a man a half foot shorter. As the duel was about to begin, Lincoln lifted his blade and lopped off a tree branch, giving pause to Shields and time for the seconds to intercede and discuss a modus vivendi. The duelists ended up leaving, unbloodied and with all appendages still attached.

Not far from the lapping of the Mississippi, Lort and Stengel counseled with their seconds, both of whom recommended a truce. The contestants declined, and Hancock motioned us to the dueling ground where the men took positions twelve yards apart. At the signal, they raised pistols and fired.

One slumped to his knees, the other fell backward, each stifling groans. I sent Deems to the kneeling man, Lort, and I examined the alderman. The bullet had penetrated his thigh, fortunately missing his femur and femoral artery, but remained in the flesh to limit hemorrhage. Not so with Lort whose grazed temple was, as such wounds will, bleeding profusely. With a compress from my bag, Deems stanched the flow. Having only a single litter, the seconds first carried Stengel to the skiff before quickly returning to tote Lort. In the bottom of the boat, we laid traducer shoulder to shoulder with calumniator. The Negro ferryman shook his head—not in sympathy, I think, but at what he saw as the lethal stupidity of white men. With both duelists stable, Nicodemus said, "Tell me, gentlemen, have we settled whether or not God sanctions slavery?"

Once again in Saint Louis, with considerable dispatch we transported the duelists to the city hospital where a surgeon removed the bullet from Stengel's leg and I put a fresh bandage on Lort's wound. As I did, he thanked me for the field treatment. I said, "Perhaps shock from the injury erased your memory of the event, but it was not I who stanched the bleeding. It was a young Negro whose black hands saved your white life. That same man will speak tonight on the need for medical education without regard to race."

Leaving the hospital, Deems asked whether dueling occurs in England. I said that bequeathals from the mother country are great but not without impediments. He scowled. I digest what I said:

In an aristocracy, the goal of a duel is preservation of a social order. Upholding a class system. Acceptance of hierarchy is necessary to privilege. Duels help maintain rank. In American democracy where class is largely an economic expression available to any who have money to rise—or lose it and fall—a duel can be more a pique attached to a mind wanting to teach a man a lesson. When perceived equality of station is the rule, a pistol becomes the enforcer of choice.

Deems scoffed. "So the purpose of American dueling is to open a hole in a man and expose flaws of his inner character?"

"A duelist anywhere is a man of conceit who takes it upon himself to determine another's lifespan."

Nicodemus went off to visit Patsey, bringing her a bouquet from a street cart, and I stopped in a bank to draw once more upon my letter of credit, then on to the post office to send Sophie my long missive written here and there over the past days. To my joy, awaiting me in general delivery was a letter saying she and the Hunt children were recovering from the Russian fever; she wished I could have been the doctor treating them.

I wrote a note advising not to leave a fever-bed too soon and that I would check with the post office at Fort Leavenworth for a letter from her. I regretted my western journey increasing— not lessening—the distance between us, but reason cautioned me against expressing too quickly endeavors of the heart. Yet it is true: not since stepping off the *Narwhale* had I questioned my dedication to exploring the grand American experiment. When I saw Deems, I asked him to discourage any weakening in my resolve to continue he noticed in me. Sophie might be flattered by the strength of her allure, but I doubt she would respect a man unable to keep a commitment.

I wandered off to the college to observe two classes: the first a lecture about rheumatism and the second (joined by Deems) on vertebrate physiology. Watching his eagerness in pursuing his goal—instead of falling in love with the pretty woman seated in front of us—bolstered my drooping determination to continue. I owe my perseverance to him.

Still, his example was not enough that night to ward off my pursuing phantom. As usual, I smelt her favored scent coming from the dark miasma enveloping her, but this time at her side she carried a knife. The image startled me upright, which startled Nicodemus awake. He said, "Again?" I needed not answer. "Maybe she's not in pursuit of you," he said. "Maybe she wants to cut the throats of your thoughts about Sophie."

"Thoughts have throats?"

"How else could they talk to us? By the way, wasn't I recently warned about hobgoblins? So who treats the physician?"

12 July

This morning I told Deems I would like to read the papers Patsey gave him. I append several below. The yellowed pages are sequentially numbered, and the handwriting is legible if unpracticed.

THIS BE MY STORY

1

my name be patsey. lord knows how old i be. i dont know. lord he dont tell me. it be said i be born when general washington be president. one time mama seen him ridin his horse of a morn. right by the plantation. she pick me up and she say look baby. there be the president. wave your

arm at him. so i done wove it. us coloreds was own by the
chetwin family on their plantation. in virginia. tobacco.
they own about thirty coloreds. marster chetwin be a
lawyer. white folks obey him. so did us. he was good to his
coloreds. the missus she was good too but that dont mean
she wouldnt slap you down. but she never put a whip on
me. exceptin once. she teach me what stealin meant after i
took a gingerbread boy offen a kitchen tray. he was in the
winda coolin down. i dint want to eat him. i want him to
be my doll. he be brown. big dark eyes like mine. they was
raisins. i give him a kiss and done broke his head off. then
his arms went to fallin off. so i had to eat him. that be how
i got caught. gingerbread on my lips. but she never whip
hard cause she took to me and that be why she teach me the
alphabet. she knowin all along teachin me against the law.
teachin a colored to read. or do numbers. i wasnt no good at
numbers but i could read natural like a bird sing. she teach
me to spell rhythm. and contumacious. she say that be me.
and conglomeration. that word missus teach me so i could
swank in front of white folks come to visit. she tell me to
stand and say welcome folks to our humble home. what a
excellent conglomeration we have here tonight. another she
teach me be obsequious. she say for me not be obsequious.

2

they was a man from down at the flanders plantation. he
come see mama on christmas. and easter. he be a overseer.
mama be pretty and of light skin color so gentlemens pay
her attention. black or white it dont matter. but he be not
my pappy so peoples ask who be my pappy and i just say
a ol turky buzzard lay me in a egg in a field over across the
river and the sun hatch me out. then peoples leave it be.
they see i grow up mostly as good as anybody in the county.

white folks dont always know black folks have rules just for
themselfs. if a black man hits his wife white peoples dont
give a hoot. but if he do hit her then he better have a reason
or the colored preacher get on him. or maybe her brother.
i never seen no black man take the lash to another black
man. they uses fists. once in the field a black man he took a
knife to a mean black man and for that there be a whippin
for both. the whippin for puttin slaves lifes in danger. a dead
slave be loss of property. death cost marster money. when
mamas baby after me die she bury baby boy in the colored
corner. next year on his birthday as best she could figure it
without no calendar she set a rock on his grave. for twelve
months she hunt up a proper rock. one she find be round
like a baby head and she scratch two eyes and a smile on the
rock. baby never had no name. just baby. she know baby was
goin to die cause a week before the birthin a ol owl flown
over the cabin and that be a sure sign death on the way. that
be why a owl hoots at night. he be sayin to somebody get
ready a grave. death acomin.

3

marster chetwin he keep us in cabins we call huts and they
all was built better than on other plantations. they was line
up and had board floors and chimleys but most of all they
had beds we build for ourselfs. every fall and spring i tote
my tick sack out to the woods and cram it with fresh pine
needles that smell so good for a while. i had nice dreams in
the spring and fall but sometime a dry needle poke through
and stick me in my behind. momma use to bake ash cakes.
made with cornmeal. salt and water. and i think lard if we
had it. she pat them out round. then she rake up coals in the
fireplace and set the cakes on the hot bricks. when cakes be
cookt she put hot ashes on top. when they nice and brown

she brush away ashes. nothin she cook up for us was gooder then her ash cakes. but i never seen no white chiles like one. they just spit them out. momma say white people cant taste as good as colored folk. they tongues be not right cause of cussin at black peoples. the lord be a good man cause he dole out punishment for those not lovin thy neighbor. they on the road to whats below preacher say. one of my tasks when i was a girl chile was gettin missus little folks to bed. they had to have a story tolt so i learnt to make somethin up. the favorite be about the ugly oger who live in the chifforobe. it be so frightsome i be warn not to tell it again. except the chiles beg for it so i trade a secret tellin for decent behavor. that seem fair to all.

4

if a slave come down sick missus had three kinds of medicine for a cure. one be call vinegar nail. one be rosin pills and one be tar. vinegar nail for aches in the stomach. she make it buy droppin a pound of iron nails into a jug of vinegar and shakin it then lettin it set. on a sick night she give us two rosin pills. raw pine rosin rolled in a ball and dunk in molasses. for tooth ache or ear ache she fix a bad tooth or a ear with warm pine tar. all the girls and boys wore shirt tails until about sixteen. it was a long frock come down to the knees. even in winter time we never have but one garment. it was cotton or flax wove on a loom kept goin year round. we et twice a day. sunup and sundown. work hands et in the huts but the colored chiles sometime be aloud to carry our gourd bowls to the big kitchen to get filled with cabbage soup. or bean soups. some such. special times we be aloud to go to the table after white folks done et and snatch pieces of bread left there. we use wooden spoons. food be not the best eatin but it was enough to get us growed till

we could do real work. or be hired out. i had a pet. a ol mud
turtle name vernon. he come crawlin out from under our
hut one morn like he showin up just to say hey. he was too
lazy to run off. fixins was too easy. suet. and boy howdy did
he put hog lard away. i dint much like collards but he did so
we be a good match till somebody stolt him. probably for a
soup pot. that be his reward for growin too fat. i miss him. i
never did fine another mud turtle.

5

when i turn nineteen. maybe twenty. marster he hire on a
new overseer. white man. forty some years old. he act the
gentleman in front of missus and marster. obsequious.
but around us he be crafty roughneck and he turn stormy
without no warnin. he missin one ear bit off in fight. even
feel hands done stay clear of him. his name mike baines. i
was attach to the house so how i gone keep out of his way?
when he pass by me he whisper unclean things to me. he
smell of liquor. i dint know where to turn for protection.
i got no brothers and the house need him more than me.
cause i had some looks to me and i had development he
never miss a chance when he caught me alone to whisper in
my ear unclean words. and times he say to me hows it my
little nigga girl get so uppity? i dint know how to protect
myself. one morn i had to help in the pig lot and then i
know. that night i fill a old medicine bottle out of a pool
of pig piss. when next i see overseer man comin on i toss
stink on my garment. he dont care none. he still whisper
at me. mama she know about him but she have no place to
do nothin. he say he gone tell marster to sell my boy deems
down river. my little cuff. down river. i pray for somebody to
catch monster man in the woods and leave a knife deep up
in his ribs where his heart beat. some day

12 July, evening

Tonight I asked Deems about the abrupt ending to Patsey's account. Here is the story she told him:

One afternoon she was sent out to the old, rat-infested barn to fetch a harness. She came upon Baines, who shoved her into a horse stall and tore her shirttail. Cussing her for being uppity, he said she needed a lesson, and undid his belt and hit her across the legs. Then he popped a loose board from the stall and pulled out a quart of rum stashed behind, and took a big swig, all the while eyeing the terrified girl lying at his feet. With the toe of his boot, he lifted her shirttail so he could see what was exposed beneath. He began to undo his britches.

About that time Chetwin entered the barn and yelled for Baines to saddle up his horse for him. Patsey jumped up and ran, but she kept silent about what had happened. The next day Chetwin and Baines went off to a cattle auction, and she returned to the stall. In her hand was a box of rat poison used on barn rodents. From its hiding place, she removed the bottle of black rum and poured in a measure of powder and shook it vigorously before replacing it behind the boards.

Two days later Baines was found dead in the very stall where he had assaulted her. Beside him was an empty liquor bottle. His pants were down around his ankles, and it was *assumed* vigorous self-abuse caused his heart to fail. He was buried without a Christian ceremony.

Understanding a finish to the fifth page of her autobiography would be a warrant for her death, Patsey never finished her pages. Now, with her beloved son as confessor, she has come clean, and when her final hour arrives she can pass peacefully and be laid to rest in the colored cemetery, her headstone carrying a carved cross.

13 July

Soon after morning light, George Hancock appeared at the hotel to take us across the Mississippi to Illinoistown and on to the ancient earthwork called the Great Mound or Monks Mound. Saint Louis is known as "Mound City," and indeed its environs are sprinkled with multitudes of earthen structures of indeterminate age, but all certainly constructed before the arrival of the earliest Europeans in this area, perhaps a thousand years before. The mounds are commonly shaped into conical hills or rectangular platforms or linear ridges. The number of them raises the question, Why are so many clustered here?

For some reason, this location near the middle of America once had a larger geographical and spiritual meaning, but how could those people know they lived at the center? Did they comprehend the distances to the eastern and western oceans? George pointed out that the key structures—called "heathen hills" by doubters with a biblical persuasion—lie within a radius of the heart of the city of no more than a dozen miles. Other than all the gigantically heaped-up earth, the ancients left behind few answers. But a current map of the territory suggests a most plausible solution: within that radius is the conjunction of the two longest rivers in America, the more than five thousand miles of the Mississippi and Missouri. And only twenty miles beyond is the mouth of another major river—if lesser in length—the Illinois. Only a hundred twenty miles south the nine hundred miles of the Ohio join the Mississippi.

Amidst the continental cordilleras of the Appalachian and the Rocky mountains, in America there is no other confluence of equivalent magnitude: the earthworks are here because a grand congregation of waters is here. Like the ribbons around a package, these four rivers join to carry the largest portion of rain falling between the massive parallel mountain ranges. That means the giant mound on the banks of Cahokia Creek sits at the hydrological heart of America.

And yet, in their frequent indifference to the past, whether human or natural history, Americans pay Cahokia no respect. Hancock said, "You'll see what ought to be the location of a grand monument to identify and honor the site of the first city in what is now the United States. North of the Rio Grande, no other edifice can compare, and still the earthworks in Saint Louis suffer from a dedication to level them for commercial endeavors that could be set down almost anywhere else."

Guiding us to narrow Cahokia Creek, delineated by its wooded margin, he led the way towards some several mounds of varied configuration and size. The soil here being entirely alluvial, *any* noticeably raised structure is without doubt from human hands. Along the bank of the creek we came upon a truncated mound I can describe only as *unexpectedly stupendous*. Its domination of land and sky a millennium ago would have been even more overpowering. In general outline it is a trapezoid reaching upward nearly a hundred feet. Slopes on the south and west sides are interrupted by level aprons, the one southward showing a less declivitous slant and giving the appearance of a ramp leading in two segments to the top. I paced off the circumference of the base and found it to be close to the measure I took last year of the great Egyptian pyramid west of Cairo. The volume of this Cahokian mound I estimate to be commensurate. (I append my quick sketch of it.)

Our climb up the ramp was rigorous, but once on top I counted forty other, much smaller earthen structures proximate to the grand mound, their locations made apparent by overgrowth. The regularity of placement indicates a definite plan for what was formerly a populous settlement deserving the term *prehistoric city*. Yet, said Hancock, a few visitors believe the mounds are a result of differential erosions of the Mississippi alluvium, an explanation free of hydrological science, and manifestly preposterous. Others, believing the aboriginals incapable of the constructions, say the work was done by Persians or Hindus or Tartars or Greeks or Romans or Vikings or a lost tribe of Israelites. Such denial of Indian capacities supports the notion attached to the imperium of conquest holding that native peoples have no current claim to these lands.

From the top of the Great Mound, the bluffs marking the changeable course of the Mississippi over the eons are quite visible although several miles distant. Below us on the first terrace of the structure itself, were a couple of collapsing frame buildings, one the remnants of a chapel built by Trappist monks to serve not white settlers but the Cahokian Indians. Hancock said the purpose of the monastery had been to evangelize among the natives with the goal of converting them to support French dominion in America, thereby obstructing British influence. The effort—more imperialistic than religious—failed soon enough.

As we started down to ground level, I was overwhelmed by questions: How much time and how many baskets of soil carried by how many humans had this colossal structure required? What kind of political system had coordinated a population and kept it at labor for generations? Above all, what was the motivation to build it?

The monumental work lends credence to the truth of the intelligence of indigenous peoples, whose claims to sovereignty are continually assailed. Citizens can believe Joshua made the sun and moon stand still for a day, but they are reluctant to credit Indians for having built the great Cahokian mound.

Residents here routinely raze ancient earthworks. Mounds of prodigious size disappear to make way for fashioners of silk hats and peddlers of teapots and sellers of turnips. In this nation, to look back is to think backwardly, leaving Americans to think on the riches of tomorrow, thereby denying themselves awareness of a past deep in riches of a different sort, a wealth of perceptions that could guide them.

To stand under a night sky atop the Great Mound and perpend what primitive incantations and mummeries might have been recited atop it, what talk of polity and religion, what stories to explain the meaning of human existence—such contemplation can give bearings to a life, to a nation. But in the American mind, the past is naught but a useless land of the dead. Unless the past is printed as holy writ.

13 July, evening

At supper, Hancock reminded me of Charles Dickens's account in *American Notes* of the author's recent excursion to the Great Mound:

> Looming in the distance, as we rode along, was another of the ancient Indian burial-places, called The Monks Mound in memory of a body of fanatics of the order of La Trappe, who founded a desolate convent there many years ago, when there were no settlers within a thousand miles, and were all swept off by the pernicious climate: in which lamentable fatality, a few rational people will suppose, perhaps, that society experienced any very severe deprivation.

This single, if long, sentence is the *entire* response Dickens made to the unmatched construction. Hancock averred that *no* part of that paragraph is correct. The function of the mound, said he, is not primarily, if at all, for burials. Trappists I have met, said I, despite my not sharing their views, deserve not the term *fanatics*. And the word *convent*, Hancock commented, properly belongs to an order of nuns, not monks. Further, the hundreds of whites now living near Cahokia Creek prove false the idea of a "pernicious climate." Yet the celebrated author passes on these distortions.

Dickens traveled America with his wife and her maid as well as his male secretary—none of whom appear in his book. Aloof and insular, his entourage moved through the country as if constrained within a windowless coach with a stuck door they were loath to pry open. When he did step out and happen upon an American, too commonly he turned the encounter, in the book, into clumsy satire and vain attempts to represent American speech. He generalizes from the smallest detail, but only if it reflects negatively on the country. As a boy might filch a plum from a pudding, Dickens plucks an item here and there, swallows it without truly tasting, and stays not to partake of the whole dish.

The only portion of his book evincing genuine interest in penetrating the sentiments of the nation lie in three visits: to an orphanage, another to an asylum, and one to a prison. Of the ordinary citizens he meets along the way, Dickens presents American men as slow-witted and incapable of articulate expression. And, to his eye, whilst American women are *uncommonly pretty*, they too are unburdened by ideas and lack informed articulation. Of woman suffrage, he is silent.

And what of the indigenous residents? His lone Indian is a man he comes upon in the grand saloon of a steamboat. The writer's understanding of Indians fails by an unbridgeable margin to match what he gives to a white thief, a deranged white wife-beater, or a physically disadvantaged white child. For him, it is as if the disparaging, discrediting, disrupting, and dispossessing of aboriginals in America does not exist. The result is an Englishman who travels best when seated in a hotel room where he can allow assumptions and imagination to do his legwork.

By frequent echoes of pejoratives from Frances Trollope, his report intimates Dickens read her *Domestic Manners of the Americans*, yet he seems innocent of Tocqueville's considerably more cogent and informed *Democracy in America*.

Once returned to the safety of his chamber at home, Dickens laments the cruelty of American slavery, but nowhere during his six-month journey into the States does he report a conversation with a Negro slave or a freedman. Did he never meet either a slaveholder or slave hunter? An Abolitionist? His comments on slavery he cribs from an abolition tract, *American Slavery as It Is*, but uses it only as an afterthought to a chapter compiled in England. Most damning is his refusal to mention the dominant role English slavers and settlers played in establishing in the new land an economy and social order based on human bondage. American slavery is a British gift.

14 July

The morning of our departure from Saint Louis came on clear and mild after a storming night flushed the streets of the stench of quadruped ordure. George Hancock, of whom we have become fond, unexpectedly joined us for breakfast, and offered accompaniment to the levee and our westward-bound boat, the *Osage*, a name appropriate given the number of that tribe we have seen in this city, many of whom are engaged in the fur trade of the Missouri River country.

Before we embarked, he presented Nicodemus with an elegantly wrapped package. Inscribed on the flyleaf of *A Physician's Guide to Common Ailments* was thanks for his words encouraging Negro medical education, a proposal generally well received. (No more than a half dozen whites walked out.) Deems was moved by the inscription from Hancock.

To the time when people of any color or creed
may enter the halls of Hippocrates to learn
the alleviation of human suffering.

Tucked within the *Physician's Guide* was an envelope containing a hundred-dollar bill and a note:

Thank you. —A. B. Lort.

A surprised Nicodemus murmured, "Maybe I should set up a practice on Bloody Island to close wounds and open minds."

Hancock said to him, "Have you the interest, we may be able to find an enrollment for you in our college. I can't promise what will happen, but I *can* promise I'll try to *make* it happen."

As for my talk, reception was modest, with one commentator complaining I danced along the edge of *nullifidian godlessness*. (Perhaps his definition of God could be larger.)

We outfitted ourselves in new duds. Deems selected another chapeau carrying a loud message of *Look at me!* I said, "Does a smart peacock announce his presence among foxes?" He put the hat down, and we boarded the *Osage*. I asked were he ready for the American West. Answered he: "Ready, willing, and able! Said the match to the tinder."

Like horses waiting at a hitching-rail were thirty boats nosed in towards the levee, and it took us nearly the length of the paving to reach the *Osage*. She is, I must say, not just a tub but a *decrepit* tub, although her pedigree is an honored one: the *claim* is she is sister to the doughty *Omega*, the steamboat that carried the great naturalist—born a man of the Caribbees—John James Audubon up the Missouri in search of animals for his illustrious book *Quadrupeds of North America*. Only four years ago, Audubon left this very levee, and he managed to survive *his* version of a floating powder-mill. May we emulate his success!

In place of Bristol fashion, the *Osage* has history, character, and compact maneuverability appropriate to the sharp switchbacks and narrow channels of the Missouri. I felt immediate affection for her as well as hope she would not (our bunks situated directly above the high-pressure boilers) blow us to Abraham's bosom, not an unusual fate for a steamboat, especially one contending with the Big Muddy.

From the far end of the levee, the mouth of the Missouri lies less than twenty miles upstream. Had the surface geology up there been of rock, as is the riverbank in Saint Louis, the city would have been built at the juncture of two gigantic rivers in the manner of Pittsburgh. Of all the waters contributory to the Mississippi, the Missouri is by much the most significant, its power fully capable of stealing the character of the Mississippi and transforming it into its own. Through force of speed, color, current, and numerous deadfalls, the Mississippi south of the confluence is so the child of the unbridled Missouri some geographers say that below the juncture the river should be called the Missouri.

At the convergence, water pouring out of the west whacked the *Osage* and made her labor, our boilers under noticeably increased strain to overcome the downstream afflux. In this early season, the chaos of currents surpassed those of the Mississippi, further evidence of the western river being greater than a mere tributary. Since the waters of the world are one, to give separate identities is of more use to a cartographer than a hydrographer or traveler. Within the first mile of the Missouri, I was sensible of civilization slipping away and all of wild America opening ahead. As thrilling as intimidating.

The *Osage* is a side-wheeler, but Missouri River captains often prefer the narrower beam of a stern-wheeler to maneuver around impediments almost beyond enumerating: shoals, boils, whirlpools, ice floes, sandbars, gravel bars, snags, sawyers, eddies able to spin a boat like a dreidel, and swiftly moving fallen trees—many still in leaf while trunks of others are bleached from age and thick with wickedly sharp branchings ready to break any hull challenging their native authority. A downstream boat is at risk because of its speed of descent, and one bound *upstream* is in danger from the speed of descent of driftwood.

The contrariness of the Missouri is evident even in its variations of flow, perhaps nowhere more obvious than in the illogic of a large snag carried upstream on one of the peculiar opposing currents. Such contradictory motions, often surging along the shore, were capably employed by Captain Meriwether Lewis only forty-some years ago to assist crewmen laboriously towing their cumbersome keelboat upriver.

These dilemmas—including the force of the Missouri freshets and floods—are typical of this river antagonistic in most of its phases: perverse where it is not adverse, flowing east when not running west, moving calmly until it moves with violence as if suddenly enraged. A calamity avoided is little more than a catastrophe promised. The voice of its silent power is the thump and clunk of floating cottonwoods and sycamores mingled with the screech and scratch of cedars against the hull. At first these sounds are unsettling, but for a traveler of stalwart spirit—and confidence in the pilot—the noises become simply aspects of a day on the Missouri. So I am told. Nevertheless, to spot a snubbing tree and tie up for a spell will come as relief.

For a better look at what was rolling towards us, Nicodemus and I climbed to the hurricane deck. The varying agitations of the Missouri, stirred by no visible cause, are actions perceivable only through imagination. I wanted to view its underbelly to fathom the unfathomable, to see it *truly* because the source of its machinations is hidden beneath its occluded body. To observe the surface kicking along, shaking entire sycamores as a canine does a jawed snake, is to glimpse only its hide: underneath a pelt is flesh; under flesh, a skeleton; under bones, a beating heart; and the heartbeat of the Missouri is gravity, without which the river would die.

Although the angle of descent of the Big Muddy over its almost three thousand miles is modest everywhere—the Great Falls an exception—it has immeasurable expanses of drainage pushing it forward and preventing its retreat: each tributary trickle, runnel, and creek insists it on. When precipitation comes down between the Rockies and the Mississippi, between the Canadian border and the north slope of the Arkansas River, most of it goes as fast as the terrain concedes into the Missouri, which shows no interest in staying home in ponds or lakes, no allegiance to any channel, no commitment other than to keep moving.

The waters of the Missouri, like the human residents on its shores, are immigrants desiring to get on, to roam, and that is one reason it strikes me as a most American river, one not just determining and shaping its own territory but demonstrating the character of the nation. Unruly and often spoiling for a fracas, democratically demonstrating no preference for what it gathers up and carries along, it expresses itself in the very soil composing it—alluvial residue brought from mountain and plain. I suspect all components in a human anatomy exist also in the turbidity of the Missouri: if dust could make Adam, then Missouri mud could make an American who might sing, *O new found land, I am of thee.*

The river, exclaiming itself every league, does not hesitate to flaunt its nature, boast its puissance, and challenge boatmen who would ride its back on beyond the sunset. Within our initial twenty miles, even before Saint Charles, it spoke what it is: *I am the Missouri. I am the way west. If you cannot come up me, you do not belong.*

When Deems, thinking of the eastern rivers he knew, heard me call the river unruly, he responded, "*Unruly?* It's uncivilized to a fare-ye-well. And that's what I'm here for."

Stretching out far ahead and moving under low-angled shafts of sunlight transmuting the opaque water into a continuing golden filament, the reflected river flourished its length, disappearing only behind its bends and oxbows, coming forth to wind and wander eastward across half a continent.

We stood long enough near the bow of the *Osage* for sundown to come on and hang above a long blur of thinning altocumuli gradually smudging the sun into an observable disk, atmospherically magnified to disperse over the sky a flagrant radiance one might expect at the first—*or final*—sunshine on an Earth ready for either impending glory *or* disintegration. Alpha or omega? I asked Nicodemus which he saw, and he said, "Every sunset is somewhere somebody's sunrise."

When the disk began vanishing at the shut of day, I heard him murmur: "O America!" Now, as I write this, I am trying to hear his tenor. Maybe what he said was, "Oh, America." Was it belief in citizens fulfilling the promise of the land? Or was it a premonition no people could *ever* fulfill a covenant with such a munificent land?

14 July, nightfall

Following supper, we returned to our quarters. We had not registered for separate cabins, instead—as if to save money—we requested under our aliases a shared room. Mr. Cuff feared we were getting reckless in covering our trail. He was thinking of a brief notice in a Saint Louis newspaper about my lecture to the medical college and his call for Negro education. Although he was not named—referred to only as a *young colored*—I was identified. I reminded him Ferrall was illiterate. Deems replied, "And if there's a henchman who isn't?" I pointed out that we boarded the *Osage* just as the papers arrived, and we had watched all passengers coming up the gangway.

Scowling, Deems shook his head: "Am I going to be a damned runaway all my life? I've heard so many stories about slaves being recaptured long after their escape. Even from free states." I asked *how many* of them had been captured beyond the Missouri River country in what Americans term the Far West. The question heartened him. He said, "In Virginia, people claimed true liberty was across this or that *divide*, but I never knew where any of those divides were."

"This very minute," said I, "you're moving ever farther west atop one of them. One *big* one."

A sharp rap on our cabin door sent Nicodemus diving beneath his berth. I asked who it was. A woman's voice apologized for mistaking her cabin number. Deems crawled out and said calmly, "I'm through with this game. I'm going to buy a pistol."

"In a border state," I said, "isn't a black man carrying a pistol a confrontation ready to happen? Don't discount *two* of us are protecting your *liberty*. And my *life*."

"Only a dinky pistol."

"We've foiled him twice."

"I want to kill him just once."

"I can't tell you what to do," I said, "but if it would help, I'll consider arming myself with a pocket pistol."

He rubbed his face, sat to think, then said, "I wonder whether life on the moon is this lunatic. One day I find my mother years after she was sold *down* the river, and two days later a crimp is trying to capture me somewhere *up* a river."

"The crimp hasn't found you, and nobody has found me."

"Yet."

"Deems, perpetual anxiety creates a hellish existence." He gave no response, so I added, "A man who can survive slavery can surely win out over a single, ignorant slave hunter." He said nothing. I tried again: "Would you like me to carry a pistol?"

"I'll think about it."

"Until then, why not distract yourself with this powder mill we're sleeping on top of? Any moment it could obviate further worries."

The 14th inst.

Navigating the deceptions of the Missouri in darkness extends beyond being *unwise* into *damned foolhardy*. With nightfall and a sky absent of moonlight, the *Osage* tied to a snubbing post at the landing in Saint Charles, the last American village captains Lewis and Clark left behind to begin their ascent into the newly acquired territory, land theretofore home of the indigenous: Indians and bison, prairies and plains, all ruled by the autocracy of the Missouri which so determines what goes on here. Leaving late on a rainy afternoon, the Corps of Discovery gained all of four miles the first day.

Boatmen say the Missouri is the longest of American rivers— although its length cannot be precisely determined because it refuses to remain in one place long enough to be measured with exactitude. If water can be said to *fidget*, then the Missouri fidgets: moving down *this* channel today, shifting to *that* one over yonder tomorrow, forever snaking to and fro across its continually improvised route to the sea. This, incidentally, is one more characteristic it imparts to the Mississippi below the confluence where riverine changes can snatch a piece of one state and tack it to the shore of a neighbor: on a Friday a farmer in Arkansas may go to bed contentedly knowing his spring plowing is complete, only to arise on Saturday to find he now has sixty unplowed acres of Tennessee.

Our captain, goat-bearded and barrel-chested and more approachable than he appeared, talked this evening about the Missouri, and these are adjectives he used: *shifty, inconstant, treacherous, false.* He said, "Old man river has more tricks up his sleeve than old Merlin. If your course is upriver, you're headed for a couple thousand miles of ensnarements and concealments. Seventy percent of the steamboats here end up in wreckage, a good many of them splattered into a splintery heap to hazard other boats. The average length of service of a steamer bucking the Missouri is less than two years. If a transport company is going to make money, it better do it fast. That tells you our gal *Osage* is on borrowed time."

Deems and I made a night stroll through the streets of Saint Charles. We began with Main, which rests on ground no higher above the river than the top of a tall, long-eared horse, and that is especially so during floods: in April from spring rains and in June from snowmelt off the Rockies. Between the north bank of the Missouri and the hills, there is not enough space to lay out more than one street capable of holding parallel lines of narrow row-houses in brick or stone. To walk perpendicular to Main is immediately to wade into the river or, going the other way, to start up a steep slope. The village sits in this challenging location because these hills offer elevated land near the confluence. This geological up-rumple gave the town its birth but now keeps it from becoming a second Saint Louis. In winter, even a mule can struggle to reach the top.

Saint Charles until recently was the temporary seat of state government whilst builders were cutting a new capital *and* capitol out of the forest 120 miles upstream. In the interregnum, legislators spent time here arguing whether to allow free Negroes to settle in the state, a division—at least in the minds of citizens—two decades later still not decided. On Main Street, we overheard almost as much German as English, an intimation that the abolition question in Saint Charles will soon be tilted if not decided by immigrants.

15 July

I awoke at first light from the noise of getting underway. On a packet, cabins are typically along the inscrutably termed *boiler* deck, but the boilers are below, on the *main* deck. Atop what lubbers term the *roof* and rivermen the *texas* deck stands the pilothouse—a windowed box—immediately behind the tall smokestacks. Port and starboard are paddle wheels contained within gaily trimmed housings. Cabins—ambitiously termed staterooms—occupy virtually the entire boiler deck, entry to them from the river side.

Her length is 140 feet but she's only twenty-two in beam, making our limited complement of travelers companionable. Though not diminutive, this lesser size puts the *Osage* at certain disadvantages against the might of the Missouri. Watching her face up to her handicaps, I found myself twice refer to her *pluck*.

At our departure I was on the texas to observe our passage upriver—Deems off I know not where—when I was joined by an elderly man, an immigrant from Bohemia, his name Vinko, who served with the Americans during the recent conflict with Britain. The War of 1812—often termed here the Second War of Independence—is still recalled by some citizens with a degree of animosity and on occasion thus expressed to me. Speaking a functional English, Vinko marveled at the Missouri country but soon fell into comparisons and reminiscence of life along his native River Labe. As he talked, he withdrew a small New Testament from his pocket for me to examine. It was bound, he said, in horse leather.

"In one of our persecutions in Bohemia, all who own Bible get order to give it up. In our village was only thirty families. One morning soldiers arrive to take Bibles. My grandmother, she see men going house to house while she is making the breads. Before they come to her door, she wrap oilcloth around Bible and stick into baking pan and pour batter over it. Pumpernickel, you say here. Two pans go in oven. When soldiers hammer on kitchen door, she welcome them come in, and they search cottage. Whole time they smell delicious baking breads. Soldier say to her he buy him some bread. And he give her coins. But now she no remember which loaf has Bible. He pull out his saber for to make share with corporal. He whack open loaf. Inside is not Bible. Soldiers is eating pumpernickel when they leave. On table is other loaf. She is picking up to see how heavy. And it is heavy because inside is Bible. Now in your hands is Bible to escape soldier's sword."

15 July (later)

Deems sauntered up, after examining the compass in the pilothouse, to say, "If this confounded river runs straight for a mile, it atones for the mistake by going crooked for the next ten."

His words put me into thinking a human life never for long follows a straight line. Such a course is unnatural. If it did, we would go mad with the boredom of being locked into sameness. The best travel throws sameness aside for a spell and seeks reprieve from the monotony of undeviation and bends the straight lines of our days into the thrill of unexpectation.

To stand at the bow of the *Osage* as she ascends the bent Missouri, is to watch a painting that moves in an ever-shifting point of view, a daguerreotype of a scene changing moment by moment. A picture in motion. On average, the Missouri requires two miles to gain one linear mile, as if the river is enamored of a compass, wanting always to embrace more of its 360 degrees.

On the walls of my childhood bedroom in Saint Kitts, my mother allowed me to paste up sections of maps, one joining the other, England next to Egypt, Samoa against Swaziland. To enter the room was like walking into a cockeyed globe where no place ran true compass points. I would fall asleep looking at a road in Macedonia and wake up looking at a village in Mongolia. On the ceiling I drew constellations, they too in disarray. I so loved beautiful Orion, I painted a sky with two of them so I could lie abed, facing right or left, and see the Hunter and his sword.

This remembrance must be occasioned by the troubles hitting me a year ago: it was then I began seeking a road to elsewhere, and that is the reason these months later I am so far from home and looking up to discover Bonhomme Island Bend, a whereabouts I never knew existed, and beside me is a good man whose existence was also then unknown to me. My course here has been as far from straight as up is from down, as a sphere from a cube. Corrupting predictability can be highly salubrious. So postulates the physician.

16 July

The *Osage* spent the night at the landing in Washington, Missouri to take on several barrels of burley tobacco, all of it in thick twists for the Indian trade. The captain sent the first mate to ask me to check on a passenger in her cabin located near the stern and yielding a fine view downstream. Her quarters far surpass ours and are fully suitable to the Sultana of the Stage, Miss Lilly DuVallee (née Ethel Vale). Accompanied by Nicodemus, I expected another instance of dyspepsia brought on by the American habit of eating too fast or dystrophia from a diet of excessive consumption of maize ("Indian corn," Americans say): they mix cornmeal with lard to make cornbread, corn pone, corn dodgers, corn cakes, corn grits, and they love hominy, corn on the cob, corn oil, and corn whiskey. Americans stuff a mattress with corn shucks, smoke tobacco in its hollowed-out cobs, and even address human posteriors with them.

The Sultana is an effusive woman of amplitudes in all its measures: voice, breadth of beam and shoulders, and a height putting her eye to eye with most men. Her size allows her to assume a leading role wherever she finds herself—on stage or off, in costume or not—resulting in a personality of amplitude to match her other amplitudes.

She was pallid, but her lively greeting was as if she had known me since boyhood (she has a couple of decades on me). In a pronouncement likely heard across the river, she said, "I'm singing for the troops at Fort Leavenworth in three days! I can't perform with half vigor in half voice!"

My ears ringing, I wondered what possibly could be *full* voice. I asked the Sultana to describe her indisposition.

In her alto at half volume, she sang—not spoke, but *sang* out, "Worms! Worms! Inglorious worms!"

I had to nudge Deems not to smile. I asked her to give me all the details she could, which she did with an accuracy to make diagnosis certain. I said pinworms were more common among children than adults, and she vociferated, "Of course! I'm a child at heart!"

Deems and I took my medical kit to the galley and there prepared a tincture of water, bitter root, and a smatter of peppermint to ease the acridity. We returned to her and I explained that the tonic should expel the problem; my able intern would bring her the decoction three times a day.

The 17th

This morning when the Sultana entered the salon for breakfast, her lips now painted brightly and her eyes deeply shadowed, she looked ready for the stage. She came to us, threw one arm around me and the other around Nicodemus, pulled us tightly against her shoulders, and declaimed for all to hear, "These gentlemen have made it possible for my pipes to sing as if I descended from the choir angelic!"

The boat has a shelf of books for perusal by passengers, most of the volumes related to rivers or boats with but a single novel, *The Adventures of Robinson Crusoe.* One of the others is a selection of journal entries by captains Lewis and Clark on their voyage and trek into the newly gained territory of the Louisiana Purchase that has so reshaped the face of America.

The written expression of the captains is able yet distinct one from the other. Clark writes in a familiar, direct, and congenial manner about practical matters, never rising into anything I would term philosophical, thereby creating a counterpoint to the more learned and finely wrought, reflective mode of Lewis. To read their words is to glimpse the inner man—his soul, if you will—and come away with a notion of why Lewis died young (by his own hand, so it is reported) and Clark passed but recently just shy of his seventieth year, a man of means earned to a degree through negotiated dispossession of native peoples, particularly those whose name this boat bears.

I just read Clark's report on the loss of one of his men:

> We made a warm bath for Sergeant Floyd, hoping it would brace him a little. Before we could get him into this bath he expired with a great deal of composure, having said to me before his death that he was going away and wished me to write a letter. We buried him on the top of a high, round hill overlooking the river and country for a great distance.

Earlier I came upon Captain Lewis ruminating on his thirty-second birthday, an age near mine. Five years later he was dead.

> I have in all human probability now existed about half the period which I am to remain in this sublunary world. I reflected that I had as yet done but little, very little indeed, to further the happiness of the human race or to advance the information of the succeeding generation. I viewed with regret the many hours I have spent in indolence, and now sorely feel the want of that information which those hours would have given me had they been judiciously expended. But since they are past and cannot be recalled,

I dash from me the gloomy thought and resolve in the future to redouble my exertions and at least endeavor to promote those two primary objects of human existence by giving them the aid of that portion of talents which nature and fortune have bestowed on me; in the future to live for mankind as I have heretofore lived for myself.

17 July, evening

The *Osage* made good time before she grounded on a narrow wing of a sandbar invisible under a sun glaring off water. Reversing her paddle wheels was insufficient to free her, and the crew's long push-poles were of no avail. The river was rising, but to wait for its effect would entail a delay of unknown duration. The captain asked among our hardy complement of passengers whether any would wade into the shallows to shove on the hull. Eight of us entered shoal water only to our knees. We took up positions to try to move the boat towards the downstream current, the paddles churning mightily and at last freeing her to regain the channel. Standing at the edge of deeper water, we cheered. From then on, I remember nothing.

What happened next, so I am informed, was this: one of the wheels sucked in a small piece of drift and kicked it back, striking me above the occipital bone. Deems saw me slip into the downriver flow, bobbing half-conscious before going under. I am told he lunged to grasp my left arm just as the river got hold of me. Against the swiftness of the current, he pulled me towards the sandbar, where he kept my head above water until the skiff reached us.

Stretched out flat on the steamer deck, I came to, opening my eyes to discover a perfect circle of worried faces peering down. Deems propped me upright so I might finish coughing up my personal draft of the Missouri River, the sediment noticeably granular in my mouth. With mind fixed on molars grinding grit carried a thousand miles from the Rocky Mountains, I did not comprehend what had occurred. Vinko knelt to show me a thing the size of an apple, likely a pine knot from an old plank. Said he, "This is wood to hit you. I throw back in river."

"No!" Deems said. "What fails to kill a man ought to be preserved." Then, remembering the pattern in his coffee in Saint Louis, he added, "I'll carve it into a death's head." Now, as I write, the eroded knot with its resinous rings stares at me from my table to remind me how nigh oblivion is at every moment.

The grounding prevented the *Osage* from making the scheduled destination, so we stopped at the landing for the new capital in Jefferson City. Given the boundary irregularities of Missouri, the town is placed as close to dead center of the state as feasible whilst still keeping the streets near the river for accessibility. As to the confident positioning of the capitol itself, it hangs on the edge of a river bluff so precariously a single torrential rain and mudslide could send senators and their desks holus-bolus into the Missouri, a result a number of citizens would heartily cheer.

The building, constructed of what is termed here *white marble*—actually limestone—is said to be fireproof. Despite its being not quite finished, it is open for governing. Handsome in a simplicity of columns, dome, portico, rotunda, and twin chambers, it bears the common design delineating the locus of the American political process. The classical architecture and structural work, however, is the expression of numerous English and French immigrants who settled in Saint Louis.

It is curious the building faces not the famous river but the state penitentiary, a proximity some here believe deliberate to remind politicians to weigh temptations offered them. Beyond the penitentiary, the view on eastward is nevertheless a fine sweep of wooded bluffs for miles downstream; to the west the vista is of similar midwestern beauty.

From its inception, the statehouse has been the source of contention for innately disputatious Americans, and still today they are quarreling over various aspects—its leaky dome, even its very location. I am often surprised Brother Jonathan can accomplish anything at all, so politically quarrelsome he is. The Erie Canal— which created widespread prosperity not just for its immediate territory but for the nation as a whole and turned New York City into the leading port—was also argued over *prior to* construction and squabbled over *during* construction, the wrangling continuing *long after* construction. It may be discordance is in the nature of a mercantilistic democracy, with its acceptance and encouragement of self-interest and the equality of opinion: the result, contention.

Once again the national motto, *E pluribus unum*, rings hollow, as it often does—until an outsider criticizes the country or tries to take territory; then, truly, Americans act as a body politic united. To see how deeply *belief in land* is built into their thinking, one need only to suggest the nation give up a single square foot of ground. American democracy stands on several foundations, and none is greater than the soil itself—and its acquisition. If the Quaker adage "Thee must never relinquish principal" holds, then any American might say, "Thee must never relinquish acreage."

At the foot of the capitol bluff is a substantial limestone building—in part a hotel, trading center, and warehouse. A three-level balcony extends the length of the structure and opens to the river, and there we found clean if plain quarters. Leaving our clothing with a laundress, we washed river mud from ourselves, and by day's end, we were seated on the balcony to observe the Missouri roll its mute power eastward. That utter silence overwhelmed as does the inaudible movement of stars across an unclouded sky. Nicodemus said, "We're so close, I could pitch a peach pit into the river." Had he a pit, he would have pitched.

To test my recovery Deems asked: where I was born, my year of graduating from Cambridge, who the current President is, and concluding with, "Do you know anybody in Buffalo, New York?" Having passed the concussion test, I recommended a celebration. He went below to the bar and returned with a small flask of sour-mash Missouri whiskey, and we drank to surviving the Big Muddy. I said, "One's brain is on loan. Best to preserve it to use wisely before it must be returned."

I added it is always a special day when one does not die, and Nicodemus answered, "Then all our days are special till the final one. Although, *dying* seems particularly special." Raising a following toast, I thanked him for keeping me traveling along in the human train rather than as a bloated corpse washing up on some muddy levee. "A remarkable friendship it is," said I, "when each owes the other his life."

Answered he, "One saved neck deserves another."

Our supper—taken on the veranda—was roasted vegetables and canvasback, a duck I had heard unqualifiedly praised from the Chesapeake to the lower Missouri. Indeed, it was superbly toothsome, enhanced perhaps by another pour of distilled corn mash, all the while the force of the Missouri sliding past without so much as a gurgle.

Many times I have wondered whether I have ever seen the exact location where one day I will breathe my last. Watching the flow, I smiled at having avoided one more biddance to rejoin the grand cosmic flux that engenders all. For the nonce, I was happy to sit high and dry with my friend who is responsible for my *being* high and dry and alive enough to withstand another jigger, this one leading into goosery of song: I taught Nicodemus two verses of "I Likes Me a Drop of Good Whiskey, I Does."

18 July

We were dressed and aboard the *Osage* as she began building steam. Off we moved into the next leg of our ascent, this one of twenty-five miles to Providence Landing, a place of three haphazard structures, six pigs wandering, four cows uncorralled, two hitched horses, and one lazy-legs who responded to my greeting as if I were the county assessor come to knock on his door. Deems said, "You think he has a door for the assessor to knock on?"

To our satisfaction, at riverside a pair of stalwarts were loading a wagonful of whiskey barrels onto the *Osage*; the drayman allowed, on his return, he would have space to haul us to Columbia, a few miles distant. For a dollar. Whiskey, tobacco, hemp, and higher education are the economic underpinnings of Boone County, the first two drawing censure from the local Baptists, the third cultivated by them, and the latter often ignored by them. The road to town ascended rather steeply and windingly from the river onto a rolling terrain of trees, opened here and about by cramped clearings often holding a cabin and a compact field of corn or oats—so I presumed from the seedlings. Nutriment for man and beast—a portion of the nutriment destined to be *poured*, a result some citizens lament as sin and others laud as salvation.

It was beautiful territory. Were there meadows instead of forest, the lay of the land would remind me of the English Midlands. One homestead in particular caught my eye, a small tobacco plot surrounded by oak woods and lying just beyond a pair of natural ponds formed by the collapse of a limestone cave here called a sinkhole, a term defying the charm of what it describes. Limestone is one reason for the local whiskey-making: water infused by magnesium carbonate being a natural concomitant to a tonic of joy.

I said to Nicodemus, "Those ponds, the oaks in that setting— I'm going to bring Sophie here and build her a house so she may sit on a porch and watch wood ducks and herons and whatever else comes to visit."

He clapped me on the back. "Well then, my countryman, welcome to America."

18 July, evening

Columbia, only recently established as the location of the new state university, centers on accurately named Broadway. South is the college and its main hall, a structure of three floors and six large limestone columns in the Ionic order and a dome with a windowed cupola. The building directly fronts the county courthouse of four Ionic columns five blocks north. Citizens here quarry the limestone beneath their feet and turn it into *public* architecture and use its geological influence to distill *private* ardent spirits. At the entrance to the campus is a lakelet formed by a chalybeate spring, its iron salts making it salutary as well as scenic.

After finding lodging near the campus, we walked to Academic Hall to look in on Professor Martin Larousse, foretold of our visit by George Hancock. The professor was in the lab and invited us to observe his efforts to isolate certain alkaloids. I never met him at Cambridge, but I knew of him there before he gave up medical practice and emigrated to the States to teach and conduct research. He is midway through his sixth decade, affable, of slender physique making his head appear too big for the shoulders, furthered by a sprawl of white hair.

On the laboratory bench were several bowls of powdered distillates, each of a slightly different tint of reddish brown.

Nicodemus asked what they were. The professor told us to sample a powder; we did and immediately tried to wipe away the bitterness and clear our nostrils of its acrid odor. Larousse smiled and said, "You've just tasted raw laudanum, my latest formulations from opium I'll distill into a tincture. Some call laudanum a gift of the gods, some say it's God himself, and others say it's Satan in a bottle."

The professor invited us to his home for supper prepared by the housekeeper. Larousse speaks professorially and was pleased to explain his work.

"As long as humans remain biological creatures—*organic* beings—our existence will be determined predominantly by chemistry. My role as a chemist is to find ways to improve our biological inheritance. When we talk about human *intention* and *values* and *meaning*—things distinguishing us from other biological matter—we're talking about functions of our brains, about chemistry. I refer to issues at the center of being human."

He stopped to think how to proceed.

"When I was a young physician in London thirty-some years ago, I was often called into tenements to treat people. The living conditions were abysmally wretched. Coal smoke filled the air, drinking water crawled with what only recently we've identified as bacteria. Humanity crammed in together. Disgusting personal hygiene. Inadequate food, and much of what people did find to eat could sicken the abundant rats sharing their rooms. Dysentery and cholera were common. Consumption, rheumatism. And the physical injuries! Broken bones and infections. Once I had to scare off a rat eating afterbirth of a newborn human baby."

Nicodemus, agitated, remembering a plantation hut, let drop his pocket memorandum. Larousse paused only long enough for Deems to retrieve it.

"The misery overwhelmed me," he said. "Animals in the forest have healthier lives. Inured to difficulty as those people were, their sufferings exceeded human endurance. Unlike beasts, we have little capacity to suffer in silence. I wanted to quit. Then it came to me. Even if I couldn't cure all the illness I encountered, I could do *something*, and the most useful *something* would be alleviation of physical pain. About then I learned of the work of Thomas Sydenham, a physician who survived the great plague in London. He studied a compound known at least since the birth of writing. A substance produced by *Papaver somniferum*, the opium poppy. I'll wager, Doctor, you have one of its derivatives in your medical bag."

"I have laudanum," I said. "I'm aware, of course, of those who declaim against it, but they're never in pain when they turn righteous."

Larousse nodded, "Show me a man with a seriously fractured leg who will not pay any price for relief of pain. Or a woman with stomach cancer who will refuse. A child with a rotten tooth. Because sooner or later we all experience bodily misery, my quest is to develop an opium derivative able to block pain until recovery from the injury or disease. A recovery free of addiction. And it's there I face difficulties. Not in the chemistry, but from commercial purveyors of various opiates. Manufacturers of patent medicines well understand the value of a patient who becomes a permanent *customer* incapable of refusing a medicament even after the anodyne is no longer necessary."

Observing Deems writing in his memorandum, Larousse said, "Several companies supported my research until they heard my focus is to remove the addictive element. Then they began circulating stories I was a mad scientist bilking the university."

Deems requested Larousse to look over his notes. The doctor corrected the spelling of *anodyne*, then said, "If I succeed in creating an addiction-free palliative, next I'll undertake removal of greed from the human brain."

19 July

We had a pair of choices to proceed westward by water: return to a boat at Providence Landing or go forward via stage to Franklin Landing, one of the jumping-off settlements for seekers bound for the West. Out here, *West* has a capital letter to distinguish a destination from a mere direction. Deems decided the question with, "Pilgrims don't backtrack." I asked were we now pilgrims, and he said, "This journey feels like a pilgrimage even if I don't know the sacred path. Not yet." I took his point: maybe the greatest pilgrimage is to a place beyond an unknown bourn. After all, *destination* and *destiny* differ only as egg to hatchling. And so we caught the stage for Franklin. The thirty miles were over good and dry lanes, and the coach was roomy with only two others to share it.

Of the aptitudes an able traveler should carry along, few are superior to learning how to greet a fellow rambler. The key, as Cedric of the Road posited, is to remember we all are at each moment departing the Land of Now, and often we differ not so much where we *have* traveled as where we *wish* to travel. In the instance at hand, one of our wayfarers chose not to divulge anything about where she was bound, and the other wanted to divulge opinions on everywhere he had been within memory. His disquisitions brought to mind another attribute of a happy vagabond, a most practical characteristic: the ability—*when needed*—to doze off even in a rocking coach.

To our surprise and relief, the *Osage* lay snubbed to a post at Franklin Landing; she had grounded a mile downstream yesterday evening and managed to escape only after dawn. We greeted several familiar voyagers, and were soon underway once again. The steamer whistle disturbed a large hawk from a cottonwood into westward flight, the bird using the open sky above the Missouri as its path to follow the river as a farmer a furrow.

Having no reason to stop at Arrow Rock on its high bluff, our little tub continued unencumbered by contrary wind or current to steam smartly onward as if the *Osage* were queen of the waters and the Missouri her footman. The lone challenge for the pilot was glare off certain reaches of the river that disguised impediments capable of delaying a vessel for an hour or forever. Deems counted three remainders of broken-up steamboats, one of recent occurrence. I spent half the afternoon with my journal at a table under our cabin window, now and then glancing up at the shore of the Missouri country. A green and woody land it is.

Supper was filets cut from a single blue catfish the size and weight of a ten-year-old farm boy. Served alongside was river-sturgeon caviar prepared by the cook himself. Bold is the diner who looks closely before partaking of a freshly caught sturgeon, with its spines and primordial protuberances and a face proclaiming *misbegotten!*

After the meal, for all to examine, the captain had a boatswain set out on the foredeck a dead and desiccated paddlefish found on the gravel bar last night, its cartilaginous exterior blanched by the sun. If ever there is truth to the phrase *Here be strange beasts* once inscribed on ancient maps, *Polyodon spathula* qualifies for inclusion. At the front of a shark-like body was a snout two feet in length and shaped like the paddle of an Indian canoe. Overall, the brute was six feet long and before drying out had to weigh more than a hundred pounds. Its gaping mouth looked capable of swallowing a stray cat, although our cook said the fish is toothless and eats only "invisibles," probably meaning plankton and larvae. Were such a critter to show up in an English stream, there would be panic in the village at the arrival of Endtime. A tourist said to Deems, "How could God create that creature?" to which he suggested perhaps God had not been consulted on paddlefish design, and she said, "I should think not!"

Among our passengers are seven Osage men and four women traveling from their village on the distant Neosho River, their present home territory. They are making for Fort Leavenworth to demonstrate various aspects and skills of their native customs: horsemanship, archery, dancing, even a re-enactment of a raid on their ancient enemy, the Pawnee. Through the active presence of the American military, relations have changed just enough to lessen intertribal hostility; in fact, one of the troupe was born a Pawnee, yet he is now content to play the role of a dying enemy warrior—right after sitting peaceably at table with enemies from an earlier time.

When not performing, the Osage wear a mixture of European and tribal apparel. One man sports Indian-style leggings and moccasins of tanned deerskin and a soiled, frilly shirt of red cotton with a smoke-stained, Scotch-plaid blanket thrown over it. With a coxcomb's pride he adorns himself in a gaudy turban. Another man, also in leggings and cotton shirt, paints his face with two irregular patches of cobalt and vermilion in a pattern to induce alarm in any white unprepared for such a visage, a reaction amusing the troupe. Young males shave their heads, leaving a scalp lock on the crown they dye red and hang with feathers; this style of coif, so I learned, began as a challenge to an enemy to try to steal it. The women's sullied raiment is, by comparison, drab to the point of raising in me sympathy for their assigned lot, although on some female arms are wonderfully elaborate tattoos in a spider web pattern.

Steamers are forbidden by government regulation from serving alcohol to any Indian, and farther upriver the Army will search boats for liquor before allowing entry into territory with a native presence. So far, only one of the men in the troupe has spoken a little understandable English. The women remain silent. I must remark, females are held in observable subservience. The oldest among them is quite stooped from years of bearing burdens: papooses, baskets of hides, bedding. Similar spinal deformation awaits the younger women.

Earlier, on the texas deck, my journal writing attracted considerable interest from the Osage, not for its content but simply for the act of inscribing, called by them (in translation) *drawing*. With hand gestures, a brave indicated for me to *read* aloud a drawing; I selected a short paragraph about their dress. They paid rapt attention, not understanding a word of it but nodding wisely when I concluded. To them it was a chant. Now, in Osage I am He-Who-Draws-Worms. Not *words*, but *worms*.

The 19th (later)

I have neglected to mention: at Jefferson City we were joined by a young geologist on his way west to prospect for minerals. He lent me his copy of Henry Brackenridge's *Journal of a Voyage up the Missouri River in 1811.* The author's pen is full of energy and capable expression. Of the Osage he says they are "the tribe most attached to the Americans." Of what I have seen, the oft-repeated comment on Indian taciturnity reflects not only their language incomprehension but also disaffection stemming from dealings with whites—especially in the matter of land. Virtually every transaction has concluded with Indians losing ever more ground. And so today they may listen to an American but will say little: when standing before a man out to bilk you, silence is well advised.

These exploitative practices cannot further trust, especially when carried out by whites who openly refer to Indians as *savages,* and in all dealings express hauteur and condescension amounting to flagrant disrespect. Mr. Brackenridge, an astute observer, holds an enlarged and uncommon view of the natives we are about to meet along the Missouri.

Many are the reports of the considerable stature of the Osage, the men not uncommonly in excess of six feet. Several visitors to Osage country have referred to them as "giants of the prairie." Based on my early evidence, that opinion somewhat stretches accuracy, although those traveling with us are indeed big; no man in the troupe fails to top both me and Nicodemus and all of our crewmen. The women, except the one with stooped shoulders, are but slightly taller than American women aboard.

The Osage call themselves Wah-sha-shay, namely, People of the Middle Waters. When they are not on the far prairies for an annual bison hunt—which feeds them without the drudgery of animal husbandry—they live in soi-disant villages. This partly settled way of life and their large population have made them a force for Americans to recognize and has earned them dominance in the fur trade of the lower Missouri Valley. In exchange for furs and pelts—bison, beaver, mink, muskrat—they desire European manufactured goods—weaponry as well as kettles and cutlery and cloth and decorative trinkets. And, when clandestinely offered, whiskey.

The commerce has kept the Wah-sha-shay from warfare against whites. Notably, almost alone of tribes living near battlegrounds in the recent war, the Osage did not side with the British. Yet the American response since then continues to push them from their homelands.

With the Pawnee, however, the Osage are more bellicose, ready to address frictions still capable of assuring mutual harm. But there too, growing trade has helped reduce disaccord. Once again I point out Washington's understanding that the success of American democracy in no small measure depends upon commerce. What a monarch is in Europe, money is in America.

Currently, a local grievance with whites exists over a few Osage sub-chiefs' agreeing to the sale of terra firma under tribal control, the men having no authority to sell lands in the possession of them all. The Osage believe their domain belongs not only to those living but also to their posterity. Because Americans want acreage for which there is no legally established evidence of ownership beyond occupancy, whites execute native dispossession through treaties lacking legitimacy and fairness.

Of the aboriginals on this continent who have long been disregarded and displaced by European economic practices, the Osage have survived better than others in avoiding extermination by weapons or disease or assimilation. They have developed means to live alongside white supremacy while preserving their own ancient practices. The troupe aboard the ironically named *Osage*, to be sure, inclines towards cooperation; after all, the performers earn their way by effectively selling to whites demonstrations of traditional arts and customs. We pay to watch costumed dances and to applaud drums and chants. With us their trade is in differences, transactions benefiting all; in that practice I see hope—if, *if* citizens recognize democracy will not long abide under egregious divisions.

Evening of the 19th

By sundown our boat steamed past the hamlet of Glasgow and continued under the light of moonset to the quiet side of a sandbar, and here we are to lay up until dawn. The Osage troupe took opportunity of the beach to rehearse its performance three nights hence: dance, song, and a remarkable exhibition of archery by the senior member—carrying the honorific *sachem*—a sinewy man, not so tall as the others, with thinning white hair parted on the side and when he performs drawn into a pair of braids interwoven with beads of garnet.

From a quiver at his back, he deftly drew arrows and let them fly in a single motion. Although the distance between the old fellow and his target was not great, his aim was usually true, including that in a trick shot released from behind his back. Between arrows, he spoke in Osage through a white interpreter about hunting the sacred buffalo, often mocking himself by miming the declining strength of his arms and legs.

Deems was in utter fascination with the bowmanship and the chance to stand so close to (in his terms) a "live Indian sachem." After the demonstration, he approached the archer to say slowly and with unnatural enunciation, "Me Nicodemus. You good with bow. What you name?"

The Osage elder listened intently, looked at those of us around him, and then with the theatrics of a veteran performer said distinctly and formally, "Your words lift the spirit of this old warrior who once was a brave. It is good when the young show curiosity about the old ways. That is the way the Grandfather

Spirits pass along knowledge of the world. It is right to come with questions. You ask my name. I have six names, my son, but only three are for the white man, even for a black white man."

At this response, Nicodemus stood embarrassed by his presumption the archer could not speak English. Deems himself had met with presupposition from whites that he, a Negro, would not know about the voyages of Odysseus or Caesar's *Commentaries* or understand terms such as *ablution* or *litigation* or *sanction*.

Noticing the chagrin, the old sachem politely said, "I also speak some French and, *if forced*, a little Pawnee. Years ago I was called— to say it in English—Young Archer. Now I am Grandfather-With-Bow, although the young like to make it Old-Fart-With-Bow. I have forgotten how to say that in Osage. In Osage I have a second name, but it is too difficult for an American to say. And that is good. If a white man knows it, he can gain power over me. In English it is harmless. To you, I am Two Hearts."

Nicodemus interrupted. "But how—."

"My English," said the old fellow, "is a gift from the sisters at Saint Botolph's Mission Boarding School where I was sent. They wanted to implant a tiny white man inside an Indian boy. There is an ugly Osage word for the custom, but I don't remember it. The nuns named me Ralph, but Osage has no *r* or *l* or *f* sounds. The stupidity of the name is harmless because it comes from the white man and has no power. So goes the theory."

20 July

I have become so accustomed to the noises of getting underway this morning I slept through them, waking to a cabin empty of Deems. My languor may be a delayed result of the blow to my cranium and indication of need for a day of rest. Rain dimpled the river unvexed by wind, and the steamer chugged steadily upstream at a good clip. Ignoring breakfast, I accepted an invitation from Deems to join him and Two Hearts and four other Osages to take advantage of the warm rain and bathe on the hurricane deck out of view of women. I shared my bar of lye soap with the men, who soon began tossing it in a game they called—in translation—"catch the slippery pig," but with the word *slippery* attended by an Osage word for *coition*. The soap ended up in the Big Muddy.

On the nape of the old warrior's neck I saw an inflamed nodule, perhaps a boil. Would he like me to examine it? He said he is accustomed to Osage treatments which usually operate through the *calendar cure*, viz., *time*, a medicine man's greatest poultice. Along with favorable *coincidence*. "However," said he, "my calendar is running short of pages, so I will submit to the medicine of the white man."

In our cabin I sat Two Hearts in a chair and asked him to remove from his shoulder the quiver and bow he always carries as a badge of his days as a brave. Around his neck he wears a single eagle claw in a silver mount. Deems laid out several instruments, and I examined what appeared to be a furuncle ready to point. With Nicodemus observing as understudy, I deterged my hands and the sachem's neck. Explaining the procedure, I lanced the thin covering of skin to drain off the exudate before dressing the lesion. I told the old sachem infection is not uncommon with such a boil and to let me see his neck each morning. Whilst he rested, I sketched him.

When I finished, Two Hearts studied his portrait and said, "Before the white man also sees his people vanish, I hope he never goes through what he has put upon the red man. And the black man."

He rose slowly, his years (which he otherwise carries well) manifesting clearly, and he said, "I have seen many winters, but of those born before me, they all are gone. To live long is to go on alone. I am left to bear witness and carry the wisdom of the Grandfathers to those who are yet in high feather. But the young, do you think they have interest in a windy old man? The regrets I could save them, *those* they will have to face on their own. Maybe that is the way the Grandfather Spirits intend. Learning and memory work better through *hurting* than *hearing*. Although with time the will to continue to learn falls like dusk. But in night is comfort. For the aged, it is good not to look beyond the dawn."

Nicodemus said, "I believe Two Hearts is an ancient philos opher."

"No, my son. I am only an ancient codger rasping on. Do you know the word *garrulous?* When the arms and legs begin to fail, the tongue takes over. Jawbones are the legs of the old."

"You're more than old jawbones. In you, I still sense a young buck."

"Thank you, my son. Tonight I will tell the buck within me of your words. Maybe then he will stop whispering to me to set him loose. His dreams remember when women looked at him with desire, and he has not forgotten it is a good day when a penis is of service."

I asked Two Hearts would he prefer to remain in the quiet of our cabin to rest in my berth, and he said, "If you spoke Indian, you might make a good medicine man." He lay back and was soon softly snoring. He had told Deems he was trained never to snore louder than a night-bird calls. Noise can scare off game. Or alert an enemy to one's position.

21 July

Many passengers are napping away the rainy morning. In the nearly empty saloon, Deems studied his newest medical book, and I wrote a letter to Sophie I will leave at the next landing. I mentioned to her the bond building between Nicodemus and Two Hearts, describing the sachem at length and saying the link was more that of grandson to grandfather than son to father, both of them finding something lost. I opined the old Osage, whilst knowing Deems is educated in white ways, considers the lad's race as setting him apart from some of them. Each man comprehends things unperceived by me.

I do believe, though, following my treatment of his furuncle, Two Hearts now has trust in me. In Nicodemus, the old fellow sees a young man who also has experienced contempt at the hands of a race that has made difficult his own life. A sachem met on the great prairie is the grandfather Deems never had. It is inspiriting to watch the two of them together, although I confess to feeling usurped, a reflection of excessive self-regard. After all, it is my own society of whites that for generations has excluded Two Hearts and Deems, making it natural for them to share a bond, one now, for me, thwarted by *my* skin.

Rain ceased before we arrived at the landing at Lexington, some three hundred miles up the Missouri from our start. Alone, I disembarked to exercise my legs in the hamlet mostly located well above the river. Settled by Kentuckians—hence the name—the trade here is in tobacco, hemp, cattle, and what riverboats bring in: gamblers, slave traders, land speculators.

The warm afternoon led me to quench a thirst in a riverfront bar, an enjoyable moment right up to noticing a pair of hooligans of the kind the river washes in as it does dead fish. They were palavering about the slave trade and the danger of abolition ruining what they termed *business*. To my dismay, I saw holstered to one of them a pearl-gripped pistol on his left hip, and on the other a bowie knife. Pulling down my hat brim and lifting my beer mug to cover my lower face, I took a close look at the man's profile: the best description of my response is simply, *my heart sank.* Indeed, it had to be Hell Bent Ferrall talking to another slave hunter. I turned away to think of something I could do to interfere further with his pursuit. Say, a scalpel across a criminal throat.

Ferrall wants Deems for remuneration, and me for the satisfaction of retaliation. To him, against a man who shamed him, revenge outweighs reward. In us he sees one captive and one corpse.

I left the bar, I trust without notice, and boarded the *Osage* to take a position offering a view of all entering after me. Of them, not one was our nemesis. I was happy the captain used both the rising river and the rising full moon to fire the boilers into driving the wheels hard, each rotation extending the distance between us and maleficence.

Joining Deems and Two Hearts at supper, I spoke about stumbling onto the hunters. Nicodemus received the news stoically, and the old sachem listened with great interest. At last he said, "When a hungry panther trails its quarry, one of them will die." There followed a long silence, eventually broken when he added, "Tonight I will smoke my pipe and chew the fat with the Grandfather Spirits. They are wise in the ways of the panther. That is the theory."

22 July

Sometime after midnight a knocking at the cabin door: I rose to whisper, "Who is it?" but answer came there none. Unfolding my clasp knife and keeping it low at my side, I opened the door a few inches. There stood a masked figure wearing a flowing white robe. The thing pulled aside the mask to reveal the Woman in White who thrust at me a blue baby, the umbilical cord around its neck. My recoil woke us both.

Deems asked, "The dream again?" and waited for me to recover my senses before he said, "Shouldn't you address this phantasm?"

I set down here, in brief, what I told him in hopes describing my haunting might assist finding a remedy for it. He noted I had earlier written to Sophie, and once again thoughts of her coincided with an appearance of the apparition. His observation forced me to recognize—*to admit*—the figure had to be an eidolon of Caroline. Having introduced my wife into the topic, I had unbolted the door to her death in childbirth and the concurrent loss of our infant daughter. I could no longer repress my guilt. They died because a physician did not know enough. Malpractice from ignorance.

Rattling on, seeking excuses, making excuses, I explained we were then living in an isolated cottage in Devon. And help was not available. And the child arrived prematurely. And I was fresh out of medical college. And I had received little training in parturition. *And, and, and, and.*

Here Nicodemus stopped me to retard such excusing and effusing. He suggested I shut my eyes, calm myself. When I regained a degree of equilibrium, I said, to know something well, one must comprehend its many ramifications. Yet ramifications are infinite and human knowledge is finite. Regardless whose it is, what a brain knows is woefully superficial and precariously imprecise and often lethally incorrect. But when ignorance condemns one's wife and child, mere awareness of limitations is empty because it is useless.

I said, "If only, *in some way*, I could have done more. I was worthless to them."

Deems went to the cabin window now admitting the first rays of morning light, then turned to me, "Need I remind you? You *have* done more. I stand as proof. *I am alive!*" With those words I was too overcome to speak further, and he said, "I'm going to fetch Two Hearts. He might know something about ghosts."

An hour later the pair entered the cabin. Two Hearts, reasonably flexible for a man of his years, sat on the deck in a cross-legged manner. He removed his deerskin jerkin so I could examine his neck. The lesion was healing properly.

His thin, ropy chest carried a large tattoo: an azure line spiraling away from a central point, increasing in circumference until it almost reached from one scrawny shoulder to the other. I asked about it, and he said, "All things try to be round. It is their nature because all things begin in a center. The journey, if it is to be true, must go outward to become round. But going out makes a traveler lonely. Then he wants to circle back to rejoin the source and come home again. I was born on the prairie, but I come from the stars. As do we all. Even the white man. *So it is said.*"

Looking at Nicodemus, Two Hearts smiled, then continued, "To forget the source is to lose the high blue road towards harmony. Forgetfulness is a path to sorrow. When sorrow comes before you, it is important to remember what you love. This tattoo is a map to show me the circling of all things. From the stars and back to the circling stars. Some warriors tattoo their scalp with the count of every enemy they have killed. I do not wish to boast how many enemies I have killed. And white men—I have killed none. Now, I am old and my neck is stiff, and it is hard to look down to my tattoo and be reminded of the great blue road. And so in my age, I carry a small journey tattoo on my left wrist above the blue blood lines from the heart. Forgetting is the worst of death."

"I can't forget," I mumbled, "and death still haunts me."

"Maybe the way has changed and you do not recognize it," he said. "Twice I have begun my life again. Changed the desire of my heart. When I was sixteen my father was killed and scalped by a Pawnee known as I-gah-shi-tha. That means *Stone Club.* After much counsel with the Grandfather Spirits, I went north to find him. At the end of the tenth day, I came upon him in a thicket. In sport with a noisy woman. I told him to let her loose and come out and stand. When he did, I struck him down. But I did not scalp him. He was the first man I killed, and because he was

Pawnee, I earned respect among the Wah-sha-shay. And my life as a warrior began."

Deems said, "And so you became Two Hearts?"

"Not then. On a spring hunt, my natural son, a boy of ten, was thrown from his horse. He fell under the hoofs of the buffalo stampede. Once the herd rumbled on north and we could get to him, he was recognizable only by his trampled moccasins. In my sleep, I still see his face and body, but I will not describe them. I consulted with the Grandfathers for a season of nights before I could heed their wisdom to start my life all over. My second life is to kill no more. To live as a sachem."

We waited for him to continue, and I thought he had nodded off. Then he said, "I feel the third beginning approach. It comes on like a road rising ahead of me. I hope it is the good blue road. Three can be a good number. The road is the way in this third world for two-leggeds to confront beginnings. There is an Osage word for that, but I cannot remember it. Only those who do not quit can go forward. Each evening, with my pipe, I counsel with the Grandfather Spirits, and I ask them to reveal to this old man the way onto the blue road."

Eyes closed, he sat in silence, and again I thought he had fallen asleep when he spoke.

"It is clear. I have *come* forth and now I must prepare to *go* forth. For you, the white medicine man, you could ask the Grandfathers the way, but they will not tell you because you do not believe in them."

Discerning disappointment, Two Hearts said, "I will shoot the breeze with the Grandfathers tonight and ask for you. I will apologize for your ignorance of things, and explain you cannot help being a white man. I will remind them white men do not understand circles and roundness and cannot see the blue road. And that is the reason they misbehave."

He looked at me intently before continuing. "The Grandfathers like a good joke. Do you have one? Best are ribald jokes."

I could not recall even a child's jest. Two Hearts said, "I will tell them a couple of mine and say you gave them to me to pass along. Then, *then* they *might* advise. I know a good one."

"Tell me."

"It does not work in English. English lacks subtlety. I hope the Grandfathers have not heard it. It is about a nun, a cactus, and testicles."

23 July

We arrived in the late afternoon at Westport Landing, scarcely more than a line of thrown-together frame buildings set onto a low and level limestone outcrop serving well as a levee substantial enough to hold against the outside current of the combined Missouri and Kansas rivers conjoining less than a mile westward, the latter (or Kaw River) delivering a considerable tribute of sediment to the Big Muddy. Beyond the steep bluff above the landing and five miles south is Westport, the name signifying it as a portal into the American West. Activity along the riverfront was almost entirely given over either to moving cargo *off* boats to get it to Westport for stocking Conestoga wagons or to moving cargo *onto* boats for shipment upriver to Fort Union and Fort Benton.

The place was a vortex of topsy-turvydom, commotion and pandemonium, racket and ruckus, a conflux of heterogeneities: aboriginal, American, African, Asian. I heard words spoken or shouted in English, French, Spanish, and at least two Indian tongues. It was as if living flotsam and jetsam from the good ship *American Experiment* had been tossed ashore here to be sorted and reorganized to see what would come of it all: among the westward bound were Chinese men headed for railroad construction, a Negro woman pushing through to retrieve a wandering child, an Indian whacking at an intemperate mule, a red-faced sodbuster cussing at something I could not discern, all of us equally sweating under a hot sun.

The *Osage* will remain overnight to unload barrels of this in exchange for crates of that, to replace passenger X with traveler Z, and (above all, to our pleased eyes) to bring aboard a supply of wood for the voracious boilers to keep us moving away from any trailing malevolence. We had time to bang around in the rowdydow to gain the feel of a frontier town that could be named Anything Goes. With us was Two Hearts, his quiver and bow as always over his shoulder in case a bull buffalo came charging into the throng. Nicodemus and I kept him between us to assist his occasional unsure steps, even though Deems said to him, "I notice the young buck inside you is having a good time."

"Yes," Two Hearts answered, "but he lives on memory of what was. The past feeds his days. That is the purpose of yesterdays. So goes the theory."

As sundown quickened, the hubbub quieted, and Two Hearts thought it time for a meal; we ascended the bluff to a primitive chophouse with a fine view of the confluence. I had a sense of standing at the edge of what we loosely term civilization where roads return to trails, where woodlands yield to grasslands, where white society must vie with what it terms savage, where scales of justice are melted down into pistols, tornadoes supplant summer showers, and the fundamental condition of humanity is not convenience but contention. This raw place—untamed, untilled, untried—is certain to reframe the American experiment as did the earlier frontiers farther east. With the crossing of each boundary, Americans take yet another step away from their European antecedents to become ever more American. Westport Landing, within a day's ride of the center of the nation, holds resident a power waiting to rise, a force begun and now unstoppable except by cosmic intrusion.

I had an uneasy and overwhelming impression that what lies here restive and imperfectly visible is getting ready to make itself known, and when it does, nothing anywhere will be left unchanged. Whatever that potence proves to be, it will be awesome because it is a collusion of differences headed for collision with all coming before it, the result a convergence of things not yet seen and scarcely comprehended.

The chophouse was about to shut down, but I persuaded the cook, a large man who perhaps had consumed a few too many servings of his specialty dish, to toss together some eggs and sausage, all of it superior to offerings on the steamer. Before we could begin our meals, a man entered with deliberate noise. He, side-armed with pistol and bowie knife, sauntered to our table, and said to me, "Liken them sassages, Doctor? You take em bloody?" and with that he pulled his long blade and in a stroke whacked open a sausage.

Then he said, "And how bout you, black boy? Yourn need cuttin too?" and he split another sausage. Turning to the Osage, he rasped, "Hey, you redskin devil! While I'm cuttin and carvin, I might as well take care of what you got. This country dont want nothin what's sittin at this here table."

As he waved his knife at the old warrior, Two Hearts rose instantly, only to be shoved against the wall and onto the floor. Deems immediately confronted Ferrall as I helped up the sachem. I heard, "So this is the nigga of my five hunnerd dollars. Double iffen I drag it back alive. And you can be sure of that. You made me come a long ways to see yer goddamn face, and that gets me in the mood to put the whet leather to my knife. I'll tell yer black ass this—it's about to be took back to the plantation what owns it. Yer Master Reilly wants a little ol prittle-prattle with his runaway, and a shotgun'll do all the talkin."

Then our hellhound turned to me, coming close enough I could recognize him by his rancid breath: "And heahs my ol nigga-lovin fren. Good to lay eyes on you agin, fren. Now *you*, you aint agoin back to the plantation because once you git outta reach of the law, I'm puttin a bullet inta yer stinkin ear. For all the trouble you done give me."

The cook had come out when he heard Two Hearts hit the floor and Deems yell at Ferrall. His presence ended the confrontation, and with a smirk, Ferrall slunk out. The Osage wore an expression I had not seen on him before, a look carrying the fire of a young brave. He was limping from his fall, and he was locked in silence. I asked were he all right, and he said, "Hell no. My eggs ended up on the floor."

I had a notion Ferrall followed us to the *Osage*, but too many people were milling about for him to act. Whatever fraction of the law there may be beyond the Missouri, I am certain that, if we dare to proceed westward, we are likely to find out.

24 July

Our steamer plugged off at dawn into the thirty-some miles to Cantonment Leavenworth—fast becoming an Army fort—and we arrived in time for me to find the postal station. As I stood expectantly for whatever might await in general delivery, I deposited my missive to Sophie. The clerk took an unconscionable time to return, and when he did he had nothing in his hands. Never have I seen hands so empty. It would be unmanly to write I was *crushed* at not receiving a letter, so I will use the watery word *disappointed*. I had turned towards the door when another clerk called out, "Tom's new here. He missed these," and held up three letters. *Oh, benighted humans! Too soon dejected, too soon elated!*

I moved fast to the *Osage* to get aboard before she was to pull out. A deckhand told me there was no hurry: a bad boiler will likely detain her for two days.

To Nicodemus I suggested we leave the river and take off for the prairie. The Osage troupe was talking about the seasonal migration of bison heading north, and I was keen to travel beyond the edge of cultivation to where the plow is all but unknown—at least for another few years. Good ground to shake Ferrall.

Deems was nonplussed. I tried to counter his dubiousness by saying we could return to the river after we witness the migration of a thousand bison, more than a million pounds of beast, 750 tons of American buffalo moving en masse in one of the great spectacles of the natural world. Congregate the animals and they would overwhelm any town in the West.

Thinking a moment, he said, "What if we invite Two Hearts?" And he was off to bring him to our cabin. The old warrior tried to sit on the floor, but his fall left him too stiff to bend down. As he took a chair, he said, "It is not good for an Indian to sit like the white man. It will make him weak. Do not tell the others about this."

Nicodemus proposed my idea. Two Hearts considered only long enough to prepare to speak clearly in his mellow voice. "My son, I have smoked with the Grandfathers to ask how to proceed towards my next beginning. They have remained silent as they do when they must hide they do not know an answer. But you suggest an answer. For the last time, I want to see the passage of the buffalo spirits in the land where I became a brave. Such a journey will complete my circle."

Here he raised his left hand to examine his tattoo as if it were a cosmic map. He said, "The troupe will not miss an old archer whose strength is declining. I will show you, my son, the country of the Grandfathers and their buffalo. The land where many things begin. My heart sings at your words."

Slowly and unsteadily he stood to say, "And now, it is good to ask, *When the hell do we leave?*" adding as he opened the door, "This excitement has made me hungry. I will need strength to face the buffalo. Their spirit is strong."

25 July

Last night was riddled with dreams, but in this instance not mine. Nicodemus dreamt Ferrall dragged him in chains up to the door of the plantation house, where Reilly had a shotgun ready. Deems woke and required time to regain sleep just before dawn.

Two Hearts came to our cabin to mend an arrow broken when Ferrall knocked him to the floor, and he told of *his* recent dream. He was sitting under an unclouded prairie sky to stare at the Evening Star. He said, "I have never seen Wah-tse-do-gah so bright and so big and so near. One of my arrows could reach it. It grew bigger until it was the size of the moon, and still it grew until night turned to day. It was then I woke and realized the Grandfathers sent a message."

Scowling, he shook his head. "They worry me. They like messages to be puzzles so they can wager over my intelligence. They think I am old and gone simple, and they do not believe I know there will come a good day to die. The secret of a good death is do not live past your time."

We gathered our equipage as Two Hearts, bow and quiver over his shoulder, waited impatiently on the landing. He pointed up at a red-tail, and said, "Before a journey, it is a good day when wah-sah-shin-gah tonga is above. Even better when it flies *west* to follow the path of the Sun. Hawk spirit leads the way and Wah-tse-do-gah will light our way. We cannot go wrong." Perhaps so, but once off the levee, we turned the wrong direction and had to backtrack.

As if, however, to confirm omens, the old sachem had that morning met a dozen Omaha Indians going west to join a band of bison hunters. He explained, "We speak the same tongue, but they mispronounce many words," and demonstrated their numerous embarrassing mispronunciations. (Before the day was out, two Omaha had corrected *his* words.) He said, "It is good the

Omaha can be trusted because we will have to buy two horses for you. To me, they will lend one."

Observed closely by a squad of soldiers to certify we were after bison and not white scalps—a certification helped along by the presence of two non-Indians—we assembled under the Omaha sub-chief Sho-say-wah-he, in English, Bone Heart. Whatever a heart of bone is, I have no idea. No! In fact I have several ideas, none desirable in a leader, although Bone Heart accepted us and negotiated a fair price for a pair of mounts. He calculates our presence will be continual notice to all that we are not a war party.

Two Hearts introduced us in Osage, calling Nicodemus Young-Black-Grandson, and me, using English, Sawbones, which the Omaha heard as "Zawbo." Now, among them, that is my name. I have had worse. Deems is quite honored by his, and his gait is almost a strut. I am amused and inspirited by our blood admixturing that will do more than merely allow us all to get along.

Nicodemus needed say nothing to create trust from the Omaha, but for me their trust hangs on my being a zawbo who might be able to relieve pain or save a life. Even before we left the cantonment area, an Omaha came to me with a rotten bicuspid. I administered a dose of laudanum to dull the throbbing, and through Two Hearts I indicated I would extract the tooth in the evening to rid him of pain altogether. The rapid relief from the laudanum made him believe me.

And so we started off into the great American prairie. Never have I felt so keenly alive. Deems said, in the cockiness of youth, "Shall we invite Hell Bent to join in?"

Said the Osage, "We already have."

26 July

The presence of the Omaha Indians, so I hope, may keep Ferrall at a distance if he shadows us, allowing our journey to continue without let or threat. At some point—today, tomorrow, next week—we surely will have shaken free of the blackguard. I will not watch my life be circumscribed by a man, in the words of Two Hearts, "not worth a thimbleful of belly mud." The old sachem added sadly, "I have forgotten the Osage word for *belly mud*."

The horses are the best mounts yet, although the Omaha mock us for using saddles, which, incidentally, cost far more than our steeds. Nicodemus is invigorated by fulfilling a boyhood dream of riding onto the prairie with *wild Indians*. I feel a modicum of exhilaration myself.

We westered, the country changing from woodlands to grassy hills with trees growing only in the shelter of creek vales; where grass had not burnt, it grew to the haunch height of our horses, and a small man could take a few steps into a spread of big bluestem and quite vanish. The farther west we traveled, though, the grass became ever shorter, with large swaths little more than green shoots rising from the ash of the fires Indians set last autumn to draw in deer and bison. What a symbiosis it is—fire, grass, bison, human—one consumption after another repeated and repeated in the cyclic law of this land. Another of the sachem's circles.

The Omaha, who make their bed pallets from hides of bison—furred side towards the sleeper—laugh at our brightly colored woolen blankets, but they have offered to trade for them—not for bedding but to wear: one pony for one striped blanket. Had we known this value before joining them, we could have done a good business. The physical appearance of the Omaha is similar to the Osage, but they are not quite so tall nor so prideful. They are drawn to Nicodemus to the degree his self-esteem has become rather puffed up. Considering the humiliations he endured in his boyhood, he is due a measure of admiration.

This evening, one of the several women with the hunting group (including families) went into labor. It was her first delivery—she is but sixteen—and there were difficulties enough to bring the Omaha chief to me to request assistance. Given my previous failure with a birth, I had to school my nerves. Upon seeing her struggle, with nothing but a strip of bison leather to bite down on to control pain, I asked Deems for my kit even as memory of Caroline's suffering and death threatened to unman me.

Nicodemus saw my expression, my shaking hands. He spoke calmly, encouragingly, and still I hesitated. Then he said, "If you don't assist, she's going to die." He held up my medical bag, shook it at me, and I fumbled for an ampule of laudanum, opened it, and removed the girl's bison strap. Two Hearts told her to swallow. As the pain eased, I asked Nicodemus to help her sit. With the next contraction, the old medicine man translating, I directed her to exert herself, and soon I could grasp the infant and assist it into the light. He is well formed.

I placed him in the mother's arms, and the Omaha women who had been standing by stepped forward to bless and clean mother and baby. I was shaking to the point of almost falling. Deems said, "You did it! Now you *know* you can do it. You have re-begun." After dark, under a full moon, the Omaha drums and chants celebrated new beginnings for mother, father, baby. And, unbeknownst to them, a physician. I think I shall never again see the Woman in White.

27 July

At dawn, dam and her child were helped onto a travois assembled from two lengths of cottonwood saplings cut from the creek edge where we had camped. Off our contingent went. After the mother's departure, I extracted the rotten tooth of the brave. In the two administerings of laudanum, the Omahas observed the effect of powerful medicine, and I fear I will not have sufficient opiate tinctures to ease all the pains that now may be brought to me. Two Hearts warned me to keep watch on my medical bag. In order to protect the chemical *magic*, he let the people know *white man's medicine* works only under a Blood Moon; at the next one, I trust Deems and I will be back in the world we come from.

In western Europe are many vistas that could belong to an American landscape—forests, lakes, mountains—but the tall-grass prairie is a distinct face of this nation. As we jogged along among the indigenous people, I rode immersed in the country as if it had enwrapped me. Deems and I became, briefly, a part of the land and its natives, whose language we did not speak but whose welfare was important to us, as was ours, I do believe, to them. Their features so different from either his or mine, and ours so different one from the other. Nevertheless we all ride across the prairie in a shared mission: theirs to find food, ours to witness a great passage of that food. For a traveler, nothing is finer than to be able to say, "It is for all this I have come."

As we crossed the first of the large tracts of newly sprouting grass of tender and moist shoots sought by deer and bison, the Omaha discerned no animals had yet passed through, but a scout gave assurance the beasts were moving our way. On a level-topped rise above a broad depression that will serve to funnel the bison into an eruption of rocky hills, we pitched camp. When it is time for the mounted Omaha hunters to enter a migrating herd, we can watch from above.

With tents set up, mostly by the women, the men began lazing about, addressing their attire and facial appearance, evidencing the vain behaviors of a French dandy. They plucked whiskers and eyebrows, or experimented with designs for face paint, or stretched out in the warm sun like canines, dozing and scratching, and sometimes rising for a conjoining with a woman inside a bison-skin tepee. Only recently the Omaha were diminished by smallpox; now, to this physician, it looks as if the tribe is dedicated to rebuilding its population. On the plains, to become few is to become none.

Nicodemus and I were also lying in the warmth of morning when thundering rose from the far side of the hill where we camped. The noise grew louder, and the Omaha women hurried to gather the children out of sight. The warriors leapt onto horses and indicated for us to do the same. With no time to saddle up, and without stirrups, I did a poor job of mounting up, but the men were too occupied with the threat to laugh.

We had just formed a line when a swarm of horsemen came over the brow to charge directly at us, pulling up only when in range of a human voice.

Two Hearts said to me, "This is not welcome. They are Pawnee."

Heavily and intimidatingly decorated with paint and feathers, four Pawnees approached near enough for their horses to whinny and sniff at the snouts of the Omaha steeds. One of the men, a warrior of serious if not deadly mien, approached Nicodemus, to study him before brazenly reaching over and roughly wiping fingers across my friend's forehead. The Pawnee examined them. Two Hearts whispered, "He is looking for war paint. He has never seen a black white man." The warrior laughed and held up his hand to show the others there was no color, and they joined in his laughter. I understand now why the Osage term for *enemy* and *Pawnee* is the same. In an excess of swaggering, the imposing leader rode forward and directly approached me and spoke. I turned towards Two Hearts for translation: "Word is out. He asks if you are the white medicine man who gives cure to all ills. He's a half-breed renegade the Army calls Joe Blood. In Pawnee, his name means *Slash Knife*."

"Not all ills," I asked him to translate. The chieftain scowled and dismounted and motioned for me to do likewise. He said something, then peremptorily raised his breechcloth to reveal his organ of regeneration. On it was an early-stage chancroid, almost certainly a non-syphilitic lesion.

I nodded and pointed to the nearest tent and advised Deems to join in and bring along the medical bag. The chief adjusted his breechcloth and strutted before me into the tent. I treated the chancre with an application of mercury, adding my counsel, delivered by Two Hearts, to avoid venery until the lesion completely healed. To help convince the chieftain of the cure, I administered a dose of laudanum. The rapid—if temporary—palliation will support belief in my power, and if a cure, will insure our safety. Rearranging his garment with all dignity possible under such circumstances, he departed, saying not a word. Two Hearts whispered, "We must hope the silver water works. If it fails, say goodbye to your scalp."

How strange is this newly found land where a man may get a reconfigured hairline because of another's unhealed chancroid.

28 July

The Pawnee have not returned, and I now have amplified appreciation of the god Mercury and his caduceus, the symbol of my profession. Two Hearts directed Nicodemus and me on an expedition to see a buffalo jump not used since the old sachem was a boy. It was a ride of an hour.

Parallel rows of stones led to the edge of a cliff. In another time, Indians hid behind the rocks before rising and shouting and waving blankets to stampede entering bison over the precipice where those surviving the fall were slaughtered. The manner of hunting today is to ride into a herd and thrust lances or shoot with arrows or bullets—a less wasteful practice at a time when bison numbers are in decline.

To demonstrate the old system, Two Hearts and I assumed the role of harriers and took position out of sight, and Nicodemus acted the part of a bison charging towards its death. In this game of *playing Indian*, he became a boy again, laughing, snorting, ready to gore a careless hunter. I watched through my spyglass as he ran in utter joy along the lines of stones.

Out of nowhere, a horseman riding hard came from the rear to trail him, and closed in to knock Nicodemus onto the ground. I thought the rider was a Pawnee, but Two Hearts growled no Indian would attack like that. He said, "It is a white man."

My glass revealed something worse than a Pawnee standing above a prostrate Nicodemus. I started for him, but the old warrior pulled me back. I shouted the man drawing his long knife was Ferrall.

"There is a better way," Two Hearts said. Then, in a sequence happening so fast and seamlessly I can only describe it as orchestrated: from his quiver the old archer withdrew an arrow and let it fly to strike Ferrall's boot. Hell Bent jumped back to see where the shot had come from.

Spotting us beside the rock wall, he pulled his pistol to draw a bead on me. I shouted at Two Hearts, "This time, don't miss!"

He breathed deeply, half-exhaled as his venerable arms worked to steady the bow. He released a second shaft at the same moment I saw smoke from the pistol and heard a ricochet.

Ferrall recoiled as if dodging another arrow, then his head leaned unnaturally to one side, his knees buckled, and he collapsed atop Nicodemus. As we approached the men, Two Hearts held his bow level and set with a third arrow. Ferrall lay prostrate, one leg moving slowly to bend at the knee, his left hand twitching but still gripping his pistol. From his lungs came a hollow exhausting of wind. Except for the shaft stuck in his boot, we found no other arrow although his trachea was sliced open, and a jugular cleanly severed. I knelt to check his pulse. Feeble, then nothing. I told Two Hearts the malfeasor suffocated before he bled to death, and the sachem said, "It is good when the bad die twice."

We pushed the corpse off Nicodemus who was groaning and coming to. He asked, "Am I dead?"

"You are *not*. But our nemesis is. And you, *you* are truly free. The final chain is cut." Then to the old warrior I said, "I'm grateful you didn't miss the second time."

He answered, "I didn't miss the first time. The angle was wrong. I had to turn him. This seemed a good day for him to die."

After we ascertained Nicodemus was uninjured other than a bruised shoulder, our task was to attend the corpse. Two Hearts had become unstable. When I looked him over I noticed dark stains on his left moccasin and legging. Hell Bent's bullet had ricocheted to nick the sachem and draw enough blood to require binding. Deems and I helped him lie down. He said, "It is good for an old man to see he still has blood in him and know he has not yet dried up. I have great affection for my red blood. When I was a tyke, I thought the white man was pale because his blood was white. Then I saw my first gut-shot white man."

To change the topic, Nicodemus said, "Grandfather, without your arrows, I'd be hog-tied now and on my way downriver. And the doctor's brains would be running out his ears." Touching his boot to the corpse, he added, "For this human dunghill you've rewritten his nickname from *Hell Bent* to *Hell Bound*."

Said the Osage, "It is a good day when a man can send a bad man to Hell."

Having no shovels, we dragged the corpse to an outcrop of sandstone, and after taking his weapons, with difficulty we gathered broken rocks to entomb the body despite Two Hearts advising to leave it. He said, "The sooner coyotes eat his liver and squirt him out, the sooner his journey to the next world can begin and he can be made into something else. I hope it is not as an Indian. We have no need of a white man like that."

Disregarding the counsel, we completed the heaping of rocks. Then I took a flat piece of sandstone and scratched in the date, and Deems added "RIH"—for Rest in Hell but which could also be taken for a man's initials—and laid it on the pile.

We managed Two Hearts into a sitting position to make certain his wound was sufficiently bound for our return to the Omaha camp. I passed him a water skin to drink all he could, and Deems thanked him again, and he nodded, "Last night, the Grandfathers advised me to help out."

Deems said, "A good red man killed a bad white man to save an ordinary black man. I think you rewrote a pattern in American history."

"My son, I must speak the truth. I was never good at white man's history. The Grandfather Spirits say the stories of the white man are unpleasant and in them are many Indian deaths."

When Deems was sturdy enough to stand, I handed him the bowie knife and I kept the pistol, and we all mounted up for the encampment. The day was clouded though warm, and we moved slowly, taking along Ferrall's horse. Its brand had been crudely obliterated by a knife, scars useful to further his disappearance.

We had made only a couple of miles when a bevy of renegade Pawnees surprised us in a carefully laid ambush. They outnumbered us by only four warriors but by eight rifles. Two Hearts struck up a parley involving considerable gesturing towards Deems. Once finished, the Osage surprisingly gave Ferrall's pistol and steed to the Pawnee, and the renegades took off fast. I was relieved—for some reason I was more concerned about theft of my compass than losing a horse I could replace. Two Hearts watched them flee, and he said, "It is a good bargain to trade one horse and one lie for three lives."

Moving again, I asked his meaning. He said, "I told them Nicodemus carried the *black sickness*. Yesterday he had been as white as you. I tipped them off the sickness is worse than the smallpox, and the white medicine man has power to turn anyone black. Because I am old and immune, I have the duty of taking you both to a remote valley to bump you off. Unless the Pawnee wanted to change color, they had better allow an old man to complete his

job. I believe I clinched their decision when I mentioned the black
sickness also causes the penis to fall off."

Said Deems, "I guess I'm only half sick."

"It is told," said Two Hearts, "that long ago when the white man
took servants, he painted them black to identify them. Thereafter,
when the servants had children born to them, the little ones came
forth black. But I do not believe that theory."

He waited for a response, but our silence led him to
continue. "Often," he said, "a man can save his skin, but once in
a while his skin can save *him*. We were lucky. Pawnee have no
affection for an Osage, and for a white man they have only hatred.
But for you, my son, today is a good day to be born black."

"At last!" Nicodemus said.

29 July ??

(I am writing in arrears and can only guess at the date.) On the
western horizon we saw smoke rising from a stretch of prairie,
perhaps ignited to direct the movement of bison making their way
northward. Or it could be wildfire. Two Hearts advised stopping
to assess the direction of the flames and take on a little sustenance.
He brought from his saddlebag three cakes of pemmican given
him by an Omaha woman who is, in his American words, sweet
on him.

Said he, "She traded the food for certain affections. An Indian
believes copulation transfers wisdom from the old to the young.
Among old white men our belief is held in high regard."

Her recipe was dried and pounded strips of bison mixed with
bone-marrow grease and dried sand-cherries. A hungry traveler
can find it surprisingly palatable.

As we chewed—and *chew* we did—Two Hearts spoke of
his hope of seeing the massive bison passage any day now. He
said, "The white man has no understanding of the buffalo except
as a thing to be killed, and that happens because his heart is not

connected to what is greater than his own life. He kills the buffalo not for food but to starve an Indian. The Wah-sha-shay, we kill a buffalo only after honoring him, for his spirit is large. He carries the power of the plains. Even the panther fears him and prefers the crippled or newborn. The white man eats buffalo and learns flesh made out of water and grass is good. I do not know how grass turns into meat, and it bothers me. From blades of grass comes a powerful beast. Sap turns into blood and big humps of muscle. I have asked the Grandfathers about this, but they do not tell me. Maybe they do not know either. They are not good at admitting ignorance. My son, can you tell me?"

"No, Grandfather, I can't, but I'm good at admitting ignorance."

On we rode, the old sachem working up something to say to Nicodemus. It was this:

"From the buffalo the Indian makes leggings and jerkins and tents and shields and spoons. Glue and coracles. Ribs make good sleds for the snow. He cooks and heats his lodge with dry turds of the buffalo. From snout to tail, he uses it all, and when the beast is gone, then the Indian borrows its spirit to give him courage and remind him to respect things. Nothing is wasted. So runs the theory."

Sure of his receptive audience, he kept going. "At the Indian boarding school nuns taught us that in white religion people eat the body of their spirit man and drink his blood, but to me it tasted like crackers and juice of the grape. When an Osage eats of a buffalo, it is real flesh and blood. The white man says we are 'heathens' and 'savages' and says we are ignorant and must be wised up, but a man who calls crackers 'flesh' and juice of the grape 'blood,' maybe *he* should be wised up. I do not begrudge whites their strange beliefs, but I cannot figure why they have no respect for ours. Maybe they could think better if they were made of buffalo instead of crackers."

Knowing the old sachem was still working on his history, we rode waiting for him to speak. At length he said, "In Saint Botolph's Indian School, we poor Indian boys were taught about this business called miracles. But I could not understand how an impossible becomes possible. It worried me. It is not enough just to say it is so. Already I could see things not in front of me, but they were things I had seen before. Dead warriors in the icy grass, their blood frozen on their arms and faces. I was told such seeing is not a miracle. It is imaginary. I wished it was imaginary, then the dead warriors could arise again as I was told some white men do.

"I did not understand why what I had seen and *still* could see was not a miracle, but what I had never seen and could not see *was* a miracle. In my head, to carry pictures and voices of those I had known, *that* must be the miracle. But I could not explain it, and it worried me."

Nicodemus said not a word. Then, from the sachem: "I did not understand believing what no one alive has ever seen but *not* believing what I and the warriors saw. Instead, the nuns said I must see what I have not seen and believe in what I could not see. They said it is the invisible that is the truth."

We stopped for Two Hearts to urinate, he advising us to join him. Once again on his horse he said, "Now, in an old one's dreams, he sees the land before the white man appeared. It is good to be reminded. But how, *inside my head*, can there be pictures and people who speak? That is impossible, so they must be a miracle. It is good to be too far gone to worry about it."

The sky clouded over and obscured the advance of the smoke. Our horses were becoming skittish, and our water-skins nearly dry. Two Hearts said, "We will have to be like the buffalo and use our noses to tell us which way to go. Do you know what a man does in a prairie fire?"

"Runs like hell," Deems said.

"No, my son. A two-legged cannot outrun a prairie fire. If flames catch up and trap him, he must find a barren swale and flatten himself in it. Then he pisses straight up. It is good to shut the eyes. And the mouth."

"What does a woman do?"

"If she is alone, she dies. It is a hitch in the design of woman, but the Great Creator atones for the decision by giving her longer life. A mistake cannot be undone, but it can be apologized for. The lifepan of woman is an apology. There is an Osage word for this fire-pissing, but I cannot remember it. It means *body-water-gives-life.*"

We stopped to mark the progress of flames now near enough to be visible through the smoke. Two Hearts said, "The old medicine dance is worth a try unless the doctor has something better in his bag."

He dismounted and bent forward as far as his ancient spine would allow and began stepping, his feet barely leaving the ground, moving in a small circle, all the while vigorously chanting not words but sounds any Grandfather Spirits in the vicinity would hear. He was soon winded, and we faced west to watch the fire line encroach on the base of the ridge where we were. Two Hearts whispered, "My chant was to the Grandfathers to lend us a hand. If the fire climbs the slope, we may be goners. Fire runs faster uphill than down. And if the flames create whirlwinds, the dust devils can catch us and choke us to death."

The smell of smoke was now strong in our nostrils and ash from the fires fell as we drank the last water from our skins. Deems said he needed relief. "No, my son. If the Grandfathers did not hear me, you must hold it. And you might have to help me. Old men do not piss as well as the young. Their trajectory is short and the aim untrue."

The ash was coming down faster. I cannot say with exactitude it was raining, although the sky was leaking something neither drips nor drizzles but of sufficient dampness to darken the dry grass on the slope. The fire-line became low enough to jump, its roar lessened, and we felt droplets, and slowly the crackle of flames died. Deems stood to look down the hill, and he said, "Grandfather! The fire's out! You danced it to death!"

Two Hearts turned to the west, and gave his crafty smile. "Sometimes the old magic works. And sometimes it does not." Mounting up, he added, "Once was a time when I could dance up a thunderstorm. It would take all day. Maybe two. The longer dancing went on, the better it worked. A sachem learns ways to use inevitability."

We descended the hill, crossed the blackened ground now safe from flames for another season, and went on to find the Omaha encampment. The old sachem understood how to locate it: he followed a stream.

30 July

Comforting it is to be again with people who know the land and can read the sky to predict return of the bison: when the sword of Orion turns to point towards their approach. This evening Two Hearts sat cross-legged outside his tent and beyond the firelight of the camp, holding his long pipe with two hands in a meticulous and loving manner. He had been, said he, *jawing* with the Grandfather Spirits, but when Deems and I sat beside him they went mum.

"I do not mind your interruption," he said. "The Grandfathers were telling ribald stories. They do that when they have nothing to say. It frightens them to be silent too long. All they have is voice, so if they do not speak, they cease to exist. It happens with age. Years ago, I was told they once had bodies, but when the white man arrived, the Grandfathers found it better to keep themselves among the old stories where the strangers cannot find them. Else he will steal their secrets and kill them. But going mute is a mistake. The Grandfathers should try to share. Their selfish attitude, it worries me. Perhaps when I meet them face to face they will explain their reasons. Instead of telling ribald stories. Which are not useful."

To light his pipe, he snared a coal from the ashes of his small fire but did not immediately touch it to the bowl. Instead he studied it before blowing it into flame. "I have asked the Grandfathers about the nature of fire. And where grass goes when fire eats it. I do not understand that. Maybe the white medicine man can explain."

I said, "Heat from fire can change matter into gasses."

"What kind of grasses?"

"*Gasses.*"

Two Hearts considered, then said, "I have never seen these gasses. Where do they live?"

"They are everywhere around us. And *in* us. In you now are gasses. Each has a name."

"Of course. All things must have a name. Even ones we do not know. Are the gasses in me the same as farts?"

"Some of them."

"Then I know them, but I cannot remember the Osage word for them. When I was young, I have seen them. Boys lit them. They are blue. They are beautiful although they stink. The polecat too is beautiful but strong of odor. But here is a contradiction: if I blow hard on a burning stick, the flame can disappear."

"Your breath's a different gas with a different name."

"All this is good to know. Otherwise, when I light my pipe I could blow myself to Kingdom Come. I have often heard the white men speak of that country, but they do not say where it is. It sounds like a good destination."

Deems answered. "It's wherever you dream it to be."

"Ahh. That is very Indian."

Rain came on this evening to soak the prairie, and Deems said, emulating the old sachem, "Sometimes the old dance medicine works better than white man's chemical medicine." I countered I was taught how to deal with *pain*. For *rain*, the white man uses roofs. Nicodemus answered, "Roofs burn."

July the Last

Two Hearts slept poorly, and I saw signs he was failing, but he requested no medication. Word went around about a herd of bison moving north, pursued by Osage and our Omahas riding alongside *and* among them to let fly arrows and stab a few with lances. We three joined the women above a broad draw to watch until the hunters emptied their quivers. The initial passage was even faster than I had imagined: the pounding hooves, the rising dust, eyes of the bison enlarged and red with alarm, yet the beasts followed their ancient intelligence to avoid being separated from the mass to be readily picked off. They had learnt to run from men as if running from pack wolves.

The old warrior wanted to return to his tent for rest. Nicodemus on his left, near his heart, and I on the right, we escorted him back to camp. Deems stacked our saddles so the old fellow could half recline. I knew, sooner or later, he would want to talk. It was his way. When he recovered himself, he said, "I am thankful to see the buffalo spirits one last time. Tonight I will ride north with them."

"Grandfather, you're not ready to ride a horse."

"I will not need a horse, my son."

He dozed off, waking only when his devoted Omaha woman, surprisingly young, served him a bowl of dog stew, which he accepted but ate slowly, stopping to say, "She's a good woman. Not pretty but good in the actions of copulation. She lends a hand to keep me from thinking about death, and that is good for the young to do for the old. But the young are busy humans, and they forget about such things until they are old. *Then* they remember and regret being so busy because now they understand what it is to be forgotten."

Once more his eyes closed, and when he woke he said, "While I slept, I dreamed, and I thanked the Grandfathers for some victories. But I did not bring up the defeats. I also thanked them for restoring a son to me. And I mentioned they could have introduced him to me sooner. I asked them to look after him, to converse with him and not be fearful of his color. I assured them he would have been born Osage if he had the choice. Who would not?"

Two Hearts smiled. He said, "I asked the Grandfathers to help him become wise in medicine even if it is medicine of the white man. I told them he was raised by the Americans so he is ignorant of much, and he will need help in finding the blue road leading to all things else. I asked them to lead him away from the white man's fear of otherness for it is otherness we are born into. I do not understand why the way is so hard for whites to find when it is everywhere. That worries me."

For a time, a long time, he lay still, and Deems whispered, "Is Grandfather dead?"

The old sachem mumbled, "I heard that."

And again he slept. When he awoke, he said to me, "You are a good man. You also cannot help you were born a white man. To be born a two-legged of any color is to be born to bear a burden. Alone among all creatures, it is not fair we have to chew things over in order to live wisely and honorably, but the Grandfathers do not care about fairness. They care about strength of heart and mind because that is the only way they can talk to us. I apologize for them, but I do not believe they will talk to you because you do not know the language. In the boarding school I learned they at times will talk through the books of the white man. Grandfather Spirits respect the white man's books because some of those words help him towards finding the good blue road. If he finds it, he lives with more respect. It is good to live respectfully."

He slipped off once again, this time his breathing so soft, I felt his pulse. He opened his eyes and said, "Old men take a long time to piss and to die. They cannot help it. There is an Osage word for *slow pissing*, but I do not remember it."

Two Hearts turned to Deems and requested paper and pencil. He said, "These are white man's tools, but they can be of service when they are not used to tell lies."

Nicodemus gave him my journal to hold across his lap. Two Hearts, shakily, began to draw. When he finished he said, "I will ask a favor. It is to build this drawing on a hill. You will need four poles forked at one end. It is a platform for what a white man calls 'burial.' He uses that word because when his time comes, he digs a hole and hides himself. He acts like a groundhog because he is ashamed and fearful he has not troubled himself to find the good road. At his end, it worries him, but his worry comes too late to be of use."

Deems and I studied the penciling. Two Hearts said, "Strip my body to my loincloth, wrap me in my blanket, and tie me to the top of the platform. Consider it a stage station where a traveler waits for a coach to take him on to the next station of his journey. A white man can understand that, even if he wants angels with wings to carry *himself* away. I have looked for these angels, but I have seen only birds with wings, so I will count on *them* to move me along. Crows, ravens, magpies, vultures, eagles—they are good at helping. I have heard their voices many times, but I have never heard an angel. Once I thought I smelled one in the boarding-school chapel during prayer, but it was a boy farting. He was an Oto. The Oto are onion eaters."

The old sachem asked for water, not for thirst, but to wet his throat so he could speak clearly, as a sachem should. "I am going to miss talking like a human being, and it worries me."

"Grandfather, eagles may have wings, but they also have claws and beaks. They will tear you apart and eat you."

"That is the way, my son. All life, sooner or later, must be eaten. Life is born to be eaten. Every flea, every catfish, every buffalo. The nuns told of mummies buried in tombs in great stone pyramids so the mummies will not be eaten. But when their time comes, something will be there to eat them. I want the birds whose songs I recognize, I want *them* to do the job. I prefer a hawk to fly off with my heart—but a crow will do. Carry it into the sky. Let brother crow take me up in his paunch and squirt me down here and there so my parts can begin to turn into seeds to rise again. My innards, made from buffalo, they will help brother crow fly, and the thrush sing. There will be three of us up there. I cannot explain it, but I know that where birds squirt, there the grass is greenest, and deer and buffalo desire it. Maybe the white man's science will one day explain this, and if I return as a white man, then I will understand."

Two Hearts asked me to remove the single eagle claw from his neck and put it around Deems. "If you allow it, my son, it will remind you to respect things and watch for the blue road the white man finds so difficult to travel."

He lay back, looked to the sky, closed his eyes, and said, "The buffalo took my son, and now they bring me a grandson. He arrived almost too late. But now, he is here with me. And that is good."

When his eyes shut again I checked his pulse. Without opening them, he said, "You are making it hard to die, and this is a good day to die. The secret of a good life is don't live past your time. Do not cause me to miss my hour. I cannot remember how to say that in Osage."

Reaching a hand to Deems, the other to me, he clasped us tightly. I was surprised at the strength in his ancient grip. Then it loosened, and his arms fell to his sides.

August, 1848

---

1 August

IN THE MORNING, I persuaded an Omaha warrior to trade me a hatchet for twelve tobacco twists. Using the travois constructed to tote the Omaha mother and her baby, we secured Two Hearts to it and saddled up to find a fitting height to erect a scaffold for our honored sachem. In a coulee thick with cottonwood saplings, we cut four with sturdy forks, and also a passel of pieces to serve as stabilizers. The Omaha woman dedicated to looking after her beloved friend had given us a batch of bison-leather strips to use as lashings. As we worked, Deems became pensive. Was he holding strong? He nodded, "Until now, I've never known any of the grandfathers I've lost."

On we rode. Emerging from the low horizon was a hill appearing to rise from an unseen center. Whilst Nicodemus trimmed branches and dressed the poles, I used the hatchet to dig four postholes to anchor the forked uprights; then we lashed in the platform ribs to lock things together. The frame was sturdy enough for us to stand on.

We carried Two Hearts from the travois and lifted him. Rigor mortis made the hoisting easier than had our charge been freshly passed. Deems laid out a soft bed of two bison hides, fur-side up, but he wanted me to tie his grandfather to the platform. He murmured, "Will you speak a few words?" I declined. Benediction should come from him. Said Deems: *"Me?"*

"Remember your Caesar. Imagine a noble Roman eulogy."

Climbing onto the platform, at the feet of Two Hearts he affixed a bison head, one of several along our path today. Atop the scaffold, trying to employ the formal parlance of the old sachem, Nicodemus delivered his thoughts with careful enunciation, pausing between sentences to think and collect himself:

"Hello, Grandfather Spirits—and any others listening. We bear to this hill a man *almost* accurately named. *Almost* because he had more hearts than two. A better name could have been Heart-In-Hand. He was open to most of what he met: creatures that fly, swim, crawl, run on four legs, and even many that talk with words. He did his best to respect the white man, no matter how difficult he found it. I believe his medicine of counsel must have helped Indians in ways our version cannot. Every day he wanted to learn. I also believe this Wah-sha-shay came as close to discovering the center as a human being can, and he tried to mark the trail for others. And now, as he might say, it is a good day to begin the next journey to find the blue road."

After Nicodemus descended I sketched the scaffold. As I did he said, "For me, never before were words so difficult to speak, and never before did I so know *what* to say."

We walked our horses down the slope and mounted up. Deems asked, "Which way, O Doctor of Science?"

Not precisely sure where we were but believing it was a little northwest of the middle of America, I said, "The bison are moving towards the Missouri River. That seems like an expedient direction." Off we went, but I soon pulled out my compass to allow white man's science to confirm the big beasts knew where the hell they are going.

When last I looked back at the scaffold, three magpies were perched on it, and overhead a red-tailed hawk led us forward. It was a good day for Two Hearts to be getting on down the road beyond the sunset.

The Omaha woman had packed us pemmican into a bag made from a bison paunch. Shortly after noon we stopped in a shaded coulee with a briskly flowing spring, drank, and began chewing. I broke our silence. "I believe your grandfather was content to die once he saw the bison migration for the final time. And, *even more*, after he found a grandson."

Nicodemus nodded. "And also after doing a final great deed."

"What unusual deed?"

"Saving the life of a white man."

"*And* saving a black man from being returned to bondage?"

Smiling, Nicodemus said, "Do you think he had preference for one of those salvations?"

"At this point in his years, for such differences he cared not a damn. I've never known anyone of age so successfully avoid regressing into selfish stupidities."

"I miss our old sachem."

"Birds will carry on his heart, and your heart will carry on his memory. That is the theory."

We remounted and rode northward, silent until I said, "Nicodemus, these are not the best circumstances to bring it up, but I have to say it—we may be in a little difficulty."

"When haven't we been? So what's it this time?

"A white man and a black man roaming in red men's country. They have rifles, ammunition, numbers, food, and a full portion of suspicion and ill will. And, I might add, they know the territory. They know where water is, where cover is. All we know is a direction. One somewhat dependent on an animal proven to smell better than it sees."

"We also know our nemesis is buried under rocks and inescapably bound for Hell."

Half a league on, Nicodemus said, almost in irritation, "I'm waiting to hear what we should do."

I wanted to say, *As am I.* Instead I offered, "Unless you have a superior idea, let's continue deeper into the American experiment."

"I can't see Grandfather turning back."

And so, we proceeded on.

Afternoon of the 1st

Beyond the platform, we covered a good many miles. The faster we move, the more we reduce opportunity to be overtaken by Indians hostile to a pair of foreign ingressors. Our mileage was indicated on our buttometers: if we no longer suffered from saddle soreness, we were still subject to saddle weariness.

I have not found a truly serviceable traveler's map of the western prairies, and from the one in hand I can reckon only we are south of the Platte River, and that makes us rely on the simplicity of holding our course due north to intersect per force with the Missouri River.

We came upon a crooked and creeked vale able to block a distant view of a small campfire. Happy to call a halt to the day and sit down to pemmican and a few drafts of spring water, we were even happier to be out of the growing stench of the Omaha hunting camp: a bloating pony dead from a rattlesnake bite, butchered and rotting bison carcasses, pools of horse urine and piles of manure mixed in among the ordure of the swarming dogs—some of which rolled in the strongest substance they could sniff out—the growing foulness drawing ever more flies.

In villages and towns, the human animal lives largely unaware of the immense quantity of his and his animals' excreta. Prairie Indians are not known for policing their camps, their practice being to consider rank ground a sign to travel on and set up again, thereby marking out a pattern across the land. Surely will arrive a day when coprology is a recognized archeological discipline through which petrified dung will reveal as much as a skull.

Nevertheless, safety in human numbers can make tolerable the befouling of a camp. Deems and I, alone and unarmed but for a couple of knives, would not complain to have with us a few human producers of feculence, men able to bear arms.

Nicodemus followed the creek upstream to find its source and check its potability. He came bounding back. "It's a hot spring! A deep pool! Big enough to hold two or three men! What do you say?"

We stripped and waded in. The water was pellucid and wonderfully warm, and we hung in the depths letting the heat ease our tired muscles and the vigorous current wash us clean. When we climbed out and stood in the rays of the setting sun to dry, I said, "Deems, how does a house servant come to be so well built?"

Peering down as if *that* was my referent, he said, "Just nature," I guess.

We opened our bedrolls, and I laid a fire, adding a few green leaves to smoke away winged insects with unknown names; then we reclined to listen to critters of the night that sing but sting not. With music from the insectivorous chorale wafting under a prairie sky of a clarity I never saw in smoky London, my friend and I rejoiced in a rare chance for contemplation.

At last he spoke. "Was Ferrall the cause of Grandfather's death?" I said I didn't think so. The ricocheting bullet had only nicked him.

"Remember," I mused, "Two Hearts was ready for the passage. If felonious Ferrall had any hand in the death, then it was nothing more than an assist to the timing so that your grandfather could move on with the bison. *And* with a restored son at his side."

"You believe that?"

"When his eyes closed, I've never witnessed an expression as calm as his. It wasn't acceptance. Rather more akin to *expectance*. He was content the Grandfathers sent you to him. If only you and I depart with such dignity and serenity."

"On this prairie," Deems said, "that seems unlikely."

We lay a long time, silent and looking up, before he said, "Do you see the bright star to the south? Above the horizon. Flickering blue sparks."

I said it was Sirius, one of our nearest stars, but the travel time of the flickers measures in years.

"I don't know why I've never noticed Sirius until tonight. Maybe Grandfather is saying goodbye. Or maybe it's a 'Hello!' A hello from his new, high blue way."

"If so, he'll send you greetings for the rest of your life."

Said Deems, "He told me, 'Where human beings are few, stars are many.'"

After another long quiet, Nicodemus asked were I awake. I was, and he said, "Has the Woman in White come calling recently?" No. "Has Sophie been on your mind recently?" Yes. "Lying here, I'm thinking how we were both in bondage when we met. Not just *my* slavery—*your* slavery too. A nightwalker controlling your dreams. Limiting you."

"What are you saying?"

"Your apparition possessed you. I had a hemp noose at my throat. You had a memory at yours. The manumission the doctor needed was freedom from a nightmare."

He waited for me to respond. I said nothing. Then he continued. "You remember about the Virginia plantation? About why I had to run away? Why Reilly wants me dead?"

"You're referring to the white woman who visited you in the night?"

"My version of a woman in white. In some ways, her visits were not unwelcome. I was slow to realize how close to death she was putting me. And *your* woman of the night, the vengeful specter, your self-perceived guilt, it wanted you—*or Sophie*—dead."

Again we were quiet under blue Sirius. Then Deems asked, "If you'd known this morning you'd die tomorrow, would you do the same as you did today?"

"Ride till I'm exhausted? I would not."

"What if tomorrow's our last day before joining Two Hearts on the road to elsewhere?"

"I don't believe you can live with that as a guide. Not for long. Perhaps now and then for stimulation."

I was almost asleep when Nicodemus said, "It's comforting to have half a continent between me and, and, and—. *The plantation.* But on a beautiful and cool evening like this, thinking of those nights, a warm and naked body in my bedroll would be welcome."

2 August

Even a chill prairie dawn should not make getting out of a snug bedroll the most difficult of undertakings. But it did. With effort, I can come up with two or three other possibly greater challenges, but at sunrise I could not. Deciding to face it, I moved quickly with a wash more stimulating than required. I roused Deems and built a small and smokeless fire, and we began gnawing pemmican.

I was imagining a hot English breakfast: eggs, sausage, grilled tomatoes, hot buttered scones. To corrupt the poet: *Oh, to be in England now that . . . August's there!*

My partner was unusually silent but said he was not unwell. The truth is, the prairie—becoming ever more the plains, with its many restraints on vegetation—was beginning to wear on us. I have no doubt a human can learn to love this territory, but it would take time, especially for a man whose first memories are of blue Caribbean lagoons below volcanoes at the edges of green acres of sugar cane.

I do not know whether the pemmican or the chewing revived Nicodemus. Perhaps it was his jogging horse; nevertheless he whistled a merry tune—but softly to keep from announcing our presence. Bison hoof prints appeared and vanished only to reappear farther along whenever we crossed damp ground, and trampled soil became our compass needle. Over short-grass prairie we travel more easily than in the tall grasslands we recently left. Whenever bison sign evanesced, my prized compass gave reassurance.

We climbed a rise leading to a good vista northward, where I hoped to see reflections off the Platte River. Instead, *rearward*, I saw something else: several dark shadows moving our way over the route we had just used. "Bison," I announced and raised my spyglass. Bison the shadows were not. They were six mounted Indians, each wrapped in a fur robe against the north wind. I whispered, "I think we're being trailed."

Between us, we had a bowie knife and a clasp knife with a four-inch blade. Nicodemus moved the horses behind a pile of rocks, and we both lay belly flat to watch. I pointed my glass at the figures. Although bison robes covered their attire and prevented me from recognizing their tribe, I said I thought they were not Osage or Omaha. He asked, "Pawnee?"

I could not say, but I knew we were far enough north to have entered the country of various Sioux tribes. Traveling with the

Osage and Omaha, I had learnt the hand sign indicating *Sioux*: a flattened palm drawn quickly against one's throat in a slashing motion. On the shadows came, following the bison trail leading directly to us. Deems piled question on question: "Can we hide? Should we make a run for it? Do they just want to say hello? Maybe all they want is our horses."

"And maybe," I said, "all they want is our scalps. I doubt they have a black one in their collection. Whatever they're after, they know where we are."

On the plains, one improves chances of survival with long vision. I again aimed my spyglass towards the horsemen. By then, we could hear their steeds snorting as they labored up the hill. Then the scope revealed a most welcome detail: two of the horsemen were *horsewomen*. Would a raiding party bring along young females? I decided our best defense was to bluff. Saddling up quickly, we kept the rocks to our backs and our horses facing the interlopers. I hung the bowie knife boldly from my belt.

The warriors closed in but remained mounted. The eldest gave an aggressive, "Ou-eh!"—*hello* in Osage and Omaha and Kansa. I answered the same. Forcefully he spoke several utterances, concluding them by pointing to the bowie knife and saying, "Mo-hi!" And so began a reciprocity of shaking heads and gesturing over what a long-bladed *mo-hi* is worth compared to a rifle. The exchanges went on for some time, evidence of how much Indians enjoy bartering. Clearly, the warrior intended to leave with the knife one way or another. Motioning towards it, he approached me. Not letting go of it, I allowed him to examine the sharpness of the blade, the glint of the steel, a weapon superior in his view to his beautifully crafted and just as lethal an instrument made from the rib of a bison. Were we in a different place, I would have delighted in swapping a steel knife for his elegant *mo-hi*.

I indicated my interest in two rifles and a full cartridge belt— about the value of four bison robes in the fur trade. The Kansa, as I decided he must be, signified he wanted to take the knife and heft it. I signed I would hold his rifle so he, an arm's length away, could wickedly thrust the blade towards me. He handed over the gun, and I gave it to Deems, still mounted, who laid it over his left arm and directed it towards the Kansa. By now the warrior was mad to have what had been the slave hunter's weapon.

He tapped the spyglass around my neck. With reluctance, I passed it to him. He lifted it to his eye, object lens aimed the wrong way, then dropped it and shook his head to show the thing was defective. I turned the proper end towards his eyes. Scanning the horizon, he smiled and nodded.

I gestured again at a second rifle. "No!" he said in English. With even greater reluctance, I held up my compass. My beloved compass. The sun cast a gleam onto it, and he reached forward. I pulled it back and motioned to a brave's rifle more or less aimed at me, and I held up two fingers. The warrior scowled but even in his pro forma refusal he could not mask his fascination with the device, although he likely had no idea of its purpose. Perhaps to him it was a beautiful jewel, a war medallion.

On the prairie grass I laid out the compass, the long knife, the spyglass, and—ceremoniously—our last twists of American tobacco. As he studied the rare goods, I gesticulated to a loaded cartridge belt across the chest of a young brave. The warrior, dramatically, shook his head and turned away. I took that to be a sign to gather up my offers, but as I began he stopped me, and from the brave he removed the cartridge belt, and from a boy a worn rifle, and placed them both next to my goods. Deems still had the first weapon cradled towards the leader. I nodded. Remarkably fast, he snatched up his acquisitions, putting the compass and telescope around his neck and the knife under his belt, giving the tobacco to his cohort to share. He made a stiff wave, mounted up, and turned the band back down the slope.

Once far enough separated from them, I asked Deems, "Can you handle a rifle?"

"*Handle* one?" he said. "Yes, I can *handle* one. But if you mean *fire* one accurately, I remind you, plantation slaves are not trained in weaponry."

We were off the hill and moving north when he said, "Well, Doc Zawbo, we've become true members of the American frontier. You've swapped our instruments of knowledge for instruments of death."

"Yes," I said, "but it's not yet decided whose death we may have addressed."

3 August

Yesternight we discussed our route toward the Missouri River and which way to go on it. Whether or not to wester onward. We decided nothing more than to continue.

In darkness I had a sense the River Platte was not far distant, but I could see nothing of it, even from the vantage of the hill where we encamped. Rising with dawn, I looked north in some expectation and indeed, *there she flowed*, golden sunrise reflecting off her eastward passage across a wide and flat valley, the river laced with sandbars and shallows, enough to render it unnavigable to anything but a lady's teacup. Due west across the plain, I discerned the spread of Fort Kearny and its two companies of Mounted Riflemen who serve to protect the growing numbers traveling westward over the Oregon Trail. In Westport we had heard of a discovery of gold-bearing creeks in northern California, and the profusion of wagon wheels raising dust below us—so early in the morning—seemed to confirm the report.

We ate the last of the pemmican—grateful for having had it *and* thankful it was gone—and hurried down to take up the Trail towards the fort where we found considerable frontier activity. The Missouri River, I learned, is a couple hundred miles north or east, farther than I had calculated. In a tent set up by two Ohio women earning their way westward with their aptitude for grill and griddle, we ate our first hot meal in days, and delectable it was, more so because of our recent deprivation. We sat on the ground by their hand-lettered sign:

> You shoot it dead,
> by golly,
> we'll cook it good
> and make you jolly.

Rolling past were trains of wagons ranging from big Conestogas to simple oxcarts. Deems again wondered what our plan should be now that we know a steamboat is leagues distant.

The geometry of our possibilities was a distorted right triangle with an obtuse-angled base: the hypotenuse being the most direct course to the upper Missouri River but running squarely through territory under the almost total sway of various Siouan tribes, none recognized for tolerance of the American encroachment forcing them ever farther north and west. "The two of you traveling alone," a soldier here told us, "are *flat out asking for it*." The comparative safety of the Oregon Trail would mean more miles but under watch of the Army.

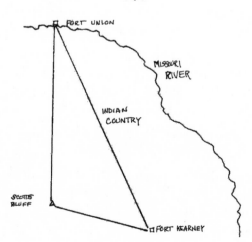

Nicodemus said, "From one hour before I met you until now, I've become accustomed to men wanting me dead. I'm used to it. *However*, to be honest, I lean towards mixing with the Trail folks. I want to continue exploring westward."

My own motivation for joining them is greater assurance of reaching Fort Union to catch a downriver boat. Further, to take a risky shortcut just to read a letter a few days sooner would be the height of self over fraternity. Said I, "The Trail it is then!"

We bought some portable grub—dried beans and jerky—from one of the several traders near the post. A fellow who noticed us packing our horses strode over to ask, "You boys intersted in thowing in with my lot?" (When a man enters the American West, he at once shuffles off years and becomes a *boy*.) His *lot* proved to be his wife and two girls and a freeborn Negro woman. The moment Deems laid eyes on her, I saw our answer had to be "You bet!" She is a quadroon from Memphis who is seeking a changed life in the be-your-own-woman American West. If I had to put words to expressions, Deems was saying to her, *Here's the best man you'll ever meet,* and she was saying to him, *Prove it!*

The man, Lloyd Murdock, is a goldsmith intending to open an assay and refining business north of San Francisco Bay. He confided to me as we prepared his wagon for the inequalities of the road, "The easiest gold's not in them creeks. It's in miner's pockets." He will share food with us if we use our rifles to bring in a little fresh meat. The next thing I realized, we were a mile beyond Fort Kearny: in two hours since dawn, our lives had taken yet another abrupt and unexpected turn. Such is life in America.

Murdock's spouse—too thin, I think, to face rigors of the Oregon Trail—is Irma, and the Memphis woman is Cassandra—Cassie to the children who ride in the wagon, although they are often allowed to walk alongside. Following us all is Jane, a milch cow to help feed the girls. The oxen are Margaret and Florence. Murdock said, "If you count, them females have me seriously outnumbered. Even with you boys, they still have us by more than double." That may be why, farther along, he invited Sergeant Sims of the U.S. Army to join us.

As for us—with Ferrall forever off our track—Deems and I dropped our aliases so this family can know us as we are. Nicodemus rides as close to Cassandra as a horse can get without knocking her over, often dismounting so she may ride, either way making me aware how uncompanioned my journey would have been without him.

4 August

The north bank of the Platte, recently the route of the two-year Mormon migration, is now used by immigrants of many orientations. To stay out of the way of romance, I often ride beside Sergeant Sims, who points out pieces of history: "Over by the river is Dirty Woman Ranch," he said at one point. "The name has nothing to do with absence of soap and water."

Occasionally Deems and I lift a daughter onto our saddle to sit before us. Murdock is beset with their begging him to trade the milch cow for an Indian pony. He said, "I knowed way back when how a girl and a horse got hatched out of the same egg."

The Trail is no longer a single path but a web of braided erosions, often ruts, and the Platte, except when blocked from view by box elder trees, is frequently visible. I had never imagined something so shallow and silted could be called a river, despite its great length. When snowmelt comes off the Rockies, so I hear, the character of it quite changes from what we are witnessing: more seep and ooze than flow. To fall in it now would be to get stuck rather than drown. For us, *our* persistent hydrological problem is rain for pasturage of horses and oxen, causing a portion of each day to be lost in moving quadrupeds off the Trail to find grass.

On our arrival at Scott's Bluff

Keeping my journal is just short of impossible now: we ride from sunup to sunset, and using a pen and inkhorn to scribble-scrabble in a book spread across my knees by the light of a campfire produces not comprehensibility but illegibility. The best I can do is use my memorandum for later transfer. But these impediments can serve: the logbook is running short of blank pages, and that restriction means I must contract, compress, condense, compact, constrict, concentrate, and curtail my entries, something I have decidedly not done in this sentence. What the hell. To have to shrink and shrivel is to remove joy from writing.

But the great plains assist: part of the experience of traveling here lies in addressing the tedium arising from their miles of sameliness suggesting the sea out of which they arose. How difficult, after days of them, to describe a long and level line as beautiful; instead, how pleasant to remember things curvilinear and sinuous, to imagine not arid hills of shriveled prickly pear but wooded slopes, to dream not unending shades of umber but rather the dozen shades of green in an eastern forest. I do appreciate the beauty here, but it is beauty of the minimal, a sere land deprived of all but openness, where creation is prodigal with scantiness.

There I go again: an outburst of wording to leave me with not enough pages to record arrival. I must note, though, Nicodemus and Cassandra have begun holding hands with the fall of night when the children are asleep. Sergeant Sims believes Deems and I—with our medical skills—would be welcome to ride with his squad patrolling the territory north to Fort Union.

Because we are independent of an organized emigrant train, we move more rapidly, a welcome consequence for a fellow roving buffalo country and foolishly desirous of a letter from Buffalo, New York. But so it is.

On our twelfth day, we arrived at Scott's Bluff, in an area of remarkable and welcome features disrupting the flat horizon and awakening the dulled gaze of immigrants hungry for relief—both emotional and topographic. Appearing first was Castle Rock, a massive sandstone protrusion standing well above the level plain; to this point on the Trail, it is the most notable natural monument visible. Even more rousing, it indicates the long trek through Nebraska territory is nearly at an end. Twenty miles west is Chimney Rock, a hard, sandstone shaft rising from a rounded pyramid of friable ground. Other fancied resemblances of sandstone are Steamboat Rock and Coyote Rock, expressions of human imagination wanting escape from monotony and crying out for something—anything—*vertical* on this planar land.

Deems persuaded the Murdock family to take a day to rest the mules, an interval he spends with Cassandra. I hardly see him. Already he has arranged to write her letters to be sent to a post office north of San Francisco where she and the Murdocks will settle.

Departing in the morning for Sioux country, Sergeant Sims has ready his squad; Nicodemus and I have signed on as a volunteer medical unit and will receive Army pay. I am moved by my friend's dedication to stand with me when his heart is urging him on west.

Few blank pages remain. What chance is there a trader at a remote garrison will carry such an item as a logbook?

?? *August*

With horses rested and fed Army oats, our patrol left Scott's Bluff at dawn. We will cover the sixty miles to Bordeaux's Trading Post—nothing but a log-and-mud hut with a sod roof, so I hear—in about two days because all we do is ride, ride, and ride on, with scant opportunity to talk. Around the campfire at day's end we sit in silence. Because of our weariness, it is wise to keep our mouths closed.

Two days later

We arrived at Bordeaux's to be greeted with good news: of late the Oglala have been living quietly in hope of no further white incursion into their lands. But observing the unending vanguard moving westward, I conclude that a vain wish. Land and gold— those are continual topics among the immigrants, and once again I wonder what happens when those assets run short.

Americans think in terms of infinitude, rarely permitting the finite to shape their plans. The notion is: all before us today will still be there for the taking tomorrow. And the indigenous peoples, in their unfamiliarity with European ways, they too fail to reckon changes driven by increasing human numbers and new technologies. Neither side can imagine an end to their worlds. Red or white, no one sees *temporariness* as eternal. But I fear something in this confliction is going to get exterminated.

If the current peace remains unbroken, we should arrive at Fort Union soon, a brave wish for a fellow who spends his time on a horse by thinking of letters from the east. My almost obsessive ruminations have not brought the return of the night phantom, and so, astride my horse, I compose missives in my mind and in the evening jot down phrases in my memorandum book to be assembled at Fort Union for posting to Sophie. I jog along and I see her more than the land before me. Realizing my failure this morning, I try to restrain dreaming and take in the territory.

We passed the eastern front of the Black Hills—*greenly* beautiful and made more so by looking back to the aridity we are slowly putting behind. I know now why the Lakota consider the Hills as the home of their Great Spirits: were I one of the Grandfathers, I too might reside here, especially if I had a Grandmother Spirit to share it. There I go again.

Call it mid-August

I have lost track of days. This noon we reached Castle Rock Buttes after a good many miles of scrublands striped with erosional gulches plugged with pines, terrain to my tired eyes more peculiarly interesting than beautiful in spite of my resistance to becoming one who travels only for beauty. My keenest memories of my American tour include a slave market, a mummified wife, a throat sliced open by a well-launched arrow. *And*, friendships.

Our troop raised a hullabaloo as we saw the rocky cliffs of the Little Missouri, a tributary differing from the big Missouri as mustard to custard. From there we finally descended a long declivity to the juncture of the Yellowstone River with—to my surprise—the nearly limpid waters of the Missouri. At the union of the rivers, as if envious of clarity, the muddied Yellowstone does to the Missouri what *it* does to the Mississippi. On the north bank of the conjoined flows, a few miles west, stands Fort Union. No sailor ever greeted a port with deeper joy than did I at that rude post. It is possible our Sergeant understood why Nicodemus and I linked arms and danced.

With dispatch we entered the tent of one of the several traders to sell our rifles and cartridge belt. A military post is not the place to peddle armaments. We received only a palmful of low-denomination coins. Deems said, "As it pans out, you've traded your beloved compass for a rifle and it for a dinner in Saint Louis."

I answered, "If Sophie is present, it's a trade to be treasured."

In the fort mail room the clerk looked me over carefully before saying, "Ah, Doctor! Been wanting to see the man who can get such correspondence as these." He handed over six envelopes addressed in the elegant cursives of a woman trained in the Prussian system. He asked, "Your sweetheart?" I said I hoped so—if I can survive a couple of thousand miles of the Missouri River. Said he, "Most do. Not all, but most."

He believes the next steamer for Saint Louis will arrive in four days. "That is," according to him, "*if the American Democracy* don't blow up. She's rigged out with them high-pressure boilers, and Captain Avery likes to burn them hot." Thought I: *Let 'em roar, Cap! Let's live on the edge!*

Arriving tomorrow will be a downbound fur-trade boat to pick up not passengers but mail.

Settled in a barracks, I read Sophie's words. She described life with the Hunt family, saying she was learning American history with the children. In the most recent missive she wrote that her brother had found employment in a Saint Louis bank; to assist German immigrants opening accounts, he can tender her work as both an interpreter and translator of documents. She is about to be on her way there. The letter ended with, "I so much look forward to seeing you again!"

25 August (so I learn)

At sundown Nicodemus bought a pint of whiskey we carried to the riverbank. He asked how I measured my exploration of the American experiment. I quote myself: "I've shaken off a woman of the night for a woman of the light, one I hope will join me in that wooded county with all the limestone columns and good whiskey. Our friend, Professor Larousse, told me the college needs an instructor of human physiology."

Today I kill time by squeezing notes from my addendum book into this journal, all the while hoping the *Democracy* is running at just below explosion speed. Deems has signed on as an Army medic to be attached to a hospital unit soon to depart for the gold fields not far north of San Francisco Bay—*and* Cassandra. Her presence explains his becoming Private Nicodemus Trennant. Even better, he is now a federally sanctioned freedman, and in uniform he will command admiration from his inamorata, his Dulcinea. Every day he writes her. And I, too, each morning add a few lines to a continuing letter I will send off to *my* Dulcinea when I see smoke from the next downriver fur-trade boat. I know what my closing sentence will be: *I hope to find you in Saint Louis where I will offer my hand in marriage.*

26 August

Deems and I returned this evening to the riverbank to watch its flow, as mesmerizing a natural event as I have witnessed. We poured beverage and took our time before speaking. We both feel the impending separation. I asked how he views our long tour. Here is a digest of his rumination:

"Even if our journey of four thousand miles is not quite ended, it's a good day to arrive alive. As Two Hearts might put it."

He was quiet again, then continued. "Four months ago I was a slave owned by a man who controlled my body *and* a goodly portion of my mind. Slavery runs deeper than chained limbs. Now, after our miles, I'm a free man serving as an Army medic on his way to meet a woman of his dreams. Since crawling from under your bed in Baltimore, I've found a grandfather I'd been deprived of. *And* a friendship unlike any I've ever known."

We sat in silence until he said, "In a country where such things are possible, I've discovered a trust I never knew, *and* greater hope for what you've been exploring. I'm wearing the uniform of that experiment because, despite my origins, I believe in the way forward, however stumbling it goes." He put his hand on my arm, and said, "Tell me. Do you think we found the blue road?"

Said I, "Ask me again in forty years."

He raised his glass to mine and said, "Indeed I will."

27 August

This journal has only a half page to hold I know not what because I see no end to the exploration that began with the alleged horn of a unicorn. Perhaps words about the grand American experiment and a pledge not to betray it but to help fulfill it, and to keep always in mind the shocking speed humans and their institutions grow old and fail.

Well, well, well. *American Democracy* is in sight, coming forward in a flurry of steam and wood smoke and frantic whistle-blowing to urge us aboard with dispatch. The captain is not blessed with patience, and for once I think that a splendid disposition. The name of the boat recalled to me the story of the woman who approached Benjamin Franklin as he left the final meeting of the Constitutional Convention to ask, "Well, Doctor, what have we? A republic or a monarchy?" Franklin answered, "A republic—*if* you can keep it."

Deems accompanied me to the wharf. I put my arms around him as he did me, both of us silent, neither having learnt words appropriate to such a parting. To break the awkwardness, I said, "Nicodemus, you're the finest dust-ball I ever found under a bed."

He said, "Glory be Nathaniel Trennant was the first to find me!"

With that I crossed the gangway and hurried up to the texas deck to witness departure and the beginning of a life I could hardly have imagined when I boarded the *Narwhale* in Plymouth Harbor. The good vessel *American Democracy* turned into the current, her whistle blowing farewell to those on the dock, and as the Big Muddy took hold, I spotted Nicodemus waving both arms, and I shouted to him, "Know that I love thee!"

A BOOK REQUIRES MORE THAN A WRITER

Were Nathaniel Trennant alive today, he'd thank copy editor Gloria Thomas for her dedication to the job at hand and her keen knowledge of the English language, editorial qualitites no longer common. He would also thank the accomplished and amiable staff at the University of Missouri Press: David Rosenbaum, Andrew Davidson, Drew Griffith, and Robin Rennison.

And, above all, a book requires a reader, so to each alert reader of his words, the good Doctor would, I have no doubt, say *Thank you and be well.*